Praise for *New York Times* bestselling author Susan Mallery

"Megastar Mallery provides plenty of holiday cheer...
[W]onderful...heartwarming."
—*RT Book Reviews* on *Christmas on 4th Street*,
4.5 stars, Top Pick

"Fans of the Fool's Gold series will enjoy
this Christmas interlude."
—*Publishers Weekly* on *Christmas on 4th Street*

"A sweet, heartwarming Christmas romance."
—*Kirkus Reviews* on *A Fool's Gold Christmas*

"In her second Blackberry Island novel, Mallery has
again created an engrossing tale of emotional growth
and the healing power of friendship as these three
'sisters' meet life's challenges."
—*Library Journal* on *Three Sisters*

"The wildly popular and prolific Mallery
can always be counted on to tell an engaging story
of modern romance."
—*Booklist* on *Summer Nights*

"Mallery infuses her story with eccentricity, gentle
humor, and small-town shenanigans, and readers...
will enjoy the connection between Heidi and Rafe."
—*Publishers Weekly* on *Summer Days*

"Susan Mallery is one of my favorites."
—#1 *New York Times* bestselling author
Debbie Macomber

SUSAN MALLERY

Christmas
on
4th Street

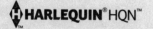

ISBN-13: 978-0-373-77899-7

Christmas on 4th Street

Copyright 2014 by Harlequin Books S.A.

The publisher acknowledges the copyright holder of the individual works as follows:

Christmas on 4th Street
Copyright © 2013 by Susan Macias Redmond

Yours for Christmas
Copyright © 2014 by Susan Macias Redmond

PLEASE RECYCLE

Recycling programs for this product may not exist in your area.

HARLEQUIN®
™ www.Harlequin.com

Printed in U.S.A.

To those who serve our country. Soldiers, support staff, healers and those who sometimes have the most difficult job of all...waiting at home. May your holidays be a time of love and happiness.

To my cheerleaders—I adore each of you. Thank you for all you do.

Finally—to my readers. You inspire me every day. In return, I try to make your Fool's Gold dreams come true. As promised, in this book is a scavenger hunt. Sixteen objects, suggested by readers on Facebook. You'll find the list on the Freebies page at SusanMallery.com. It's under the Members Only tab. If you're not a Member yet, you can join for free, and it only takes a few seconds.

Christmas
on
4th Street

CHAPTER ONE

IN REAL LIFE, snow was not nearly as delightful as it appeared in movies and on TV, Noelle Perkins thought as her spinning car finally came to a stop in a snowbank. She'd been driving up the side of the mountain, not making any sudden moves, when it happened. Although she wasn't exactly sure what the *it* was. There'd been a swoosh and a swerve and then the world twirling around her. There might have been a scream or two, but as she was alone, she wasn't going to admit to that.

She glanced around, noticing how the nose of her car was firmly planted in the wall of a surprisingly firm drift. The good news was she was pretty close to her destination. The bad news was she was going to have to figure out a way to get down the mountain when it was time to leave.

That was for later, she told herself as she turned off the engine then unfastened her seat belt. First she had a puppy to let out.

Noelle opened the door and started to stand, only to discover why her car had gone whirling around. Snow, it seemed, was slippery. Her feet started to go out from under her and she had to grab the door frame to keep from falling.

"This is so wrong," she murmured, finding her balance and carefully closing the car door. She started walking very tentatively toward the house at the end of the long driveway.

Snow had come early to Fool's Gold. There had been several inches in late October, then it had all gone away. More had fallen in early November and now this blast the following week. But it was different in town, she thought as she felt her left foot slowly sliding out from under her.

She waved her arms and managed to stay on her feet, then started forward again. In town, roads were plowed and sidewalks scraped. Someone put magical stuff down so it wasn't slippery. She never had any trouble in town.

Growing up in Florida, followed by a career move to Los Angeles, had not prepared her for a real winter, she thought as she made it to the porch. Her feet started slipping again. She lunged for the railing and managed to hang on as her lower body slipped and stretched until she was nearly parallel to the ground.

She dug her toes into the snow and ice, hoping to find some traction. At last she managed to get her legs back under her and straighten. It was like being a cartoon character, she thought grimly. Only with the possibility of breaking bones.

"This is so not what I expected," she said aloud, thinking that Felicia's request had seemed so reasonable. With everyone running around, Webster, her friend's eight-month-old puppy, had been left home alone. Could Noelle go and let him out?

Felicia had been a good friend to Noelle. When Noelle had opened her own store—The Christmas Attic—over Labor Day weekend, Felicia had been right there, helping stock the place and offering suggestions. When Noelle wanted to participate in town advertising with the other local retailers, Felicia had helped her navigate the maze that was local government regulations. When Noelle worried that she would never find a man for... well, you know, let alone love, Felicia had reassured her that it would happen. So helping with the family puppy seemed the least she could do to pay back her friend.

"I am capable," Noelle told herself as she made it up the stairs. They were surprisingly not slippery. Whatever that magic stuff was, they must use it here, she thought.

She walked to planters on the railing and felt around for the spare key. Only there wasn't one. She checked all the planters, sure that was where Felicia had told her to look.

Nothing.

Unsure what to do next, she walked to the front door and heard a soft snuffling sound.

"Hey, Webster," she called.

The puppy yipped excitedly.

Noelle reached for the door handle and found it turned easily. She pushed it open.

Two things happened at once. A very excited fifty-pound German shepherd puppy bounded out toward her and she saw a duffel bag in the foyer.

Noelle automatically patted the enthusiastic dog. He licked her hands and wiggled before dashing down the stairs and heading for the trees on the side to take care of business.

"It's slippery," she called after him, only to realize he had magical feet because he returned at the same hyperspeed with which he'd left and never skidded once.

"Good boy," she said, hugging him.

Problem one solved, she thought. Which only left the mysterious duffel and the open front door.

The bag could be Carter's, she thought, picturing

Gideon's thirteen-year-old son. Or it could be the proof that some evildoer had broken into the house and was, even as she stood there, ransacking the place. Either way, she had to find out.

She stepped cautiously inside, the eager dog at her side. By the front door was an umbrella stand. She grabbed the biggest, most threatening umbrella she saw and held it in her hands like a club. She was tough, she told herself. After all, she'd taken a self-defense class earlier that fall. Of course her instructor had warned them all against walking *toward* trouble.

"If you're in here to steal stuff, I've called the police and I'm heavily armed," she yelled as she walked through the open area of the main floor. There was a big living room and a huge kitchen. She knew there were bedrooms at each end of the house and more living space downstairs.

Webster enjoyed the game, staying at her side, his wagging tail thumping against the wall at regular intervals.

"Just walk out with your hands up and no one will get hurt," she continued.

She paused, listening. There was a sound from the hallway. She turned, umbrella poised. If necessary, she would hit the guy, then run. She was pretty sure Webster would run with her, thinking this was just more happy puppy fun.

The bathroom door opened and a guy stepped out. A tall guy wearing nothing but jeans. He had a towel in one hand and was using it to rub his just washed hair. In fact, staring at the tall, well-muscled man, Noelle would guess he'd just washed the rest of himself, too.

She paused in the middle of the hallway as several

thoughts moved through her brain. First, few burglars bothered to shower while on the job. She didn't have actual working knowledge of that as fact, but was willing to assume it was true. Second, while she knew she'd never seen the man before, something about him was familiar. Third, he was really handsome, with light brown hair and dark blue eyes. And had she already mentioned the body to her brain? Because it was good, too.

They stared at each other and she remembered her list. Right. Fourth... Her gaze dropped and she swallowed. He had a nasty-looking cut on his left hand—complete with raw flesh, black thread from stitches and—

"Oh, no," she whispered as the edges of her consciousness seemed to fold in on herself. "Not blood. Anything but blood."

For someone who had been through what she had, it was pretty funny that the sight of blood made her woozy, but there it was. Life with a sense of humor. Her stomach roiled, her skin got clammy and she knew she was about an eighth of a second from crumpling to her knees. If that happened, she didn't think Webster was up to saving her.

She bent down to shorten the distance to the floor and hopefully save herself from a lasting brain injury.

GABRIEL BOYLAN STARED at the half-collapsed blonde. "This is why I hate the suburbs," he told her as he dropped his towel and moved toward her.

"Can you hear me?" he asked, speaking loudly.

She waved toward his hand. "Keep that away from me."

Her voice was weak and she seemed to be swaying. He swore under his breath, noticing even as she started to go down that she was still brandishing that ridiculous umbrella in his direction. Great. His brother had fallen for someone insane.

He grabbed the umbrella and twisted it out of her grip, then lowered her the rest of the way to the floor. She groaned. He took in her paleness and rapid breathing and figured she was close to fainting.

The annoyed, I-really-don't-like-people side of him wanted to let it happen. At least unconscious she would be less trouble. But the doctor in him knew that wasn't the right decision. He shifted her so she was on her knees, then pushed her head down.

"Head lower than the heart," he told her. "Slow your breathing. You're fine."

"You can't know that," she managed to say.

"Want to bet?"

When it seemed like she was going to stay conscious, he returned to the bathroom and quickly wrapped his left hand. The deep cut was still tender and oozing. He was lucky—he'd been stupid to get injured in the first place, but while it was ugly, no permanent damage had been done. A good thing considering he needed his hands to make a living.

When the tape was secure, he shrugged into a clean, long-sleeved T-shirt, then walked back into the hallway.

The woman had straightened and was staring up at him. Her gaze dropped to his hand, then darted away.

"Thank you for covering up," she said, her voice low.

He assumed she meant the wound and not his chest. "You're welcome."

The puppy settled next to her, leaning heavily on her, ready for the next round of whatever it was they were playing.

"You're sensitive to blood," Gabriel said.

The woman winced. "I know. It's ridiculous. I always have been. You'd think I would get over it, but no. Oddly, I can deal with getting a shot, as long as there's no bleeding. Otherwise, I have to close my eyes." She drew in a breath, then looked at him. "Who are you?"

Gabriel frowned. "Gideon didn't tell you?"

"I haven't talked to him recently." She paused, as if trying to remember how long it had been. "I guess I've seen him in town but we haven't spoken."

Now Gabriel was confused. "You're not Felicia?"

The woman scrambled to her feet. She was a tall blonde—too skinny for his taste, but pretty enough. She wore black jeans and a ridiculous sweater decorated with tiny Santa heads. Like he'd said before—the suburbs sucked.

"No, I'm Noelle," she said. "Who are you?"

"Gabriel."

He was going to say more but her blue eyes widened. "Gideon's brother?"

He nodded, unable to figure out why someone he'd never heard of was chasing people with an umbrella in his brother's house. Not that there was an appropriate place for that sort of thing.

She smiled. Whatever else he was going to grumble about faded as her mouth curved. Because the second she smiled, he felt a whole lot better about nearly everything. His hand hurt less, he wasn't as tired and the avalanche of regret he felt at showing up in Fool's Gold reduced itself to a small rock-slide.

Talk about a trick.

The smile widened. "Oh, wow. I didn't know you were coming for sure. You're the doctor, right? Felicia mentioned she'd asked you to stay for the holidays, but I thought you'd said you couldn't make it. I'm Noelle Perkins. Felicia and I are friends. I have a store in town and I know Gideon, of course. And Carter."

The son his brother hadn't known he had, Gabriel thought. There was a situation.

"Gideon and Carter are shopping in Sacramento. Felicia got stuck in town and asked me to come and let Webster out." Her smile faded. "Oh, no. I attacked you. I'm really sorry."

"It's okay," he told her. Mostly because it was and partially because he wanted to see the smile again.

"I couldn't figure out why the door was open and the spare key wasn't where she'd said."

"Gideon told me about the key, too, and I used it."

"Of course."

The smile returned and his breathing relaxed.

She bent down and collected the umbrella. "I took a self-defense course a few weeks ago. Just a Saturday afternoon of basic stuff. My instructor would so kill me if she knew what I'd done, so if you could not say anything I'd appreciate it."

"Not a problem."

She glanced quickly at the bandage, then away. "Um, what happened to your palm?"

"I was an idiot."

"It happens to all of us."

"I should know better."

She flashed the smile again. "And the rest of us shouldn't?"

"Fair point," he told her.

She waved the umbrella. "I'll put this back." She started down the hall. "Do you want some coffee?"

"Sure."

She went into the kitchen and pulled out mugs and two small pods filled with coffee as if she knew her way around the place.

He was still having trouble wrapping his mind around the fact that his brother was engaged and had a son. Not that the two events were related. Carter's mother had died a couple of years ago. As for Felicia… Gabriel frowned as he realized he didn't know how she and his brother had met. The fact that he hadn't spoken to anyone in his family in over a year might have something to do with that.

Webster followed Noelle and looked hopeful as she collected spoons and started the coffeemaker. She eyed him.

"I'm pretty sure you've already been fed," she told the dog.

He wagged his tail.

She sighed. "You're so demanding. Fine. I'll give you a cookie."

Webster woofed at the word and followed her to the pantry, where a plastic container of bone-shaped treats sat on a shelf.

"But just one," she told him, waiting until he sat to give it to him.

He took it gently and bolted from the room.

Gabriel watched him go. "He's not much of a guard dog. He let me in without a growl."

"He's a puppy," Noelle said. "Felicia wants him to be friendly rather than aggressive. He's supposed to be Carter's dog, but she's the one who takes care of him. He's been to a few obedience classes but they don't seem to be taking."

She motioned to the large table, and he moved forward to take a seat. Noelle added the first pod and pushed the button, making sure the mug was positioned underneath.

She leaned against the counter. "So, you're here for the holidays. To be with your family. That's nice."

"I haven't seen them in a while," he admitted, trying to remember the last time he'd joined his parents and brother for Christmas. More than a decade, he thought. Fifteen years? Longer than that? Maybe it had been before he'd left for college. "Feel free to fill me in on what I've missed."

"I've never met your parents," she said cheerfully. "I know Gideon, of course. He moved here before me. It was last year. I just got here in the spring." She wrinkled her nose. "It was before the whole snow thing. I'm going to have to take some lessons or something. It's a lot more slippery than I realized. I know there's an ice element, but I didn't think it was, you know...*ice*." She made air quotes as she spoke the last word.

He chuckled. "You have a lot to look forward to."

"You mean aside from warmer weather?" She turned back to the coffeemaker and pulled out the mug. "How do you like it?" she asked, already moving to the refrigerator.

"Black is fine."

"That's such a guy thing."

She pulled out a container of flavored coffee creamer, then handed him his mug and returned to the counter. She obviously knew her way around the kitchen. Because of Felicia, he told himself. Women who were friends hung out a lot doing stuff like having coffee. He supposed it wasn't that different from going out and having a drink.

She stuck in a second pod, put a mug in place and hit the button.

"You know Gideon bought a couple of radio stations," she said.

He nodded.

"He does an oldies show every night. Lots of songs I've never heard of but most of them are good. Felicia runs the festivals in town. She's very organized. Carter's in school, of course." She glanced at Webster, who sat with his tail wagging. "What about you, young man? Any career plans?"

The puppy barked.

"Impressive." She glanced up at Gabriel. "Sorry. I talk to everything."

"It happens."

She got her own coffee and poured in the flavored creamer then set the container back in the refrigerator. She took a seat across from him and tilted her head.

"What else can I tell you?" she asked. "I have guilt about trying to attack you."

"With an umbrella."

She laughed. "I'm not sure if that makes it better or worse."

He liked how amusement danced in her blue eyes and the flash of teeth when she smiled. He wanted to keep her talking because the sound of her voice soothed him. A ridiculous claim, but there it was. What he couldn't figure out was why. Why her? He was around women all the time. Other doctors, some of the nurses and techs, soldiers, administrators. But Noelle was different somehow.

"How long has Carter been around?" he asked.

"He showed up this past summer. His mom died about

a year before that. He was in foster care with his best friend's family. They'd made arrangements with Carter's mom before her death, I think. But they started having marital trouble and he was going to have to go into the system. He didn't have much to go on—his dad's name and that he'd been in the military. But he found him and made his way here. I don't think I could have been that resourceful at his age."

"Me, either," Gabriel admitted.

He cupped the mug with his good hand. The wound on his left palm throbbed in time with his heartbeat. If he were his own patient, he would tell himself to take something. That being in pain didn't reduce the time to heal. But he also knew he wouldn't listen. That he didn't want the mental wooziness that was a side effect and that he was a long way from the threshold of what was unbearable.

"You know they're getting married, right?" she asked. "Gideon and Felicia."

"I'd heard."

"There aren't details yet. At least not that I know of, but I can't see them waiting." She paused and raised her mug. "I should probably warn you about her."

"Felicia?"

Noelle nodded. "She's really smart. However smart you're thinking, you're not even close. She's beyond genius level, although I don't know what that's called. And she speaks her mind, which I adore, but it can surprise some people. She just flat out says what she thinks. So you don't have to be subtle around her. Oh, and she's super beautiful. If we weren't friends, I'd have to hate her."

The last statement was delivered cheerfully.

"You're good at speaking your mind, too," he said.

She shook her head. "Not really. I try to be honest. You know, not waste everyone's time with game-playing. But it's a tough habit to break. I'm not advocating being mean at all. That's not right, either. But I think the world would be a better place if we all stuck a little closer to the truth."

She paused and the corners of her mouth turned up. "I have no idea where *that* sermon came from." She stood. "I should get back to my store before I start boring you with my theories on the meaning of life."

"You have theories?" he asked as he rose.

"A few, but trust me, you don't want to hear them. Anyway, I also need to get back to my store because in an effort to save money I hired part-time college students instead of full-time regular people."

"College students aren't regular people?"

"Not usually. And especially not when there's a dusting of fresh powder up on the mountain. I live in fear of returning to my store and finding the door propped open and no one inside. Well, no one who works for me." She paused. "It's weird because the high school kids I've hired are really responsible. So I guess at nineteen they regress."

He had no idea what she was talking about but that was okay. Just listening to her voice was soothing. He also appreciated the information about his family. A case could be made that he should have known it all himself, but he didn't.

"It was nice to meet you," she told him. "And I am sorry about the umbrella."

He waved off the apology. "You okay to get down the mountain?" he asked.

She blinked at him, then her eyes widened. "Crap and double crap. My car's stuck in a snow drift."

Crap was her idea of a swear word? She wouldn't have lasted in Kandahar an hour, he thought, amused.

"I don't suppose you know anything about winter driving?" she asked.

"As a matter of fact, I do. I went to medical school at Northwestern and I've been stationed in Germany more than once."

"Whew. Good. Then maybe you wouldn't mind backing my car out of the drift? Then I can sort of point it down the mountain and I'll be fine."

Instead of answering, Gabriel walked to the front door. Despite being barefoot, he headed out onto the porch and saw her small import nose-first in a bank.

There were skid marks on the driveway and a couple of places where it looked like she'd fallen on her way up to the house.

"This really is your first winter," he said.

She moved beside him and sniffed. "I have other talents."

He was sure that was true and he wanted to tell her they were likely far more interesting than an ability to drive in the snow. But she was a friend of his future sister-in-law and this was a small town and he wouldn't be around for very long. All good reasons to only say, "I have no doubt."

He stepped back into the house and waited until she'd joined him to close the door.

"Give me a second to put on boots and I'll drive you back to town."

"You don't have to go to that much trouble."

"Someone has to. I doubt you can make it on your own. Pointing the car in the general direction of town is not an option."

NOELLE NODDED AT the nice, handsome doctor before he turned away and retreated to the guest room. She sighed, thinking it just wasn't fair. He was single—at least she thought he was—she was single. She wasn't sure what else they had in common, but there had to be something. Regardless, she obviously hadn't impressed him in the least.

Oh, well. There were worse fates, she told herself. Just as soon as her busy season was over, she was going to get into a relationship. Maybe she would join one of those online dating services, or see if there were clubs for singles in town. If nothing else, she could put the word out with her friends. Most of them had recently fallen madly in love.

Maybe there was something in the water, she thought as Gabriel walked toward her, taller now in sensible-looking snow boots.

"Keys," he said as he approached.

She dutifully held them out. "I'm sure once I'm out of the snowbank I'll be fine."

"I doubt that," he said, shrugging into his jacket. "You'll be a menace until you hit flat ground."

"That's not very flattering."

He looked at her, his blue gaze steady. "Isn't it true?"

"Sure it is, but you're being kind of blunt about it."

"I thought you liked blunt."

"Not as much as I thought."

She made sure Webster was secure in the house before closing the door and following Gabriel to her car. He told her to wait while he backed the car out of the snow, which he did in one easy move. The tires didn't even skid—something she considered a personal betrayal. When she got her car back in the garage, they were going to have a little one-on-one conversation.

Gabriel stopped beside her and opened the passenger door. She climbed in, instantly struck by how close the seats were and how much broader his shoulders were than hers. She fastened her seat belt and as she did, she glanced at him.

He had a nice face, she decided. A little guarded and there were shadows under his eyes, no doubt from his hand injury and maybe traveling. But he was someone she would instinctively trust. Not that her instincts were anything to brag about, she thought. Look what had happened with Jeremy.

Or not, she thought, facing front.

"Is that the way?" he asked, motioning with his left hand.

Instantly, she felt herself getting woozy. "Be careful with that," she murmured. "It's like a weapon."

He glanced at the bandage. "There's hardly any blood."

She leaned back and closed her eyes. "Just the *B* word itself is bad. Yes, go down this road about three or four miles. At the bend in the road, turn right. Follow the signs and you'll be heading into town."

She pressed a hand to her stomach and told herself to think pure thoughts. Or at the very least, distract herself.

"You picked a really good time to visit," she said, knowing she was about to babble and not caring. Babbling was better than fainting. Or throwing up. "There are always festivals in Fool's Gold, but more so during the holidays. There are a couple of parades and a live nativity. I can't wait for that because there's going to be an elephant."

"In a nativity?"

"Don't judge. You don't know for sure there wasn't an elephant at the birth of baby Jesus."

"I'm actually pretty confident there wasn't."

"Priscilla is a part of a lot of celebrations in town. She's a member of the community, too."

"Priscilla the elephant?"

"Do you know any other Priscillas?" She risked opening her eyes and was pleased to see that there was no bloody bandage in her peripheral vision.

"She would be the only one."

"Okay, turn there," she said, pointing when they reached the bend. "Follow that road into town. You'll turn right on Frank Lane."

"Who's Frank?"

"I have no idea. It's by 4th, which is where my store is. But yeah, Frank. I guess there's more town history I have to learn."

"You know about the elephant. That should count."

He was nice, she thought, wondering if there was a subtle way to ask him to coffee. Or dinner. She glanced at his large hands resting on the steering wheel and wondered how badly things would go if she mentioned a sleepover.

She pointed to her store, and he pulled in front and parked the car.

She turned to him, prepared to offer a heartfelt thank-you, only to realize there was a problem. "How are you going to get back to Gideon's house?"

"I thought I'd go find Felicia."

She risked a quick glance at his hand, then turned away before she got faint. "Are you up to it?"

"I'll be fine. Just point me in the right direction."

She looked into his eyes and smiled. "I thought you didn't believe in that."

"My concerns were specifically about your driving."

"I want to take offense at that, but there's the whole snowbank issue that makes it less valid."

They got out of the car and she gave him directions to Felicia's office. He handed over her car keys.

"Thanks for the ride back," she said, wishing she was better at the boy-girl thing. She used to be relatively okay at it. Obviously the lack of practice was showing. "I hope we run into each other again. Not literally," she added, glancing at the snow still lodged in her fender.

"I'd like that," he said.

She returned her attention to him, trying to judge what he was thinking. But his dark blue eyes gave nothing away. He smiled and gave a wave, then turned and started in the direction she'd told him.

Noelle watched him go. When he turned the corner, she hurried toward her store, only to come to a stop when she saw the sign on the door.

Gone skiing. Come back later.

CHAPTER TWO

THE TOWN OF FOOL'S GOLD was like something out of a cheesy made-for-TV movie, Gabriel thought as he followed Noelle's directions. There were plenty of people on the streets and every single one he passed greeted him in some way. Women walked arm in arm, the sidewalks were shoveled and sanded and all the storefronts were decorated with turkeys or leaves or painted with some Thanksgiving tableau. Talk about surreal. He half expected dancing lampposts or singing forest creatures to escort him.

The last time he'd seen his brother, Gideon had been malnourished, bruised and mentally shattered. His brother had been taken prisoner by the Taliban and kept for nearly two years. He'd been in a cell with several other Americans, all of whom had been tortured regularly. Gideon had been the only one to survive.

Gabriel had visited him in the military hospital where he'd recuperated before being discharged. From there Gideon had gone to Bali, where he'd worked on getting himself back to whatever his degree of normal was going to be. Gabriel couldn't reconcile the soldier his brother had been, or the broken prisoner, with anyone who would live in a town like this. What the hell had happened?

He knew he wouldn't get an answer until he got the chance to talk to his brother himself. In the meantime, he kept moving until he found the office he was looking for. He ignored the jabbing pain in his hand and how tired he was.

He went inside and walked down the hall to the office marked Fool's Gold Department of Festivals. He knocked once and entered.

The room itself was large, with a big desk, chairs for visitors and color posters of more fantasy events in the freakish town. But what really caught his attention was the tall redhead who stood when she saw him.

She was beautiful. No, that wasn't the right word. She was stunning, with green eyes and pale skin. A sweater showed off perfect curves. Her eyes widened as she hurried around the desk.

"Gabriel! You're here. Noelle just called and told me you had brought her into town. I appreciate you helping my friend. She's not a very good driver in the snow. I've done my best to explain the theory of staying in control on a slick road, but she seems to learn best by doing. I suppose winter driving is a skill more easily mastered through practice."

She paused and put her hands on his upper arms. "I see so much of your brother in you. There are variations, as well. How interesting. I have no siblings, so all my observations about the subtle differences and similarities within a biological unit have been with friends or people I work with."

Noelle had warned him Felicia was intelligent. She obviously hadn't been kidding. Smart *and* beautiful, he thought as she stared at him. Funny how despite that, the smile that had most affected him today had been Noelle's.

Her mouth trembled slightly as that smile faded.

"I feel compelled to hug you," she admitted. "Is it too soon?"

"Go for it," he said, holding open his arms.

Felicia stepped into his embrace. She hung on with more strength than he would have guessed. He hugged her back, thinking Gideon would have his hands full with this one.

She stepped back and motioned toward one of the chairs by her desk. "How was your trip? Are you tired?" She sat back down.

"I'm okay."

She stared at his hand. "That's the injury Gideon told me about? I understand there's no tendon or nerve damage."

"I was lucky."

"You were. Based on placement you could have easily severed…" She paused, then sighed. "You would know that better than me."

"Maybe not."

She grinned. "I'm sorry. When I get nervous I talk too much." She bounced back to her feet and crossed to a table by the window. Once there she picked up a box and brought it to him. Inside were rows of crisp, red apples.

"They're grown locally," she said. "The last of the season. Delicious."

He took one, but didn't bite into it.

She took her seat again. "Carter is very excited to meet you. He and Gideon are in Sacramento, doing some shopping." She paused. "You know about Carter, right?"

"Gideon's son. Yes, he told me."

"Good. He's so interesting to have around. He does have occasional emotional outbursts, but I'm sure they're the result of hormones. For the most part, he's fun and enjoyable. He's responsible, too. He takes good care of Webster." She bit her lower lip. "I'm sorry. You've never met him and my observations have no value at this point. It's just…your approval would mean so much."

He frowned. "My approval about what?" The dog? The kid?

"I'm marrying your brother."

Her voice was soft, tentative. Gabriel wanted to bolt for the door. She wanted his approval because she was joining the family? Was she kidding? Didn't she know he hadn't seen his parents in over a year and barely had any contact with his brother? They'd spoken more arranging his visit than they had in the past decade.

"I'm sure you two will be very happy," he said, hoping he sounded friendly instead of trapped.

"We will," she assured him. "Gideon and I are well suited. We have a shared love of the town and Carter, of course. I was in the military, so I have a basic understanding of what he went through while he was abroad. We're both committed to our relationship and the family unit and there is excellent sexual chemistry."

She paused, her eyebrows drawing together. "I shouldn't have mentioned the latter. That's more of a girlfriend topic."

Despite the throbbing in his hand, the exhaustion clawing at him, he laughed. "I can handle it," he told her. "Just don't give me details. We're talking about my brother."

She smiled. "Yes, of course. I don't want to make you uncomfortable." The smile faded as she paused. "Your parents will be arriving soon."

"I'd heard. It's going to be one big family Christmas." He glanced down at his hand. A tiny spot of blood had seeped through the white gauze. No doubt what had caused Noelle to nearly faint. She was a lightweight, he thought humorously. She wouldn't last thirty seconds of his workday. Not that he would want her to see what he'd been dealing with on a daily basis for the past decade.

"Do you think you could tell me what they're like?"

It took him a second to realize Felicia meant his parents and not his life as a trauma specialist in the army.

"I'm not sure what you want to know," he admitted, returning his attention to his future sister-in-law. "My parents were very traditional. Mom took care of business and Dad told us all what to do."

Felicia frowned. "There's information in your statement, but I don't understand it." She waved her right hand. "While I'm exceptionally well-schooled, my social cues aren't perfected. I'm mostly concerned that they bond with Carter and that they not tell Gideon he shouldn't marry me."

"Grandparents are hardwired to love their grandkids," he said, impressed with her bluntness. "As for you, what's not to like?"

"Thank you for the compliment. I could compile a list of my flaws, but I know that's not what you're asking." She drew in a breath. "I'm very nervous. Gideon always speaks of his mother fondly but he has more ambivalence about his father."

"And he was the good son," Gabriel said drily.

"You weren't?"

Gabriel didn't believe in dwelling on the past and he wasn't going to start now. "My father was a drill sergeant. Great for the military but hell on the kids." At least Gideon had always wanted to serve. "Just don't let him boss Carter around."

Felicia nodded. "We have a routine that is beneficial to all of us. I'll be sure to protect that."

He made the mistake of flexing his injured hand, then had to hold in a curse. "I should let you get back to work. What time do you head home?"

"Five." She looked at him. "You must be tired. I can drive you up the mountain now, if you'd like."

"I'll be fine," he told her. "I'll wander around town until you're ready."

He gave her his cell number, then stood. "It's nice to meet you, Felicia. My brother is a lucky man."

Her expression softened and what could only be described as love filled her eyes. "I'm the lucky one. I'm glad to finally meet you." Her mouth curved. "Whenever Gideon's in a bad mood, I remind him that he once shared a womb with you. He finds the image so uncomfortable, he's usually distracted from whatever is bothering him."

Gabriel was a doctor and even he didn't like to think about being in his mother's belly or sharing the space with his brother. "You're a twisted woman. Like I said, Gideon chose well."

She came around the desk and hugged him again. "I'm so happy to have an extended family," she said. "Even if it is by marriage."

This time he was more comfortable hugging her back. She wasn't anyone's definition of normal, but to his mind, that concept was highly overrated. He had a feeling that she and his brother fit the way a couple was supposed to. He told himself to let his usual cynicism go and simply be happy for them. After all, it was that time of year.

He left her office and started walking through town.

While the sky was clear, the temperature was cold enough to make him grateful for his bulky coat. He ignored the steady pain in his hand and occasional stumble. He could make a couple of hours. Once he was back at Gideon's he would crash for a couple of days and wake up healed. At least that was the plan.

The small downtown was bustling. Even on a weekday afternoon. There were lots of stores, including a coffee place called Brew-haha. He stopped in for a drip to go and got a cupcake while he was at it. He wandered by the park, then saw Noelle's store across the street. Not sure of his purpose, he crossed at the corner and walked toward the building.

She was in the window, putting a Help Wanted sign in front of the decorated Christmas tree. When she saw him, she smiled and waved, then motioned for him to come in.

The store was big and well-lit. There was more Christmas paraphernalia than any one person could want. Overhead beams simulated an actual attic and two or three train sets ran around the perimeter of the store. The air smelled of apples and cinnamon, and holiday music played in the background. A couple of women browsed what looked like the world's largest teddy bear display.

"You found Felicia?" Noelle asked.

"I did." He chuckled. "You were right. She's smart."

"And beautiful. It's an annoying combination, but she's my friend and I love her. Which I think makes me a superior person."

Noelle laughed as she spoke. Her blue eyes were bright and happy. Everyone had secrets, he thought, but he would guess hers were the garden variety. No dangerous ghosts, no great loss. This was what home was like. Regular people living their lives. Like nearly every soldier, he'd enjoyed knowing that ordinary life had existed somewhere. The difference was he didn't know if he could return to it or not.

"What's with the sign?" he asked. "The college help let you down?"

"You have no idea. When we got back, the store was closed. Both my salespeople had taken off to experience the fresh powder up on the mountain. I'm trying not to hope they fall and break an arm."

NOELLE STUDIED THE tall man in front of her. He'd been pale the last time she'd seen him, but now she would swear there was a gray cast to his skin. The shadows under his eyes seemed darker and his mouth was pulled in what she would guess was pain.

"Are you okay?" she asked.

"I'm fine. Jet-lagged. Felicia is going to take me back up the mountain when she gets off at five."

Noelle winced. That was three hours away. "It's my fault," she told him. "I shouldn't have let you drive me back to town."

"I wasn't going to have you drive yourself and crash."

"I might have made it."

"*Might* being the operative word. I'll be fine."

"No offense, but you don't look fine. Are you sure I can't drive you back?" She held up her hand. "Never mind. I already know what you're going to say."

The worst part was, he was right. Until she got some more practice, she shouldn't be doing any winter driving outside of the plowed streets of town. But she couldn't leave the poor man swaying from exhaustion.

"Come on," she said, motioning for him to follow her.

She led the way to the back room, where she kept extra inventory and had a small break area with a table and four chairs.

The table was actually salvaged from an estate sale in town. Noelle loved the deep mahogany finish and the graceful legs, but what had most appealed to her was the writing etched into the top. As if the previous owner had spent long hours writing letters.

Now she pulled a blanket from the pile on one of the chairs and folded it into the shape of a pillow, then pointed to the sofa. "It's more comfortable than it looks."

Gabriel shook his head. "I'm fine." He seemed more wary than interested in resting.

"You're practically unconscious. This is a Christmas store. I really can't be explaining the strange man slumped on the middle of my floor." She collected a second blanket. "You don't have anything else to do until Felicia picks you up. Come on. No one will bother you here."

"You're coaxing me. I'm not some wild dog you're trying to rescue."

She grinned. "I can't help it. It's a girl thing."

He grumbled something under his breath, then finally walked to the sofa and shrugged out of his jacket. He lay down. He was too tall to stretch out, but he was able to turn on his side, with his legs not too bunched. She draped the second blanket on top of him.

"You don't have to sleep."

"I won't."

"Of course not. I'll be back a little before five."

She walked out of the storage room and went to help her customers. They each bought two bears. A family with a toddler in a stroller came in and wanted to talk about the train set. Ten minutes later they left with one, along with three holiday DVDs and an angel doll for their young daughter. Noelle tiptoed back into the storage room to check on her guest.

Gabriel's eyes were closed and he didn't stir as she approached. Good, she thought as she backed out toward the front of the store. He needed the rest. It was the best way to heal. While she'd never been cut as badly as he had, she knew something about what it took the body to recover.

THE AFTERNOON PASSED quickly. Noelle was kept busy with customers and brainstorming sales and events. Important when one was in retail, she thought. About ten minutes before five, she walked into the break room and stopped by the sofa. Gabriel didn't look as if he'd moved at all, but his color was better and some of the tension seemed to have faded. She put a hand on his shoulder.

"Hey," she began, her voice soft. "It's nearly—"

He sat up instantly, his eyes wide with alarm. "What?"

She kept her voice low and calm. "It's Noelle. You're in my store. You've been sleeping."

His dark blue gaze locked on her face. "I cut my hand. I don't have a brain injury."

"Just checking," she told him as she straightened and walked to the refrigerator. She took out her pitcher of water and poured him a glass. "Felicia phoned. She'll be here in about ten minutes."

He shifted until he was facing front. "She didn't have to leave work early for me."

Noelle handed him the glass. "It's nearly five. You've been asleep for three hours."

Gabriel took the glass. "I was tired," he admitted. "Thanks for letting me crash."

She turned one of the dining chairs toward him and sat down. As always, by the end of the day, her feet were ready for a break.

"It's the least I could do," she told him. "You drove me down the mountain. Of course I could have done you in with an umbrella and chose not to, so maybe *you* owe *me*."

"Not likely."

He drank the water. She tried not to notice how appealing a warm and sleepy man could be. His light brown hair was mussed, his expression relaxed. She was sure the wariness would return soon enough, but it was nice to see him without his guard up.

For a second she allowed herself to think what it would be like to crawl up next to him—to feel his arms around her and maybe snuggle on the sofa. She hadn't been in a relationship in what felt like a millennium, but was actually just about two years. Long enough for her to be lonely, she thought.

He finished the water then set the empty glass on the table by the sofa. "Thanks for all of this," he said, motioning to the blanket and the sofa. "You were right."

"I usually am."

His mouth twitched. "And modest."

She shrugged. "I live with the burden."

The twitch turned into a smile. "Are you thinking sainthood or just a tasteful plaque?"

"We'll start with a plaque." She studied him. "You're still exhausted. Jet lag?"

He nodded. "I spent the past two days traveling."

"Where did you come from?"

"Germany. There's a big hospital there." He looked like he was going to say more, but didn't.

"How'd you get back to the States? Military transport?"

"Part of the way. Then commercial. There was snow in Chicago."

She looked at the lines around his eyes and mouth. "Your hand is bothering you," she observed. "Can I get you something for it?"

"I'm fine."

"You're not." She didn't risk glancing at the bandage. "You're forgetting I saw it earlier."

"How could I forget? You fainted."

"I didn't. I *nearly* fainted. There's a difference."

He leaned back against the sofa, looking more relaxed. "Not much of one."

"You're trying to change the subject."

One eyebrow rose. "From?"

"How you acting like a macho idiot isn't going to help you get better."

"This would be your medical opinion?"

She ignored that. "Pain is stress and stress inhibits healing. I read a lot," she added, knowing she wasn't ready to tell him why she knew what she was talking about. "Would it help if I said I wouldn't tell?"

"No."

"You're so stubborn."

"Do I get a plaque, too?"

She held up both hands. "Fine. Don't heal. Have an open wound forever. See if I care."

He stood slowly. She was tall, but he was taller. He looked all manly in her storage room, she thought. Out of place, but in a good way. If that was possible.

"I should go wait out front," he said, reaching for his jacket. "So Felicia doesn't have to park."

"You up to this?" she asked, thinking that he hadn't seen his brother in a long time. "Dealing with all the emotional stuff? If it gets too much, tell Felicia you're still recovering from blood loss. She'll force you to go lie down. Oh, but if you do that, don't resist. She knows things."

The amusement returned to Gabriel's eyes. "What kind of things?"

"You know. Scary military stuff. Like how to twist you up like a pretzel and make you scream like a little girl."

"I wouldn't have guessed that about her."

"It's true. She's not as good as Consuelo, but she has skills."

He studied her for a second. She felt the heat of his gaze and hoped he was thinking how he'd like to rip her clothes off and have his manly way with her. Then he leaned close and kissed her on the cheek.

"Thanks for not running me through with the umbrella. And for the nap."

"Anytime," she murmured, holding in a sigh. Apparently Gabriel found her very resistible. Just her luck.

She walked him to the front door and was about to say she hoped to see him again when an older lady called for help by the glass ornaments.

"Be right there," she said and turned back to say something to Gabriel.

But he was already gone.

CHAPTER THREE

"GREAT VIEW," GABRIEL SAID, tipping his beer bottle toward the darkness beyond the deck that wrapped around his brother's house. During the day the side of the mountain was visible, but now there was only the outline of trees and the starry sky above. A little light spilled out from the house. Enough for him to make out the man sitting next to him and the railing of the deck. But beyond that was only the night.

Dinner had been more comfortable than he'd expected. Carter had done most of the talking. He'd asked a few questions, then gone on about his day and his friends. He was a good kid, Gabriel thought. Well-adjusted and friendly. Felicia had kept the conversation going, as well, but she'd been carefully watching Gideon, as if concerned this was all too much for him.

After the meal, she'd shooed the brothers out of the kitchen to "get caught up." They'd come out on the deck, where it was cold and quiet.

"I like the light," his brother said.

Gabriel thought of all the skylights in the house. He only knew the broad brushstrokes of his brother's imprisonment, but suspected he'd been held somewhere indoors. It made sense to want to see as much sky as possible after that.

He sipped his beer, conscious of the constant throbbing in his hand. Later, when he was ready for bed, he would take something. Over-the-counter only, he amended, thinking that Noelle would mock him if she knew.

"Sweet setup," he said. "You've done well."

"I got lucky. I didn't plan to settle here when I came to visit. Hell, I wasn't planning to stay anywhere. But then I saw the radio stations for sale and I figured I might as well give it a go."

"Because you know so much about radio."

Gideon grinned. "I learned. I like what I do."

"Oldies." Gabriel shuddered. "Why?"

"It's real music. Not everyone wants to listen to LL Cool J."

"Then they're missing out. Carter prefers my music over yours."

His brother leaned his head back. "You're guessing."

"Maybe, but I'm right."

"Everyone has flaws." His brother turned toward him. "He's impressive, isn't he?"

"Yeah."

"I want to take credit, but I can't," Gideon admitted. "It was all his mother. She did better than I ever could have. Then she got sick. That forced him to grow up fast."

"Does he talk about her much?"

"Some. Felicia's fine with it. She encourages him to make sure he has her picture around and that he tells stories about her. Keeping the memories fresh."

"She's great, too."

Gideon nodded. "I can't explain why she loves me, but she does. She's fiercely loyal. Determined. When I was ready to give up on being part of a family, she wouldn't. She was willing to take Carter and raise him herself." He sounded impressed and a little in awe. "I didn't want to let her in, but I couldn't help myself. And once I stopped trying to fight her, it was easy to admit how much I loved her."

Gabriel understood the concept of family. He'd been in one, had friends with families. He got that people loved each other. Some bonds couldn't be avoided, but romantic love? It wasn't worth the trouble. Life was tenuous. It could be over in an instant, so why bother?

"You've come a long way," he said instead.

"I didn't think I could make it," Gideon told him. "But this damned town healed me. I can't say how, but it did. I started to get involved." He chuckled. "There are festivals practically every weekend. Wait until you see how they celebrate Christmas here. It's an eye-opener." He turned to his brother. "I know you only came because you got injured, but I'm glad you're here."

Gabriel was having trouble keeping up. As a kid Gideon had been open and friendly, but his time in Special Forces had changed him. The adult Gideon he knew was a taciturn soldier—a man who would rather cut off his right arm than discuss his feelings. Yet here he was, talking about belonging and love and connection.

"I should check the back of your neck for some kind of pod," he mumbled.

Gideon laughed again. "I haven't been taken over by aliens. I'm who I always was. Before everything else happened." His humor faded. "Sometimes it's hard, but Carter and Felicia are patient with me. I get through."

Which sounded rational, Gabriel thought. Not like his brother, but healthy. "What happens next?" he asked.

His brother took a swallow of his beer. "We survive the parents' visit."

Something Gabriel didn't want to think about. "How long will they be here?"

"Through Christmas. They have a vacation rental in town. They won't be living here."

"That's something." He couldn't take too much of their old man.

"How you feeling?" Gideon asked.

Gabriel was about to point out that not everyone wanted to share at this meeting when he realized his brother was looking at his hand.

"It hurts."

"What happened?"

Gabriel settled deeper into the chair. "A bunch of nineteen-year-olds got drunk."

"It always starts that way."

"You know it. My patient and his buddies got in a fight and one of them went through a plate glass window. They drove him directly to the hospital, which saved his life. There was a large piece of glass and I forgot I didn't have superpowers and pulled it out bare-handed."

The move had been stupid. He knew it and everyone in the E.R. had known it, too. One second he'd been a rational doctor, doing what had to be done to save his patient, and the next he'd been spurting blood everywhere.

Gideon raised his bottle. "We all have moments."

"Not like that." He'd tried to keep working on the teen, but there was no way. His team had stepped in and another doctor had seen to the kid. Gabriel had stabilized his own bleeding until the crisis was over and he could be looked at without endangering anyone. Unfortunately, he'd lost more blood than anyone had realized.

"I ended up having to be admitted myself," he grumbled, then swore. "What was I thinking?"

"You weren't," his brother reminded him. "You were reacting."

"Not well and not in the right way." There was no point in reliving a past he couldn't change. "I was lucky—there's no permanent damage. It hurts like a son of a bitch. My CO told me it was time to go home on leave, so here I am." Otherwise he would have worked through the holidays, like he did every year. He always volunteered to stay so others could be with their families. This time he hadn't had a choice.

"I'm sorry you got hurt, but I'm glad you're here," Gideon told him.

"You want someone to take the pressure off with Dad around."

"That, too. Although I figure we can throw Carter in his direction. From what everyone tells me, grandparents can't resist grandkids."

An interesting plan. "You're not worried about what the old man might do to your kid?"

Gideon smiled. "Nope. Felicia will protect him. She's tough and fierce. I wouldn't want to go up against her."

"Good to know. Then I'll stay out of her way."

"Just don't threaten Carter and me and you'll be fine. Oh, I guess the dog falls under that umbrella now."

Gabriel started to say something, but the word *umbrella* reminded him of the woman he'd met earlier. Noelle, who'd been willing to defend her friend's house with nothing more than bravado and an umbrella.

He was glad she'd seen the error of her attack. Had there been a real intruder, she would have been in trouble. But he'd been no threat and he had to admit she'd been an unexpected distraction.

For a moment he allowed himself to wonder how his evening would have been different if she'd been the one sitting out here with him instead of his brother. He grinned. For one thing, they wouldn't be so far apart. And they sure wouldn't be talking.

"What are your plans for after the holidays?" Gideon asked. "Staying in?"

By *in* his brother meant the army. His smile faded.

"I don't know," he admitted.

He'd always planned to stick around long enough to get his twenty years. He would still be young enough to move into a regular job at a hospital. But lately, he wasn't sure he wanted to. Or could.

It was the flights, he thought grimly. Those years of shepherding injured soldiers from Iraq and Afghanistan. They were in no position to be moved, but needed the more intense care only a permanent military hospital could provide. So they were patched up and flown out. He and his team spent the hours dealing with one crisis after another. The conditions were cramped, the patients critical. Space and weight limited the equipment.

When he hadn't been on the flights, he'd been working in field hospitals. Those on the front line suffered from PTSD, while those who cared for them battled compassion fatigue. Watching the endless parade of injured, continually fighting against impossible odds without ever knowing who lived and who died, left a person drained. Even his rotations to the hospital in Germany didn't provide much relief.

Gabriel knew that was where he was now. Exhausted and empty. Which increased the likelihood that a person made mistakes and he had the hand injury to prove it. He needed to get away. His brother's invitation had provided a place. Going to spend time with the family at the holidays required no explanation.

The door to the house slid open. Felicia stepped out into the night. She crossed to Gideon and placed her hand on his shoulder. He put his fingers on hers.

"I'm sorry to interrupt," she said, her voice quiet. "I wanted to give the two of you plenty of time to connect. A strong relationship between brothers would be beneficial to each of you and it would provide Carter with a view of how siblings interact."

Gideon smiled. "How could I have resisted you?"

Felicia smiled. "You didn't—at least not physically. It was your resistance at giving your heart that was the cause of your delay in admitting your feelings. I'm glad you're more open now. We're going to have children and I want Carter to be comfortable as a brother, but also a member of the family. I don't want him to worry he's being pushed out."

"Which is not what you came out to tell us."

"No. Your parents just called."

Gabriel felt the tension in his shoulders. "Giving us an ETA?"

Felicia looked at him. "Yes. They're so excited about meeting me and Carter that they decided to drive straight through. They're only an hour or so outside of town." She returned her attention to her husband. "I knew you'd want to mentally prepare for their arrival."

Gideon's humor faded. He was on his feet in a second, already moving toward the far end of the deck. About fifteen yards away, he stopped and turned back.

Gabriel recognized the need to bolt. He was feeling

it, too. Unfortunately he didn't have anywhere to go. Although he remembered seeing a couple of hotels in town.

No, he told himself. He wouldn't leave tonight. But the morning was a whole other matter.

THE BOYLAN FAMILY could trace their service roots back to the Civil War. Each generation of Boylan men enlisted. They weren't officers, they were never famous for their exploits, but they gave to their country and had the medals to show for their courage.

Gideon had wanted to be a soldier from the time he was little, but Gabriel had wanted something else. As a boy he'd dreamed of seeing the world, of visiting great museums and studying other cultures. Gideon had been loud and athletic. Gabriel had preferred reading to playing in the tree-house fort their father had built in one of their many backyards. He'd preferred theater to baseball and debate to football.

The summer he and his brother turned fifteen, his father had taken him for a long hike. When they were alone in the woods, the older Boylan had demanded to know if Gabriel was gay.

Gabriel knew he was different from his brother and his father, but there were other guys like him. Guys who wanted more than hitting a ball. And it had nothing to do with whether or not he liked girls.

He'd said he wasn't and had known his father didn't believe him. On the bright side, when Gideon got caught with a cheerleader in the back of the family car, he'd been grounded for a month. When Gabriel had been found with the pastor's daughter in a very compromising situation, he'd gotten a slap on the back and unexpected praise. So there had been compensations.

But on the whole, it hadn't been easy being his father's son. Now, all these years later, as he waited in the cold for his parents to arrive, Gabriel told himself there was no need to head for the hills. Or in this case, the mountains. He might not have his brother's Special Forces training, but he figured he could make a run at surviving for a few weeks on his own. Not that disappearing that way was an option.

They were all lined up on the porch. Even Webster, who had no idea why the pack was shivering in the cold but happy to be a part of things.

An aging Ford Explorer pulled up in front of the house and parked. Gabriel watched the couple that stepped out.

His first thought was that they were older than he remembered. It had been years and the time showed— more on his father than his mother. His second thought was that his father seemed smaller somehow. Not the imposing figure he'd always been.

It wasn't easy to grow up with a drill sergeant for a father. There were expectations for behavior in the community that other kids didn't have. Norman Boylan had always been more bogeyman than parent, at least when Gabriel had been young. Now, looking at the man, he realized that he was at least two inches taller. His father wasn't a threat anymore—he was little more than a man close to sixty who had once been the center of his sons' small world.

Gabriel's mother, Karen, was still pretty. There'd always been a softness to her and he saw that now as she took in the sight of both her boys. Then her gaze shifted to Carter and tears filled her blue eyes.

She'd been the one who comforted, the one who tried to explain why their father had made the rules he had and enforced them with an iron fist. Gideon had accepted her hugs and kisses, then run off, healed. But Gabriel had resisted, asking why instead of apologizing for their father, she didn't try to change him. He remembered she'd said changing a man wasn't so easy and when he got older he would understand.

Felicia and Carter were the first ones down the stairs. Karen hugged her future daughter-in-law, then put her hands on Carter's shoulders. Webster joined them, racing to Norman's side. Gabriel half expected his father to ignore the bounding puppy. Instead, he crouched down and petted him, then ordered him to sit. Webster, like any young recruit, did what he was told.

"We'll go into town and get drunk," Gideon said as he and Gabriel started down the stairs.

"How about we get drunk in Morocco?"

Gideon flashed him a smile, then stepped onto the path and held out his hand to his father. Gabriel did the same. What they said was "Dad" but the tone was "sir."

Norman didn't try to hug them. He studied each of them in turn, stepping back when their mother rushed toward them.

"My boys," she cried, holding out her arms to them and pulling them close.

She hung on for a long time. Gabriel gently patted her back, waiting for all the emotion to pass. Finally she stepped away and wiped her tears.

"I can't believe how long it's been since we were all together," she said, her voice trembling. "This is so wonderful." She turned to Felicia. "Thank you for inviting us."

"We're happy to have you," Felicia murmured.

Gabriel waited. From what he'd seen, Felicia usually

said more. A statement or two on the importance of the family unit or an unexpected observation about connection. But there was nothing else.

Gideon leaned close. "She's trying to tone things down for the folks."

"They're going to find out you're marrying a genius sooner or later."

"She wants it later so she doesn't scare them off."

"She's great. They'll like her."

"That's what I said," Gideon told him. "But she won't listen."

Gabriel wanted to take her aside and point out that Gideon wasn't looking for their approval, but doubted that would make her feel better. She would have to figure it out for herself.

They moved into the house. Norman fell back to keep pace with Gabriel.

"Still slacking off at the cushy hospital job?" his father asked, slapping him on the back.

Gabriel thought about the horrors he saw, the hours he worked and how there was never an easy day. He remembered the countless times he'd been forced to tell a brave, young soldier that yes, his leg, arm, eye or more was gone. He thought of the screams and the blood and knew there was no point in talking about any of it.

"Still slacking off," he said, shutting the door behind him.

NOELLE HURRIED TOWARD Brew-haha. Her friends had invited her for coffee before she opened her store. While she was busy, she'd never thought to say no. Since moving to Fool's Gold, she'd met wonderful women who were very much a part of her life. They had sustained her in ways they didn't even know about.

She walked in the coffee house right on time and saw that Patience, Felicia and Isabel were already at a table together. There was a plate of muffins, a latte at each place and a slightly guilty expression on each of their faces. Noelle had no idea what was up but she knew the guilt didn't come from eating an extra muffin that morning.

"Hi," she said as she took her seat. "What's up?"

Patience slumped in her seat. "I'm so bad at this. I just can't keep a secret. Not from anyone I care about. I'm a blabber. It doesn't matter if I don't say anything—it shows on my face."

Felicia studied her. "In the gambling world, it's called a tell. The twitch of a muscle or a nostril flare. I could show you what you're doing and teach you how to control your involuntary reaction."

"Or she could simply accept the fault and move on," Isabel said cheerfully. She picked up her latte. "I'm just saying."

"I don't think I'm very trainable," Patience admitted.

Noelle relaxed and reached for a muffin. Obviously whatever was up with her friends wasn't a crisis.

"If you want to try, I'm here for you," Felicia said, then she cleared her throat. "Gideon's parents arrived last night."

"They weren't due for a couple of days," Isabel said. "Or did I get that wrong?"

"They were early," Felicia admitted.

Noelle thought about Gabriel and how tired he'd been yesterday. She didn't know the man very well, but from the little she'd seen, he wasn't exactly a family kind of guy.

"Did everything go okay?" she asked.

"It was awkward," Felicia admitted. "Norman and Karen seem very nice, but there hasn't been much contact between all of them in a while, so that makes a difficult situation worse. Carter is thrilled and Webster offers an excellent distraction. We talked for a couple of hours, then we all went to bed."

She held on to her mug. "This morning Norman was up and fixing breakfast at six. I found him easy to talk to but then I don't have any kind of past with him. It's going to be more difficult for Gideon and his brother."

"Can we help?" Patience asked. "Host a dinner or something?"

Isabel nodded. "Ford is a master at dealing with a big family and we can all be buffers. Just say the word."

Noelle nodded, not wanting to say anything in case she sounded too eager. Because where there were Felicia's soon-to-be in-laws, there was also likely to be a certain handsome doctor. Maybe he would like her to rub his back or gaze adoringly into his eyes. She was up for either. Or something more adult.

Which only went to show she had been manless for far too long.

"Thank you," Felicia said. "I appreciate the show of friendship." She pressed her lips together. "Enough about me. We wanted to talk to Noelle for a reason and she has to be at her store soon."

The three women turned to her. Noelle had a sudden need to worry about having something stuck in her teeth. "What? Don't freak me out. This is my busy period. I couldn't take the pressure."

Patience reached for her hand. "We have something to tell you."

"It's a good thing," Isabel added quickly, then sighed. "The best."

"We're getting married," Felicia added.

Noelle exhaled a breath she hadn't realized she was holding. She squeezed Patience's fingers, then picked up her latte. "Duh. You're all wearing engagement rings. I'm blinded on a regular basis."

It was true. Each of them sported a diamond ring of impressive size. Noelle resisted the urge to cover her face and moan, "My eyes, my eyes." But she wasn't sure her friends would get the humor.

"You know I'm happy for each of you, right?" She sipped. "Do you worry I'm upset?"

"No," Isabel told her. "It's not that at all."

"Then?"

"We're getting married at Christmas," Patience said in a rush. "Christmas Eve. After the Dance of the Winter King."

"Oh, wow. That's great."

Noelle had never seen the Dance of the Winter King, but she'd heard all about it. Fool's Gold did Christmas in style. Christmas Eve day began with a live nativity and ended with the production, put on by the local ballet school. Afterward those attending went to midnight services at the various churches around town.

"We haven't told anyone," Felicia added. "Our fiancés know, of course, and Dellina. She's assisting us in planning the weddings. We thought with having everyone already at the convention center, it would be convenient."

Isabel rolled her eyes. "And romantic. It will be a surprise."

"But we wanted you to know," Patience added.

"Thanks for telling me. This is a great idea. I can't wait." Noelle felt a slight twinge and knew that was about wanting to be in love herself. While she was totally happy for her friends, she wanted a little of that love magic, too.

It would happen, she told herself firmly. She only had to believe. She knew that life was a precious gift. She was going to enjoy all of it, including her friends' triple wedding.

"We want you to be our attendant," Felicia told her.

Isabel grinned. "Look at it this way. You only have to buy one hideous dress." She held up her hands. "And it won't be hideous, I promise. I've already pulled three different dresses that are great."

"I'm honored," Noelle said sincerely. "For all of you thinking of me. This is going to be such a surprise for everyone. Let me know if you need any help with anything."

"You're extremely busy with your store," Felicia pointed out. "But your offer of assistance is very supportive. Thank you." She smiled. "Consuelo also offered to help, but I knew she didn't mean it. She was backing out of the door as she said it." The smile broadened. "Maybe I'll invite her to be a bridesmaid."

Patience's eyes widened. "Are they to that point?"

Isabel shook her head. "I'm sure Kent would propose in a heartbeat, but Consuelo needs a little more time to settle into what she calls the hell of being normal."

Noelle chuckled. "That sounds like her." She glanced at the time on her cell phone and groaned. "I have to get the store open. Thanks for telling me your secret. I'll keep it to myself. And thank you for making my first ever Fool's Gold Christmas even more special."

Noelle waved as she dashed out and headed for her store.

She was pleased to find she really *was* genuinely happy for her friends. They were all in love with terrific men. Men she had absolutely no interest in. She told herself that what she would take from the upcoming wedding was that love was in the air and if she was lucky, she would catch a little for herself.

She turned on 4th Street and raced toward her store. She still had to restock the stack of throws she kept by the stuffed animals. They had been a last-minute addition to her inventory and were huge sellers. Apparently, Christmas was when everyone wanted an extra blanket or two to toss on the sofa.

She was reaching for her keys when she saw someone standing outside of her store. A tall, handsome someone with piercing blue eyes and a smile that made her stomach start the Macarena.

"What are you doing here?" she asked Gabriel as she approached. "Did you decide you really need a nativity made out of local gourds?"

Gabriel stared at her. "You have one of those?"

"Of course. I pride myself on stocking the unusual."

"Or the extremely strange."

"It's Christmas," she pointed out. "Or it will be in six weeks. When else would someone want a gourd-based nativity?"

As she spoke, she opened the front door and flipped on the lights. He followed her inside. She turned on the trains, then started the music. She was unwinding her scarf when she shifted back to find him standing in the middle of the store.

He looked better than he had. More rested, less gray. Although he still seemed tired. The shadows remained in residence beneath his eyes.

"What's up?" she asked, shrugging out of her coat.

"I want to talk to you about a job."

She laughed. "Right. If you're looking for a present for your mom, I can give you some suggestions. We have some really pretty ornaments she might like."

She disappeared into the back room to put her coat away and tuck her handbag into her desk's bottom drawer. When she straightened, Gabriel was standing close enough that she could see the various colors of blue that made up his irises. She could inhale the clean scent of him and catch a hint of the heat the man generated.

"I want to come work for you," he said.

"That's insane. You're a doctor. This is retail. I sell Christmas stuff."

"I know what you do. You need help and I need…"

She waited, confident this had to be a joke. When he didn't speak, she shook her head. "I'm sure they would be thrilled to have you volunteer your services at the local hospital."

"I need a break from that. You're looking for someone to stock shelves and work the cash register. I can do that."

"You're injured."

"Just my left hand. I'm right-handed."

She put her hands on her hips. "What's going on? Are you filming this for a YouTube video? Famous doctor punks innocent store owner? I'm not eating a live bug for you."

"No live bugs."

"Not a dead one, either."

"Why can't I apply for the job?"

"Because you're grossly overqualified." She touched his arm. "What is this about?" she asked again.

He drew in a breath and stared into her eyes. "I need to be doing something with my day. I'm stuck here for over a month and I have nothing to do. I can't work in a hospital right now." He opened his mouth, then closed it. "I can't."

Noelle hated to admit she didn't know all that much about the wars her country had been fighting for over a decade. She saw what was on the news and those special reports on the magazine shows, but that was it. Her only firsthand knowledge came from what she'd learned from the men her friends had gotten involved with.

This past year a bodyguard school had opened in town. The principals were all highly trained former military people who had risked their lives to protect those at home. Isabel's fiancé, Ford, had been a SEAL. Consuelo had served and done secret stuff, Gideon had been in the army, and so on.

She'd heard bits and pieces, knew there were ghosts and nightmares and the kind of damage that couldn't always be seen. It made sense those helping the injured would suffer in their own way.

"I'm going to make a series of statements," she said slowly. "I'd like you to respond to them."

"Now you sound like Felicia."

"I should be so lucky." She drew in a breath. "You're in town because of your hand and maybe what you do for a living. It's something you need a break from."

He nodded cautiously.

She hesitated, feeling her way through an emotional minefield. "You don't see your family very much."

Another nod.

"So being around them is intense. And parents are inherently complicated. Plus there's the whole they don't know Carter and what do they want from you."

Nod.

"My amazingly charming store has a good emotional vibration and you feel comfortable here. Plus, you're really excited about the gourd nativity. Did you know they're made by a guy named Lars, a local farrier, who also trims Heidi's goat's hooves."

His mouth curved up. "Now you're making stuff up."

"I'm not." She paused. "You really want to stock my shelves and ring up my purchases?" Noelle had to press her lips together as she wondered why a perfectly normal question suddenly sounded incredibly dirty.

"It would be the highlight of my holiday season."

"I can't pay much more than minimum wage."

"Not a problem."

"Even though you don't need this job, I have to be able to depend on you."

"I promise not to go snowboarding without clearing it with you first. But the day after Christmas, I'm gone."

"My busy season ends the day before Christmas, so we don't seem to have a timing issue." She hesitated, sure there was something she was missing. Only she couldn't figure out what it was. The bottom line she needed help and a responsible, attractive man was offering. She couldn't think of a single reason to say no.

"Okay then. I guess you're hired."

CHAPTER FOUR

NOELLE OPENED THE store the next morning with an expected burst of anticipation and enthusiasm. Sadly, she knew the cause. In a perfect world, she would be able to fool herself for at least a few days. But she'd never been very good at convincing herself of anything that wasn't true. She had always had a streak of realism that now reared its ugly head.

She had a thing for Gabriel. The handsome, wounded doctor pushed all her buttons. He was funny, nice, kind and elusive. Or in the feline vernacular—catnip.

She didn't know why it had to be like that. Why couldn't she be wildly attracted to some normal, local guy who'd been living here for fifteen generations and wanted to get married and have five kids? She supposed one of the reasons was that she hadn't met anyone like that.

"Well, if I do, I'm all over him," she murmured as she went through her pre-opening ritual. She turned up the heat, made sure the trains were running, checked the selection of Christmas music on her iPod and then moved toward the cash register. She had just finished counting ones, fives and tens when someone knocked on the still-locked front door.

Her stomach gave her a name before she even looked

up. Sure enough, Gabriel stood there, right on time, still tall and, worse, smiling.

"Hi," she said, unfastening the lock and letting him in. "You're here."

"As promised."

"That's nice. Where did you park? I like to save the spaces out front for customers."

He shrugged out of his coat. There was a light dusting of snow on his hair and he wore a navy sweater that brought out the deeper blue tones of his eyes. He could have stepped out of one of those funny "woman to woman" Christmas cards.

"I walked."

She stared at him. "Down the mountain? It's, like, five miles or more. Are you insane? It's freezing cold and snowing. You can't walk that far in this weather. Oh, my God, I've hired a crazy person."

He dropped his coat onto the counter and put his hands on her shoulders. "Breathe."

"I'm not going to faint."

"No, you're going to pop a blood vessel. Breathe."

She was less interested in breathing than the feel of his *large* hands holding her. If only he would pull her closer or maybe cop a feel, she thought wistfully.

"I'm staying in town," he said. "My parents rented a little apartment for the holidays. It's not much more than a studio. They decided to stay at Gideon's when they saw how much room he had, so I took the rental instead." He dropped his arms to his sides and shrugged. "It's plenty big enough for me and they get more time with Carter."

She decided not to comment on the sudden lack of hands on her arm and instead focused on the conversation. "It was getting too intense?" she asked.

He grimaced. "My mother carted photo albums with her. Last night we relived our childhood, year by year."

"There had to be happy times."

"There were. When we were younger, we moved around a lot. Once my dad became a drill sergeant, we settled."

Which didn't exactly say when the happy times were. "Camp Pendleton?"

He smiled. "Don't let my dad hear you say that. That's in San Diego and it's the marines. We're army. We were at Fort Knox, Kentucky."

Somewhere she had never been. "I'm sure it was lovely."

"That's one way to describe it." The smile faded. "My dad and I were never close. He was a tough guy and I wasn't a tough kid."

"I'm sorry."

"Don't be. I got through it then and I'll get through it now. It's only for a few weeks, right?"

She nodded, thinking how much she wanted to tell him to be grateful he had family at all. She'd never known her dad—he'd run off before she'd been born. But that had been okay because she'd been raised by her grandmother and her mother. The two women had been warm and loving and she'd had a blessed and happy childhood.

Even after she'd moved to Los Angeles for law school, they'd stayed close. The two women had driven out to spend every summer with her. They'd been there to celebrate with her when she'd landed her first real job at a prestigious law firm in Century City and had screamed and celebrated with her when she'd passed the bar.

Only they'd been killed during a twenty-five-car

pileup on I-10 while driving back to Florida. Noelle missed them every day of her life and would give anything to have them back.

But she'd also learned that telling people that only made them feel guilty. That Gabriel would have to figure out for himself the need to appreciate what he had, while he had it.

"All right," she said. "Let's get you settled. I'll show you where to put your stuff. I need you to fill out a W-4 for my accountant and then I'll give you a tour of the store."

Fifteen minutes later, it was official. Gabriel Boylan was an employee of The Christmas Attic.

She walked him through the basic layout. "I keep baskets up front," she said, showing him the stack of lightweight oval baskets. "Most of what we carry is small. Encourage the baskets. Otherwise, when a customer gets her hands full, she tends to head for the register."

"Makes sense."

"You can see we have sections. Ornaments and home decorating over there, the nativities on that wall."

"Including gourds?"

"You think I'm kidding. You need to go check it out."

"I will."

"The bears are over there, with all the kid stuff close by. We have some books, but mostly send people looking for Christmas books over to Morgan's."

"Don't you want to have Christmas books here?" he asked.

"No. Not with a perfectly good bookstore less than a block away. I'm not stepping on any toes. What if every other store started carrying ornaments and teddy bears?"

"Or this," Gabriel said, picking up a Santa pin from a display.

She leaned close and moved the hidden switch on the back. Santa's nose lit up.

Gabriel stared at the bright nose and slowly shook his head. "I don't know what to say."

"Something along the lines of, 'Why Mrs. Smith, your mother, aunt, granddaughter will love that pin, I'm sure.'"

He nodded and turned off the switch, then returned the pin to the display. "Point taken."

She was pleased with his response and even more excited to see there wasn't any blood on the bandage.

"Then there's the bear section."

He followed her around the corner and came to a stop. "I saw this before, but it seems bigger."

"I've put out a few more. Bears sell."

Three large sets of shelves rose to the faux rafters. Each shelf was crowded with different stuffed animals, mostly bears. Brown bears and white bears, bears that were fuzzy and plaid. Some played music and some you just wanted to squeeze.

"I have a layout in the stockroom," she said, leading the way. "That will help you when you have to put things out. And now I'll teach you the mysteries of the cash register."

Gabriel learned the system quickly. Noelle had chosen a credit card service that didn't give as many reports, but was a whole lot easier to deal with on a daily basis. Right at ten, she unlocked the front door and let in a couple of waiting customers.

The next few hours passed quickly. There was a steady stream of business. Just before noon, a pretty woman came into the store. She had short brown hair and looked to be in her late fifties. Noelle was about to greet her when she saw Gabriel staring at the woman. Something in his expression told her this wasn't just any customer.

Noelle walked over. "Hi. Welcome to The Christmas Attic."

Gabriel glanced between them. "Noelle, this is my mother, Karen Boylan. Mom, this is Noelle Perkins. She owns the store."

"It's lovely," Karen said, unbuttoning her coat. Underneath she wore a bright purple sweatshirt with a shell logo and the words Blackberry Island. In smaller print, the sweatshirt proclaimed Stay for the Wine.

"Great color," Noelle said. "Where is Blackberry Island?"

"Washington State. Just north and west of Seattle. Norm and I went there a couple of years ago. We did the whole west coast, heading north through the summer. Then we drove home. It was a very nice trip."

"It sounds like it."

Karen turned to her son. "Your dad and I sent you a few postcards."

Gabriel nodded. "Right. They were great." He looked at Noelle. "I should run those errands now. Before it gets too busy. I'll be back."

He was gone before she could ask what on earth he was talking about. Seconds later he was in his jacket and heading out the front door.

She opened her mouth, then closed it when she saw Karen's face had settled into lines of deep sadness.

"That was my fault," his mother said. "He's running away from me. I don't want you to think badly of him."

"I won't," Noelle said, then glanced around the store. It was quiet, at least for the moment. "Why don't I fix us both some tea?"

She led Karen into the back room and filled two mugs with water. After putting them in the microwave, she turned to Gabriel's mother and offered a slight smile.

"How are you settling in for your stay?"

Karen blinked several times and drew a breath. "Fine. It's beautiful here. What a sweet little town. Norm and I have traveled a lot and we've never been anywhere like this. I'm excited about all the festivals."

"Me, too," Noelle told her. "I moved here in the spring, so this will be my first Christmas. I hear it's crazy busy. There's a parade on Thanksgiving and the day of giving. I plan to throw myself in the center of all of it."

"That's a good attitude."

"Thanks." Noelle noticed the other woman's earrings. "Are those garnets?"

"Yes." Karen touched the earrings. "They're part of a set that's been handed down in Norm's family. There were only boys in his generation so I was fortunate enough to inherit them. There are several other pieces— a necklace, bracelet and ring. I love them." She twisted her hands together. "Have you known my son long?"

"Not at all. I met him shortly after he arrived." She thought of the umbrella incident and grinned. "He's a good guy, though."

"I think so. His father… Growing up, the boys weren't as close to Norm as I would have liked. There were a lot of rules. I suppose I should have stepped in more. Been a buffer. Norm tended to run the house the way he ran his recruits."

The conversation was that awkward combination of vague and intimate, Noelle thought, grateful when the microwave beeped and she could busy herself making tea.

"He's mellowed," Karen continued. "But I'm afraid it might be too little, too late. I was hoping this trip would help us reconnect as a family. Gabriel said he wasn't coming but then he hurt his hand and changed his mind. I took that as a sign."

She paused. "Sorry. I'm going on and on."

"It's fine," Noelle told her, handing over a mug of tea. "Have you talked to Felicia? She's great and may know more about where your sons are coming from."

Karen's expression relaxed. "I know. She's wonderful. So intelligent, but still very warm. Being with Gideon can't be easy—not after all he's been through. And then dealing with Carter. Not many women would be so accepting of having a thirteen-year-old boy suddenly show up, but she's embracing it."

"What do you think of Carter?" Noelle asked.

"I can't get enough of him. I wish I'd had the chance to meet his mother. Norm is in heaven with Carter. And he's bonding with Webster, which surprises me. My husband is not a pet person."

Karen sipped her tea. "So my son is working here?"

"I know, strange, right? It's just while he's in town. I think he wants to be distracted."

"And avoid us," Karen said, before holding up her hand. "You don't have to disagree with me. We both know he moved into town to have a little less family time. I accept my part in what happened. Now I have to change it."

Noelle found herself liking Gabriel's mother. She'd

obviously made some difficult choices and was now accepting the consequences.

"You know," Karen said slowly, "Gabriel isn't seeing anyone. At least as far as I know. He's never married." She paused. "Oh, dear. I'm turning into a meddling mother. That can't be good."

Noelle laughed. "Don't worry. I won't tell. And while I appreciate the sales job, I'm not sure Gabriel is my type."

"You worry he has commitment issues? He's reached that age where I'm starting to wonder why he's not married."

Noelle hadn't thought of that. "I'm more worried that he's leaving. I want something more traditional. A husband who plans to stick around."

Karen nodded. "I understand. Speaking as a woman who's been married for thirty-five years, when it works, there's nothing better."

"And when it doesn't?"

Karen chuckled. "It helps to have girlfriends who are willing to listen. Are you free for Thanksgiving?"

The change of subject startled Noelle. "What? Yes." Each of her friends had invited her over, but she'd declined. They were all newly in love and forming family traditions. She wasn't comfortable being a part of that.

"Please join us for Thanksgiving dinner," Karen told her. "Felicia is cooking and I'm going to help. It's just the six of us. Very casual. You seem to understand Gabriel, and I think he would like a friend around."

Noelle wasn't sure if she could be considered a friend, but she liked the assumption. With Felicia's future in-laws and Gabriel in the house, not to mention Carter, Felicia and Gideon weren't expecting a romantic evening.

In truth, Noelle wouldn't mind being with other people and hanging out with Gabriel would be interesting.

"Thank you," she said. "That would be nice."

She made a mental note to call Felicia and let her know about the invitation.

GABRIEL RETURNED ABOUT three minutes after his mother left. Noelle put her hands on her hips. "You were lurking."

"Maybe," he said, sounding unrepentant.

"She's your mother and she loves you. Talk to her."

"We talk."

"All evidence to the contrary?"

He ignored that and put his coat away. When he returned to the main part of the store, she wanted to say more, but several customers chose that moment to step in from the cold.

A little after noon Ana Raquel Hopkins breezed in with a basket of sandwiches. Ana Raquel, a young and talented chef, had run a food trailer all summer. She'd fed locals and tourists alike out by the park. The changing weather and an unfortunate accident—a car backed into her trailer—had ended her seasonal business prematurely. Now she worked up at the Café with her fiancé and did a sandwich delivery to the local businesses in town.

"So, you're new," the petite blonde said as she walked over to Gabriel.

Noelle held in her humor as she watched him deal with the larger-than-life personality that was Ana Raquel.

"Yes," he said slowly.

"But you look familiar." She snapped her fingers.

"Oh, right. You're that old guy's brother. The one on the radio. Gideon."

"We're twins," Gabriel said drily.

"I'm one, too." Ana Raquel apparently missed the point of his tone as she studied his face. "Not identical, right? Because you don't look alike. Fayrene and I are identical. Less now than when we were little."

"Because you're so big now?"

She grinned. "You're upset because I said you were old. I'm sure your wife thinks you're totally hot."

"I'm not married."

"Huh. Not ever?"

Gabriel drew a deep breath. "No."

"Wow. You're brave. Because seriously, you're reaching the age when people start to ask questions if you've never been married. Like is there something wrong with you." She paused expectantly.

Noelle stayed by the counter, where she could keep an eye on customers while watching the show.

"There's nothing wrong with me," Gabriel said, his teeth clenched.

Ana Raquel tilted her head. Her long ponytail slipped across one shoulder. "If you say so," she murmured, her voice making it clear she wasn't convinced. She turned back to Noelle and handed over two bagged lunches. "Be careful with that one," she said in a loud whisper. "I think he might not be right in the head."

Noelle nodded solemnly. "Thanks for the warning."

Ana Raquel left.

Noelle did her best not to burst into laughter as she passed over one of the bags. "I forgot to mention I provide lunch, or she does."

Gabriel stared at the bag. "She cooks?"

"Yes, and incredibly well. She and her fiancé wrote a cookbook. *A Fool's Gold Cookbook.* You can buy it anywhere in town." She pointed to the small display in front of the cash register.

He walked over and picked up the book. "This is her?"

She waved the sack lunch. "Trust me, you'll love it. Their sandwiches are always so interesting. And there's yummy salad."

"Not just any salad? Yummy salad?"

"I accept that you have to mock me to regain your sense of power because she called you old."

"She called my brother old," he clarified.

"You're the same age."

"Not the point." He took one of the lunches. "You're sure she's able to do this without adult supervision?"

"Very funny. You're going to love it." She paused. "By the way, your mother also worries that you're too old to never have been married."

He groaned. "Please be kidding."

"Sorry, no. By the way, she also asked me to join your family for Thanksgiving."

He stared at her intently. "Please tell me you said yes."

"I said yes."

"You'll come early?"

"You're that worried about spending a day with the family?"

"Holidays are brutal."

She smiled. "Fine. I'll come early. Go eat your lunch. Then you need to stock shelves."

He picked up one of the bags. "We're having a run on gourd nativities?"

"You'd be surprised."

He started to leave, then turned back to her. His bandaged hand came up and lightly grazed her cheek. She felt the heat of his touch all the way down to her toes. The contact was as unexpected as her visceral reaction.

"Thank you," he murmured.

"You're welcome."

She thought about mentioning he could thank her in other ways. Like kissing. Or walking around shirtless. But he just headed for the back room, apparently unaffected by their brief contact.

Just what every woman needed for the holidays, she thought dreamily. A man crush.

THANKSGIVING MORNING Gabriel sat on his brother's front steps, sipping coffee and ignoring the cold. His mother had insisted he show up for breakfast. The request had been unexpected and he hadn't had time to figure out a lie. So he'd been stuck arriving at eight.

It hadn't snowed for a couple of days, so the roads were clear. A good thing considering Noelle was driving up by herself. As he watched the driveway, waiting to see her arrive, he realized they hadn't discussed a time. *Early* could mean a lot of things, especially considering dinner wasn't until five that afternoon.

He continued to hold on to his mug of rapidly cooling coffee, pleased he could almost stand the pressure of the cup against his wound. He was healing. The searing pain was just a dull ache. The stitches pulled when he moved. Good signs. His work at the store hadn't set him back at all. Not that he cared if it did—he liked what he did at The Christmas Attic.

He'd taken the job on an impulse. Keeping busy meant less time to think—something he appreciated. In his regular job there was too much thinking. Too much worrying. Once a crisis hit, there was only reacting, then later, second-guessing. Folding throws and making sure the teddy bears were in a straight line would get old in time, but for these few weeks, the job was exactly what he needed. A place to retreat.

When he had his flashbacks—the sound of an explosion somewhere out of sight—he was able to stay calm. He kept breathing and the urgent sense of having to go help, to save, bled away with the sound. He was left back in this time and went on with his day.

Now he turned toward the driveway, but no car appeared. Damn.

He wanted to see her, he realized. Not just for the way she would be a buffer between himself and his parents, but because she would make him laugh. She would poke fun at him and breeze in and out with a graceful sway of her narrow hips. She would be endlessly patient, as she often was at the store. She didn't care that some old lady took nearly an hour to pick out two ornaments with a combined value of less than ten dollars. She wanted every customer to be happy, whatever it took.

Integrity, he thought, finishing his coffee. She had integrity. And long legs, he mused, thinking how good they would feel wrapped around him as he—

Gabriel slammed the door on that line of thinking. No, he told himself firmly. That wasn't going to happen. For one thing, Noelle was sweet and soft and not the kind of woman who thought sex was a game. For another, there were no secrets in Fool's Gold. He'd figured that out the first day. If he slept with her, everyone would know. Then he would be gone and she would be left with the consequences. He liked her so he didn't want to hurt her.

He heard footsteps on the porch behind him. He was hoping the person joining him was his brother. Or even Felicia. He could handle the company of either. He doubted Carter was up yet, otherwise he would take the kid.

But no, he thought as his father settled next to him. His luck wasn't that good.

"Here," his dad said, handing over a travel mug. "If you're going to be fool enough to sit out here, you need to keep warm. Your other coffee will be cold by now."

"Thanks."

"You waiting on a woman?"

He was, but didn't want to have the conversation. It would mean explaining why and that would take both of them places they didn't want to go. His father had spent his life in the military but had seen little actual combat. It was a timing thing. While Gabriel hadn't been under live fire, except when the field hospitals were attacked, he'd been plenty close to what went on. Gideon had lived it, of course.

Regardless, their father would feel he was one of them and want to talk about it. Gabriel had never been able to figure out what to say.

"Just enjoying the morning," he told his father.

Norm nodded. "Beautiful country."

"So it seems."

"I heard you had a job in town."

Gabriel opened the travel mug and drank the hot coffee. Warmth filled his stomach. "Just for the holidays."

"Retail?"

From the tone it was obvious his father thought retail was as distasteful as having to clean up the local dog park.

"I like it."

His old man turned to him. "You can't mean that. You're a soldier."

"I'm a doctor and I'm not suggesting a career change. I have a lot of time on my hands. This is good, honest work. Different. Seeing people all excited about the holidays reminds me what the fight is about."

Most of the words were true, he thought with some surprise. He didn't have enough to fill his day and the store was unexpectedly pleasant.

"Just don't get any ideas," his father grumbled.

"About?"

Gabriel knew it was wrong to bait his father, but did it anyway, even as he continued to watch the driveway.

"Leaving. You're staying in."

"You asking or telling?"

"Leaving's not an option," Norm told him. "You owe them."

"I've paid that debt. I gave the army what they asked in return for my education."

"It's not enough. This isn't about the letter of the law, it's about the spirit. You have to do the right thing, boy. That's how you were raised."

Gabriel drew in a breath, then faced his father. "You're saying I can't leave."

"Yes. Stay and get your twenty. You'll still be young enough to get some fancy hospital job and earn your millions." Each word dripped with distaste.

"You think it's about the money?"

"What else? It's like those jet jockeys who take their

training to some airline. Disgusting. They should stay in until they're released. Leaving isn't right."

"You think service isn't a choice? It's indentured servitude, with pay and medical? Once you sign up, you're in for life."

"That's how it should be," his father told him. "If you're thinking of leaving before your twenty, you're dishonoring this family. I should have known you'd be like this. You never understood the importance of what was right. Never understood the history you'd been born into. When I was your age—"

Whichever of the stories he'd been about to launch into was cut short when Noelle drove around the corner. She managed to stay in the middle of the driveway, right until the end. Gabriel saw the triumph in her blue eyes. Then she hit the brakes a bit too hard and went sliding.

He heard her shriek and guessed she was spinning the wheel too hard. Sure enough there was a sweep to the right, then to the left, all in slow motion. Her car came to a gentle rest against a snowbank by the porch.

He stood and started toward her. Norm stayed on the porch, muttering something about female drivers.

Noelle opened her car door and stepped out.

"That is so unfair," she yelled. "I was careful. I went slow and it was perfect right up until the end."

"You hit the brakes too hard."

She glared at him. "You think?" She turned and kicked her tire. "I'm not good at snow driving. Why is that?"

Instead of answering, he put his travel mug on the roof of her car, then pulled her close. She had on a thick coat and a red knit cap. Her long, blond hair spilled over her shoulders. She looked like a model for a ski ad. Ignoring her inability to travel in bad weather.

He wrapped his arms around her and was pleased when she returned the action, holding on to him.

"If you're going to mock me, don't," she told him, staring into his eyes.

"I'm not."

Behind them, the front door closed. The older Boylan had gone inside. They were alone.

"Are you going to kiss me?" she asked.

There were a dozen reasons not to kiss her and only a couple as to why he should. But the latter were more compelling. Or maybe it was just because a woman like Noelle wasn't easy to resist. Either way, he lowered his head just enough to brush his mouth against hers.

CHAPTER FIVE

GABRIEL'S KISS WAS sadly brief, Noelle thought as she felt the warmth of his lips on hers. There was contact, a sensation of heat, and then he raised his head. She wanted to insist on more, but perhaps the front yard of his brother's house with both his parents in residence wasn't the place.

"Thanks for coming early," he said.

"You're welcome. Felicia called me a little bit ago with a last-minute grocery list." She smiled. "I've never heard her so rattled."

"I wouldn't know. I've been banned from the kitchen. All the men have. This is Felicia's first Thanksgiving dinner."

They were still standing very close together. If not for the layers of coats and sweaters, their pose could be considered intimate. She liked how his hands rested on her hips and the way he was looking at her—like a man looks at a woman who intrigues him.

"We should get inside," he said. "You're freezing."

She could stand the cold a little longer but nodded anyway and stepped back. She got the two grocery bags out of her car. Gabriel took them from her and together they walked inside.

The house was bright and warm. So far there weren't any smells, but it was barely eleven in the morning. If they weren't eating until five, the turkey wouldn't have been in the oven very long.

Karen and Felicia stood together talking in the open kitchen. Felicia glanced up and saw Noelle, then hurried toward her.

"You're here. Thank you for stopping at the store. I don't know how it's possible I forgot anything. I made lists and I checked them at least twice."

"Just like Santa," Gabriel murmured.

Noelle took in her friend's slightly frantic expression and did her best not to smile. "It's okay. I'm happy to help. Where are you in the meal preparation?"

She asked the question before realizing she was hardly an expert. Her lone Thanksgiving cooking experience had been two years ago—shortly after the death of her mother and grandmother. The meal had turned out, but she hadn't really cared either way.

This was better, she told herself as she took the grocery bags from Gabriel and put them on the counter. This time she was happy and healthy and the meal wasn't her responsibility.

"I read an article online," Felicia began as she emptied the bag. "About a woman who does a just-in-case turkey the night before. At the time I remember thinking she was wasting a lot of time, but now I completely understand and I think she's brilliant. I need a just-in-case turkey."

Noelle moved next to her friend. "While I'm enjoying the meltdown, because you're normally so unflappable, let's be rational for a moment. Has anything happened to make you concerned the turkey won't turn out?"

"No. It's only been in an hour. It's barely started cooking. I followed the directions precisely for cleaning it and then filling it with stuffing." She turned to Karen. "You were with me, helping. Did it appear everything was in order?"

Gabriel's mother nodded. "You need to take a breath. There's no crisis."

"I forgot whipping cream! Who forgets that? What if I forgot something else?"

Gideon walked into the kitchen and took Felicia in his arms. "Hey," he said, staring into her green eyes. "I love you. Carter loves you. We have a home and a dog and family. It's one dinner. Get over it."

Noelle knew about Felicia and Gideon's relationship, but she'd never had much of an opportunity to observe it firsthand. Now, as Felicia visibly relaxed in her lover's arms, Noelle felt a twinge of envy. While she was happy for her friend, she wanted that kind of love for herself. The safety and sense of belonging. Life was short and it was important to hang on to whatever happiness was available.

Her gaze wandered to Gabriel and she sighed. While he was nice eye candy and a surprisingly efficient stock person, he wasn't anyone she could have a long-term relationship with. He was leaving and she was staying. She had no sense of him wanting to connect in any way. He wasn't close to his family and according to Ana Raquel and his mother, had nearly reached the age where an explanation on the question "Why aren't you married?" was going to get awkward.

All reasons to remind herself that he was not good boyfriend material. Not that he'd been, you know, asking.

He turned and caught her studying him. One eyebrow rose in inquiry. The movement was oddly masculine and very sexy. It made her wonder if she was worrying about the wrong thing. So she wasn't going to marry Gabriel. Big whoop. Maybe she could simply mention they could do the wild thing while he was in town.

Before Noelle could decide if she was being incredibly contemporary in her thinking or simply delusional, Felicia stepped out of Gideon's embrace.

"You're right," she said firmly. "The dinner will be fine. I understand the safest temperature for our dinner, so no one will get food poisoning. Everything after that is simply a bonus." She glanced at the clock. "We need to get to town or we'll miss the parade."

"I thought you were in charge of the festivals," Karen said as they all moved toward the front of the house.

"I am, but this isn't technically a festival, so I don't have to worry about it. However, I will be dealing with the Christmas tree lighting on Saturday."

Gabriel moved next to Noelle and held out her jacket. "Not a 'holiday tree' lighting?" he asked.

"No. Here in Fool's Gold we've decided to throw political correctness to the wind and call it a Christmas tree. I know because there was a very vigorous discussion about that exact topic at the last business association meeting. We took a vote."

He nodded slowly. "You voted for calling it a Christmas tree."

"I did."

The large group was sorted into two cars. Gideon stayed behind to watch the turkey. Noelle saw Felicia whisper something into his ear before they left. She suspected it had nothing to do with cooking.

The trip down the mountain didn't take long. Felicia directed Norm to a parking lot a few blocks away from the parade route, and they walked the rest of the way.

Noelle found herself next to Gabriel, which was nice. She told herself it was because he was tall and broad, so he could block the wind, but in truth, she liked speculating about him. And if that caused a tingle or two, all the better for her.

They stopped by several street carts and bought hot chocolate and popcorn. The sidewalks were crowded with families. Because it was Thanksgiving, there were fewer tourists than usual for a parade, but plenty of residents. It was as if most of the town had turned out to watch.

"Over there," Felicia said, leading them to a viewing area by the Fox and Hound. The corner spot allowed them to see down two streets.

"Nice," Norm told her. "You *are* good at logistics."

Carter settled on the sidewalk. Karen sat next to him. Norm and Felicia were behind them. Noelle noticed that Gabriel did his best to keep his distance from his father.

She wondered about their relationship. Gabriel hadn't said that much, but there was obviously tension. Despite the fact that Carter had showed up in Gideon's life over the summer, Norm and Karen hadn't come to meet him until a few days before. Felicia had been the one to invite them to visit for the holidays. What had happened to cause both sons to become, if not estranged, then at least disconnected from their parents?

Not a question to ask minutes before the parade started.

She sipped her hot chocolate, grateful for her coat and the sweater she wore beneath. The sky was blue, but the temperature couldn't be much above freezing. She could see her breath.

Gabriel pointed across the street. "That guy is selling chestnuts," he said. "Are you sure this town is real?"

"Mostly. I don't think I like chestnuts. Now, if he had fudge, that would be a different story."

"You eat chocolate?"

She glanced up at him. "I'm a fully functioning female, so yes. Why are you surprised?" She held out her to-go cup. "Hello, hot chocolate."

"I thought you only ate healthy stuff."

Because she was skinny, she thought, knowing that just over three years ago, she'd been curvy and completely happy with her body. Then she'd gotten sick. Weight had seemed to melt off her. It wasn't exactly a diet she would have recommended to anyone.

In the past year, she'd gained back about a third of what she'd lost. It was slow going, but she was determined that she would see her curves again.

"I love chocolate," she said firmly, and swallowed the last of her drink. Again, discussing the whys of her thinness wasn't a subject for this second.

The sound of music drifted to them.

"It's started," Carter said, scrambling to his feet. Norm held out his hand to Karen as she stood. They all turned and looked up 4th Street, straining to see the beginning of the parade.

"Are there floats?" Gabriel asked.

"I don't know. I hope so."

Felicia glanced at them. "There is the local high school marching band, some vehicles from the fire stations, a few old cars and some oversized balloons." She shrugged. "I saw the list."

"That's it?" Gabriel asked.

Noelle poked him with her elbow. "Attitude, mister. It will be magical. You'll see."

"Oversized balloons?"

"Maybe it's like the Macy's parade in New York."

He grinned at her. "I'm sure it's exactly like that."

The music got louder. Soon they could see two teenagers with a banner welcoming them to the annual Fool's Gold Thanksgiving parade. An old convertible went by with Mayor Marsha perched in the back. She waved regally as she passed.

There were a few balloons, including a charming Christmas penguin with a bright red cap.

"Aren't penguins in the South Pole?" Gabriel murmured in her ear.

"Stop talking."

"Where it's *summer?*"

She looked at him. "You're not getting into the spirit of this."

"It's the best parade I've seen in years."

"You're just saying that."

He surprised her by putting his arm around her. "No. I mean it."

She allowed herself a moment of enjoying the warmth of him next to her, then turned her attention back to the parade. The marching band came by next, blasting a rock version of "Jingle Bells," then a couple of police cars and a fire truck. The latter had a fireman's hat on the hood with the number 46 on it. There were wreaths on the side of the truck and a plastic Santa sitting on the bumper.

A block or so away, people started yelling. Noelle turned but couldn't see what was causing the fuss. The sounds were happy—mostly surprise and delight. She raised herself on tiptoe.

"Can you see what it is?" she asked.

"Not yet," Gabriel began, then swore softly. "No way," he said. "No way."

Felicia glanced up the street. "Oh, that's right. I forgot about them."

Norm and Karen both looked at her. "How could you forget?"

Noelle shifted forward, trying to get a look. "Forget what?"

Then the crowd seemed to move back and she had a clear view of Priscilla…dressed as Santa.

"Is that an—" Gabriel began.

"Elephant?"

"Uh-huh."

"Yes." Noelle squeezed her hot chocolate cup and danced from foot to foot. "Do you see what she's wearing? I know it's just a jacket, but still."

"How do you get a jacket on an elephant?" Gabriel asked.

"In pieces," Felicia told him. "They're held together with industrial-strength hook-and-loop closures." She turned to Gideon's parents. "There's a ranch outside of town. Mostly they have goats, but there is also an elephant, some llamas and other animals. It's very eclectic, which suits the town."

Noelle didn't care about that. She began to cheer at the sight of Priscilla the elephant strolling down the street.

Most of the Stryker family walked with her, each of them dressed for the holidays. Rafe and Shane pulled wagons with their children in them. As Priscilla got closer, Noelle saw that she was trailed by a goat and a pony, each dressed as a Christmas elf.

"I'm never moving," she said with a sigh.

Gabriel still had his arm around her. Now he pulled her against him. "Was it ever a question?"

"No, but now I'm completely and totally sure."

AFTER THE PARADE, the family drove back up the mountain. Once in the house, Felicia headed for the kitchen. Noelle and Karen went with her while the men headed downstairs to watch whatever game was on. The smell of roasting turkey filled the air and made Noelle's stomach growl.

Felicia crossed to the oven and turned on the light. "It would make me very happy if you could cooperate," she whispered, then glanced over her shoulder. "I do understand the foolishness of talking to my entrée. I just can't seem to help myself."

Karen nodded sympathetically. "I've had many a conversation with my meals," she confessed. "It's nothing to worry about."

Carter flew into the kitchen, Webster at his heels.

"I'm going to take him out," he said, crossing to Felicia and hugging her. "Then I'll be back. I'm going to peel the potatoes. You remember that, right?"

"Yes. I remember," Felicia told him.

The boy and the dog headed outside.

When he was gone, Felicia turned to them. "He wants to help. It's so nice. We've been very fortunate with his personality and how he was raised. His mother did an excellent job. I hope when Gideon and I begin a family that I can be half as skilled."

Karen moved toward her and touched her shoulder. "You'll do great."

"I have doubts," Felicia admitted.

Noelle was about to reassure her when she heard a

sharp, angry voice. It took her a second to realize it came from downstairs. Karen and Felicia both turned in that direction.

"No," Karen said firmly. "They're not going to fight on Thanksgiving."

She spoke as if this had happened before, but didn't explain any further. But when she started for the stairs, Felicia and Noelle went with her, all three women hurrying down to the lower story.

The voices grew louder.

"This isn't about you," Gideon growled. "It's not your choice."

"I get a say," Norm shouted. "You're both my sons and you will respect my opinion."

The three women raced into the family room. The men faced each other. Tension was thick with more than a hint of anger. Noelle saw Gabriel's back was stiff, his shoulders set. A muscle twitched in his jaw.

She had no idea what the fight had been about, but she knew he was in pain. As she moved toward him, Karen grabbed Norm's hand and physically pulled him toward the stairs.

"You stay out of this," he told her.

"No," Karen said, still pulling. "You're coming with me until you can cool off. We talked about this."

"You don't understand."

"I understand plenty."

Felicia went to Gideon and murmured something. He nodded and they went down the hall behind the family room. Which left Noelle with Gabriel.

He crossed to the window and stared out toward the mountainside. "Sorry about that. It's a family thing. My dad has… He has expectations."

She thought about making a joke that he was a doctor and what more did his father want. Only she didn't know what the fight was about and couldn't be sure she wasn't stepping on toes. She wanted to help and didn't know how. A frustrating combination.

Gabriel stood alone and in that moment, as she watched him, she wondered how much of his life he spent like that. Solitary.

Without knowing what else to do, she crossed to him.

"Hey," she said, touching his good hand.

He turned his face to her. Pain darkened his eyes, along with something she could only assume was hope. Hope that she would somehow make it all better.

Panic seized her. She had no idea what to say. What to do. A distraction was called for but short of yelling "Fire," there was nothing that…

"You could kiss me again," she blurted.

In that split second before he responded, she braced herself for dismissal, sarcasm or pity. Which probably didn't make her a poster girl for mental health, but then she'd never believed in lying to herself. The fact that *she* found him attractive didn't mean the interest was returned.

One eyebrow rose. "I could," Gabriel said, right before he lowered his head and did just that.

The first touch of his mouth on hers was soft. Not tentative, she thought, closing her eyes. More discovery than passion.

He had nice lips. Warm and tender, but masculine enough to keep things interesting. Although she expected him to straighten right away like he had that morning, he didn't. He lingered.

Nerve endings began to fire. Instinctively, she stepped

toward him just as he wrapped his arms around her and pulled her close. They touched everywhere and still it wasn't enough.

She rested her hands on his shoulders. He was muscled and strong. He shifted slightly so he was kissing her cheek, her chin, her jaw. Heat radiated from every point of contact. When he trailed light kisses down her neck, her breath caught.

It wasn't just that she hadn't been kissed in what felt like forever. It was that she hadn't ever been kissed by *this* man before. She hadn't felt the solid pressure of his chest flattening her breasts, hadn't experienced his large hands splayed against her back, hadn't known the depth of wanting that left her practically trembling.

He returned his mouth to hers. She parted her lips without him asking and was thrilled when his tongue swept inside. At the first hungry stroke, she knew she couldn't refuse him anything. Or if she could, she didn't want to. She ached all over. Her breasts, between her thighs. She wanted him touching her, exploring her. She wanted to touch him in return, learn everything about his body. She wanted to yield and then she wanted to take.

The need was so great, so overwhelming, she was suddenly terrified she was the only one at the party. She drew back, doing her best to control her breathing. Gabriel stared at her, his expression hungry.

"You're unexpected," he murmured.

"I could say the same thing." She cleared her throat. "I wanted to distract you."

"Well done." The corner of his mouth twitched. "I knew you'd be trouble, but I didn't think you'd surprise me."

She smiled, liking the sound of that. But before she could say anything else, Carter clattered down the stairs, Webster at his heels.

"Hey," the teen said as he bounded into the room. "What's the score?"

Gabriel glanced at the big-screen TV, muted but still tuned to the football game. "It's tied."

"I should get back upstairs," Noelle said. "See if I'm needed in the kitchen."

Gabriel nodded. "Thank you."

For the distraction? For the kiss? For making him realize she was exactly who he'd been looking for all his life? Okay, the latter was a little unlikely, but a girl could dream.

"IT'S A FAMILY TRADITION," Karen said, when the food had been put on the table. "I'll go first. I'm thankful to be with my boys again." She nodded at her husband.

"I'm thankful we have the strongest fighting force in the world," Norm said.

Karen sighed. "It's Thanksgiving."

"And I'm giving thanks."

Felicia cleared her throat. "I'm thankful for my wonderful family. Immediate and extended. And for my friends." She smiled at Noelle.

"I'm thankful for my family, too," Carter said, squeezing Felicia's hand. "And Webster."

Gideon agreed with Felicia and Carter, and Gabriel was thankful for those who made it. Noelle finished with thanks for finding where she belonged.

As Norm began slicing the large turkey, Carter leaned toward his uncle. "You're like my dad, right? Serving in the army."

"As a doctor. Your dad saw real action."

"But you carry a gun," Carter said.

"Sometimes," Gabriel told him. "Not often."

"Did you always want to be a doctor?"

Norm snorted. "Hell, no. If it was up to him, he'd have studied English literature at some fancy university and become a college professor."

Carter and Noelle both turned to Gabriel.

"Is that true?" the teen asked.

Gabriel shrugged. "It wasn't an option."

"You're right about that," Norm said, putting slices of turkey onto the first plate and passing it to his wife. "In our family, we serve."

Karen looked desperately around the table. "This is all so lovely, Felicia. I don't know why you were concerned. Everything turned out perfectly. Thank you so much for doing this."

"You helped," Felicia said. "Although I am pleased with the turkey."

"Maybe talking to it made the difference," Gideon teased.

Conversation shifted to the threat of snow and the upcoming holiday festivals. Noelle wasn't sure if Norm's outburst was forgotten or simply politely swept under the rug. Either way, she reached under the table for Gabriel's hand and took it in hers. He turned to her.

"You okay?" she asked quietly.

He nodded and squeezed her fingers before releasing her. She accepted the information because it was the polite thing to do and she didn't know him well enough to push. But she couldn't help wondering if this exchange was the exact reason he hadn't seen his parents for so long. Under the circumstances, she couldn't blame him.

She was sure Norm was acting from some misplaced sense of doing right by his family. She just wished he could see that the price of that was losing the very thing he wanted to hang on to.

GABRIEL WALKED TOWARD Noelle's store early on Friday. She'd warned him that they would be busy and open extra hours in support of Black Friday. He'd been out of the country so long, it had taken him a second to remember what Black Friday was. He had trouble believing that people made such a production of shopping for a holiday that was still a month away, but then he wasn't the Black Friday target audience.

Besides, he owed Noelle. She'd been there for him the previous day. From her enthusiasm for the parade, to distracting him from his fight with his father, she'd been by his side.

He sipped the coffee he'd bought at Brew-haha and crossed the street. He had to give her credit. She was unconventional. He grinned at the memory of their kiss, remembering how the exploding need had nearly knocked him off his feet. For someone who danced with excitement when viewing an elephant in a Santa suit, she was one sexy woman.

He was still grinning when he rounded the corner and saw a group of people waiting outside The Christmas Attic.

No, he amended. Not people. Women. Lots of women. They formed a line and were all talking animatedly. When an old lady toward the front of the line spotted him, she called out.

"When do we get this show on the road?"

Gabriel stared at her. "We, ah, open at eight."

The old lady glanced at her watch. "You've got five minutes. If you think you're going to be late, you're wrong."

He nodded instead of answering, then hurried past her and opened the front door to step into the store.

Noelle was already there. She'd put on her cheerful red apron with the store logo on the front and was counting out bills as she put them into the cash register.

"There's a line," he said, pointing.

"I saw." She looked up, her gaze slightly unfocused. "I don't think I'm ready."

"Not being ready isn't an option. They seem determined and hostile."

She pushed the cash register shut, then drew in a breath. "Okay. It's going to be a long day. We'll pace ourselves and do the best we can. If you get tired, you can rest in back. Or leave early."

"I can make it through my shift."

"I don't want you relapsing."

"Wouldn't I have to lapse first?"

Her lack of smile told him she was nervous. He crossed to her and put his hands on her shoulders.

"You'll do great. The store is charming and you have customers waiting. Let's open a couple of minutes early and get this day started."

She stared into his eyes. For a second, he thought instead of opening early, he should take the minute or so they had and kiss her. Of course, kissing would lead to him wanting more and this wasn't the time or place. But it sure would be nice.

"Hey, you in there! It's freezing out here."

The comment came from outside and was accompanied by an insistent knocking. Noelle squared her shoulders.

"Okay," she said as she marched to the front of the store. "I'm ready."

"Me, too."

Although it turned out he was wrong. He wasn't ready. There was no way to *be* ready for the onslaught of customers. They arrived in groups of twos and threes, they lingered and they bought. Bears and trains, CDs and throws. No corner of the store went unexplored. If he wasn't restocking, he was bagging. Every now and then he carried bags to a waiting car.

"Excuse me, young man."

Gabriel turned and saw a pleasant-looking woman leaning heavily on a cane covered with painted purple flowers.

"Yes, ma'am. How can I help you?"

"I'm looking for a menorah for a friend of mine and I noticed the one in the side window. It's so pretty. Having it made of glass is very unusual and I like that the candles are all different colors. Can you get it for me?"

"Of course," he said, already heading for the stockroom. "We have one in a box."

He passed Noelle, who smiled wearily. Five minutes later, the lady with the cane had her menorah and was heading out of the store. He was about to check on the bears when another woman stopped him.

"You're Gabriel," she said, eyeing him. She had white curls and wore a bright purple track suit. "Gideon's brother."

"Yes."

"I'm Eddie." She smiled. "I need you to carry this to my car."

She handed him a box about the size of a soda can. He stared at it.

"You want me to carry that?"

"Uh-huh." Eddie nodded. "I'm old so you have to do what I say. Come on. The day's a-wasting."

He had no idea what was going on, but wasn't about to tell the seventysomething woman no. She led him out of the store and down the sidewalk. They walked to the corner and she pointed to a late-model sedan. When they reached it, he handed her the package.

She smiled. "Thank you."

"You're welcome."

Still confused about what she'd wanted, he turned, only to feel her pat his butt. He spun back. Her expression was both innocent and satisfied.

No, he told himself. He'd imagined the light touch. And if he hadn't, there was nothing he could do about it.

"Ah, have a nice day," he mumbled before backing toward the store.

The steady stream of customers continued until Noelle closed and locked the door at six-fifteen. They'd both been on their feet since seven that morning.

"My feet hurt," she said, untying her apron. "My back hurts and I'm starving."

"Me, too, and an old lady patted my butt."

Noelle looked at him and started laughing. "You're making that up."

"I swear it happened."

"Eddie or Gladys."

"Eddie."

"Then I believe you. Did you get lunch?"

"No."

"Me, either. Want to come by my place? I'll order the biggest pizza you've ever seen. You'll love it."

She had a smudge on her cheek and dust on her jeans. She looked as weary as he felt. But as she invited him over, all he could think was that what he really wanted for dinner was her. Because when he was around her, the world somehow righted itself. Even if he was being harassed by seniors.

For a second he wondered what she would say if he told her the truth. He figured he was at even odds for her wanting the same and slapping him. Which meant the most sensible course was to say, "Pizza sounds great."

CHAPTER SIX

Noelle pushed open her front door and flipped on the lights. The place was small—a two-bedroom starter home with a single bathroom. A classic ranch style, built in the fifties.

Gabriel walked in behind her. "Nice," he said, glancing at the black leather sofa. "That looks comfortable."

"Throw yourself on it. Seriously, I plan to do the same as soon as I order the pizza."

She waited until he'd moved into the living room before sinking onto the bench by the door. She unzipped her boots and tugged them off, then stretched her aching feet. She hadn't been kidding before—every part of her hurt. Even her hair. She couldn't remember ever being this exhausted. And the thrill of it was she got to do the same thing tomorrow. At least she didn't have to open until her regular time.

She stood and limped into the small kitchen. Once there, she pulled the pizza menu free of the magnet on the refrigerator door.

"All meat?" she asked.

Gabriel stood in the doorway of the kitchen. "You like that?"

"No, but I'll get it on half."

He crossed his arms over his chest. "You can eat half a large pizza?"

"Yes."

"That I want to see."

"You will."

She placed the order, adding a pint of Ben and Jerry's, then put the phone back on the counter. She opened the refrigerator and pulled out two bottles of beer.

Gabriel's expression of surprise returned. "I would have said you drink red wine."

"I have mysterious depths."

"I can see that."

They headed back to the living room.

Her sectional sofa took up most of the floor space, but she didn't care. There was a chaise that was perfect for stretching out to watch movies and she had a great reading light. She'd bought a nice big television because she wanted to see all the period details in *Downton Abbey*. Maybe an apartment would have made more sense, but she liked having a yard. Her landlord, local retired cyclist Josh Golden, had told her she could plant whatever she wanted. This past summer she'd gone crazy with berries. Next year she was going to experiment with a few vegetables. If her cash flow improved, she would buy a place, but for now, the tiny house was plenty.

Gabriel sat at one end of the sofa while she collapsed on the chaise. She wiggled her toes, wondering when her feet would go from seminumb and sore to seriously throbbing. She pointed to the coffee table.

"Feel free to put your feet up. I bought that at a garage sale for twenty bucks. It's indestructible."

He hesitated for a second, then bent down to unlace his boots. He pulled them off and then raised his stocking-clad feet on the battered wooden surface.

"Thanks. I'm used to standing all day, but for some reason this was different. Harder."

"I know. I'm used to running around, too, but I'm completely exhausted. I think it's the intensity." She picked up her bottle of beer and took a sip. "You remember the gift bazaar is coming up, right?"

He leaned back his head and closed his eyes. "Don't remind me. What is it with this town?"

"We love to celebrate."

"You need a twelve-step program. Hi, I'm Fool's Gold and I'm addicted to festivals."

She smiled. "I'm actually really excited about the bazaar next weekend. I stocked it with some really interesting items. Now you remember you can simply direct people to the store, right?"

"Yes, my goal is to sell as little as possible."

"I need something to throw at you," she grumbled. "Of course you can sell things, but you don't have to. If they want it in a different color or whatever, tell them to come to the store. But that's for next weekend. Tomorrow we only have to get through the post–Black Friday what-if-I-didn't-get-everything-I-want shopping frenzy."

She shook her head. "I should have taken part-time jobs in retail while I was in college."

"What did you do?"

"Internships when I could get them. I was a nanny for a couple of summers and I temped in offices. I was a waitress. The usual. What about you?"

"I didn't have summers off. I got through college quickly. Once I was in the army and they were paying for medical school, there weren't any breaks."

She angled toward him, taking in the strong profile

and determined set of his jaw. "Did you really want to be an English professor?"

He glanced at her. "I don't know. I didn't want to be a soldier."

"Yet you are one."

He shrugged. "Not really. Being a doctor was a way to honor the family legacy and still do something I wanted to do. Hard to do that while writing a thesis on great American writers of the twentieth century."

"Your dad pressured you."

"That's one way of putting it." He drank from his beer bottle. "My dad was determined. He talked about Gideon and me going into the army from the time we were born. Doing anything else wasn't an option. Looking back, I tell myself I should have stood up to him."

"You were a kid. Did you even know there were other choices?"

"Not really," he admitted. "I just knew I couldn't go do what Gideon did."

She'd been lucky with her family. They wanted her to do whatever made her happy. But not all parents were like that.

There was a knock on the door. She stood and groaned as her feet and legs protested, then hobbled to the door. Gabriel beat her there and pulled out his wallet.

"I've got this," he said.

She grinned at him. "You're such a guy."

"Thank you."

Ten minutes later they were seated at her small table. She put out plates and napkins, and they were digging into the pizza.

The crust was crisp on the outside and soft on the inside. The melted cheese was hot, the grilled vegetables the perfect texture.

Gabriel stared at her half of the pizza. "Vegetables? Seriously? On pizza?"

"I know. I can't help it. But you have your manly all-meat." She grinned. "Beer and pizza. Later you'll probably feel the need to go challenge some teenaged boys to a drag race."

"Or I could just watch wrestling on TV and have my manhood affirmed that way."

"Really? Wrestling? Don't they wear tights?"

"It's not tights. It's—" He sighed heavily. "Why do I bother?"

She laughed and took another bite of her pizza.

When they'd polished off every slice, she leaned back in her chair. "That was great. And later, there's ice cream."

"A gourmet meal?" he asked.

"One of my favorites."

He started to say something, then stopped. She had a feeling it was going to be to ask her if she ate like that, how come she was so thin. And she didn't want to talk about her weight or how she was still working her way back to what she had been.

"Any pizza where you were stationed?" she asked.

"Sure. The army provides. In Germany there were a few places around the base. In Afghanistan and Iraq, it was more of a challenge to find. The mess had it, but it wasn't exactly the same."

She got up and walked to her refrigerator, where she grabbed a second beer for each of them. "You were close to the front line, weren't you?"

"Sometimes."

She remembered what Felicia had told her. "You were also the doctor on the plane, right? The one who flies with those being medevaced to Germany?"

He nodded cautiously.

She could tell he didn't want to talk about it. She would guess he'd seen a lot of horrible injuries on those flights. From what she'd read and seen on news reports, the injured were in pretty bad shape when they were flown out. Gabriel and his team would have been doing their best to keep everyone alive while working in really cramped conditions.

"It must have been intense," she said.

"My work mostly is. I see the soldiers when they're first injured. Get them stabilized and ready for whatever surgery they're going to need." He relaxed a little. "The hours are long and when I was in a field hospital, the injuries just kept coming."

"How did you unwind?" she asked.

She was waiting for him to say volleyball or video games, or maybe make a joke. Instead, he stiffened and seemed to be looking at everything except her.

Her brain processed the change in him and tried to fill in the blanks. Then she felt herself starting to grin.

"Sex?" she asked, not bothering to hide her amusement. "Are you saying that there's sex in the military?"

"I was on a softball team," he grumbled.

"Is that what they're calling it these days?"

He met her gaze. "Yes, sometimes sex was a way to escape."

"Horndog," she said cheerfully. "So is that why you never married? Because I think you're going to need to give Ana Raquel an answer on that one. Not to mention your mother. Not that she's going to want to hear what you've been doing in your spare time."

"I don't care what Ana Raquel thinks about me, you won't tell my mother and no, that's not the reason I'm not married."

He opened his mouth as if he were going to say more, then closed it.

"Gabriel?" she asked quietly, wondering what he was thinking about. "What happened?"

He looked at her. "There was a woman. A doctor. I liked her a lot. We'd been dating for a few months. It was…different."

"You cared about her."

He nodded. "A few of her friends were going out in a Humvee. Just the girls. She went with them." His mouth twisted. "One second they were driving away, laughing and the next they were hit by a rocket."

Noelle gasped. Her stomach clenched and she regretted all the pizza she'd eaten.

"They were gone," he said, staring past her. "All of them. Just gone. It happened so fast."

"I'm so sorry. That must have been horrible."

"It was. Everything about it. But it also affirmed what I've always believed. That there's no point in getting married."

She stared at him. "Excuse me? You're dismissing the entire institution?"

"Sure. Life is tenuous at best. We could all be dead tomorrow. I've seen it again and again."

"I know what happened is a tragedy, but you learned the wrong lesson."

"No. I didn't." He glanced around. "I'll admit it's less

likely to happen here than where I was, but we still don't know what tomorrow is going to bring. Why risk it?"

"All the more reason to risk it," she told him. "We should grab happiness while we can, because you're right. There's no promise of more time."

"I'm not saying other people shouldn't get involved and get married. Just not me."

"What about a family? Don't you want kids?"

For a second, his expression turned wistful, but then the softness was gone. "I don't see that happening."

"You're going to be one lonely old guy."

"Ana Raquel will enjoy being right about me."

She wanted to say more, to tell him he was wrong, but she knew there was no point. Gabriel was an intelligent man who had obviously thought a lot about his future. He'd seen that life was tenuous and had decided to avoid future pain by not getting involved. She'd learned the same lesson about life's tenuousness, but with opposite results. She'd thrown herself into her new life in Fool's Gold—buying the store, making friends, having plans.

"I'm thinking about getting a cat," she said firmly, because a pet was the next step for her.

"I like cats," Gabriel told her. "They make you earn their respect. Webster would go home with anyone."

"He's a puppy."

"You think he'll be any different when he's older?"

Noelle thought about the friendly dog and how he seemed to adore the world. "Probably not," she admitted. "But he's really sweet."

"A good quality in a large dog." He picked up his beer. "How did you come to live in Fool's Gold?"

"I wanted to make a change. I'd been practicing law for a while and—"

He raised his eyebrows. "You were a lawyer?"

"Yes. You don't have to sound surprised."

"You're not ruthless."

"No, I'm not. That was part of the problem. I went into the profession with the idea I could help the world. Unfortunately, I was seduced by an offer from a corporate firm." There had been a guy involved in that decision, but she didn't want to go into that.

She sipped her beer. "I didn't love my work but I also didn't want to quit."

That decision had been taken out of her hands when she'd gotten sick. She'd taken a leave and when she'd returned, she'd been taken off all the important clients. Instead, she'd been relegated to research and writing reports. The firm wouldn't outright fire her for what had happened, but they'd made it clear they didn't trust her anymore.

"Eventually I knew I had to walk away," she continued. "I spent a few weeks figuring out what I wanted to do with the rest of my life and kept coming back to my family. Mostly my grandmother. She loved Christmas so much. It was a huge deal for all of us. She would tell me stories about when she was a little girl and all the magical things stored in the attic."

"That's where the name comes from."

She nodded. "I decided to open a store. The only problem was finding a location. It didn't seem like an L.A. kind of establishment. I wanted someplace smaller. So I spun until I was dizzy, then put a pin in a map of the States."

He stared at her. "You're kidding?"

"Not even a little. Under the pin was Fool's Gold,

which I'd never heard of. I moved here a few weeks later."

"And the rest is history. You were determined. I'm lucky you didn't attack me with that umbrella. You could have disemboweled me."

She laughed. "I was only going to try to knock you out. I could never disembowel anyone."

"That's right. You'd faint. Probably for the best. It keeps the rest of society safe." He studied her for a few seconds. "You'd never worked in retail but you packed up your life to move to a town where you didn't know anyone and you opened a store?"

"Yes." She waited for him to tell her she'd been an idiot.

He raised his bottle toward her. "I applaud your bravery."

"Thank you. Life is short. You have to do what you can while you have the chance."

His gaze sharpened. "Is that what you believe?"

She nodded. "Same as you, with an entirely different theory. I want it all. Love, kids, an IRA. I could go tomorrow, but what if I live to ninety-seven? What if you do?"

"Then you can join Ana Raquel in being right."

"The possibility doesn't change your mind?"

"No."

Not a surprise, she thought. He'd seen too much to have faith. She wondered why he'd chosen to go there, rather than where she had—with the belief that all opportunities were welcome.

"It's getting late," he said, rising to his feet. "I should go."

She stood, ignoring the whimper from her feet. "Are you mad?"

He smiled. "No. I'm not mad."

Do you want to have sex?

She wasn't sure where the question came from, but once formed, it didn't want to go away. Not that she was going to speak the question. Her fearlessness had limits.

Still, the kiss yesterday had been very nice.

"Thanks for all your hard work today," she said. "It was even more than I expected. We'll be busy through the season, but I think this is the worst of it."

"This is making me appreciate my day job," he said, carrying his plate to the sink and putting his bottle into the recycling bin.

"You're saying you don't want a career in retail?"

He faced her. "There are things I like."

"My sparkling wit and charm?"

She was standing by the table. He walked toward her and put his hands on her waist.

"That's part of it," he murmured even as he lowered his mouth to hers.

She wrapped her arms around his neck as he pulled her against him. In her stocking feet she had to shift her head back a little more than she had before, but the kiss was worth it.

His mouth was warm and hungry against hers. He moved back and forth a couple of times before settling in and brushing his tongue against her bottom lip. She parted her lips for him, welcoming the sensuous stroking along with the clenching low in her belly.

She tilted her head. Their tongues circled in that age-old dance of sexual need. He slid his hands up her back. She stepped even closer so that they were touching everywhere possible. Her breasts flattened against his chest, her belly pressed against his groin and in a matter of seconds she felt proof of his arousal.

Her fingers instinctively tightened their grip on him. What she really wanted to do was cup them against his need. Which would first require undressing him. She remembered how he'd looked in jeans and nothing else and had to hold in a moan.

Her bedroom was just down the hall. All she had was a full-size mattress, which meant there wouldn't be a whole lot of room for both of them. They would have to snuggle close and that could be fun.

He broke the kiss to nibble his way along her jaw, then over to her ear. He drew her lobe into his mouth and then bit down gently. Shivers raced through her.

They definitely had to go to her room, she thought, desire making her frantic. Get in her bed and—

"I should go," he said, dropping his arms to his sides and stepping back.

She blinked at him. "What?"

"It's late."

"It's eight."

"I know, but if I stay…"

They were going to have sex. She was fully aware of that. It was kind of the point.

"I don't understand," she admitted.

"I don't have an IRA."

Had she been drinking more than she realized? She glanced into the recycling bin and saw that no, she had only finished one beer and started a second. Even with her empty stomach, that shouldn't be enough to get her into an altered state of consciousness.

"An IRA?"

"I'm not what you're looking for," he said.

Really? Because the quivering in her belly said otherwise.

"It's not that I don't want you," he continued.

"Oh, good, because if you'd tried that one, I would have pointed out the obvious."

He gave her a slow, sexy smile that had her quivering. Then the smile faded. "I like you, Noelle."

Crap. She might have been out of practice with the whole dating thing but even she knew that any conversation that began with "I like you" was not going to end well.

"But?" she asked, bracing herself.

"But you want things I don't believe in. You want forever. You want love. I can't give you that. I'm leaving and even if I weren't, that's not me."

"And if I just want sex?"

She happened to be glancing down as she asked and had the satisfaction of seeing his erection surge slightly.

"I don't think my luck is that good," he told her.

"You're saying I'm not that kind of girl?"

"Something like that."

She wanted to say he was wrong, only he wasn't. She was old-fashioned. In her world, sex and love went together. Or if not love, then extreme like with the possibility of love.

Did she want to make an exception? Hold her heart carefully apart while giving Gabriel her body?

The girl bits were screaming "Yes, please. Take me now." The rest of her was more cautious. Did she want to have what it took to be that disconnected from her feelings? Did she want making love to be that casual?

He brushed another kiss across her mouth. "You know I'm right," he said firmly.

"I don't like it," she said, following him into the living room.

He put on his boots and tied the laces. "Me, either."

She looked at him. Sexy, charming, a doctor, honorable and not having sex with her. Was there a complaint card for life, because if there was, she had a few things to say.

He rose and crossed to the door. She handed him his jacket. As he slipped it on, she pressed her hands against his chest.

"What if I change my mind?" she asked.

"Get the big box of condoms."

She grinned. "Extra large?"

"You know it."

GABRIEL HAD BEEN to some of the largest cities in the Middle East. He'd haggled for food, for rugs and even, when he'd been engaged, for jewelry. He knew how to deal with the crowds, the heat, the bugs. What he wasn't prepared for was the women of Fool's Gold.

The morning had started out innocently enough. He'd gotten an extra shot of espresso in his usual black drip because despite being exhausted, he'd spent the night tossing and turning. Kissing Noelle had left him restless. He wanted her and he knew he shouldn't have her. Not a comfortable combination. The good news was his hand had stopped hurting and he would be visiting a local doctor to get the stitches out in a couple of days. The bad news was without his hand to distract him, he'd had more time to think about Noelle.

He'd arrived at the store on time, had found Noelle

already there and sorting through boxes that had arrived the day before. Conversation had been easy and all about business, including the fact that she'd hired some extra help. As if the kiss from the previous night had never happened. Only it had happened, as his dick kept reminding him. He'd felt her body against his and now he wanted more.

He'd thought the arrival of the customers would be a distraction, and in a way it was. Only customers in Fool's Gold were different. For one thing, they got personal. An attractive woman in her fifties stopped by to look over the display of bears.

"I have new grandbabies," she said with a smile. "I knew having six kids would eventually pay off. So, you're Gideon's brother, right?"

"Yes," he mumbled, wishing someone else would come up and claim his time. Maybe he could excuse himself to put away something. Or make a coffee run.

"Max and I listen to his show most nights. The music is a little before my time, but still fun. You're a doctor?"

Gabriel wondered if this would be where she mentioned one or all of her daughters weren't married, and if so how to gracefully duck out of the conversation. But before he could figure anything out, a pretty teen with red hair and green eyes walked over.

"Gabriel, right?" she asked, then turned to Denise. "Hey, Grandma."

"Melissa." The older woman hugged the teen. "What are you doing here?"

"I got a job."

"Then I should leave you to it." The older woman hugged her again, waved at Gabriel and walked away.

"I'm Melissa Sutton," the teen said, holding out her

hand to shake. "Noelle just hired me to help for the holidays. I'm working this weekend, then I have another week at UC San Diego before I take finals and then I'm home through the first of the year. She said you guys were really swamped."

As she spoke, she moved through the store, straightening as she went. She fluffed the fur on a stuffed bear, then turned back to him.

"What?" she asked at his pointed stare.

"Are you old enough to be in college?"

She laughed. "I'm eighteen. Don't worry. I'm not like her other temporary employees. I'm not coming home to play. I want to earn money." Her expression turned impish. "My folks are paying for college, but I'm responsible for providing for my own fun. And I have a latte habit that chews up cash. I blame Patience. She's the owner of Brew-haha. I worked there when the store opened last spring and got totally hooked. Of course the caffeine helps on those long nights of studying. Mom says you're a doctor."

He had no idea who her mother was so didn't know if they'd met. "Yes," he said, wondering why everyone found his occupation so fascinating and how it was they all knew what he did.

"In, like, the army, right?"

He nodded.

"I want to be a lawyer. Noelle used to be one, but she doesn't talk about it much. She swears she'll give me some inside info on my shifts and I'm going to make sure she does."

A few more customers came in, and Melissa took care of them quickly and efficiently. Gabriel was able to return to keeping the shelves stocked, which was his preference. Noelle manned the cash register when she wasn't helping customers. The store was crowded and busy, just the way it should be.

Sometime close to noon a blond woman with a couple of toddlers stopped by. The older child—a little girl— had a small stuffed giraffe clutched in her hands.

"Hey, you," the woman said, stopping to hug Melissa. "I heard you were back."

"Just for the long weekend. Then I have finals. I'll be home for the winter break by the seventh." Melissa turned to Gabriel. "This is my aunt. Dakota Andersson, this is Gabriel Boylan."

"Nice to meet you," Dakota said, shaking his hand. "Gideon's brother, right? You're twins?"

"Fraternal."

The little girl was waving frantically at Melissa, who scooped her into her arms. "How's my best girl?" She looked over the girl's head. "Dakota is a triplet and they're identical. She's one of six. Her brother, Ethan, is my stepfather." Melissa paused. "Is that right? If Liz is my aunt and he's married to her, then he's my step uncle, maybe. Whatever. He's my other dad."

Dakota picked up her young son and held him. "We have a complicated family."

"I met your mother earlier," Gabriel told her, remembering Melissa's grandmother.

Dakota laughed. "Be grateful we're all married or she would be talking up her daughters."

News that didn't surprise him.

Just before Dakota left, she turned to Melissa.

"You're not going to miss the tree lighting, are you? Noelle knows about it. She's closing the store early."

Melissa smiled. "I'll be there, I promise."

Dakota waved and walked away. Melissa looked at him.

"You look trapped."

"No, I don't," he said automatically, although maybe it was true.

"The town is a little intense. I grew up here and sometimes it gets to me. When I talk to my friends at college about what it's like here, they don't always believe me."

"So there's a tree lighting," he said. "Why am I not surprised?"

"Yes. There's a city tree and it's huge and tonight it's lit for the first time this season. You may have noticed the storefronts are all decorated."

"They have been," he said, remembering the pumpkins and paper turkeys in windows.

Melissa's expression turned pitying. "That was for Thanksgiving. I'm talking Christmas. We take our holidays here very seriously."

"I've noticed that."

"Between last Wednesday and this morning, the decorations have all changed. And tonight is the tree lighting. You're going to be there, aren't you?"

He could think of a dozen things he would rather be doing. Only he had a feeling that Noelle would want to be a part of things and because of that, he would go with her. Because he liked being near her. He liked her enthusiasm and belief in what was possible. He knew she was wrong, but he respected her position.

"I'll be there," he said.

Three women walked up then and started looking at the nativities. Gabriel checked the rest of their stock and was about to make a run to get more bears when he noticed his mother moving toward him.

Tension threatened, but when he saw she was alone, he relaxed. He wasn't ready to go another round with his father, he thought.

She looked different than she had when they'd first arrived. Happier. She held shopping bags in each hand.

"You've been busy," he said, taking the bags from her.

"Mostly gifts," she said, giving him a hug. "A few things for Carter. A couple of baby gifts."

"Who's pregnant? Felicia?"

"Not that I know of, but she's made it clear she wants children. I'm planning ahead." Her blue eyes softened. "She's going to be a wonderful mother. I'm just so happy for them both."

He had a feeling tears would be next. He glanced at Noelle and held up both bags. She nodded, understanding he was going to take them to his mother's car.

They walked toward the front door.

"This time we'll be a part of things from the beginning," his mother continued, then looked at him out of the corner of her eye. "What about you? Any babies in your future?"

He swore silently. "No."

"Noelle seems nice."

"She's my friend, Mom. We're not dating."

"Oh. I thought you two had a connection."

They did, but he wasn't about to discuss the fact that he found Noelle incredibly sexy with his mother.

"Is there someone special?" she asked.

"Not right now."

An evasive answer, but it beat dealing with the truth.

"I was worried about Gideon," she admitted as they walked out to the parking lot and she pointed to where she'd left the Explorer. "After what happened to him. Does he talk to you about it? Being held captive?"

"Not really. I know the broad strokes."

"He hasn't said a word to me. Your father says I shouldn't push. That I couldn't understand what he went through. I suppose that's true, but I want to be there for him."

"You should talk to Felicia," he said. "She knows Gideon better than anyone. She'll have an idea of the best way to deal with his past."

His mother nodded. She opened the back of the Explorer, and he put the packages inside. She touched his arm.

"You know I love you, don't you?" she asked, her gaze intense.

"I know, Mom."

"I let your father have things his way. I've always regretted that. I know he was difficult. It's just…" She paused. "He's an honorable man."

Norman Boylan's honor wasn't in question. It was how he'd chosen to deal with his sons that Gabriel had a problem with. And that his mother had let her husband determine all the rules.

"I don't want to lose you," his mother said, tears filling her eyes. "Please tell me I haven't."

He drew her into his arms. "I love you, Mom. You haven't lost me."

It was the truth. He would always love her, but he'd found that love existed best from a safe distance.

"Are you going to stay in the army?" she asked.

"I don't know."

"For what it's worth, I'd like you to get out. Settle down somewhere. Fall in love. Get married."

"Give you more grandchildren?" he teased, mostly to distract her.

"Exactly." Some of the sadness left her eyes. "I'm proud of you, Gabriel. You work so hard and you save so many soldiers. I know their families are grateful. But now it's time to do what you want."

"I like being a doctor."

"We both know why you became one."

He shrugged. "It was a long time ago. It's what I know. And, as you said, I help."

"I worry you would have been happier doing something else," she admitted.

"I don't."

He'd chosen his path and there was no going back.

She rested her head on his shoulder for a moment, then straightened. "All right. I've kept you long enough. You need to get back to work. I'd hate to be the reason Noelle fired you."

He chuckled. "I don't see that happening, but okay. I'll see you later, Mom."

She nodded and kissed his cheek. While she got into her SUV, he turned and headed back for the store. On his way, an older woman waved him down.

"Young man! Young man! Could you help me with my packages?"

She had a couple of bags and a box. He eyed them, then her, before nodding slowly.

"Happy to help, ma'am."

He picked up everything and walked with her to her car. But as he lowered the items into the trunk, he was careful to keep his butt faced away from her. Maybe he'd imagined what had happened yesterday, but he'd learned that in a place like Fool's Gold, a guy didn't want to take any chances.

CHAPTER SEVEN

ONCE THE SUN went down, the temperature dropped quickly. Noelle burrowed deeper into her thick coat, grateful for the scarf she'd grabbed at the last minute. The sky seemed lower than usual, as if heavy clouds were pressing down on the town. She might not be an expert, but she would guess there was snow in the forecast.

She'd closed The Christmas Attic an hour early and raced home to change into jeans and winter boots. She'd barely finished tying the laces, when Gabriel knocked on her front door. When he'd mentioned the tree lighting and she'd said of course she was going, he'd offered to pick her up at six-thirty.

Not a date, she told herself firmly. If it was a date, that would mean they were dating. Thinking a guy was hot and wondering if she should sleep with him was very different than the whole "going out" thing.

Now, as they walked toward the center of town, she tried to figure out why the ceremony was so appealing to him.

"You don't strike me as the tree-lighting type," she said as they waited at the corner for the light.

"I heard it wasn't to be missed. By the way, Melissa is great."

"I know. When she came and asked if I still needed help, I grabbed her." She laughed. "I actually clutched her sleeve and begged her not to apply anywhere else. When she was still in high school, she helped my friend Patience through the opening of her store and she was terrific. On time, friendly, a hard worker. She's a dream employee." She paused and glanced up at him. "Not in your league, of course."

"Of course."

Gabriel was bundled up, too, in a heavy coat and boots. But enough of his face was visible to remind her he was one good-looking guy. Those blue eyes, his mouth. Her gaze lingered on the latter. She sure could use another couple of kisses, she thought wistfully.

"Over there," he said, pulling her hand out of her pocket and taking it in his. "Hot chocolate." He guided her toward the stand setup and started to laugh.

"What?" she asked, seeing only a growing crowd and, in the distance, the looming shadow of the dark Christmas tree.

He pointed and she saw Ana Raquel manning the stand. "I know she's going to ask me why I'm not married."

"She's too busy," Noelle assured him, liking that a petite twentysomething made the sexy doctor nervous. "But if she says anything, I'll tell her you're a god in bed, and that will shift the rumor mill into a more acceptable direction."

He winced. "I'm not sure I want that out there."

"Of course you do. Doesn't every guy?"

"Then I'd have a reputation to live up to. I don't want you disappointed."

She paused on the sidewalk and pulled her fingers free of his, then planted both her hands on her hips.

"There's an assumption." She glanced around, then lowered her voice. "I haven't said yes."

"You haven't said no, either."

She was about to agree when she suddenly remembered what had happened. She leaned close so she could speak even more softly. "You're the one who told *me* no." She poked him in the middle of the chest.

"I was doing the right thing."

"Like that matters," she grumbled, even though she knew it did.

He put his arm around her shoulders and drew her toward the stand. "You need liquid chocolate in your system," he told her. "Hot, thick and delicious."

It did sound good, she thought. "With whipped cream?"

"Sure. Otherwise, what's the point?"

They waited in line, then placed their order. Ana Raquel talked them into some brownies she'd baked, made change efficiently and shooed them on their way.

"See," Noelle said as they joined the crowd standing around the tree. "You were practically anonymous. Feel better?"

"I'll admit to being wounded by her inattention."

She laughed. Now that he'd relaxed a little and gotten to know her, she'd figured out Gabriel was a lot of fun. He didn't take himself too seriously and he had a unique view of the world. Both really good qualities.

He kept one arm around her, which meant she had to feed him bits of cookie as his other hand held his hot chocolate. She liked the feel of his lips against her fingertips and the warmth of his breath. Around them, Christmas music played and she could see several lit storefronts.

"I like how all the businesses decorate for Christmas," she said. "My store always celebrates the season, but it's nice when everyone else joins me."

"What do you do at the other holidays?" he asked.

"This year I didn't open until Labor Day and it was all Christmas. But I have those two small windows on the side. I thought I'd change them out for the regular holidays. Hearts at Valentine's Day, that sort of thing."

"You could have a section in the store for different holidays," he said. "From January to, say, October. Once the locals find out they can buy a cute Easter bunny at your place, they'll come in more."

She stared at him. "That's a really good idea."

He kissed her nose. "Thank you for sounding so surprised."

She laughed. "You're not a retail guy, but it's brilliant. I'll do it." She snuggled close to him again.

"This time of year always reminds me of my family," she told him. "My mom and grandmother would have loved Fool's Gold."

"They're here with you," he said.

"You believe that?"

He nodded. "We might go at any time, but there's something that goes with us. I've seen a lot of soldiers die and when they do…" He paused. "Sorry. Not moment-appropriate conversation."

She shifted so she faced him. "Gabriel, you don't have to edit yourself with me. You can't shock me."

"Want to bet?"

"Okay, you can, but that's okay. I'll get over it. If you want to talk about anything, I want to listen."

Gabriel thought about what he'd been through on his various tours. The screams, the horror, the blood. There was no way he was going to tell her how an IED ripped a soldier to shreds. How the first hour was all about stopping the bleeding. That more than shrapnel was blown into the ravaged body. That rocks and dirt and plant matter had to be dug out of the wounds. That when the soldiers were wheeled off to surgery, he sometimes wondered if there was enough of them left to make it.

He wasn't going to say that like every other soldier he knew, he had nightmares, moments of cold sweats and disorientation. Despite her offer, she didn't want to know. No one did. The images, once embedded, couldn't be removed.

He stared into her blue eyes and smiled gently. "Christmas was a big deal at our house, too," he said. "My mom baked for weeks and my dad was pretty mellow." The smile turned genuine. "Gideon and I believed that came from the amount of rum she put in Dad's eggnog. There were always lots of presents and we sang carols and went to church at midnight."

"That sounds nice."

"It was. Once my dad was a drill sergeant, we stopped moving around. That was good, too. Gideon and I went to the same high school all four years. He got to play football and I…"

"Read obscure books and made your father crazy."

"Something like that."

She was beautiful, he thought absently, the crowd around them fading as he took in the curves of her face. Somewhere along the way they'd finished their hot chocolate and tossed the cups. Now she placed her hands on his chest.

Through the thickness of his coat, he couldn't feel much more than the pressure, but even that was nice. Nicer would have been both of them naked, but the tree-lighting ceremony didn't seem the right place for that sort of thing.

Still, he leaned close and kissed her. Lightly, without expecting any more. He lingered, wanting to taste her, feel her softness, enjoy the intimacy. When he drew back, she sighed.

"You're a good kisser."

"Thank you. I'm glad you appreciate my skill."

She laughed. "At last the doctor's large ego rears its ugly head."

He moved so his mouth was next to her ear. "That's not my head."

She laughed again, then leaned against him. An older woman stepped onto a small podium and the crowd quieted.

"Good evening. For those of you who don't know me, I'm Mayor Marsha. Welcome to our annual tree-lighting ceremony."

The mayor went on to explain about the tradition and outlined events that would take place over the holiday season, including a lighting of the large menorah on the first day of Hanukkah. Gabriel didn't know where they planned to put the menorah, but he wouldn't be surprised if it was right next to the Christmas tree. Fool's Gold was that kind of place—all faiths would be welcome to join in.

Noelle leaned against him. He wrapped both arms around her, wanting to be as close as he could. Whatever happened to him, wherever he went, he would remember these few weeks in this odd little town. He would remember the tree and the elephant in the parade and the butt-patting old ladies. But mostly he would remember *her* and when it got too bad, he would let those memories wash over him.

FELICIA'S DIRECTIONS HAD been accurate, Gabriel thought as he pulled into the parking lot of his brother's radio station. Damned if Gideon hadn't really bought the place. From soldier to DJ. It was a tough transition to imagine. He could only guess how difficult it had been to live.

He walked around back and hit the buzzer. Less than a minute later, his brother opened the door and grinned.

"I already have the beers out," he said by way of greeting.

"She told you I was coming."

"Sure. She said talking to you would be good for me. That it would strengthen our fraternal bond and allow us to feel more connected. It would also remind me why it was good to have a sibling so I could explain that to Carter when he had to deal with a half brother or sister."

Gabriel followed his brother down a narrow hall. "That sounds like your girl."

"I know." Gideon's voice was full of pride. "I'm a hell of a lucky guy."

They went into a control room. There was equipment all around them, including several computers and a control panel that looked complicated enough to run an airliner. Music played from speakers. There were bottles of beer in front of both chairs. Gideon sat in the one by the microphone and motioned for Gabriel to take the one across from him.

"I knew you were doing this," Gabriel said, lowering himself into the comfy leather chair. "But I sure couldn't picture it. A radio station?"

"I know. I didn't plan it. I was driving around town and saw the For Sale sign."

Gabriel picked up his beer and leaned back in his

chair. "I think the bigger question is what you were doing driving around town at all."

"Good point."

The song came to an end and Gideon pushed a button. "We do a combination of prerecorded and live shows," he said. "I do my show every night and a few others are produced in-house, but a lot of the shows are packaged and sold. It's cheaper."

Gabriel hadn't thought about the logistics of running a radio station but what his brother said made sense. These days there was a lot of competition for airtime. A small station couldn't stay afloat having every shift staffed with on-air personalities and necessary staff. Although as he glanced around he noticed that Gideon seemed to be the only one here.

Another song started and his brother relaxed back in his chair.

"You were at the tree lighting," Gideon said, his tone conversational.

"How do you know that?"

"I heard from more than one source. You were with Noelle."

Gabriel waited to see if there was more, but his brother was silent. This town, he thought. Nothing was kept secret.

"I went to the tree lighting with Noelle."

"And kissed her."

Gabriel held in a groan. "Barely."

"That's not what I heard." He grinned. "You gotta be careful, bro. This place has a way of getting under your skin. You think you're minding your own business but you're not. And before you know it, you're involved, doing things you never thought possible."

Gabriel picked up his beer. "Speak for yourself. I'm not staying."

"You say that now."

"I say that always."

"Uh-huh. Famous last words. Give it a few more weeks." His brother adjusted a couple of knobs, then slid in a CD. "When I first came here, I kept to myself. Bought a house outside of town, barely spoke to anyone. Then one day I saw Felicia and knew I was in trouble. Soon she was hanging out at the house and I was sponsoring a damned bowling team." He shrugged. "It doesn't happen all at once. I'll give them that. They suck you in slow and you don't notice until you can't get away."

"You had Carter," Gabriel pointed out. "That makes it different."

"True. Having a son I didn't know about show up was a game changer. I didn't know what to do with him. If I hadn't had Felicia, we wouldn't have made it."

Words Gabriel could relate to. He'd been careful with all his women, but he would guess his brother had been, as well. Having a child show up would twist a man's world around.

Not in a bad way, he thought, taking another drink. If he were the kind of guy who believed in happy endings, he would even welcome it. But then if he were that kind of guy he would be married with a few kids already.

"You get along with Carter now," he said.

"We're doing better. He's old enough to tell me what he needs, which helps. He lets me know when I'm doing it wrong. Felicia keeps us in balance." He grinned. "I could give you her technical explanation, but that would take too long."

"Not to mention require you to use words you don't understand."

"There are times," Gideon admitted. "But she's worth it."

"She helped you settle back into civilian life."

Gideon nodded. "I'd recovered from what happened as much as I was going to. The rest was all about learning to live with the past. Nightmares, that kind of thing."

Gabriel thought about all the skylights in his brother's house, the big deck where he spent a lot of time. Gideon hadn't shared much about his captivity, but Gabriel knew he'd been held by the Taliban for nearly two years. He'd been kept in an underground prison and tortured almost daily. The circumstances would have broken a lesser man. Gabriel wasn't sure he would have survived it.

"You seen the folks?" his brother asked.

"Mom stopped by the store today. I haven't talked to Dad since Thursday." Which was only two days before, but felt longer.

"He's getting better," Gideon said. "I think it's Carter's influence. Or Webster." He chuckled. "Dad's training the dog better than any of us."

Gabriel joined the laughter. "I believe it. If he can turn a green recruit into a soldier, he can get your dog to behave." He raised his bottle toward his brother. "You look happy. That's good to see."

"Thanks. A year ago, I would have told you it wasn't possible, but I was wrong. Between Felicia and my kid, I've made my way back."

"I'm glad."

Gabriel wanted his brother to be happy. If anyone had earned it, he had. He allowed himself a moment to wonder how life would be different if he believed. Only he didn't. What was the point in having it all if you could lose it at any second?

Paper Moon was a store in transition. It had been a bridal boutique for a couple of generations. As of six months ago, the Beebe family had been planning to sell it. Isabel had temporarily returned to Fool's Gold to help her parents by getting the boutique ready for the market. But life had a way of messing up the most perfect plans and now she was newly engaged, staying in town permanently and enlarging the store to include a selection of designer clothes. Which explained why there was a large hole in the side wall of Paper Moon.

"Ignore the mess," Isabel said as she urged Patience up in front of the five-way mirror. "Are these the shoes? Because you don't want to hem the dress in the wrong heels."

"These are them," Patience said, then bit her lip. "Oh, Isabel, you were right. This *is* the perfect dress."

Noelle sat in one of the overstuffed chairs by the mirror and took in the view of her gorgeous friend. "Do you ever get tired of hearing that?"

"No," Isabel admitted, bending down and adjusting the skirt. "I appreciate the validation."

Patience had been unsure about having a "real" wedding. She'd been married before and wondered if she deserved to have the whole ceremony again. But after Felicia and Isabel got engaged, they'd invited her to join them in their post-Dance of the Winter King wedding plan. While Patience had agreed, she'd resisted getting a traditional wedding dress, instead insisting she would wear an ivory-colored suit.

But Isabel had been relentless in getting her friend to try on different gowns. In the end, she'd simply ordered the one that had looked the best. Now Patience stood in a soft white gown that was fitted to the knee before flaring out. It was covered in lace. The bodice was strapless, with a lace overlay, adding a touch of modesty that was pure Patience.

"I should have listened to you from the beginning," Patience murmured.

"I can see why you like this line of work," Noelle said, loving the happiness in her friend's eyes.

"It's gratifying," Isabel admitted, stepping up on the low dais and adjusting the dress. "This is a really good fit. I'll have my brilliant alteration lady call to make an appointment with you. Get the dress tailored sooner rather than later and remember, from this day until the wedding you can't lose or gain an ounce."

"Yes, ma'am," Patience said, taking one last look at herself. She was turning when she came to a stop and her mouth dropped open. "Oh, my."

Noelle looked and saw Felicia had stepped out of a dressing room. The stunning redhead had chosen an ivory gown that was more than fitted. It clung to her perfect body in diagonal rows of what looked like pleating but was probably some kind of fancy draping. Like Patience's dress, it flared out just above the knee, but Felicia's skirt ended in dozens of massive flowers made of the gorgeous silk. They cascaded to the floor and formed a train.

"I don't know," Felicia murmured. "I can barely walk and maybe it's a little much for Fool's Gold. I don't want people to—"

"Stop," Noelle said, walking toward her friend. She

circled her, taking in the fitted back, the incredible flowers and how the color made her friend's skin glow. "Just stop. You're inhumanly beautiful. You need that dress. It's perfect on you. No one else could carry that off."

She looked at Isabel and Patience, who both nodded, wide-eyed.

Felicia stunned her by bursting into tears then pulling her close. "I love you so much. You're a wonderful friend. Thank you."

Isabel and Patience rushed over to join the group hug. Noelle let the love wash over her, filling her heart with happiness. This was what she'd been looking for, she thought happily. Closeness. Belonging. And she'd found it.

They finally disentangled. Isabel sniffed as she wiped away tears. "This was so great. But I think we should do our fittings independently or we'll spend the whole time sobbing."

"You're right," Felicia said. "The abundance of emotion is overwhelming."

"What she said." Patience waved at Felicia and brushed away tears.

"All right, I'm taking control," Isabel told them. "You two go get changed."

When the other two had retreated to the dressing rooms, Noelle turned to Isabel. "What about your dress?"

She smiled shyly. "I have it," she said, then led the way into the back.

Noelle had seen the bridal shop storeroom before. It consisted of dozens of racks filled with beautiful dresses. But the construction had eaten into the area, cutting it in half.

"Part of the remodeling," Isabel said, pointing to the makeshift wall.

"Where are the rest of the dresses?" Noelle asked, thinking storing a wedding gown wasn't like storing extra paper towels. You couldn't just rent a storage place and leave them there.

"At Dellina's. She has a spare bedroom. The racks fit perfectly and it's kept close to seventy degrees. You know, normal indoor temperatures. Perfect for my inventory." She reached for a dress and held it out.

Like the other two, it was strapless, but Isabel's skirt was full. Tiny flowers of lace and crystals covered the bodice, becoming more scattered closer to her waist before stopping just past her hips. The skirt was layers and layers of sheer fabric that rustled and swayed.

"There's a matching veil," Isabel said with a sigh. "The same flowers are sprinkled along the edge. I know it's girly rather than high fashion, but I can't help myself."

"You'll be beautiful."

Isabel put the dress back, then turned to her. "Are you okay with this? We're not making you want to slit your throat or something?"

Noelle grinned. "I don't own a knife that fancy and I'm fine. This is great. I love being a part of the secret triple wedding."

Isabel didn't look convinced. Noelle shrugged.

"Look, if I had some long-term boyfriend who wouldn't cough up a ring, I might be annoyed, but I don't. I love you guys and I'm happy for you. Besides, you got me a great dress."

In keeping with the strapless theme, Isabel had suggested a couple of different dresses for Noelle. Together they'd chosen a simple strapless cocktail dress with shirring at the bodice and an unexpected twist of fabric at the waist. The dress was short enough to be sexy but not so sexy that it was distracting. The blue-purple color flattered and it was the kind of dress Noelle really could wear again.

"I just don't want this to be depressing," Isabel told her. "I wish Consuelo had agreed to be a bridesmaid, but when I asked again, I got the sense she wanted to physically hurt me."

Noelle laughed. "That sounds like her. Don't worry. I'm happy to be the attendant friend. Really."

"If you're sure."

"I am."

They returned to the main room of the salon just as Dellina, their wedding planner, arrived with both arms full of flowers. She put down the bouquets, looked at all of them, then put her hands on her hips.

"What?" she demanded. "You've been crying. Don't try to tell me you haven't been. And I'd better not hear someone is breaking up."

"They were trying on dresses and looked so beautiful, we lost it," Noelle said.

Patience grinned. "No, Felicia looked so beautiful they started crying. I didn't inspire any great emotion."

"You were stunning," Felicia told her. "Lovely and delicate. L-like those flowers." Tears filled her eyes.

Dellina shook her head. "Was there wine involved?"

"No," Isabel said cheerfully. "We did all this completely sober."

"A frightening thought," Dellina murmured. "Are we back together now? I can move on to flowers without anyone getting hysterical?"

The three brides nodded. "I was never hysterical," Noelle pointed out.

"Good. Then we have work to do, ladies. These are some flower samples. I was thinking we'd pick a color scheme for the flowers and then each of you would have a variation of that color. That way you can have your favorites without clashing."

Noelle listened as Dellina explained which flowers would work best in a bouquet, then showed them different groupings.

Less than two years ago she'd been planning her own wedding, she thought wistfully. She and Jeremy had wanted a summer wedding on the beach. Their biggest disagreement had been about the wedding gown. She'd wanted to wear her grandmother's. She'd had the overlay of lace removed, leaving the fitted heart-shaped bodice in place. The seamstress she'd worked with had carefully reapplied the lace flowers and had added some draping. But when Noelle had tried it on for Jeremy, he'd said it was too old-fashioned.

In the end, it hadn't mattered because then she'd gotten sick and eventually he'd left her. He'd told her she wasn't enough of a sure thing for him.

She shook off the memories and returned her attention to the flower discussion.

"While you're mulling," Dellina said, pulling a tablet out of her large tote and touching the screen, "I'll mention some other details. Evie Jefferson and I talked. After the Dance of the Winter King, the girls will start a new dance she taught them. The music will change and then Mayor Marsha will take the stage to explain what's happening."

She went through the events of the evening. How the

three grooms would take their places, and Noelle would be the first down the aisle.

"I have a list of prewedding march music," Dellina said, digging for a sheet of paper. "I'm also open to suggestions. Then the traditional wedding march, then you three appear. Ceremony, ring, kiss and we invite everyone to a late supper before we all head to church for midnight services."

"You're doing the supper?" Noelle asked.

"I'm organizing it." Dellina grinned. "Trust me, I didn't get the cooking gene. Ana Raquel and Greg are handling the food. It's going to be delicious."

Felicia pulled her own tablet out of her bag. "I have a list of what's been ordered," she said. "Including the champagne."

Noelle glanced at the clock on the wall. "If you guys don't need me, I'm going to head back to my store. We're swamped and I left Gabriel in charge."

"Thanks for everything," Isabel told her. "You've been great."

"I'm happy to help. Let me know the details."

She waved at her friends, then left the store. As she hurried toward The Christmas Attic, she told herself to revel in their happiness and not think about the fact that the day after Christmas, everything would be different. Her friends would leave on their honeymoons, Gabriel would go back to Germany and her store would get quiet again. While her friends would return, they would be married and she had a feeling that could change things.

As for Gabriel, well, she doubted she would ever see him again. Not unless he started visiting his brother more regularly. And what were the odds of that? So not getting involved really made sense. Only she wasn't sure she was in a place where she wanted to be sensible.

She was about to turn the corner when Patience caught up with her. "I have to get back, too," she said. "And I completely trust Dellina with the menu." She pointed to the window for da bump Maternity. "Oh, look. She's added an animated Santa."

Noelle glanced at the window and saw a dancing Santa. There were elves, too. Cute elves she didn't remember from a couple of days ago.

"She's getting to her decorating late," she said. "It's a tough time of year."

"She's not late," Patience said. "It's the competition. I thought about trying, but with the wedding and all, there's no way. Maybe next year. Although Josh usually wins. I think he brings in people from outside to decorate. He's a professional competitor. The rest of us don't take it that seriously."

Noelle stopped to face her. "What are you talking about?"

"The competition for best holiday window display," Patience told her. "It's silly, really. The prize is some little statue. It's just for fun."

"Why didn't I know about this?" Noelle asked, gazing at the window display. "I have a Christmas store. I should be a contender."

"Uh-oh." Patience held up both hands. "I see that look of determination. I'm so staying out of your way."

CHAPTER EIGHT

GABRIEL CLOSED THE cash register and handed over the bag. "Thanks for stopping by," he said. "Merry Christmas."

Unexpectedly, he enjoyed working in the store. People were really happy when they found what they were looking for and he liked the idea of seeing the transaction through. In his day job, he patched his patients up as best he could and then they were gone. Even in Germany, when his patients left the hospital, they still had healing to do. But here, he could sell a Christmas CD and feel a sense of accomplishment.

The front door opened and Noelle burst in. She was flushed and wide-eyed, her scarf falling off her shoulder.

"What happened?" he demanded, already moving toward her. Adrenaline pumped through him as he wondered if there'd been a car accident or some other tragedy he would have to deal with. He didn't have a medical bag with him, which would limit what he could do but—

"There's a window competition," she announced. "How did I not know about this? There are prizes and everything. We have to win."

Gabriel drew in a breath and consciously relaxed his body. The chemical rush would take a while to fade, but at his least brain knew she was okay.

"A competition?" he asked. "For windows?"

"Window displays. I wish Melissa was here. I could ask her about it. There was a flyer, but I guess I didn't get it." She walked over to the computer and typed in the password to log on to the internet, then searched.

"Here it is," she said triumphantly. "The judging is the eleventh. That's next Wednesday and doesn't give us much time." She looked around the store. "I need to get organized."

"You're going to try to win?"

She gave him a pitying look. "Of course. This is important. Not only is this my first year in business, I'm the Christmas store. I need to at least be in the competition, even if I don't win."

An unexpected side of Noelle, he thought, liking her fierceness.

"How can I help?"

She smiled then and it was like getting kicked in the gut. Gabriel held in a groan as he wondered when wanting Noelle had shifted to liking her, as well. Desire was safe. It was biology and a lot about proximity. But liking was different. Liking was about personality and caring, which meant when he left he was going to miss her.

Too late now, he told himself. He was stuck.

"I'm going to walk around town and look at the other windows," she said. "I'll take notes. Then this afternoon we can strategize about what to do." She glanced toward the display in the south window. "I know we're going to need a bigger tree—that's for sure. But a real one."

"You're going to put a real tree in your window?"

"Why not? It will add a nice scent to the store and look more authentic. I wonder if Heidi would let me have one of her goats."

"No goats," he said sternly. "You can't keep a goat in the window."

"I suppose you're right. But if we made it looking like a stable and it was just for sleeping…" She shook her head. "There would be clean-up issues and I don't know how many hours a day a goat sleeps." She wrapped her scarf around her neck. "Okay, I'll be back with intel and then we can brainstorm."

Intel? Gabriel rubbed his right temple. He could already feel a headache coming on.

By EIGHT THAT night Gabriel wondered if Noelle was willing to admit defeat.

"I want to believe," she murmured, pulling up the hood on her coat. Snow fell around them and the temperature was plunging, but he knew the cold wasn't the reason for her glum tone.

She stopped on the sidewalk and drew in a breath. "You can be done with this," she added, although she didn't sound very convincing.

"You don't mean that," he told her.

"Nobody wants to spend this long looking for a Christmas tree."

"Why stop now?" he asked, not mentioning that they'd already been to all five lots in town. He would swear she'd examined every tree needle by needle but was still unsatisfied. "You can't be giving up."

"I'm not. I still think the perfect tree is out there. It has to be."

"Then you'll find it."

She looked doubtful. "Are you saying you agree with me or are you humoring me because it's the quickest way to get out of the snow?"

"Both," he admitted.

She flashed him a smile that took care of any chills.

Her cheeks were red from the cold, as was her nose. Snow landed on the faux shearling edging her hood and dusted her shoulders. She looked adorable and sexy at the same time and he suspected she had no clue as to how she got to him.

"I can't help it," she admitted. "This is important to me."

"I guessed that." He stomped his feet.

"Go home," she said. "You're freezing. I'll give up."

His gaze settled on her face. "Why do I know you're lying?"

"I'm not."

She stared at him with what he would guess she thought was an open expression. But he knew what she was thinking. She wasn't the type to give up.

"Sell it somewhere else. You're going to keep at this until you have the perfect tree and what you think is a shot at winning some ribbon."

"I heard it's a trophy."

"Well, then."

"Are you mad?" she asked.

"No. Just wondering what you'd be like if you *really* wanted something. Come on."

"Where are we going?"

"I'm walking you home. On the way, we'll come up with a plan to find the perfect tree."

She had fallen into step with him, but now she jumped in front of him and grinned. "Really? I was wondering if maybe we could drive up the mountain and cut down a tree."

"Is that legal? Aren't the mountains state or federal lands?"

"I don't know. I could find out. Anyway, it's just one tree."

"Great. An obsessed lawbreaker."

They were standing by the park, across from Morgan's Books. The sky was dark, the snow falling gently, and there were dozens of people on the sidewalks. Music was piped in from somewhere, tinny Christmas carols that reminded him of his childhood. He couldn't feel the lower half of his body. Probably a good thing considering she was staring at him as if he'd just saved puppies from a fire.

"So you'll really help me?" she asked.

"I've come too far to turn back now."

"That is so great." She bounced in place. "I'll check to see if it's legal *before* we head up the mountain. How's that? We can take my car."

"You're going to drive?"

"It'll be hard to walk back, dragging a tree."

"You're not ready for mountain driving."

She waved away his concern. "I'll be fine. I have righteousness on my side. What could go wrong?"

"Don't tempt fate. I'm coming with you and I'm driving. We'll take Gideon's truck."

She stared into his eyes, her expression innocent. "That would be very nice. Thank you."

He touched his gloved fingers to her chin, forcing her to look at him. "You're welcome."

She grinned and grabbed his hands in hers. "It'll be fun. We'll find a huge tree and cut it down. Like we're pioneers or something. Then bring it back and put it in the window. I'll win for sure."

He wasn't convinced. "You'll have to measure the window. We don't want to bring back something that's too big." He drew her against him and they started walking.

"I'll go online tonight and find out what the best trees are. We need it to last a long time and look pretty. Maybe Felicia knows. She knows everything."

He studied her. "Is this what you were like in law school? Always trying to be the best?"

"I didn't graduate first in my class, if that's what you're asking."

"Number two?"

"I was third. Besides, this isn't like that."

"It's a contest. It's pretty much like that."

Before she could answer, a little girl ran over to them. She was adorable, maybe five with shiny black hair and big eyes. She wore a thick red coat and rain boots with red polka dots on them.

"Hey, you," Noelle said, crouching down and smiling at her. "Are you staying warm?"

"I am," the girl said, smiling shyly. "We bought my grandma an ornament at your store. You helped me pick it out."

"I remember," Noelle told her. "Did you give it to her?"

The girl nodded.

"Did she like it?"

There was another smile and a quick nod. "She cried."

"Those are the best kind of presents."

The girl's mother came over and took her hand. "We were in town for the long weekend with my parents," the woman said. "Your store was wonderful. Sophie wanted you to know."

Noelle touched the girl's cheek. "Thank you for telling me about your grandmother, Sophie."

"You're welcome."

Noelle rose and turned back to him. "Does that make you want to give the world a hug?"

"You make people happy."

"I try. It's not me, it's the store, but still."

She flung herself at him. He caught her and held on tight.

He knew she was wrong—she was the one with the special touch. Without her, The Christmas Attic was simply a collection of things. She brought it all alive. While he didn't remember the little girl or her mother, he didn't doubt Noelle had taken plenty of time with them. She did that with every customer. She made shopping at her store an experience.

"We'll go up the mountain," he told her. "Find out where the best trees are and we'll go."

She smiled up at him. "You're not so tough. You pretend you're all broody and wounded but you're really a sweet kind of guy."

He wanted to tell her not to believe in him, that he wasn't a good risk. He didn't want to hurt her, but he couldn't have her faith. But those were words for another time, he thought, brushing his mouth against hers. A time when it wasn't snowing on a beautiful night a few weeks before Christmas.

GABRIEL WALKED THROUGH the cold night, grateful that the temperature would take care of any lingering desire. He'd done the gentlemanly thing—he'd walked Noelle home and left her on her doorstep without even hinting how much he wanted to go inside.

He'd read the indecision in her eyes and had known he could have easily convinced her. A few kisses and she would have started to melt. But as much as he wanted her, he needed her to be sure. To understand what the consequences would be.

A conscience was a giant pain in the ass, he thought as he turned the corner. Well, not his ass, exactly.

"Hello, Gabriel."

An older woman appeared at his side. He would have sworn there was no one else out on this snowy night. Not this late. The bustling city tended to shut down right around nine.

The woman had white curly hair and deep blue eyes. She had to be in her sixties, but she stood straight and strong. He'd seen her before, but couldn't remember where.

"Ma'am," he said, no longer surprised people he'd never met knew who he was.

"I'm Mayor Marsha Tilson," she said with a smile. "I'm glad I ran into you. I've been wanting to speak to you."

She motioned to a business across the street. He peered through the snow and saw a sign that read Jo's Bar.

"Let me buy you a coffee," she said, already stepping off the curb. "Irish coffee," she added with a laugh. "Nobody makes it better than Jo."

Somehow he found himself following the woman. He told himself to stop, that he had no business going into a bar with a woman thirty years older than him. He remembered the butt pat from the other day and wondered if he was about to get into an even more awkward situation. But somehow he kept moving along at her side, answering polite questions about how he enjoyed the town.

When they stepped inside, he found he was in the strangest bar he'd ever seen. The walls were a pale purple-blue color and the big TVs had on what looked a lot like overweight people exercising on treadmills. Was this some sports show he'd missed while he'd been gone?

The mayor led him to a table in the corner. "Irish coffees, please, Jo," she called as she pulled out a chair.

"You got it, Mayor Marsha." The woman behind the bar chuckled. "Who are you torturing tonight?"

"Jo, I never torture anyone. You know that."

"Sure you don't."

"This is Dr. Gabriel Boylan. Gideon's brother."

"Welcome," Jo told him. "Don't bother fighting her. It never works. It's like quicksand. Relax and you'll be fine. Struggle and you'll end up sinking in deeper."

The mayor draped her heavy coat over an empty chair and sat down. She wore a pale blue suit and pearls. "Jo has an imagination."

Gabriel nodded even as he wondered if Jo was the one telling the truth. He shrugged out of his jacket, then sat across from the mayor.

She set her hands on the table and laced her fingers together. "You're here through the holidays."

He wasn't sure if she was asking or telling, but he nodded anyway.

"You're working for Noelle at The Christmas Attic. That must be a change."

"It is."

"Your military service must be satisfying, but extremely difficult. There are demands on the medical personnel. We talk about the PTSD the returning soldiers deal with, as we should. But you and those like you have your own internal struggles."

"Compassion fatigue," he said flatly.

"Yes. I've read about it. What you see, what you do, drains the soul. I hope you will find your stay here healing." She smiled gently. "I wouldn't presume to know what you've been through, Gabriel, but if you need someone to talk to, I have names."

"I'm okay."

She studied him for a second. "I think you aren't just yet, but you will be."

Jo appeared with their coffees. The mugs were tall and slender and made of glass. Whipped cream floated on the top. She set down the drinks. "I was heavy-handed with the whiskey."

The mayor sighed. "You always were a good girl, Jo."

Jo laughed. "That's me. The best of the best."

When she'd left, Mayor Marsha raised her mug. "To the holidays and being with those we love."

He touched his glass to hers. "To family."

"I have a beautiful granddaughter and two great-grandchildren," she said. "And a grandson-in-law. I'm blessed. I understand your family is here now."

"They're visiting for the holidays."

Her eyebrows rose. "Are they? I was under the impression they were thinking of a more permanent move. Maybe I misunderstood."

Gabriel suspected the wily old lady didn't misunderstand very much, which meant she had information he didn't. His parents moving to Fool's Gold? Was it possible? He tried to imagine what Gideon would think about it and couldn't. Although he and his brother were twins, they were no longer close. Gideon had changed so much, he might welcome having family nearby.

"Noelle is very sweet," she said, before sipping her drink.

Was that it? Did the mayor want to warn him away from Noelle? He turned the idea over in his head and found he was pleased that she had someone looking out for her. With no family around, she was on her own. He knew she had a lot of friends, but he wanted even more people on her side.

"She is."

"The store is very special. But if you decide not to stay in the army, I don't see you finding yourself in retail."

"That's true. It's a nice break, though."

"I'm sure it is. But you're a doctor. It is in you to heal. Fool's Gold's new hospital is nearly complete. A state-of-the-art facility with a world-class trauma center."

The statement was so unexpected, he was sure he looked like an idiot staring at her. "You want to talk to me about a job?"

"I want you to consider the possibilities. You might think we're a sleepy little town, but we have more than our share of trauma victims. There are car accidents and sports injuries on the mountain in both winter and summer. We've already assembled an excellent team, including Dr. Simon Bradley. He's a plastic surgeon who specializes in burn victims. We're putting together a program to bring in patients from all over the world. Many of them will be from poor countries. We're raising the money to help them here. It's exciting work."

"I'm not a surgeon."

"Yes, I know. However your services are still very

much needed. I would like you to meet some of the other doctors here in town. Get to know them. We're also in the preliminary stages of putting together a search-and-rescue organization. We're thinking that will launch in 2015. You would be a vital member of that team."

He hadn't seen it coming. An offer like this. Stay here? In Fool's Gold?

"I can't," he said, coming to his feet.

"You don't have to decide now," she told him, still calm, still holding his gaze with hers.

But he wasn't calm. His chest was tight and he felt the walls closing in on him. In the distance was the rushing sound of chaos, of the wounded. Only the mayor continued to smile at him. Which meant the only fiery noise was in his head and he had to get out of here.

"Thank you, but no," he said, grabbing his coat.

"Of course. If you change your mind, I'm very easy to find."

He nodded and bolted for the door. Before he got there, she called him again.

"Gabriel?"

Reluctantly, he turned back to face her.

"Tell Noelle to call me and I can help her find the very best trees."

He swore under his breath. How had the old lady known about their tree search? How did she—

He didn't care, he told himself as he ducked out into the night. The snow came down harder than before. It piled up on the sidewalks and coated the parked cars. It was the kind of night that drove most men indoors.

Not him, he thought as he shrugged into his coat. Tonight he would walk until he was too exhausted to remember anything. To do anything but fall into a bed and sleep without dreaming at all.

"You're pouting," Noelle said as Gabriel turned the truck at the stop sign.

"I'm not pouting," he growled, keeping his gaze on the road.

"It seems like you are. And if that's how you're going to be, then take me back to town and I'll drive to the trees myself."

He continued through the intersection, then pulled to the side of the road. After putting the truck in Park, he turned to face her.

"You wouldn't get ten feet up the mountain," he pointed out.

"You don't know that."

One corner of his mouth turned up. "I'd take a bet on it."

He looked tired, she thought, taking in the shadows under his eyes. He'd been quiet all morning, even as he'd given her the message to call Mayor Marsha about their tree search. They'd waited until Melissa arrived to head out, but he'd never seemed very happy about what they were doing.

"Aren't you sleeping?" she asked, then took his injured hand in hers. His stitches were gone and the skin had mostly healed. "Does this still hurt?"

"I'm fine. I was out late last night."

He'd gone out after he'd dropped her off? "Oh," she said quietly, wondering where he'd gone and who he'd been with.

"Hey," he said, touching her cheek. "Mayor Marsha

dragged me to some bar for Irish coffee. That's how I got the message for you to call her."

"Are you mad about the trees? You've been really great to me and I don't want to make you do something you don't want to do."

"I said I'd help."

"I know that, but I need you to help from a place of joy."

He turned back to face the front window, folded his arms across the steering wheel, then rested his head on them. He murmured something that sounded a lot like "Kill me now," but she wasn't exactly sure that was it.

"Gabriel?"

"A place of joy?" His voice was incredulous.

"Yes. It's Christmas, or nearly. We're going out into the woods to find the perfect tree, where I know it will be waiting for us. It's snowing and beautiful and we need to have a spirit of joy."

He turned to look at her, his expression more bemused than annoyed. "You never would have made it as a lawyer."

"I have a feeling you're right about that." Or she would have gotten very good at being a lawyer and lost the wonder she felt as she looked at the soft, white snow settling all around them.

How would her life have been different if she hadn't gotten sick? It wasn't a question she allowed herself to think about very much. Would she have married Jeremy? At the time she would have said yes. That he was the one. But he hadn't stood by her and he hadn't been willing to see her as more than damaged goods. He'd walked away so easily, she'd started to wonder if he'd ever loved her at all.

Gabriel straightened. "I can't do the spirit of joy but I can manage an attitude of acceptance. Good enough?"

"Sure. We'll find your joy along the way."

"I didn't think it was missing."

He put the truck back in Drive and pulled out onto the road. Noelle got out the directions the mayor had given her and told him to turn at the private road three miles up Mother Bear Road.

"As long as we don't run in to the namesake," he muttered.

"She's hibernating. Bears hibernate."

"You'd better be right about that."

They turned at the corner and then continued up the mountain. Gabriel kept track of the distance. The road had been recently plowed and they traveled easily, but when she pointed to the private road, everything changed.

Here the snow was thick and the truck moved sluggishly through the growing drifts.

"You sure about this?" he asked. "If it snows much more, we're going to get stuck."

She looked at the paper with the instructions. "It's less than a quarter mile to the cabin. From there, we walk."

"There's a cabin?"

"Yes, for emergencies. The city owns it. Or maybe the county. The mayor says it's kept stocked for when people get lost. She said we go directly east from the cabin for a few hundred yards and then we'll find the trees." She stared up at the sky. "The snow is letting up. It's a sign."

"Lucky us."

She ignored him and watched for the cabin. When she saw it and pointed, Gabriel nodded. He turned the truck so they were facing out, then they bundled into their coats, scarves and gloves and stepped out of the cab.

The first thing she noticed was the stillness. There was only the sound of their footsteps crunching in the snow. All around them was pristine wilderness. Bare trees, naked bushes and smooth, fresh snow. There weren't even animal tracks. The cabin was dark and silent, with snow on the roof and drifts piled up nearly to the windows.

"It's like we're the only two living creatures in the world," she said with a sigh. "It's so beautiful."

"Yes, it is."

She turned to smile at him, only to find he was looking at her with anything but amusement. There was an intensity in his blue eyes, a flash of hunger that had her wanting to step toward him. But then he blinked and it was gone.

Tree first, she told herself, trying to sound mentally stern. Man-seduction later.

"Okay," she said, pulling out her directions. "We go east."

Gabriel pointed. "That way."

She was going to ask how he knew, but figured she'd been enough of a pain, dragging him out here in the first place. Besides, it's not as if she had some innate sense of direction.

"Lead on," she told him when he'd collected the ax and some rope from the back of the truck.

They made slow progress through the deep snow. Noelle quickly realized there was no way she could have done this herself. Just getting out here would have been a challenge and it wasn't as if she knew how to chop down a tree. Maybe she should have gone with one of the ones in town, she thought, then pressed her lips together. She must remember not to mention that to Gabriel.

"So, you and Mayor Marsha," she said as she struggled to keep up with him. "That must have been interesting."

"She wanted to talk to me about the new hospital in town."

"New hospital? Oh, right. The one they're building. I have a friend, Montana. She's married to Simon Bradley. He's a—"

"Famous plastic surgeon who specializes in people who have been burned. I was told. The mayor did her best on selling me the job."

"Were you interested?"

"No."

Disappointment weighed heavily in her belly. She wanted to say that Fool's Gold was a great town and the people were really friendly and that if he stayed they could… What? Fall in love? Gabriel didn't want that. He didn't want a wife and a family. He believed the risk wasn't worth the reward. If he stayed she would want to spend time with him and doing that would most likely lead to getting her heart broken. Better for them both that he disappear while she was still in emotional control.

"You're going back into the army?" she asked.

"I haven't decided." He looked up as it began to snow again. "According to my dad, I don't get to leave. I owe them until I've done my twenty."

"He doesn't want you to choose?"

"Sure. As long as I choose what he wants me to." He pointed straight ahead. "Trees," he said.

She wasn't sure if he was excited about the find or

simply wanted to get her to change the subject. Regardless, she kept moving her legs through the thick snow, and watching for the perfect tree.

CHAPTER NINE

Noelle shook her head.

Gabriel wanted to complain that this was the fifth tree she'd rejected, but he couldn't blame her. Trees that grew in nature had a lot more flaws than groomed trees grown specifically for the holidays. One had an entire side missing, while another's branches were oddly twisted. She would have done better picking one from the lot. Not that he was about to say that. She was getting more dejected by the minute.

Even though she was wearing a thick coat and a scarf, he could see her shoulders were slumped. Her hat had lost its jaunty angle and now simply hung down by her ears. He wanted to tell her that they would find what she was looking for, but he wasn't sure it was out there. The perfect Christmas tree had been elusive this year.

Snow fell harder as they waded through the heavy drifts. They'd both worn heavy boots, but were getting soaked from boot tops to knees. The temperature was dropping.

"Noelle," he began, not wanting to disappoint her, but unwilling to risk their safety. "We need to go back."

She nodded without speaking.

"Hey," he said, reaching for her. "You don't have to—"

The rest of his sentence was swallowed by a rumbling

sound as the trees above them suddenly lost all their snow. Huge clumps fell on top of them without warning, nearly burying them. Noelle screamed, then slid to the ground where she disappeared completely. He managed to stay standing, but found himself in waist-high banks.

"Noelle!"

He dove into the snow, reaching for her with both hands. She'd landed on her butt but had already pushed up her arms and was digging her way out. As he dragged her up, she pushed against the ground and managed to stand.

"You okay?" he asked as he ripped off his gloves, then brushed snow from her face. "Are you hurt?"

She stared at him, wide-eyed. "I was attacked by snow."

"Or trees. Either way, I'm thinking nature isn't your friend."

"What happened?"

As she spoke, he checked her eyes and then urged her to take a couple of steps. Her balance was steady and she didn't seem to be in pain.

"The snow got too heavy for the trees and it fell. It happens. At least it wasn't an avalanche."

She shivered. "I got snow down my back and in my boots." She drew in a breath. "Okay, I'm done. There's no perfect tree. I'm not going to win the window competition. We'll just go with what we have."

He drew her against him and kissed her cheek. "We'll find you a nice domestic tree back in town."

She nodded. "Okay. Sure."

He didn't like the resignation in her voice. His Noelle was exuberant and excited. She wanted to win the best

Fool's Gold window, or whatever the hell the contest was called.

"What happened to showing up with joy?"

"I'm too cold and I was attacked. My joy is temporarily beaten."

"Let's get you back to the truck," he said, putting his arm around her waist and helping her wade through the drifts. The ax was heavy in his free hand. "You'll feel better when you're warm."

She nodded, but didn't speak. He felt her shivering. The cold seemed more intense and the snow fell harder. They used their own trail to make the going a little easier but eventually it filled in completely.

It was only when they were within sight of the house that Gabriel realized his mistake. It was *snowing*. They weren't in town or even right off a highway. They were a quarter mile from a regular road that was three miles from a well-plowed highway. The little he could see of the truck wasn't good. Snow came up past the bumper and it was getting dark.

Noelle looked up and saw the truck. "That's a lot of snow."

"Yes, it is."

"Are we going to be able to drive out of here?"

"I don't know. We might be stuck until the storm passes."

She shuddered. He studied her in the fading light and saw that she was pale and shaking. He ripped off her gloves and touched her fingers. They were wet and freezing.

There was no guarantee he could get them out tonight. From what he could remember from the forecast, it was supposed to snow until at least midnight. He looked at the small cabin. There was a chimney and the little he could see was well-maintained.

"Let's go inside," he said. "We'll get you warm and settle in for the night. I'll see if I can dig us out in the morning."

He waited for her to make a joke, but there was only the sound of her teeth chattering.

He helped her toward the cabin. They found steps and climbed up them onto the porch. He thought he might have to go looking for a key, but the door opened easily.

Inside was much warmer than outside, but incredibly dark. Gabriel reached for a switch on the wall and was surprised when lights came on.

"They still have electricity," he said, wondering how long until it went out. "I'll get you settled and warm, then go find some firewood."

"You think we're going to lose power?" Noelle asked through her chattering teeth.

"If it keeps snowing."

He found the controls for the furnace and turned the thermostat up from forty-five to seventy. A quick tour of the cabin told him it was small—maybe six hundred square feet of open concept. A double bed was at one end, the kitchen at the other, with a living area in the middle. The only closed-off room was a small, three-quarter bath. He checked and there was still running water, although it wasn't especially warm.

He led Noelle to the sofa and peeled off her jacket. It was soaked all the way through. She must have gotten snow inside when she'd fallen and then it had melted. Her shirt was damp, as were her jeans. She was shaking.

He had her sit, then quickly removed her boots. Her socks were soaked and her feet frozen. He got up and walked to the bed, where he stripped off the blankets. There was a cedar chest at the foot of the bed with more blankets inside. He grabbed all of them and returned to the sofa.

"Stand up," he said, helping her to her feet. "We have to get you out of your clothes."

He waited for a funny retort, but she only nodded. She was shaking too hard to undo her jeans, so he reached for the button at the waistband, then lowered the zipper.

The cold, wet fabric clung to her. He eased it down, ignoring her smooth skin and long legs. She stepped out of the jeans, then pulled off her sweater. The long-sleeved T-shirt came next and she was standing in front of him in bikini panties and a bra.

She was long and lean, with small breasts and narrow hips. Her pale skin was puckered with goose bumps, and she shivered and trembled. As much as he wanted to take a moment and enjoy the view, this wasn't the time. He quickly wrapped her in the blankets and began to rub his hands up and down her arms and legs.

As he moved over her, he reminded himself that he was a doctor. His actions were purely professional and enjoying them was wrong on multiple levels.

He worked on her until she stopped trembling so hard. "Curl up on the sofa," he told her. "I'll get us settled."

She nodded, still unable to speak.

He checked the vents. Warm air drifted out, but there wasn't a lot of force behind it. No doubt the unit was small and old. It would take a couple of hours to get the cabin up to temperature. He draped her damp clothes over chairs he placed near the vents. The shirt and sweater weren't as wet as her jeans, but eventually everything would dry.

He opened the refrigerator and didn't find any food, but the cupboards were full of canned and packaged goods. He looked in the freezer and was surprised to find it full of casseroles, each labeled and dated. Most of them had been made within the past couple of months. The mayor hadn't been kidding when she told Noelle it was kept stocked.

He pulled out a couple of casseroles and took the lids off so they could start to thaw. There was a small microwave on the counter, but that would only last as long as they had electricity. He was impressed it was still going, but had a bad feeling about it lasting much longer.

He checked drawers and under the sink. In a small alcove by the front door he found lanterns, both gas and electric. He set the latter to charging, then found two more by the bed and plugged them in.

The stove was wood, which was both good and bad. They could always cook, assuming either of them figured out how to use a woodstove. The closest he'd ever come had been roasting marshmallows on a campout. He glanced at Noelle, who sat huddled in her blankets, her eyes closed. She didn't strike him as much of an outdoor girl.

There was more color in her face and she was shivering less. She opened her eyes and looked at him.

"How are you feeling?" he asked.

"Foolish. I'm sorry we're stuck out here. I guess I cared too much about the window contest."

"You're not giving up," he told her.

"We're stuck in a snowstorm. It's Sunday. Even if we get out tomorrow, that doesn't give us much time. And if we're here until Tuesday, there's no way I can get anything done."

"I thought you were the one who had faith. Aren't we supposed to be having this adventure with joy in our hearts?"

"I'll find my joy when I'm a little less cold."

He walked over to the sofa and sat next to her. He pulled her close and ran his hands up and down her arms.

"Don't give up. You're the one who believes." He kissed the top of her head.

The blankets smelled of cedar, while her hair had a floral scent. Probably from her shampoo. Even through the layers of blanket, he could feel the outline of her body. While he couldn't see anything, he happened to know she was wearing very little. A fact that had a predictable effect on his blood flow.

She raised her head and looked at him. "I'm sorry I got you trapped in a cabin," she said. "I know this isn't your idea of fun."

"A romantic cabin in the woods, where I'm alone with a beautiful woman? Yeah, you're right. This sucks."

She gave him a smile. "I appreciate the effort. You're being really sweet. I should have thought this through. I should have—"

He didn't know what she was going to say and he wasn't sure he cared. What he didn't like was her beating herself up over something that wasn't important. He only knew one sure way to quiet her, so he lowered his head and pressed his mouth against hers.

Her lips were as soft as he remembered. Warm, which was good, considering how cold she'd been. She didn't hesitate, didn't pull back. As he leaned in, she parted her lips for him. At the same time she wrapped her arms around his neck and sighed.

He moved his tongue inside her mouth and was met

by hers. Each sweet stroke was like throwing gasoline on an already roaring fire.

With her arms around him, there was nothing holding up the blankets, which meant they fell and settled around her waist. The siren call of bare skin was too great, he thought. He couldn't resist knowing what it felt like to move his hands up and down her back.

He danced his fingers along her spine and over her bra strap. He lightly traced her shoulders, then slipped down her sides.

She tilted her head and shifted her torso in what could only be called an invitation. It would take a much more morally strong man than himself to resist. He eased his hand from her side to her rib cage, then up to her breast. He cupped the curve, feeling the silky softness of her bra and tight bud that was her nipple.

As he ran his thumb back and forth across the sensitive tip, Noelle pulled back. Her blue eyes were darker, her mouth parted and swollen from their kisses. She reached for his other hand and brought it to her breast, then held his palms against her.

He'd been with women before—lots of women. He'd been seduced and done the seducing. But this was different. He didn't know if it was the damn cabin or that he was back in the civilian world or something about Noelle. He wanted her with a heat that stole his will. At the same time, he wasn't going to push, wasn't going to take. Wasn't going to hurt her in any way. He'd seen her happy and he'd seen her broken and he never wanted her to be in pieces again.

He'd told her he wasn't staying, that while he believed in love, he wanted no part of it. If she was willing to accept that, then the choice had to be hers. And gratitude for what she probably saw as saving her life wasn't the same as making an informed decision.

Reluctantly, painfully, he drew back. He allowed himself a brief image of her straddling him, letting him fill her as she rode him, his fingers between her legs, rubbing her until they were both lost to the moment. Then he drew the blankets back up around her shoulders and forced himself to look away.

"STILL THE GENTLEMAN?" Noelle asked lightly, her body tingling from a combination of warming and Gabriel's touch.

"Did you bring condoms?"

She opened her mouth then closed it. "No," she said. She hadn't even brought her purse.

"Me, either."

So stopping made sense, even if it wasn't what she wanted. Being in Gabriel's arms had made her feel strong and powerful. She'd liked the way he touched her and how she'd responded. But…and there was always a but…she wasn't sure she was ready to hand over her body when she knew the circumstances were temporary. One thing she'd learned while she was healing was that she didn't want regrets. She'd assumed most of them would be about what she hadn't done, but some could go the other way.

He lightly kissed her, then stood. "I'm going to go outside and see if I can get a cell signal. I want to tell Melissa what happened so she can close up the store and let the authorities know we're staying out for the night."

"There goes my reputation," she said with a grin.

He didn't smile back. "Are you worried about what people will think?"

"I meant it the other way," she assured him. "I have wild friends. Knowing we spent the night together in a cabin will impress them."

He stared at her intently. "Was that a joke?"

"Yikes, I must be doing it wrong if you have to ask."

He surprised her by hauling her against him and hanging on tight. "You're better."

She could barely breathe. "Excuse me?"

"You were sad when we couldn't find a tree, then freezing after the snow attack. You were barely talking. Defeated." He drew back and looked at her. "I didn't like it."

His concern was kind of sweet. She touched his face. "You're really weird, you know that, right?"

"Yeah, I've been told that before." He stood. "I'm going to try to call Melissa. Then I'll get firewood. You rest. That's an order."

"You're not the boss of me."

"In this situation, I'm your doctor and you will listen."

"Ooh, tough-guy doctor. I'm trembling."

Something flashed in his eyes. Something hot and hungry that made her very aware of her seminaked state.

If he took, she wouldn't say no, but Gabriel had already proven he needed more than that. He needed her to be the one asking. To be sure.

"I'll be back," he said as he grabbed his jacket and headed for the door. "Stay warm."

She nodded and he left. When she was alone, she stood and found her legs were steady. She was cold but no longer chilled. Wrapping one of the blankets around her like a cloak, she explored the small cabin.

The furniture was worn, but looked clean. There were bookshelves with paperbacks ranging from spy thrill-

ers to romances. A deck of cards sat on a stack of board
games. On a shelf by the kitchen was a glass paper-
weight with a rose inside. A little Statue of Liberty sat
on a windowsill.

The bathroom had running water, which was great.
There was food and even a small portable radio. She
checked for batteries and when she found them, turned
it on. Sure enough, the local Fool's Gold FM station
came in. She grinned. Later, they could listen to music.
Although she doubted Gabriel would find the oldies station very romantic. Not with his brother acting as DJ.

She crossed to the small window and tried to see
through the falling snow. The tree hunt had been a good
lesson for her. It was easy for her to fall back into her
former competitive spirit, she thought. Determined to
win, no matter what it took. That drive had propelled
her through law school and later had given her the inner
strength to defeat her illness. But it didn't make her a
restful person. She wanted to maintain her Zen self.
Which meant that she probably should have taken one
of the first trees she'd seen in town instead of making
Gabriel go up into the mountains with her.

She saw movement outside and watched him walk to
the woodpile. He brushed off snow, then lifted the tarp.
She turned back to the interior of the cabin and crossed
to the sofa. As for what was going to happen that night,
she still hadn't decided. She knew what her body wanted,
but her heart and her head were different matters.

The front door burst open. Gabriel stood in the entrance, his head and shoulders covered with snow, his
expression oddly agitated.

"What's wrong?" she asked.

"You're not going to believe it. *I* can't believe it."

She got the feeling she didn't have to panic, but still. "You're not a very good storyteller. What is it?"

"A mother cat with kittens. By the woodpile."

He continued talking, but she didn't listen as she reached for her wet clothes.

"What are you doing?" he demanded. "I can handle it."

"You'll need help. Sometimes cats are afraid of men." She pointed to the door. "Go keep an eye on her. I'll be right there."

He hesitated, but then looked her over, nodded and went back out into the storm.

She pulled on her jeans and shrugged into her T-shirt. The sweater was too wet to be any good. She struggled with her damp socks, pulled on her boots and jacket, then stepped out into the frigid afternoon.

Gabriel was pacing by the woodpile. As she approached, he faced her and shook his head. "The babies are really small. Their eyes are barely open. She's cold and starving. We've got to get her inside."

He raised the tarp over the wood and Noelle saw a mother cat had tried to make a bed by the vent from the cabin. She would guess that was the warmest place she could find. Four little kittens were huddled up against her, mewing as if they were uncomfortable.

The mama cat was small and thin, with big eyes. Her coat wasn't very long and seemed to have some tabby mixed in. She watched Noelle warily, no doubt afraid of what would happen next.

Noelle dropped to her knees, ignoring the cold and soaking snow, and pulled her gloves off her hand.

"Hey, pretty girl," she murmured, holding out her fingers to the mother cat. "It's okay. Are you lost? Do you live out here by yourself? Because it's really cold. I think you should come in with us."

The cat stared at her for a long time before finally sniffing her fingers. The action told Noelle she had to have belonged to someone at some time. Wouldn't a feral cat simply take off?

"Go inside," she told Gabriel in a low voice. "Back up slowly so you don't startle her. Look for canned meat. There's probably tuna. Open the can, then bring it to me."

Noelle stayed where she was, speaking softly, offering reassurance. He returned with an open can. She took it from him and scooped up a little with her fingers, then held it out to the mother cat.

She gulped the tuna flakes in a single bite, then stood and meowed. Noelle saw she was horribly thin and obviously exhausted.

"What happened to you?" she asked, then stood. "Come on, sweet girl. Let's get you and your babies inside."

She held out the can so the cat could sniff it, then dropped a little on the snow. The cat ate it and took a step toward her. They repeated the procedure a few times, then the cat retreated to stay by her babies.

"Get a towel," Noelle told Gabriel.

He raced back inside and returned with a hand towel. Noelle put it on the snow and reached for the cat's first kitten. The mother watched her intently but didn't try to stop her. Noelle collected all four tiny kittens on the towel and started toward the house.

"Get the tuna," she said as the mother cat followed her inside.

It didn't take long to create a bed for the mother cat

and her babies. They placed it close to a vent so she would be warm. While Gabriel poured her a bowl of water, Noelle dumped the tuna onto a dish and fed her. The mother cat inhaled her meal, then returned to her babies and began to wash them. By the time Noelle had struggled out of her clothes and was wrapped in her blanket again, mother and kittens were sound asleep.

Gabriel returned with the wood he'd gone looking for in the first place. He put it by the fireplace, then slipped out of his jacket and removed his boots.

"How old do you think they are?" she asked in a soft voice.

"A couple of weeks. They have their eyes open, but they're still blind."

"You know a lot about cats."

"My ex had a couple. One got pregnant, so I heard all about the process."

He sat on the sofa and angled toward her. Noelle watched the cats sleeping. "Did you get in touch with Melissa?" she asked.

"I did. I told her we were going to stay put until it stopped snowing. She was fine with locking up the store. She said the roads into town are temporarily closed, so no one is getting in or out."

"It's a real snowstorm."

"Does that make you happy?" he asked.

She nodded. "We're warm and safe and we now have a cat with kittens." She glanced at the sleeping family. "It's so cold out there. I don't know how she survived this long."

"Look at how thin she is. I doubt she's been eating. She probably wouldn't have made it much longer."

Noelle didn't want to think about that, but knew he was right. "If we hadn't come along," she began.

Gabriel took her hand in his. "See? Your tree obsession served a purpose."

She nodded. "We're her Christmas miracle. And don't tell me it's not Christmas yet."

"I wouldn't dare."

CHAPTER TEN

NOELLE WOKE UP to total darkness and a sense of warmth and safety. It took her a second to realize where she was and why there was an arm around her waist. As she blinked, her mind filled in the blanks. The search for the tree. The tree-snow attack, the cabin and the mother cat and her kittens.

She and Gabriel had spent a quiet evening reading and listening to the radio. Power had lasted until nearly nine, then it had gone out. He'd started a fire and they'd used the battery-operated lanterns sparingly. Their only rough spot had been when they'd let the mother cat out to use the restroom. For ten anxious minutes, they'd waited for her to come back and discussed what they would do if she didn't. But she'd appeared on the doorstep and meowed to get in.

Now Noelle wondered what time it was and how long she'd been asleep. She'd planned to make a move and think about seducing Gabriel, only exhaustion had overcome her before she could figure out how best to be seductive. She'd been asleep long before he joined her in the bed.

He was pressed up against her, his arm around her waist. In a perfect world she would roll over and do something suggestive. Unfortunately, there was a whole list of things that got in the way. For one, she wasn't sure what he would find sexy. For another, she really had to pee, and rounding up the issues was the fact that she needed to brush her teeth before kissing anyone.

Life, she thought humorously. Designed to keep her humble.

She decided to stay where she was for a few more minutes and enjoy the moment. Gabriel was warm and solid against her back. She hadn't slept with a man in a long time, she thought. Hadn't shared her life so intimately. It felt good to be with him.

Part of the healing process, she thought. While her body had gotten better months ago, it was taking her spirit longer. She'd been touched by death, had seen firsthand the evidence of her mortality. Had nearly lost everything and then had needed to fight her way back.

That was behind her now. She'd made a new home, new friends. She was safe and supported. She had let go of the past. Now all she needed was her second act, she thought with a smile. The good stuff—a husband to love and kids. Memories. She wanted lots and lots of memories.

The man next to her rolled onto his back.

"Did you sleep well?" he asked, his voice quiet in the darkness.

"I did. What about you?"

"Great, except for your snoring."

She shot up into a sitting position. "I don't snore."

"I know. I was kidding."

She glared in his general direction. "That wasn't funny."

"It was to me." His hand stroked her back.

"We need to work on your sense of humor," she told him.

"Yet people tell me it's one of my best qualities."

She heard a rustling sound by the fireplace and reached for the lantern by the bed. After turning it on, she saw the feline guest had stepped out of her make-shift bed and was stretching. The cat looked at her and meowed.

"I think that's a request for a bathroom break and breakfast," Noelle said as she stood.

She tried not to think about the fact that she was wearing a long-sleeved T-shirt, panties and nothing else. But it hadn't made sense to sleep in clothes and hey, Gabriel had stripped down to his briefs.

Nearly naked, she thought, doing her best not to watch him get out of bed. Staring seemed so rude. Still, under the circumstances, she was willing to be chastised for bad manners.

Fortunately he decided to be the one to let out the cat, so he walked across their small cabin. The fact that he came into her field of view wasn't really her fault, she told herself as she took in his broad back and narrow waist. He had a great butt, she thought with a sigh, then turned away and headed for the bathroom.

When she'd used the facilities and brushed her teeth, she returned to the main room to check on her jeans. "What time is it?" she asked. "It must be early if it's still dark."

Gabriel had pulled on his clothes and was collecting his boots. "It's daylight," he said.

She glanced toward the still-dark window. "I don't understand."

"It's snow."

She shook her head. "No. Not past the windows."

"Well past. It stopped snowing but based on how

much we got in the night, it wasn't anytime close to midnight. I would say it went until a couple of hours ago. You should have seen the look the cat gave me when I opened the door for her. She wasn't amused."

Noelle crossed to the front door and pulled it open. The cat ran back inside and shook herself off. Noelle stared at the feet of snow surrounding the house, piling up toward the room and stretching for as far as she could see. Up above the sky was bright and blue, but here on earth, it was like living in a snow globe.

"Are we going to be able to get out today?" she asked.

"I don't know. I'm going to call Gideon and find out about the snowplows. We'll need them to come down the private road. Otherwise it'll take days for me to dig us out back to where we turned."

"I can help," she told him. "Weren't there several shovels by the woodpile?"

"Yeah, but even with two of us, it'll take days to dig us out. It's a quarter mile of maybe four feet of snow. That's not easy."

He finished tying his boots, then headed for the bathroom. Noelle fed the cat and checked on the kittens before opening the freezer and quickly removing two casseroles. If they were going to be stuck here another day or so, they would need food, which meant defrosting before reheating. As for the rest of the contents of the freezer, she figured they had the rest of the day before they had to think about how to keep the food in the freezer cold. Of course, sticking it all in a snowbank would be a quick solution.

"I'll be back," he told her as he stepped out of the bathroom.

"Be careful," she told him, following him to the door.

He surprised her with a quick kiss, and then he was gone. She looked at the mother cat.

"I know what you're thinking. It all starts so casually but before you know it, you're a single mother of four, trying to make it through a hard winter."

The mother cat closed her eyes and began to purr.

GABRIEL WASN'T SURE how far he walked to get a signal on his cell phone. All he knew was that by the time he reached the top of the rise, he could barely see the house and he was cold, wet and tired.

He turned on his cell and was pleased to see three bars pop up. He dialed his brother.

"Do you know what time it is?" came the grumbling greeting. "I work the late shift, bro."

"Sorry," Gabriel told him. "I need your help."

"What's wrong?" The question was immediate and all sleep had fled Gideon's voice. He was a soldier on alert.

Gabriel explained about the search for the perfect tree in the middle of a snowstorm and how he and Noelle were snowed in.

"We got at least four feet last night," he said. "Maybe more."

His brother started to chuckle. "A cabin in the woods. Good one. Next thing you'll be telling me you had to share the only bed to keep warm."

Gabriel thought about the long night with Noelle snuggled close. Despite his exhaustion, he'd found it difficult to sleep. His body had wanted to do things with her. Sexual things. The fact that he'd found condoms when he'd checked out the bathroom hadn't made sleeping any easier. Because now there was nothing standing between him and what he wanted—except his promise.

"The cabin is on a private road," he said, ignoring his brother's comments. Gabriel described the location. "Mayor Marsha told Noelle about it, so she'll have more details. There's no way we're getting out of here until they plow up to the truck."

Gideon swore. "My truck? The truck you borrowed?"

"That would be the one."

"Great. Now I'm motivated to get you rescued."

Gabriel grinned. "Thanks for caring."

"Hey, I love that truck. Okay, I'll make some calls. You have cell service in the cabin?"

"No. I'm about a quarter mile away."

"Then I won't make you wait while I phone around. Give me a couple of hours and call back. By then I'll know something."

"Will do."

He disconnected the call and headed back for the house. When he was nearly there, he saw something moving in the snow. An animal, he thought. Something small and...

He came to a stop and swore. No way, he thought. No way in hell. But there it was. A mother cat with a kitten in her mouth. She was heading for the cabin.

While their rescues from the previous night had been a kind of tabby, this cat was gray with white paws. Her kitten was older and bigger than the others, but it was still as she carried it through the feet of snow.

He approached cautiously, not wanting to frighten her. The cat waited patiently by the front door, obviously expecting to be let in.

He opened the door and she darted inside. He followed. "We have more company."

Noelle was stirring a pot on the woodstove. She saw the mother cat and then looked at him. "Seriously?"

"That's what I said."

"How many are out there?"

"I have no idea."

The new mother cat walked over to the other one. They greeted each other with obvious familiarity. The gray mom set her kitten next to the tabby, who drew it close and began grooming it. Then the new mom headed back for the door.

"She has a family," Noelle said. "We need to get them all inside."

"I'll go with her," Gabriel told her.

Fortunately, the mother cat chose to cooperate. She led the way, occasionally glancing back as if making sure he was keeping up. She'd made her home midway up a tree, in a hole created by some other creature. There were two kittens shivering inside, including a little gray tabby that didn't have a tail.

"Hey, guys," Gabriel said, reaching for the kittens. They both glared at him and hissed. Their sharp claws ripped through his hand.

"Nice," he muttered, looking at the mother cat. "You couldn't teach them better?"

She watched anxiously as he tucked the squirming kittens inside his coat, against his chest. They settled immediately, apparently deciding warmth was more important than dealing with the abduction.

The mother cat meowed and kept pace with him as they made their way back to the cabin. Once the babies were settled by the fireplace, the two mothers curled up around their families and went to sleep.

Noelle dished up a heated chicken and noodle casserole and they sat down at the table. "We need to look around after breakfast," she said. "To see if there are any other cats in the area."

He nodded and told her about his call to Gideon. "He'll have information for me in a couple of hours. In the meantime, we'll start digging out. We work for an hour, then come in and rest before heading out again."

"Forced exercise. Experts do say to work it into your lifestyle."

"I don't think this is what they had in mind." He thought about the drifts he'd seen and how the house was buried. "The main roads are going to be their first priority. We have food, water and shelter. There may be people stranded."

She picked up her fork. "You're trying to warn me that we could be here a couple of days."

He nodded. He knew the window contest was important to her, but he doubted they would get back in time to do anything. And they sure weren't going to be looking for the perfect tree.

"I'm sorry you're stuck," she said. "I dragged you out here."

"I came voluntarily."

She smiled. "Technically, you were complaining, but this isn't the time to go into that. Melissa will take care of the store. If the snow is this bad in town, then it's not like we're going to be getting a lot of customers anyway."

She scooped up some chicken. "We have kittens, we have a radio, we have a supply of delicious casseroles. Could it be any better?"

He knew she was teasing, but that part of her believed what she was saying. She wasn't the type to look on the dark side. And she was right—they were safe and would hold out for a week, no problem.

She glanced at the kittens and smiled. He studied her profile. She was so beautiful, he thought. Giving. Unexpectedly competitive. She was nothing he'd expected for his vacation and yet now he couldn't imagine what he would have done with himself if he hadn't met her.

NOELLE STUDIED THE cards in front of her. All she needed was another two and either an eight or a king of spades and she would be out, she thought, careful to not let her expression show her glee. She'd never had much of a poker face.

It was midafternoon. She and Gabriel had already had four sessions of digging out. Snow was heavier than it looked, especially when measured in feet. They'd dug what was more trench than path to the truck, then gone to work clearing the vehicle.

Gabriel's second call to his brother had told them that the town had been slammed, as well. That while the plows were out and working, they wouldn't get up Mother Bear Road until the following morning. The good news was Mayor Marsha had promised the private road would be plowed up to the truck, so all they had to do was get it dug out and then wait to be rescued.

One more night, Noelle thought as Gabriel took another card and slipped it into his hand. He studied the cards. One more night sharing a bed. Last night she'd been too exhausted to enjoy the closeness, but tonight she planned to savor the snuggling. And maybe come up with a plan to take things to the next level.

Whoever had stocked the cabin had been really thorough. There was a fresh box of condoms in the small

medicine cabinet, along with aspirin and a first-aid kit.
As no one was injured, she found the condoms most
interesting.

She was pretty sure that making love with Gabriel
was a stupid idea, but she no longer cared. She liked
him. He was sweet and sexy and it had been way too
long since she'd been held by a man. She accepted that
he was leaving and not interested in anything long-term.
While remembering her goals was important, so was
living in the moment. And he was a real in-the-moment
temptation.

"Gin," he said, spreading out his cards on the table.

She stared at them. "No way."

He shrugged. "Look for yourself."

"You got gin last time."

"The cards love me."

She checked his runs and sets and saw that he really
had won. She put hers on the table and was able to get
rid of a couple of her extra cards by adding them to his,
then she calculated the points.

"You're annoying," she told him.

He chuckled, then got up and stretched before crossing to the counter and picking up a bottle of wine.

"A saucy red," he told her.

"I love it when wine gets saucy."

He dug around in the drawers and found an opener.
She went to get glasses. The lights flickered and then
came on. The refrigerator began to hum. She stared at
Gabriel.

"No way," she said. "That's more incredible than you
winning two games in a row. We have power?"

"Gotta love the town," he said, crossing to one of the
vents and holding out his hand. "And we have heat."

They also had access to the hot plate, she thought, carrying the lanterns over to the wall and plugging them in so they could charge. Even heating food on a wood-stove was complicated.

He carried the wine over to the sofa, and she joined him. The cats were sleeping.

"I'm not sure how we're going to transport all nine cats tomorrow," she said, after taking a sip.

He pointed to the metal box that currently held kin-dling. "I figured we'd line that with a blanket and put the kittens inside. The mother cats will be loose, I guess. It's not like we'll be going fast, so they should be okay."

"We'll have to make it work. I'm worried that once we get out, we won't be able to get back for a while and I don't want to leave one of the families behind."

"We won't."

Then she would have two new families in her small place, she thought, making a mental list of what she would need. When the kittens were old enough to be adopted, she would rally her friends to help her find them homes. The mother cats would need to be spayed, as well. It was a lot to take on, but she was confident she could manage.

The room was silent, with only the crackling of the fire as background noise. "Not exactly the fast-paced hospital life you've been used to," she said.

"That's okay. I needed a break."

"And shoveling snow for hours at a time is what you were hoping for?"

"It's good exercise."

She turned to look at him. "Would you have become a doctor if you hadn't joined the army?"

"I don't know," he admitted. "I didn't want to be a

soldier, which didn't leave a lot of options. I'm good at what I do. I know I make a difference."

"At a price," she said, thinking about all he'd told her about his work.

"It's nothing compared to what those fighting have to pay." He leaned back against the sofa. "Sometimes I think about what I could do instead. Live somewhere permanently. Have friends outside the medical profession."

"You don't have that now?"

"I avoid getting too close to anyone."

She thought about the girlfriend he'd lost so horribly and unexpectedly. "I guess that makes sense."

He nodded. "It's hard to have to patch up a friend and not know if he or she is going to make it, while still having to move on to someone else."

The realization of all he'd sacrificed made her sad. Somewhere along the way Gabriel had learned that the price of loving was too high. He was no longer willing to risk his heart because it all could be gone tomorrow. The wrong lesson, she was convinced, but she had no way to prove it to him. She reached for his hand—the one that had been injured. The wound had healed over and now there was only the scar. She put down her wine and held his hand in both of hers. There was strength here, she thought. Knowledge. He could recover, or at the very least, ward off death.

She looked back at his face and saw him looking at her. His gaze was hooded, as if he didn't want her to know what he was thinking.

In that moment, staring into his dark blue eyes, she understood that she'd never had a choice in the matter. That her destiny with Gabriel had been set from the second she'd seen him. He was kind and funny and smart and irreverent and he knew about cats. He was the kind of man who hiked through the wilderness to find the perfect tree for a window display that didn't matter to him at all. He gave his all and expected nothing in return.

She wanted to tell him that he could have her heart. He could take it with him, if he wanted, because it was his. Only he wouldn't understand the gesture as a gift. He would think she was trying to trap him, and she wasn't.

"I'll be right back," she said instead and stood. She crossed to the tiny bathroom and opened the medicine cabinet. She pulled out the box of condoms and put them on the small table by the bed, then turned to face him.

He'd risen to his feet, but didn't walk toward her. "I wondered if you'd seen those."

"I did," she said, pulling her T-shirt off and draping it over the footboard. She unfastened her jeans and let them fall to the floor.

He put down his wine. "Just like that?"

"Did you want more drama?"

"No," he said and moved toward her.

She went into his arms. He drew her against him, moving his hands up and down her back. His fingers paused on the back of her bra. She felt a slight tug as the hooks were pulled free, and then it fell away.

She pressed her lips to his as his hands slid up her sides and shifted to cup her breasts. Heat and need poured through her. She met his tongue stroke for stroke, even as she tugged on the hem of his sweater.

He pulled it off, then moved them to the bed. He touched her everywhere, arousing her with first his fingers then his tongue, exciting her until her breath came in pants and her release was inevitable. She helped him undress, silently pleased his hands trembled. After slipping on the condom, he joined with her, as the sun slipped slowly over the horizon.

"I CAN'T SEE YOU as a heartless corporate lawyer," Gabriel said, his hand moving up and down her bare belly.

They were stretched out on the bed, their bodies sated…at least for the moment. Noelle liked that they were still naked and touching each other. To her the real test of sexual compatibility wasn't in the moment. Anyone could make that good. It was after. Were there regrets? Did she want to make love again? Could they laugh?

"I wasn't heartless," she told him. "Which might have turned out to be a problem. Although I suppose I should point out that not all corporate lawyers are heartless."

One eyebrow rose.

She grinned. "Okay, *some* of them aren't. How's that?"

"I'm still having trouble believing that." He moved his hand over one breast, then the other. He paused to tease her nipples, which made her shiver.

His gaze sharpened. "You like that."

"I liked pretty much everything you did," she admitted. "I'm sure your technique has been honed by all your experience."

He groaned and rolled on his back. "I never should have admitted that to you."

She propped her head on her hand and smiled. "The fact that you used sex as a way to escape from your job pressures?" She paused. "Yeah, not your smartest conversational move. Because you can't unsay it and I will never, ever forget."

He glanced at her, the corner of his mouth turning up. "I wasn't a complete dog."

"Interesting, because I hear a distinct yipping in the background."

"When I was in a relationship, I was faithful."

"I have no proof of that."

The smile faded. "I wouldn't do that. I don't get the point. If someone's unhappy, talk about it. If you can't fix it, man up and be honest about wanting to leave."

"I know," she said, leaning forward and lightly kissing him.

He took her free hand in his and brought it to his groin. She stroked him, taking him from relaxed to aroused in about three seconds.

She'd been about to suggest they get dressed and eat, but this was so much more interesting, she thought. Especially when he drew her up so she was straddling him.

She leaned over and let her hair trail along his chest. He moved his hand between them and found her very center. He smiled slowly.

"I challenge you to a test of wills," he said. "Who can last the longest?"

She sighed as he reached for the condoms. "At last, a game I'm going to enjoy losing."

THE DOORS TO the triage center opened again. They had a distinctive squeak, so Gabriel knew a second before it happened that yet another wounded soldier was being wheeled in. There was blood everywhere, and cries of pain.

He pointed to where the soldier should go and tried

to get out of the way, but he couldn't. There were too many wounded and he was unable to make room. The doors opened again and he could see the line of gurneys stretched on forever. There were hundreds who needed him. Thousands. And he could never be enough.

He came awake with a start. In the darkness, he had no idea where he was or what was happening. Then the scent of the fire drifted to him and he heard the soft rumble of one of the cats purring. Memories returned and he was able to place himself in the cabin.

Noelle slept next to him. He put his arm around her and drew her against him. She was as warm and yielding in sleep as she had been awake. He hung on to her and steadied his breathing.

He didn't need to study psychology to understand what the dream meant. He was exhausted from his work. Drained down to his soul. It would take months to heal—maybe years. But he only had until the first of January before he had to decide and he honest to God didn't know what to do.

The decision should be about staying in the army and nothing else. But somehow Noelle had woven her way into his life—into how he thought and what he wanted to do. He'd never meant to get involved. Never meant to care. Because there was no point. They could both be dead tomorrow.

Only in her arms, right now, it didn't feel like that. It felt like there could be possibilities. And he understood that concept scared him more than any mortar shell ever could.

CHAPTER ELEVEN

NOELLE FELT GABRIEL get out of bed. She was sure it was early in the morning, but she couldn't see the clock. She sat up and turned on the small lamp by the bed. Gabriel pulled on his jeans before facing her.

"What's wrong?" she asked, taking in his drawn features. "Are you okay?"

"I'm fine. Go back to sleep."

"It's not exactly something you can order me to do." She got up and looked around for her clothes. She'd been down to her underwear the first time they'd gone to bed, and had only been wearing her T-shirt the second.

She couldn't see any clothes anywhere and started to lean over and to move the covers when Gabriel swore. She turned and saw him holding out his shirt.

"Put this on. Please."

He sounded both furious and pleading. She shrugged into the shirt and fastened the buttons. "What's going on?"

"Nothing. We have to get out of here."

"Yes, that's the plan. When the plow comes, we'll drive back to town."

He ran his hands through his hair. "That's not good enough. We need to go now."

She shifted so she could see the clock. "It's five in

the morning. The plows won't have been here. Are you going to dig us out all the way to the road?"

"If I have to."

She spotted her panties and her bra and scooped them up. She wasn't sure what had happened in the past half dozen hours, but whatever it was, it was bad. Last night Gabriel had been a warm, attentive lover. This morning he was acting as if she'd done something wrong. Or as if she wanted something unreasonable from him.

She knew neither was true and refused to let herself go there. Something was bugging Gabriel. For all she knew, it had nothing to do with her. Or maybe their great two days together had rattled him to the point where he couldn't cope. On the surface, he was a smart, charming guy. But underneath, he was as wounded as the soldiers he treated. Either way, she wasn't taking the blame for something she didn't do.

She retreated to the bathroom and dressed quickly. When she stepped back into the main room, he was gone. She told herself that if he wanted to shovel them back to town, she wished him luck.

She spent the next hour taking care of the little cabin. She fed the cats, then let them out. She washed dishes, made coffee and generally straightened up. She'd already made a list of the supplies they'd used so she could replace them later. She would talk to Mayor Marsha about how to do that. No one wanted her driving back to the cabin while there was snow on the ground.

When all that was done, she settled on the floor and played with the older kittens. They were alert and curious. As they hadn't been around people before, they'd started out a little wary of her, but a rousing game of string had them crawling all over her and settling into her lap for a quick snooze.

Sometime after seven, Gabriel returned. He was chilled and breathing hard.

"The truck is clear," he told her as he pulled off his cap and shrugged out of his coat. "The plow will be here in the next couple of hours. They're already working on Mother Bear Road."

She watched him as he spoke, hoping to see a smile or some sign that whatever was bothering him had worked itself out. But he barely looked at her as he shrugged out of his layers.

"There's coffee," she told him, pointing to the pot. "I've cleaned up and stripped the bed." She was planning on taking the sheets with her so she could wash them.

He glanced around at the empty casserole dishes, the neatly tied trash and the folded sheets. "I would have helped," he told her.

"You were busy."

For a second he looked at her. She waited, barely breathing, hoping for something. A smile, a hint that what they'd had so briefly still existed. But then he turned away and the moment was lost.

NINE CATS WERE not easily corralled. The smallest kittens protested at being put in the box, but couldn't do much about it. The older kittens wanted to explore and scramble out. The mother cats had no interest in taking a drive. After several false starts, Noelle and Gabriel stood in the center of the cabin no closer to getting the animals loaded than they had been at the start. The difference was he was pissed and she couldn't stop giggling.

"This isn't funny," he told her as he reached for one of the larger kittens again.

The animal went easily into the box, then just as quickly jumped out. Both mother cats were under the bed, yowling their protests at this kind of behavior.

Noelle laughed, then picked up the box. "Stop. Just stop. This isn't working." The truck was already loaded with everything else. They just needed to get the cats in order.

"I'll sit in the backseat," she said. "I'll put the box of little kittens next to me. You can pass me the other kittens one by one through the window. Bring the mother cats last. I'll keep them out of your way while we drive back to town."

One of the mother cats poked her head out from under the bed, saw the box and promptly retreated. Gabriel rubbed his temple.

"That might work," he admitted.

She put on her coat and took the box. He grabbed a couple of mobile kittens and started after her. When she was in the backseat, she reached for the kittens and held them on her lap.

Five minutes later all nine cats were in the rear cab of the truck, and Gabriel had gotten behind the wheel. The plow had been through, clearing the road. Noelle put on her seat belt and did her best to reassure the two families.

"This won't take long," she told them. "We'll be home soon."

Unfortunately, home was a strange place with no feline supplies, but there was no reason for them to know that. He started the engine, and they slowly drove down the freshly plowed road.

The trip back to town took less time than she would

have thought. Once they got to the main road, he was able to drive quickly. In Fool's Gold, the houses were covered with snow, as were the lawns. But the sidewalks were shoveled and the streets clear.

Gabriel pulled into her driveway and helped her inside with the cats. It took a few trips and then the family was safe. The mother cats and older kittens started exploring right away. She walked Gabriel to the front door.

"I'll go to the pet store," he told her. "Get what you need for the next few days. Food, litter, some dishes."

"That would be nice," she said. "Thank you. I'm going to take a shower, then call around and find someone who can check on them while I'm at work."

They were strangers exchanging information, she thought sadly. It was as if the past two days had never happened at all.

"Just tell me why," she said impulsively. "What happened? Why are you different?"

His dark gaze settled on her face. A muscle twitched by his mouth. She waited, hoping he would say something—anything—because that would give them a chance. If they could talk about it, they could fix it. Or at least deal with it.

"Everything is fine," he told her. "We're back. We have things to do."

"All right," she said quietly, knowing there was no point. Gabriel had to be willing to meet her halfway. Obviously, he wasn't.

She took her shower and dressed for work. Gabriel returned with the promised supplies, and she set up two litter boxes in the laundry room, then put out dishes of water and dry food. After making sure all the windows were securely closed, she left for work.

The store was exactly as she remembered. Bright and warm, with all things Christmas. Just walking inside lightened her spirits. She didn't know if she was going to see Gabriel again and tried to tell herself it didn't matter. When she realized she was lying, she told herself that whether or not she saw him, she would recover. That this was only ever going to be temporary and she had survived much worse.

A little before ten Melissa arrived, her younger sister, Abby, in tow.

"I can't believe you got snowed in," Melissa said, hugging her. "That's so scary. But you're okay?"

"We were fine. We had electricity most of the time. Hey, Abby."

The fifteen-year-old smiled at her. "I heard about the kittens. I can go by and check on them, if you'd like."

"Thanks, but shouldn't you be in school?"

Abby grinned. "It's a teacher day. Those are my favorite."

"They were my favorites, too," Noelle admitted.

She gave the teen a spare key and they set up a schedule with Abby agreeing to stop by Noelle's place right after school. They were discussing payment when the phone rang. Melissa answered it.

"That was Gabriel," she said a couple of minutes later. "He's not going to be coming in." She drew in a breath and looked at Noelle. "So, we were wondering if Abby could work here. She's really responsible."

"I'd still look after the cats," Abby promised, her fingers clenched and her eyes bright with anticipation. "Mom said I could work a few hours after school, but only through Christmas break. Once the new semester starts I have to focus on my studies."

"Having you around would be great," Noelle told her, ignoring the sense of being hit in the gut. He hadn't even told her goodbye himself. Weak-assed jerk. Only calling him names didn't make her feel any better.

"I'll show you where to put your stuff," Melissa said, leading her sister toward the back room.

Noelle walked to the front door and turned the sign to Open, then she unlocked the door and greeted her first customer.

GABRIEL WENT BACK to his vacation rental and tried to sleep. When that didn't work, he drove his brother's truck up to his place and got his car, then went back to town. He passed by the store several times, but didn't go in. He didn't have to, he reminded himself. He'd called to say he wouldn't.

Only that didn't seem to matter. All he could think about was Noelle. He missed her and wanted to be with her. Only he couldn't because he couldn't give her what she wanted.

He waited until close to six, then parked where he could see her lock up and head home. She greeted several people as she walked the familiar streets, pausing to look at the window display in front of the sporting goods store.

Gabriel swore and pounded his fist against the steering wheel. The window, he thought. The whole point of their trip up the mountain had been to get the perfect tree for the windows. Because she wanted to win that stupid contest. Only somehow that had been forgotten.

The judging was in the morning. There wasn't time to— Or was there? He reached for his cell phone and dialed.

"DAD, BE CAREFUL," Gabriel said, watching the older Boylan stretch up on a tall ladder.

"If I fall, you can patch me up," his father said cheerfully.

Great, Gabriel thought, now his dad had a sense of humor. "Bones aren't my thing."

It was late, or early, depending on one's frame of reference. His entire family was crowded into The Christmas Attic, working to make Noelle's display as perfect as possible for the morning judging.

"Just have to get this power strip in place," his father said. "Gideon, hand me that power drill."

Gideon did as requested, then returned his attention to the laptop he and Carter had brought. Karen and Felicia were sharing another computer—or rather Felicia was working the keys while Karen pushed buttons on a remote-controlled robot, dressed to look like a Christmas elf.

When he'd put out the call to his family, he hadn't known what to expect. But everyone had come through. They'd met at Gideon's house a little after six to work out a plan, then had collected everything they would need for the window display and had descended on the store around nine. The idea was to combine an old-fashioned Christmas with high-tech innovation.

The tree was the centerpiece. There were presents, some wrapped, some unwrapped. But instead of a team of elves helping Santa, there were three small robots in jaunty Christmas attire. The background was a light show, synchronized to holiday music.

"Dad, where did you find these old songs?" Carter asked.

"They're classics."

"They're not even from this century."

Gideon typed on the keyboard, then glanced at the lights his father was mounting in rows. "Nothing good is from this century."

"Hey, I was born in this century."

Gideon paused to squeeze his son's shoulder. "Okay, you're right. You're the one good thing."

Karen held up a box. "Wrapped or unwrapped?"

Gabriel glanced at the make-your-own-plushy-elephant kit. "Weird, so we'll leave it unwrapped."

He glanced at his watch and swore. It was after four. Carter yawned.

"I've never been up this late," the teen said with a sidelong glance at Felicia. "There's no way I'm going to make it through classes today."

She pressed her lips together. "Yes, I know. I should have made a bed for you in the storeroom so you could sleep."

Norm climbed down the ladder. "You worry too much, woman. An adventure like this is good for the boy. I used to take my sons out in the middle of the night to look at a meteor going by."

"Once we went into a deer blind and watched the does walk by with their newborn fawns," Gideon said.

Gabriel remembered the stillness of the predawn hours and how the babies had been so delicate as they walked by. For once his dad hadn't been yelling at him or complaining he wasn't macho enough.

"That was a good night," he admitted.

Carter and Felicia crawled into the window and began arranging the presents Karen handed to them. Gabriel and Gideon handed in the three robots, while Norm went outside with a walkie-talkie. He stood on the sidewalk, giving them direction on how to arrange the robots.

Gabriel and Gideon anchored the lights to the back of the window and tested the connection. When they all came on and stayed steady, Gideon plugged in his laptop and hit the enter key. Music played and the lights began to flash.

It took nearly an hour to get everything in place. Just as Gabriel was securing the window closed, someone knocked on the front door of the store.

Felicia hurried to let in the other woman.

"Patience!" she exclaimed.

Patience, a pretty woman with brown hair, held out two take-out trays with to-go containers.

"I heard you'd been at it all night," she said. "So I opened up a little early to bring you your morning coffee. I have regular and decaf."

"I'll take the decaf," Norm said. "Honey, you want the same?"

Karen nodded. "I'm going to try to sleep this morning."

Patience passed out the containers. She handed one to Carter. "Hot chocolate with extra whip."

"Thanks." Carter flashed her a smile.

The rest of them took the regular coffees. Patience held out a bag of donuts. "Fresh from the bakery," she said. "The window looks great."

Karen took the bag and opened it. After drawing in a deep breath, she sighed. "I love this town."

Her husband looked at her for a second, then turned to Patience. "Thank you for bringing this. I remember when I got up this early every day."

"I'm used to it now," she said with a laugh. "The first

few weeks were tough. Now I need to get back to my store. I have a surprising number of regulars who are in line by five." She started to leave, then turned back. "Oh, Police Chief Barns said to remind you to lock up before you leave."

"Of course she did," Gabriel murmured, thinking that was so like Fool's Gold. Everyone looked out for everyone else.

Carter and Gideon went outside to watch the window display as it cycled through the five songs they'd programmed. Karen and Norm headed back for the house. Gabriel joined Felicia in the cleanup.

"Thank you for asking for our help," his future sister-in-law said. "I like giving to my friends, and this was a unique opportunity."

"I should be thanking you."

Felicia smiled as she collected the leftover gift wrap. "You know, your parents are thinking of moving here permanently."

He hadn't known that for sure. "Okay, an interesting concept."

"Gideon doesn't know what to think, but I'm pleased by the news. Carter will enjoy having his grandparents around. Aside from his father, they are his only direct biological relatives. Having grandparents will add to his sense of connection and stability. When Gideon and I have a baby, your parents will be helpful."

"Won't that bother you? Don't you worry they'll get in the way?"

She shook her head. "I grew up without any family. My parents..." She drew in a breath. "I was on my own from an early age and an emancipated minor by the time I was fifteen. I welcome family, even if they are only related by marriage." She picked up several spools of ribbon. "Gideon says I have to let you be. It's the only reason I haven't asked you about staying in town."

"You listen to my brother?" he asked, mostly to distract her. "You're ten times smarter than him."

"I have more intellectual knowledge, but he's much more in tune with how regular people think and feel. I depend on him."

She was so sincere, he felt bad for teasing her. "He's a good guy and he's lucky to have you."

"Thank you. I'm lucky, as well. I'm sorry you don't have anyone special in your life. There must be a reason."

Which sounded uncomfortably like Ana Raquel's comment that he'd reached an age where he was going to have to explain why he was still single.

"Gideon believed love would make him weak," she continued. "That the only way he stayed strong was to be emotionally separate." She studied him. "I hope you don't think that."

"Life is short. It could all be gone tomorrow."

Her green eyes regarded him thoughtfully. "You don't want to take the chance."

"Something like that."

"I could provide some statistics on the likelihood of you losing your wife at an early age. Based on actuarial tables, of course." Her gaze turned speculative. "If you had someone specific in mind, I could factor in any known lifestyle or health risks."

"Asking about me and Noelle?"

"I'm curious as to the status of your relationship."

He crossed to her and took the ribbons from her hands, then hugged her. "Like I said, Gideon is lucky."

"You're attempting to distract me with a show of affection. I'm not going to forget the question."

He chuckled as she hugged him back. "And I'm not going to answer it."

She sighed. "You can't blame a girl for trying."

"No, I can't."

"You went to a lot of trouble for someone you won't admit you care about."

He thought about how happy Noelle had been as she'd planned for the contest and how everything had gone wrong. He thought of how distant he'd been, for reasons he still couldn't explain. How he'd probably hurt her.

He should have explained, he thought grimly. He should have told her...what? What would he have said? That he liked being with her more than he'd liked being with anyone else? That she was sweet and funny and with her he could almost believe in forever? But then what? He wasn't staying and even if he was, he didn't want to care that much. He didn't want to take the risk. What if he loved her only to lose her?

"She deserves someone better," he said at last. Someone who *was* willing to risk it all.

"That's the thing about love," Felicia told him. "We often get more than we deserve, and isn't that incredibly wonderful?"

"I DON'T UNDERSTAND," Noelle said as she stared at the window display. Colorful lights flashed on and off in time with the music. A beautiful tree reached to the top of the window, while three robots moved back and forth, carefully wrapping presents.

She'd spent a restless night, checking on her new cat families and worrying about Gabriel. After checking in with Mayor Marsha and explaining about their time at the cabin, she'd found herself with nothing to do. She couldn't even make replacement food for the cabin freezer. The mayor had told her there was a committee in town that handled stocking the cabin. Everything would be taken care of. Noelle had promised to drop off the laundered linens by the end of the week. Which left her with very little to do and way too much time.

She'd nearly called Gabriel a dozen times, only to realize she didn't know what to say. She'd wondered if he'd been thinking about her at all, only to discover he'd done this for her.

"We had a great time," Felicia admitted, hugging her. "The whole family worked together. It was an excellent bonding experience. I must remember this for the future. If any situation starts to get too uncomfortable, a shared task will bring people together."

She pointed to different elements of their design and then explained how to work the various remotes that controlled everything.

"I know the judging is this morning," Felicia said, "but it would be very gratifying if you would keep the decorations up for a few days."

Noelle leaned against her friend. "I'll keep them up forever."

"That's excessive," Felicia told her. "However I appreciate the spirit of your words." She studied the window. "The craft element was very satisfying. Perhaps I should take a class and learn to knit."

Noelle grinned, thinking her friend would probably come up with a more efficient way to create wool in the process. Or maybe invent a new fabric.

"I can't believe you did this for me."

"Of course we did," Felicia told her. "We love you. Well, I love you and Carter and Gideon like you very much. Gideon's parents don't know you very well and I can't speak to Gabriel's feelings, but he seemed very determined."

He wanted to help, Noelle thought. The foolish, how-he-makes-me-quiver part of her wanted to believe that this meant something. The pragmatic side of her brain warned her that one window display did not a relationship make.

"You must be exhausted," Noelle said. "Are you going to go home and get some sleep?"

"No, I want to stay awake and experiment with the deterioration of my cognitive functions due to sleep deprivation. It should be interesting."

Noelle patted her back. "You really do need to take up a hobby."

CHAPTER TWELVE

NOELLE CLUTCHED THE second place ribbon in her hand. She knew she was grinning foolishly, but she couldn't help herself. Second place! And it was her first contest. She couldn't take the credit—Gabriel and his family had done all the work, but she was still thrilled to be with the other business owners, by the big Christmas tree, hearing words of praise from Mayor Marsha.

Josh Golden, the owner of the winning window, took his small trophy and winked at her. "I think I'm going to be in trouble next year. Noelle is going to figure out what this is all about."

"Bribing the judges with donuts," someone in the back of the crowd yelled. Josh grinned.

Noelle leaned against Patience. "This is the best," she said. "I'm so happy. Next year, I'll start early with the planning. I love the animation. Felicia already said she and Carter would help me with that. I am so going to crush Josh like a bug."

Patience patted her on the back. "That's the competitive spirit we celebrate most at Christmas."

Noelle laughed. "I can't help it. I came in second!"

Melissa joined them. "I love that it all worked out in the end."

They all made their way back to their stores. Patience

ducked into Brew-haha while Noelle and Melissa turned on 4th and headed for The Christmas Attic.

Gabriel was helping a customer with a Christmas clock. He looked up as she entered. His blue eyes were unreadable, his expression pleasant, but distant.

He was back, she thought with both surprise and pleasure. She still didn't know what had happened or how to fix it. She genuinely believed she had nothing to apologize for, but that didn't mean there weren't questions. She supposed she could demand an explanation, but to what end? Letting him be seemed the wisest course of action. If he needed to disconnect, nothing she could say would stop him. If he figured it out and wanted to be close to her again, she was open to that as long as she got a reasonable explanation for his behavior. But that didn't mean she was going to ignore what he'd done for her.

She walked over to him. "Thank you," she said quietly, as his customer examined the clock. "The window is so wonderful."

"You're welcome." His gaze lingered for a second, giving her foolish hope.

She gave him a quick smile and hung the ribbon on the back of the cash register, then went to take off her coat so she could return to work.

The morning was busy. Her friend Charlie came in to look at ornaments for her mother. They settled on a delicate ballerina made of blown glass. Isabel called to say another bridesmaid gown had come in.

"I know we picked one," Isabel said over the phone. "But this one is great, too, and would so suit your skinny ass, about which I'm bitter."

"You're incredibly beautiful and Ford loves you."

"Yeah, well, I'd love me better if I could lose ten

pounds. But just saying that makes me want to eat a cookie." She sighed. "My life is complicated. Anyway, come by when you can and you can try them on at the same time and make a decision."

"My skinny ass and I will be there this afternoon," Noelle said with a laugh.

"Nativity crisis," Melissa murmured as she hurried by with two wreaths in her hands.

Noelle turned and saw a middle-aged female tourist wiping away tears.

"Gotta go," she told Isabel. "I'll be by later."

She hung up, then hurried over to the customer.

"Can I help you?" she asked, careful to keep her voice gentle.

The woman looked at her. "I'm sorry. I'm being silly. It's just these ridiculous gourds you have. Who would make a gourd nativity? Only it reminds me of when I was a little girl and I spent Christmas with my great-grand-mother because my mom was having my little brother. I didn't know Nana very well. To be honest, she fright-ened me. She was so stern and she had a strange accent. All very daunting to a four-year-old. But I learned she was sweet and funny and she had a nativity of old dried apples. Something *her* grandmother had made. It was unusual, but also beautiful and this reminds me of that."

More tears flowed.

"I have to have this," the woman said.

"You're exactly who it's been waiting for," Noelle told her with a smile.

GABRIEL WAS CLEAR on his actions. He'd been avoiding Noelle. He'd shown up for work, but he had nothing to do with her beyond polite work-related conversation. It was as if they were strangers who didn't like each other very much.

He'd expected her to glower at him. Or fire him. Something. But she'd thanked him for what he'd done and then went about her business with a friendly smile for everyone—even him. Even now, as she ushered a sobbing customer to the cash register, that ridiculous gourd nativity in her hands, she gave him a quick grin.

What he and his family had done for her window display didn't make up for his bad manners after a night of incredible lovemaking. He felt like the Grinch after stealing all the presents. The Whos down in Whoville really didn't need the trappings of Christmas to celebrate the season. They were happy anyway, and so was she.

He didn't get it. Why wasn't she pissed? Or demanding an explanation? They'd slept together. They'd been physically and emotionally intimate and then he'd turned his back on her without bothering to tell her why. Didn't that make her want to beat the crap out of him?

Either she was the best actress ever or she genuinely wasn't bothered. He suspected the latter had to be true, which only bugged him more.

Shortly after five, when they were wrapping up for the day, he followed her into the back room and closed the door behind them.

She looked at him. "What's up?" she asked.

"You're not mad."

"Should I be?"

"Yes. You should be furious. We had sex at the cabin and then I disappeared. Emotionally if not physically. I couldn't deal with you."

"But you took care of my Christmas window."

"That has nothing to do with sex."

"Good to know. Okay—you disappeared. Do you know why?"

He shoved his hands into his jeans pockets, then pulled them back out. The space was too small, he thought grimly as he tried to pace, only to find himself trapped by boxes and the small desk she used.

"It was more than I could handle," he admitted, facing her. "You, us, the cats. I can't do what you want. Be what you need. There's too much in my head. I'm going back."

"To the army?" she asked.

"I don't know. I guess I should."

"Do you want to?"

A question for which he didn't have an answer. "I make a difference there," he said at last. "I need to keep making a difference. Sometimes there are so many of them," he added, thinking of the dream he would never tell her about.

She studied him for a long time, then nodded slowly. "You think I can't handle it. Whatever you have going on. You think I'm not strong enough."

"Look, you're here in this world. Even if I could get past believing I could lose everything I care about in a second, even if I was willing to take the risk, I can't. Look at this place. It's Fool's Gold. They have elephants dressed as Santa in their parades. I think the world I know would make you a different person."

She stared into his eyes. He had no idea what she was thinking, so he didn't bother trying to figure it out. Instead, he let his gaze roam her face, taking in the sweet shape of her mouth and how her blond hair swayed with every movement.

"Let me see if I have this straight," she said. "You got too close, too fast. Because of my sparkling personality and the great sex, you couldn't handle it, so you ran. Emotionally, if not physically. Now you feel guilty, but if you apologize too clearly, I might expect more than you can give. You're also worried I'm not tough enough to handle whatever you think you have going on. Is that about right?"

While the concepts matched, he didn't like how she'd characterized him. "I wouldn't have put it…"

She raised her eyebrows. "Yes or no?"

"Yes."

"My place after closing. You need to be there. I have something to show you."

With that she opened the door to the store and walked away.

Gabriel watched her go, not sure what had happened, but if there had just been a battle between them, he'd lost on all fronts.

As INSTRUCTED, GABRIEL arrived at Noelle's small house after closing. She met him at the door, a kitten in each arm, and laughed when she handed him one.

"This is a crazy number of cats," she said, stepping over the two mother cats, as she backed up to let him in. "One litter would have been bad enough, but two?"

He saw the younger litter was still confined to a large box, but they were more active. Their eyes were open and they climbed over each other in an effort to join the rest of their friends.

The mother cats had gotten over their skittishness and wove their way about his ankles.

"They've just eaten," Noelle told him. "They're always very friendly after a meal." She set down the kitten she held.

He did the same and followed her into her tiny spare bedroom.

She'd turned the space into a home office. There was a desk with a laptop and a couple of chairs. Next to the laptop was a clear plastic bin filled with files and paperwork.

"Have a seat," she said and opened the bin.

He did as she requested, not sure where this was going. While Noelle seemed friendly enough, there was a wariness to her posture, as if she was ready to defend herself. He couldn't begin to guess what was in the bin. A criminal record? Tax fraud? Adoption records for six kids?

She handed him a file. He saw the name of the hospital printed on the front of the folder and her name on the tab.

"Medical records?" he asked.

She nodded.

"Noelle, you don't have to—"

"Just look at it, okay?"

He opened the file and read the first page. The diagnosis jumped out at him. Acute myeloid leukemia—AML. Not always a death sentence, but rare—especially for someone her age. The treatment was chemotherapy, often aggressive. If that didn't work, the next step was usually a bone marrow transplant. He didn't know much more—this wasn't his area of expertise.

The dates went back three years. Her initial diagnosis, the prognosis, depending on how she responded to treatment. His chest tightened and there was a knot in his gut. She'd had bad reactions to the chemo. She'd nearly died.

He glanced at her, at her glowing skin and shiny hair. "You've come a long way," he said quietly.

"You have no idea."

She passed him a picture of her in a hospital gown. She was thin and pale and bald, with an IV hooked up to her arm.

"I'd been sick for a while," she said, reaching down for one of the kittens, who had followed them into the study. "Just not feeling well. My doctor did a blood panel and saw some abnormalities. I figured I was stressed from having lost my mom and my grandmother in a car accident."

She cuddled the cat, who started to purr.

"But it was more than that. I went to a specialist who came up with an aggressive plan. It would be hell, but he was pretty confident we would get it all."

She gave him a faint smile. "You have no idea how many times you get stuck with a needle going through something like that. Which made my fainting when I saw blood pretty funny."

He put the file on the desk and tried to absorb what she was saying. Disbelief mingled with horror at what she'd been through. He'd been wrong about her. She knew plenty about suffering.

"You could have died," he said before he could stop himself.

"I nearly did, more than once. But I decided to fight. I believed there was going to be more to my life than my disease." She drew in a breath and looked at him. "I was engaged before. We had a wedding date and everything. It all got put on hold."

Not her idea, he realized, even as he knew what came next.

"He walked out on you," he said flatly.

She shrugged. "It was more than he could handle. I'm technically in remission. I could be here my whole life or be sick again tomorrow. No one knows. Statistically, I'm going to live until I'm eighty, but he wanted to know for sure. So yes, he left. When I went back to work at my law firm, they wouldn't give me any of the real work. They made it clear I wasn't welcome. I'd shown weakness and they had no place for that."

He wanted to touch her, to comfort her, but she didn't need that. She was stronger than he'd ever realized.

"So you stuck a pin in a map," he murmured.

"And ended up here, with a store and friends, and a life." She smiled. "I have so much to be grateful for. My own medical miracle. I might not have seen what you've seen, but I've fought my own war. I know what it's like to be overwhelmed and exhausted, all while puking my guts out. I'm tough, Gabriel. Every month I gain another pound or two. By this time next year, I'll have my curves back. I look forward to being like Isabel and worrying about ten pounds. Because that is so silly and normal and every time she complains about her hips or her thighs I vow I'll get there."

She put down the kitten and took his hands in hers. "I know about ghosts and lost opportunities and believe me, I know there are no guarantees. I'm sorry the lesson you learned from what you've been through is it's not worth taking the chance, because I believe it's *all* about taking the chance. We are the sum of our experiences and those experiences need to come from a place of wonder and curiosity."

She smiled at him. "I don't know if you're going to stay in the army or not, but I do know you're leaving

Fool's Gold. I know this isn't permanent and I still want to be with you. I want us to be friends and I want us to be lovers. And just so we're clear, if you don't want to sleep with me after hearing all this, you're not nearly as bright as you look."

There was too much for him to take in, he thought. He'd been wrong about her in nearly every way possible. He hadn't come close to guessing that she'd been sick. He'd missed all the clues. Worse, he'd misread their time together because he'd made it all about himself.

"I'm such a jackass," he said, coming to his feet and pulling her into a standing position.

"Good answer."

Sharp claws dug into his leg. He looked down and saw the kitten trying to climb his jeans. He grabbed the cat by the scruff of her neck and gently pulled her away, then set her on the ground. Then he took Noelle by the hand and led her into the bedroom.

Once the door was closed, he cupped her cheeks and studied her face. "You're so beautiful," he told her right before he kissed her.

Her mouth was soft and yielding, but as he stroked his tongue against her lower lip, he felt her respond with growing passion. The need was in him—it had never really gone away. Now it moved through his blood, heating, stirring, making it difficult to think beyond how he could touch her and be in her.

She was a gift he didn't deserve, he thought as he moved his hands across her back and then down her side to her hips. He took the return journey more slowly, savoring the feel of her body before cupping her curves in his hands.

She moaned softly. Her head fell back and he trailed his mouth down her neck.

"Tell me you bought condoms," he whispered against her skin.

She laughed and reached for the hem of her sweater. "Of course." Her eyes sparkled with amusement. "Extra large."

"That's my girl."

SOMETIME AFTER MIDNIGHT Noelle pulled on her robe and headed for the kitchen. They were too late for take-out so she was going to have to find them something to eat from what was in her refrigerator. Too bad she hadn't brought back a few casseroles from their time at the cabin. All that food had been delicious.

She found a frozen pizza in her freezer and figured they could make do. As she turned on the oven, one of the mother cats strolled into the kitchen and meowed at her. The feline gaze was both inquisitive and knowing.

"Yes, we were doing it," Noelle admitted to her houseguest.

The mother cat meowed again.

"I'm aware of the consequences. I won't get pregnant."

The cat's gaze turned knowing, as if she were pointing out there were other kinds of consequences.

"You meant falling in love?" Noelle asked, her tone light. Because she already knew the answer. She loved Gabriel. She wasn't sure when or where, but it had happened. It was a monumentally stupid thing to have done and yet she wouldn't take it back, even if she could.

"WHAT DO YOU THINK?" Gabriel asked, turning the laptop so Noelle could see the screen.

She squinted at the image. "It's a book."

"It's a set of books," he corrected.

"Because that makes it better?" she asked with a laugh.

They were sprawled on her sofa, spending a quiet Sunday afternoon together. Since spending the night with her, Gabriel hadn't left. Technically, he hadn't moved in, but in the past couple of days, he'd started bringing over clothes and toiletries.

Noelle wasn't sure what had caused the change of heart. She knew it was something about her illness but didn't know if he now thought she could understand his world better or if he thought she was tough or what. She also wasn't about to ask. If her goal was to live life to the fullest, then she needed to enjoy her time with Gabriel while it lasted and then accept that he would be leaving. When that happened, she would be hurt and have to recover.

Being with him, loving him, had made her realize that some part of her had been afraid to give in to a man again. She'd been so devastated when Jeremy had walked out on her. Intellectually, she'd known that finding out he wasn't interested in the "in sickness" part of marriage before taking vows was a good thing, she'd also felt completely alone in the world. For all of her talk of wanting a man around, she'd been afraid to take that risk again.

But now she had. She'd given her heart to Gabriel, which meant she could give it to someone else eventually. The last piece of her had healed and that felt good.

He turned the computer so he could study the screen.

"You're saying Carter won't like books for a present? I thought he enjoyed reading."

"He does. But ebooks. I know this century has been hard for you," she teased. "But there are now books you can download to your—"

She had more she was going to say, but he put the laptop on the coffee table and lunged for her. She squirmed to get away, knowing he was going to tickle her. The kittens, who had been crawling along the back of the sofa, joined in the game, jumping on her shoulder and his back. Needle claws dug in.

Gabriel straightened and gingerly pulled the kitten from his back. He held it up in the air.

"Watch it," he said, his voice softer than his words. The kitten swiped at him with one paw, then relaxed in his arms when he rolled it onto its back and began rubbing its tummy.

"Giving an ebook isn't the same," he grumbled. "How do I wrap that?"

"I'll admit the wrapping is a problem." She shifted her kitten to her lap and scratched the side of its face. "You could get him a car."

"He's thirteen."

"Yes, but he keeps telling his father it's never too early to learn to drive."

Gabriel shifted so he was facing front, then pulled her against him. He wrapped an arm around her and kissed the top of her head. His kitten started climbing his chest.

"No car," he said. "I'll keep looking. I have gifts for everyone else."

Gifts he'd ordered online in the past couple of days, she thought. They were being delivered here. He'd already told her he would need help wrapping.

"How long has it been since you've spent the holidays with your family?" she asked.

"Years. It was back in college, I think. When I was in medical school, I couldn't always get away. I needed the time to study."

"Or so you told them."

"Yeah, that, too."

She looked up at him. "Let me guess. In the army you always volunteered to work on Christmas, claiming that it was so the others could be with their families. But in truth it was so you didn't have to deal with going home yourself."

"You think you're pretty smart."

"I have the LSATs to prove it."

He smiled at her. "It wasn't about not going home. By then my parents' house wasn't home. But you're right. I didn't want to deal with them. I felt bad for my mom, but I mostly couldn't deal with my dad."

"He didn't like that you were different. He didn't understand you."

"He still doesn't."

"Men want their sons to be like them. It's difficult to let that go."

"Now you sound like Felicia," he said.

She chuckled. "Wow, that's an amazing compliment. But you know I'm right. Your dad was raised to believe in honor and service. He's old-fashioned. If it's not his way, it's wrong."

He nodded as he leaned back against the sofa. The kitten had curled up on his chest and fallen asleep. He folded his arm across his chest to hold it in place.

"He needs to get over that," Gabriel told her. "And before you tell me he's probably not going to, I already figured that out. I guess…" He paused. "I guess I don't like knowing how much I disappoint him. Rather than deal with that, I stay away."

"You're a doctor," she said, thinking Norm had to reconsider his standards.

"I'm not a soldier."

"Well, he's stupid." She snuggled closer. "I'm sorry your dad makes it hard for you to be with your family."

"I'm going to stay in touch with Gideon more. He's made a life for himself here. Carter's great and who wouldn't love Felicia? In a brotherly way, of course."

"You'd better add that," she teased. "Otherwise, your brother will snap you into teeny, tiny pieces."

"I know. Good for him."

There was something in Gabriel's voice, she thought. Was he wistful? Was he wishing he could find what his brother had? Love? A place to belong?

All questions designed to make her crazy, she reminded herself. Gabriel was leaving. Even if he was staying, she didn't think he was the least bit interested in getting involved on a permanent basis. He'd made that clear, and she would be wise to listen when he—

Her cell phone rang.

She stood and crossed to the foyer table, where she'd left it. She set down her kitten before answering.

"Hello?"

"Noelle? This is Police Chief Barns. We have a situation up on the mountain. There's been an avalanche. It's a big one and there were a lot of people skiing and snowboarding. There are going to be injuries. I'm calling to find out if you know where Gabriel Boylan is. Mayor Marsha says he's a trauma specialist. We're going to need that."

The police chief spoke so calmly, Noelle almost didn't take in the meaning of her words. Then reality slammed into her and for a second, she thought she was going to faint or maybe throw up.

"He's here," she said, turning to walk back to the sofa. But Gabriel was already at her side.

"What is it?" he asked.

She handed him the phone.

He took it and listened. While she had a feeling she'd gone pale, he stayed calm. After asking a couple of questions, he got the location and said he would be right there. He was already moving before he'd hung up.

"Stay here," he told her. "I know you want to help but you'll get in the way on the mountain. Organize in town. People will need help. Not just those hurt, but family members."

She understood what he meant. "I'll do what I can from here."

He handed her his kitten, then kissed her on the mouth and was out the door before she could catch her breath. She stared out the window, watching him drive away.

She didn't know much about snow or avalanches, but she had a feeling the outcome could be devastating. She picked up her cell phone and started making calls.

CHAPTER THIRTEEN

THE SKY ABOVE the Gold Rush Ski Lodge and Resort was an impossible shade of blue. The roads were plowed, the temperature in the high twenties. It was the perfect day for skiing or snowboarding. But with the recent storm, feet of new snow had fallen on layers of older snow. Gabriel would guess some of those layers had been more powdery, with a few inches of wet snow sandwiched in between. Then the recent dump had added weight and an avalanche was born.

He followed several police cars and two ambulances into the parking lot. People were milling about, most dressed in heavy parkas and ski pants. He pulled off to the side and parked, then sprinted toward what was obviously the command center.

"Dr. Gabriel Boylan," he said, identifying himself to a tall female firefighter who was directing people. "Trauma specialist."

"Good," she said and pointed to the large hotel. "The ballroom is in the back. They're turning it into a trauma center. You're going to be in charge of triage."

"How many people are missing?"

The woman—her badge said C. Dixon—grimaced. "We don't know. The police are running license plates from the parking lots to get names right now. We have locals, people who drive up for the day and those staying in town. A lot of schools broke early for the holidays. There could be two or three hundred people on the mountain near the avalanche. They could all be fine...." She swallowed. "Or not."

He nodded and took off in the direction she'd pointed. He had to identify himself a couple more times before being let into the hotel. From there it was an easy jog to the giant ballroom.

Emergency supplies were already being put in place. Trucks had backed up to the ballroom and were unloading supplies. As he watched, gurneys and IV stands were being put along one wall.

"Gabriel!"

He turned and saw Felicia hurrying toward him. She flung herself at him and hung on.

"Gideon and Carter were out snowboarding," she said. Her body trembled as she spoke. "Your parents were skiing, but I've already talked to them and they're fine. It was suggested I go with them, but I'm not good with those kinds of sports." She raised her head and looked at him, tears filling her green eyes. "A ridiculous thing to say. It's the shock and worry, but still. Who cares if I can't ski?"

He grabbed her by the shoulders and stared at her. "Breathe," he told her. "Breathe. You need to focus. Whatever has happened, you can't change it. But you can make a difference by helping with the logistics. Not just for Gideon and Carter, but for everyone else. We need you to stay strong."

Not the tack he would have taken with anyone else, he thought. But Felicia tended to live in her head.

For a second he thought she might burst into tears, but instead she seemed to pull herself together. "You're right. I have excellent organizational skills. Those will help everyone. Me falling apart will not."

"They've found people," someone yelled.

The huge ballroom went still for a heartbeat, then all the volunteers started moving. Gabriel hesitated for a second, but Felicia pushed him away.

"I'm fine," she said. "Go. You're needed."

He headed for the medical team by the equipment and identified himself. He pulled on a spare white coat and opened one of the large medical travel kits. Less than five minutes later, two people were carried in. They were both in their twenties, and he didn't recognize them. The woman was unconscious, while the man insisted he was fine.

"Broken leg on that one," one of the people helping the man said. "We don't know about her."

Gabriel was already moving toward her. Everything around him faded as he began his examination.

GABRIEL WAS CONSCIOUS of the passage of time, but only in the sense that it was moving forward. He had no idea if he'd been working ten minutes or ten hours. The injured came in clusters. Two here, five there. Most of the injuries were minor, although a few people had been buried in snow for some time. He diagnosed broken bones, hypothermia and shock. One woman came in screaming for her son, who had suffered little more than a few cuts and bruises.

As she fell across her teenager and babbled about how grateful she was, Gabriel told himself to be patient. That she couldn't understand how compared to a rocket-propelled grenade or an IED, this was nothing.

That any loss of life would be minimal and most of the injuries minor.

Still, the work was gratifying. More medical personnel joined him. A tall, scarred man introduced himself as Dr. Simon Bradley. Gabriel remembered him being mentioned and knew he was a plastic surgeon who specialized in burns. Gabriel directed him to where those with cuts were being patched up.

Mayor Marsha arrived, accompanied by three big guys in what looked like survival gear.

"They're from CDS," one of the nurses said. "The bodyguard school. They'll be helping with the search."

"We need avalanche dogs," another nurse said. "The town is getting so big. Things like that are important."

There was more conversation, but he didn't listen. Not while he had patients. He examined the older woman who was next in line. She was awake and alert.

"How are you feeling?" he asked, testing her pupils, then reaching for his stethoscope.

"Foolish. I could see the snow coming down the mountain, but couldn't ski out of the way fast enough. I got caught on the edge. I'm a little shaken, but nothing is broken."

He confirmed her self-diagnosis, then sent her over to the group who were probably okay but needed observation. He turned to go to the next patient only to see they had a temporary lull. Just then Carter came walking into the ballroom with his dad. There was a teenaged boy between them who was limping. Gabriel hurried over.

"Have you seen Felicia?" he asked.

Carter grinned. "She about squeezed all the air out of us. She was really worried." He sounded pleased by the information. "This is my friend Reese. We weren't in the avalanche. Reese slipped on some ice."

"I'm fine," his friend protested. "My ankle hurts. It's no big deal."

"I'll check him out," Gabriel told his brother. "How's it going out there?"

"A couple of people are missing. Teams are heading out to find them. Considering how bad it could have been, we got lucky."

NOELLE FOUND TALKING on the phone while keeping an eye on Pia Moreno was harder than it sounded. Felicia had been calling from the hotel and updating the head count. Families found themselves needing to stay in town unexpectedly. Hotel rooms had to be located and reserved.

Brew-haha had been converted into a command center. Laptops and notepads covered the tables. There was a cell-phone charging station by the front counter and dry erase boards on wheels were constantly updated with injury counts, available hotel rooms and emergency information.

Pia, the person previously in charge of festivals, had waddled in, insisting she could help. As she knew everyone and everything about the town, that was probably true. But she was also days or possibly hours away from giving birth.

Noelle finished her call, then turned to Pia. "Are you sure you're okay? You look really uncomfortable."

Pia rested her hand on her belly. "Trust me, this is nothing. Last time I was pregnant with twins. Now that was huge. By comparison, this is easy. Don't worry. I'm keeping my feet up and staying hydrated. Raoul is checking on me every fifteen minutes, and I'm not exaggerating about that. I'm fine."

She looked down at her notes. "I have information on a vacation rental for Mr. and Mrs. Boylan. They're staying with Gideon. Is it available?"

"Gabriel's been using it, but I can clear out his stuff for a couple of nights."

Pia raised her eyebrows. "So it's like that, is it?"

"For the moment."

"I'll put his place on the list and let you know if we need it."

Noelle briefly wondered if she should say anything to Gabriel, then decided it didn't matter. He would be fine with what she'd done. And if he wasn't, she would remind him it was only for a couple of nights.

Love as empowerment, she thought with a smile.

Madeline, Isabel's assistant, put down her phone. "The last missing person has been found," she announced. "We have serious injuries, but so far no deaths."

Pia sighed. "Thank goodness." She raised her voice. "All right, people, we need more beds for tonight. Get back to those calls."

THE HOSPITAL EMERGENCY room was more controlled chaos than the hotel ballroom had been, Gabriel thought as he walked inside. With the last of the missing skiers recovered, the search-and-rescue volunteers had been recalled and their vehicles had been put to use as patient transport.

As Gabriel walked through the busy waiting area, he heard a couple of people talking about the new hospital that was being built and how the town needed it. Families clustered together, looking relieved or worried, depending on the condition of their loved one.

He went to the front desk and identified himself, telling the nurse he would be available if extra help was needed. She looked harried and nodded as he spoke.

"We might be calling you," she said. "Are you going to stick around for a while?"

"Until the crisis is past."

She took down his cell number, then turned to the next person waiting. Gabriel glanced at the signage on the walls, thinking he would go find some coffee. Before he could, a dark-haired man walked up to him.

"Justice Garrett," the man said. "From CDS."

Gabriel shook his hand. "The bodyguard school."

Justice sighed. "We're never going to get them to stop calling it that, are we?"

Gabriel grinned. "Not in this town. How can I help you?"

"Just wanted to introduce myself. My fiancée, Patience, is friends with Noelle." He gave a casual shrug. "Obviously, they talk."

Gabriel was very clear on how much women talked. What he didn't know was what had been said.

Justice pointed to the two men in similar cargo pants and black long-sleeved T-shirts who joined them. "My business partners. Angel Whittaker and Ford Hendrix. Of more importance to you, these are the two who rescued your brother from the Taliban." He looked at his friends. "Gabriel is Gideon's brother."

Angel, a man with pale gray eyes and an interesting scar on his neck, moved forward. "Nice to meet you. Gideon's a good guy."

Gabriel shook his hand. He had so many questions, but at that moment he couldn't think of any of them.

"Thank you," he said, turning to Ford. "We're glad we still have him around."

Ford smiled. "Yeah, he's not so bad." The smile faded. "That was a good day for all of us. We were happy to help."

Gabriel knew what they'd done was more than help. They'd risked their lives to save his brother from a horrible death. Gideon had been the last of his team left alive after nearly two years of captivity and daily torture.

Felicia hurried up to them. She walked to Gabriel and rested her forehead on his chest. "I'm struggling to keep control."

He wrapped his arms around her. "You can't have control. This is an out-of-control situation. The best you can do is mitigate fallout. You're doing that."

He felt her draw in a breath. She raised her head and looked at him. "Thank you," she said, then turned and walked away.

Justice grinned. "Good to know her new family gets her."

"She's great," Gabriel admitted. "The smartest person I know, and that's saying something."

"Come on," Ford told Angel. "We'll go get everyone coffee."

"I'll go with you," Justice said, then looked at Gabriel. "How do you take yours?"

Gabriel chuckled. "You know I'm in the army, right?"

"You're a doctor." Justice held up both hands. "Okay, okay. Black it is."

He was still chuckling when he walked away. Gabriel returned to the waiting room. He found a family with a young boy who had a bad cut on his forehead and arm. Gabriel went over to check the bandages, then secured them more tightly. Justice brought him his coffee and they chatted awhile. When Justice left, a pretty woman in her twenties walked up to him.

"I'm Madeline. I work with Isabel, who's a friend of Noelle's." She bit her lower lip. "I'm really sorry to bother you but my niece is visiting me and she sprained her ankle. At least we think that's what happened. We're waiting to see a doctor, but they're busy with the avalanche and..." She twisted her fingers together. "Could you maybe take a look at it? I know you're a trauma specialist so this isn't anything you would normally bother with, but I didn't know who else to ask."

Gabriel thought about pointing out he wasn't with the hospital. Not that anyone seemed to care. It was the town, he thought, both frustrated and oddly comforted by the basic assumption that he was a decent guy who would step in where needed. Of course he would, but how did they *know?*

Another ambulance pulled up to the emergency room. Hospital personnel went running. If he didn't help, Madeline and her niece would be here for hours.

"Show me where she is," he said.

Thirty minutes later, the two women left. The ankle was slightly swollen, but not bad at all. A little ice, a compression bandage and she would be fine. Gabriel had sent them off with instructions, along with a promise that Madeline would take her niece to Madeline's primary care doctor in the morning.

He started for the front desk to make notes in her chart only to remember there was no chart and he had no business practicing medicine here. Well, hell, he thought with a laugh.

"What's so funny?" his father asked as he approached.

"Just wondering if I was going to lose my license."

He expected Norm to chew him a new one, but his father only nodded. "You can practice in any army facility but you're not technically licensed to practice in the state of California," he said with a shrug. "Isn't there something about helping out in an emergency?"

"Sure, but there are gray areas."

He and his father walked to the rear of the emergency room, where it was less crowded. They took seats across from each other.

"Carter's fine," his father said. "That friend of his is okay, too."

"Good. They were lucky."

"Hell of a thing." Norm leaned back in the chair. "All that snow. It's not an unexpected event, I suppose. That Mayor Marsha person was very insistent that the town needs a search-and-rescue team. Sounds like interesting work."

Gabriel raised his eyebrows.

His father chuckled. "Not for me. It's a young man's game." He paused. "You know, your mother and I are thinking of settling here in Fool's Gold."

"I'd heard that."

"Felicia swears Gideon is okay with it. Your mother and I want to be close to our grandchildren. Be a part of their lives."

Gabriel nodded, not sure where this conversation was going.

"What are you going to do?" his father asked.

"You mean there's a choice?"

He heard the bitterness in his voice and wanted to call it back. He wasn't in the mood to fight with his father and challenging Norm was a sure way to get one started.

But his father surprised him. The older man seemed to get a little smaller as he sat quietly. "I can see why you think that," he said at last. "Because of what I said before."

"You mean what you say always. The Boylan men are put on this earth to serve."

That phrase had been pounded into him from the time he was a kid. There'd never been a choice. Noelle had asked him what he would do instead and he had no way of answering that.

Norm leaned forward. He rested his forearms on his thighs and loosely laced his fingers together. "I deserve that," he admitted. "I wanted—" He cleared his throat. "You know that damn dog of theirs is pretty smart. He likes to learn new commands and he'll do about anything if he thinks he's going to get to play catch at the end of the session."

Gabriel frowned. They were talking about Webster?

"I've been working with him on basic commands. Sit, stay, that sort of thing. We're working on some others. I want to get him off-leash trained. Carter and I have been talking about putting him through agility training. It would be good for the dog and for the boy. Plus, it gives him and me a good way to connect. Something for us to talk about."

His father continued to stare at the ground as he spoke. "The thing is, if I yell at Webster, the session doesn't go well. He tucks his tail and can't look me in the eye. It's like I break his spirit and he doesn't trust me anymore. So I praise him when he does the right thing and stay calm when he doesn't. He gets what 'no' means."

His father straightened. There was pain in his eyes. Pain and maybe regret.

"You're like that."

"You're comparing me to the dog?" Gabriel asked, wondering where on earth this ridiculous conversation was going. Anger built up inside of him. His father wanted something—as he always did.

"In a way. I treated you and Gideon the same, but you're not the same. Gideon's like me. He'd rather fight or leave than talk. When he was a kid, he solved problems with his fists. The army was the right place for him and he excelled. But you, you're different."

"You mean wrong."

His father shook his head. "Your mother told me that's what you thought. I guess because I've been telling you that you were wrong for as long as I can remember. I figured if I kept after you enough, you'd change."

Gabriel hung on to his anger, because when he was pissed, it was easy to disconnect. He didn't have to care about his father. He'd learned that lesson long ago. But it had been in the face of a vocal man who'd gone out of his way to make it clear his son was a disappointment. Norman Boylan didn't apologize.

"You save people," his father continued. "You save lives every day. You're respected and honorable. Hell, a soldier like me can be found on every street corner, but not many people can do what you do. I never appreciated that before. I guess I couldn't get past my expectations so I couldn't see how proud I am of you, Gabriel."

The anger faded and with it, his defenses. "Dad," he began, only to stumble into unfamiliar territory. If his father wasn't yelling at him about his piss-poor choices, what else was there?

His father straightened. "I'm not saying we're going to always get on. We're too different. But I want you to know that I have always loved you and I always will. I tell everyone about my son, the doctor." He smiled slightly. "Then my friends all ask who your mom was sleeping with that night, because there's no way some smart, successful doctor is my kid."

Norm cleared his throat. "I won't keep you. I know you're still busy. I just wanted to stop by and say I've been watching Gideon with Carter. I raised you boys how I was raised, and how your grandfather was raised. Gideon's doing it differently and I'm thinking maybe his way has some merit."

With that his father rose and headed out the door. Gabriel sat in the chair, too stunned to absorb what had just happened. He told himself it didn't mean anything, it didn't change anything, but he had a feeling he was wrong.

CHAPTER FOURTEEN

NOELLE SAT IN Dellina's living room. They were surrounded by three bowls of personalized wrapped chocolates and a stack of little cloth bags. Each bag got two of each of the chocolates as a wedding favor. Not an especially daunting task until Noelle thought about how many people were probably coming to the wedding. It would be a large portion of the town. Which meant lots and lots of bag filling.

Dellina had pulled her long hair back into a ponytail that sat on the top of her head. She had on jeans and a bright green holiday sweater.

"Thanks for helping me with this," she said. "I know you're busy at the store. It's less than a week before Christmas."

"No problem. We're still closing at six."

Gabriel had promised to spend some quality time with the cats before heading out to have dinner with his parents. He hadn't said much but she'd noticed in the past couple of days he'd seemed more relaxed about them. She wondered if his work at the avalanche had made a difference. Something had, which was good.

She picked up two chocolates from each of the bowls, then dropped them into one bag and pulled the drawstring closed. After tying a little bow, she put the finished favor into a large white box and reached for more chocolates.

"How are the wedding plans coming?" she asked.

"We're mostly there." Dellina nodded toward the stack of papers on her kitchen table. "I'm at the going-crazy stage. A wedding is a lot to pull together, but this is all that times three, and it's a secret. Plus, Mrs. Robson is threatening to retire."

Noelle frowned, trying to place the name. "She owns Plants for the Planet?"

"Right. Our other florist moved to Hawaii, so now we're down to one. I have no idea how old she is. I want to say 106, but I know that can't be right. Still, one day she'll mean it and then what will happen? I love her work. It's fresh and beautiful and reasonably priced."

Dellina drew in a breath. "Sorry. I get tense when I think about it. The town needs another florist."

"We should put an ad in a national paper."

"Don't think I haven't talked to Mayor Marsha about it."

"Is everything else going okay?" Noelle asked.

Dellina sighed. "Yes. The menu is finalized. Ana Raquel and Greg were torturing me with all kinds of food from the Fool's Gold cookbook they were writing. I've gained five pounds in the past month. They've suggested everything from baked wild mushroom risotto to white-and-dark chocolate chunk cookie pie."

"That all sounds really delicious. Are you seriously complaining?"

"Sort of." Dellina grinned. "Okay, not. But it's been intense. Again, the issue is sheer volume. We're talking six or seven hundred people. That's a lot of food. I had to get permission to let a few more people in on the secret so we could get some help with the cooking and storage. A couple of the restaurant chefs are helping and a few of the really good cooks in town."

She tossed a completed bag into the box. "Then there are the other logistics. It's going to be late and a lot of the little kids will be tired and cranky. We've set up a quiet area with sleeping bags for parents who want their children to sleep but still want to go to the party. I've lined up teenagers to help with the babysitting, which means hiring them without telling them what it's about. Let me just say the average sixteen-year-old girl wants details before she takes a job."

She filled another bag. "There's the live band and seating for that many people. It's a logistics nightmare. I know everyone wants this to be a surprise, but I can't help thinking the weddings are going to be the worst kept secret ever."

"You've done your best," Noelle told her. "Honestly, I can't imagine how you've pulled this off. I would be curled up in the corner, whimpering."

"There are nights that end like that. Just don't tell anyone." Dellina looked at her. "What about you? Are you okay with all this wedding fever?"

"I'm fine with it." She paused, then sighed. "Okay, I'll admit to twinges of…" What was the right word? "Longing, I guess. I want them to be happy, and I want what they have, too. I wish…"

"That your hunky doctor friend wanted more than just sex?"

Noelle winced. "Is it that obvious?"

"No, I was guessing."

"Then I want you on my team the next time we play charades." Noelle reached for more candy. "He's great.

More than great. But he's not interested in anything long-term and even if he was, he's leaving. I want to stay here and dig my roots in deeper."

"I'm sorry he's not the one," Dellina said. "But the sex is great, right? Because that makes me so envious."

Noelle grinned. "So it's like that, is it?"

"Absolutely. I'm not looking for love. I just want a couple of hot nights. Or twenty."

"Not love?" Noelle asked.

"No way. My folks died when I was sixteen. I got custody of my twin sisters when I was eighteen."

"Wow, that's tough."

"For anyone, but I had it really hard. I was kind of flaky and irresponsible. My parents indulged me more than they should have. I wasn't even close to ready and then I didn't have a choice."

Dellina paused, as if remembering. "I got my sisters through high school and college. They're finally happy and settled in their lives. Now it's my turn. There is no way I want to take on any responsibility right now." Her brown eyes flashed with humor. "The only issue I want to deal with is a charming guy asking me if I want to be on top."

Noelle knew she was both teasing and telling the truth. "I get that," she admitted. "The whole fear of not being enough or the love being too much, as well as not wanting to take on one more thing."

"I believe a well-trained psychologist would say that I'm afraid of commitment," Dellina said cheerfully. "A flaw I can live with. One day I'll be ready to be in love. Just not yet."

She'd been like that, too, Noelle thought. After being sick and Jeremy dumping her. She'd been scared to risk her heart. But then she'd realized she'd been given the gift of a second chance. Was the lesson she really wanted to take away from that the idea that it was okay to live in fear?

She wanted to say she regretted loving Gabriel, but she couldn't. He was wonderful. How could she not have loved him? Only now she was left with the fact that she was staying and he was leaving and when he left, her heart would go with him.

GABRIEL'S MOTHER PASSED over another listing. "This one has stairs."

"Why shouldn't we buy a house with stairs?" Norm asked, leaning over and kissing his wife's neck. "We're not old. Look at you, Karen. Every guy in the restaurant is checking you out. They're probably wishing they were going to be me later."

Gabriel held on to his beer with both hands and reminded himself that this, too, would pass. Not so much dinner with his parents, which had been pretty okay. But his father's change of heart. Because a kinder, gentler version of the man was more than a little tough to deal with.

The quieter voice was great, as was the genuine interest in what other people were doing. Enjoying the restaurant rather than complaining was good, too. But the ongoing flirtation with Gabriel's mother was tough to take. Gabriel was glad his parents had a loving and passionate relationship. But jeez, he was their kid. He didn't want to watch it happen in front of him.

"Stairs don't matter now," Karen told her husband. "But what about when you're eighty?"

"We're still going to—"

"Dad!" Gabriel said sharply. "Give me a break, okay?"

Norm leaned back in his chair and grinned. "You should be pleased to know the sports equipment is still—"

"Norman," his wife said. "You're embarrassing our son."

"He's a doctor. He knows about sex."

Karen beamed at her husband and Gabriel waved at their server. He held up his beer bottle, grateful Margaritaville was close enough to Noelle's house that he could walk. Maybe if he got drunk enough, he wouldn't be able to follow the conversation.

A woman in her forties stopped by the table. She had dark hair and brown eyes. She smiled at him. "Dr. Boylan?"

"Yes."

She touched his shoulder. "Thank you so much for your work on the mountain. My son was injured. Several fractures and some internal bleeding. You stabilized him so he could make it to surgery. He's doing well and is expected to make a full recovery. His father and I are so grateful you were there."

He rose and shook her hand. "You're welcome. I'm happy to help. Thanks for letting me know he's going to be all right."

Her smile trembled as if she were fighting tears. "If you're not too busy, maybe you could stop by the hospital. He'd like to thank you himself."

Gabriel nodded, knowing the kid wouldn't recognize him. He'd been one of the badly injured ones—unconscious the whole time.

The woman left, and Gabriel sat back down. His father grinned at him. "Look at that. You're a superstar."

"It's different," he said, staring after the woman. "I don't usually get to hear what happened to my patients after they leave me." When he'd been deployed in Iraq and Afghanistan, his job had been to get them stable enough to make it to a better hospital or for surgery. Even in Germany, he rarely dealt with any long-term care. He was on the front line and there weren't updates on those who had been sent on.

Their server returned with his second beer, and his mother handed over a couple more listings they'd been to see. Life had returned to normal in Fool's Gold.

AFTER DINNER, GABRIEL said goodbye to his parents and started back for Noelle's house. As he walked by Brewhaha, Mayor Marsha stepped out and greeted him.

"Just the man I was hoping to run into," she said. "Can I buy you a cup of coffee? It's late, but they offer decaf."

Gabriel was tired and wanted to get home. He liked hanging out with the cat herd and looked forward to seeing Noelle. Still, the mayor was old enough to be his almost-grandmother and he'd been raised to be polite.

"Sure. Thank you."

He followed her back into the coffee shop and settled across from her.

The mayor looked as she always did. A conservative suit, pearls, her hair up. He wondered what she'd been like forty years ago—when she'd been young and her life had stretched out before her.

"I'm sure you think you've been thanked enough for what you did, but I want to make sure you know how much we appreciate you stepping in to help after the avalanche," she said.

"I'm glad I was here to help."

The college-age server walked over with his coffee. The mayor sipped her latte.

"The town is growing. Over the past five years we've had a big upswing in the population. More young couples are settling here and having babies. Our demographics are improving."

"Have you always lived here?" he asked.

"Born and raised." Her blue eyes twinkled. "I'm California's longest-serving mayor, you know."

"I'd heard that. Congratulations."

"I have a lot of years left in me. I think about retiring, but then what would I do with my time? I have a beautiful granddaughter and great-grandchildren. I've been blessed."

"Which isn't what you wanted to talk about," he said gently, knowing they were going to get to the sales pitch soon.

"No, it's not." She smiled. "Did you meet the gentlemen from CDS?" she asked.

"The bodyguard school?" He nodded. "Ford and Angel were the ones to rescue my brother."

"Yes. They've been an excellent addition to the community. Angel needs to let go of the pain of his past and fall in love again, but I'm hoping that will happen soon. We have a new PR firm moving to town. *Score.* The company is a partnership. Three former NFL football players will be moving here." She sighed. "I know they're going to make trouble, but eventually they'll figure out how to fit in. On the bright side, they'll be able to help our town advertise itself nationally."

"I'm sure that will be a good thing."

"We're continuing our planning for a search-and-rescue team," she added. "I've been thinking about it for years, but what happened last week has made the need even more apparent. Getting the necessary funding will be a challenge, but we're up to it." She glanced at him. "Your parents are staying in town."

"I just saw some of the real-estate listings they're considering."

"And you?"

"I'm leaving."

"May I ask why?"

Because...because... Gabriel stared into his coffee, as if the answers were there. "I have to go back to the army."

"Oh. I thought you'd fulfilled your time."

"Yes. I'm up for reenlistment."

"But you haven't made your decision yet," she said. "You're still considering your options."

He wasn't sure if she was asking him or telling him. Both options were slightly unsettling. Mayor Marsha seemed to know far too much about him, and he couldn't figure out how. Noelle would have mentioned any conversation with the mayor, and he couldn't see either of his parents chatting with her. Or maybe he could.

"Felicia will be pregnant soon," the mayor continued. "Gideon having a baby. That will be a show."

Gabriel chuckled. "The two of them could be very intense parents."

"Carter keeps them grounded. He's a strong soul. He's going to be an extraordinary young man. I would imagine in your line of work, you see the dark side of life. The thin thread that can be cut at any moment."

The shift in conversation caught him off-guard. "It's tenuous," he admitted. "One second a soldier is standing there, laughing, and the next, he's in pieces. You never get used to it."

"No one could," she murmured. "It's not like that here. We have our tragedies. There are accidents and people die. But we are a community in every sense of the word. In Fool's Gold, people belong. We work together to keep those on the fringes from slipping through the cracks. We're not always successful, but we keep trying."

She picked up her mug. "You're familiar with Noelle's past?"

"Yes," he said, wondering how Mayor Marsha had found out.

"I admire her courage. She went through so much and survived, yet found herself abandoned by the very person who was supposed to love her. A lesser person would have been crushed, but she pulled herself together and started over. I have great respect for her."

"Me, too."

"Then stay and prove that there is a happy ending for both of you."

He stiffened, the gentle attack surprising but strangely effective.

She took a sip, then put down her mug and reached for her large handbag. She opened it and pulled out a manila envelope.

"These are for you," she said.

The conversational shifts had left him reeling. He couldn't think of what to say, so he opened the envelope and was shocked to find dozens of cards and letters, all addressed to him. They were from former patients—

soldiers he'd kept from dying in those first critical hours. There were drawings from their kids and pictures. Men and women, some scarred and missing limbs, but smiling and happy. Home, where they belonged.

He flipped through the cards, reading words of thanks and gratitude. Notes reminded him of forgotten moments, of a kind word or a promise that he wouldn't let that particular soldier die, so not to give up.

He looked at the old woman sitting across from him. "How did you get these?"

"I have my ways. You don't get to be my age without meeting a few people." She rose and shrugged into her coat. "We need you, Gabriel. Not just for your skills, but because of who you are as a man. Fool's Gold needs you, but just as important, you need us. You belong here. Take a step of faith. I promise it will be well rewarded."

NOELLE WROTE DOWN the information. "Got it," she said with a grin. "Tell her I'm thrilled."

She hung up and put her cell phone on the kitchen counter, then turned to Gabriel. "Pia had her baby. A boy named Ryder. They're both doing great and—" She laughed. "You have no idea who I'm talking about, do you?"

"Not a clue," he admitted. "But if you're happy, I'm happy."

True words, he thought as she moved toward him, stepping over kittens as she went. They were all wide-eyed and running around the house now. Seven kittens, two mother cats and dozens of boxes from his online shopping binge a week or so ago competed for space in her small house.

Noelle reached him and plopped herself on his lap. She wrapped her arms around his neck and lightly kissed him. "You're such a guy."

"So you're not going to believe I used to be a woman?"

"Probably not. Although you certainly know how to shop."

"I might have gone a little overboard."

"You think?"

She rose. He released her reluctantly, wanting to feel her next to him. Time was moving more quickly every day. It was already the 22nd. He was scheduled to leave before New Year's. What had been weeks was now days and soon it would be hours.

"All right," she said. "We need to get organized. The best way to do this is to set up wrapping stations. It takes more time up front, but then the whole process will go more quickly. I'll clear the table for actual wrapping. We'll do ribbon in the kitchen and then stack the presents on my desk in the office."

She reached down and scooped up one of the kittens. "All the better to keep little paws and claws away from anything tempting." She stroked the kitten as she spoke.

She turned back to him. "Start going through the boxes. Get everything sorted by size. There are gift cards over there." She pointed with her free hand. "You can write those first so we'll know who gets what present."

She carried the kitten into the small office and came back with her laptop. She set it by the sink and logged on to her email program. "Oh, look. Word is spreading about Pia's baby."

He still had no clue who Pia was, but liked that Noelle

was excited for her. Mayor Marsha had been right—this town looked out for its own.

His conversation with the older woman still left him feeling unsettled. She knew too much, and he couldn't figure out where she got her information. But rather than trying to figure it out, he'd decided to instead simply enjoy the cards.

"There's a picture!"

He looked up and saw Noelle pointing to the screen. He rose and walked over to see the grainy picture of the newborn. His skin was red, his eyes tightly closed. But he was beautiful. New life, Gabriel thought.

Noelle handed him the kitten. "I have to go to the bathroom. Yell if any more pictures come in."

He took the kitten. "You'll be gone thirty seconds," he teased. "You can't go that long without knowing if there's a new picture?"

She planted her hands on her hips. "Do you or do you not want help wrapping all your presents?"

He chuckled. "I'll yell if another one comes in."

"Thank you."

He watched her walk away, enjoying the sway of her hips and the careful way she stepped over all the obstructions—both living and inanimate. Her place was a mess and it was mostly his fault, he thought. Once they got the packages wrapped, he would drive them up to his brother's. He'd also been thinking he should ask Gideon to put out the word on the older kittens. They were starting to eat regular food, which meant they would soon be old enough to be adopted. He knew Noelle was thinking of keeping the two mother cats, but there was no way she could handle them *and* the kittens, too.

Her computer pinged. He turned back and saw an email had come in. He clicked on it, thinking he would see another picture of the newborn, only to be confronted with three stark sentences.

Dr. Nelson confirmed it. The cancer is back and it's bad. I wish there was better news.

Gabriel's vision sharpened to a single pinpoint of light. All he saw was the email. The words blurred, then sharpened and he understood immediately what had happened. The AML had returned. While it was unlikely, it could happen. What he hadn't known was that she'd been worried and had been checked out by someone. She hadn't said a word.

His gut twisted, even as his mind denied the obvious truth. He thought about all she'd been through already. Of the picture she'd shown him and her talking about nearly dying. He thought about everything she'd lost and how she'd just figured out how to have a new life. She was happy, he thought bitterly, furious at the unfairness of the situation. She didn't deserve this.

Friends would rally, he knew. The town would be there for her, but that wasn't the same as family. As having someone she could depend on.

"Any news?"

He turned and saw her walking back into the living room. She looked fine. Alert, healthy. Her color was good and it was all a lie.

"Marry me," he said, not sure where the words had come from, but meaning them. "Marry me. I'll stay. I'll take care of you. I can handle it, Noelle. I won't leave. I'm not Jeremy. You can trust me to stay."

Her brows drew together. "What on earth are you talking about?"

"You don't have to pretend. I saw the email. You've been to a doctor."

"What? No, I haven't."

"It's right here," he said, pointing to the computer. "I want to help. I want to be here for you."

NOELLE FELT AS if she'd walked into the middle of a movie where everyone knew the plot but her. Gabriel looked shell-shocked, but clear-eyed. She would guess he didn't have a head injury. But still. Something was really wrong with the man.

While she was thrilled at the proposal, something about it wasn't right. He said he would marry her, but made no mention of loving her. Why would he suddenly want to marry her?

He would stay with her? What on earth was he—

She groaned. "I heard from Tammy," she said quietly, then pushed past him to stand in front of the computer. The message was brief and to the point.

Tears filled her eyes. She brushed them away and took a deep breath, then faced Gabriel.

"It's not me. Tammy is a friend of mine. We met in the hospital. Obviously, her cancer is back. She was never very strong. This is going to go fast. She wanted me to know."

There were calls she needed to make, she thought. A visit to plan. Tammy lived in San Francisco. She could go over for a few days. Tammy had a large family who would be with her, but Noelle would need to give her that last hug.

She shook her head, then turned to Gabriel, who was

staring at her as if he couldn't bring himself to believe her. "I'm fine," she said firmly. "Not sick at all. You don't have to propose. I'm not dying."

"You're sure?"

A simple question that cut like a knife.

"I'm sure."

He drew in a breath. "I thought, well, you know what I thought."

They stared at each other, then both looked away. What had once been comfortable was suddenly awkward.

He'd felt pity, she realized. He knew she was pretty much alone in the world, so he'd offered to be there for her. Not out of love, though. He'd never said he loved her.

She saw the truth then, about both of them. She squared her shoulders and prepared to put it on the line.

"I'm too strong for you," she said flatly. "I don't know why I didn't see it before. I suppose I was blinded by your good looks and charm. And how you made me feel. I appreciate what we've had together. You're a great guy, but you're not the one for me."

She drew in a breath. "I deserve someone who wants to be with me for the next eighty years, not just eight weeks. It's not about dying, because you're right. We could all go tomorrow. But what if we don't? What if I live to be a hundred? I want to be with a man who would celebrate that."

Gabriel stared at her, uncomprehending. "I wanted to help," he said quietly. "I would have taken care of you."

"I don't need that," she told him. "I can handle whatever happens. I've proven that. I've lived through things you can't imagine. I am taking chances every day and I deserve someone who will take those chances with me."

She gathered her courage. "I look at a sunrise and I see promise. You look at a sunrise and count the hours until sunset. Life is a gift and we need to accept it with gratitude and a full heart. I don't want to be with someone who doesn't believe that with me."

"I would have stayed," he said haltingly.

"I know. But for the wrong reasons."

"I'm not ready to leave you."

"Do you love me?"

He took a single step back and that was enough.

"Goodbye, Gabriel."

CHAPTER FIFTEEN

THE TWENTY-THIRD PASSED quickly. The store was busy, which helped Noelle not to think. She hurt more than she'd thought possible. Losing Gabriel was even more painful than losing Jeremy had been. But no matter the giant hole in her heart, she knew she'd made the right decision. She was all in and she needed to be with someone who was willing to be the same. Gabriel wasn't willing to take a leap of faith and she couldn't be the only one in the relationship who was.

But all the logic in the world didn't keep her from missing him, she thought as she walked home. Worse, people had stopped by to ask about him, wanting to thank him for his help or wish him a merry Christmas. Noelle hadn't wanted to go into details, so she'd said he was with his family. An explanation easily accepted in a town like Fool's Gold.

Now as she turned up her walkway, she told herself she would be fine. It was just a matter of time. She would fall out of love with him eventually. In the meantime, she could take pride in making the right decision, even though it was hard. He'd wanted to do the right thing, even if was for the wrong reason. She appreciated the effort, but it wasn't enough.

She walked into her tiny house, flipping on lights as she went. The cats raced to greet her. She petted as many as she could reach, then went into the kitchen to start their dinner service. After everyone had been fed, she cleaned up the litter box. She'd barely finished washing her hands when her doorbell rang.

"Did one of you order pizza?" she asked, walking to the door. "I believe we talked about that. Don't make me have to lock up my credit cards."

She opened it to find Felicia, Isabel and Patience on her porch. Behind them were several other women she knew, including Jo, from Jo's Bar. Jo was holding a very large, industrial-looking blender.

"We heard," Isabel said, walking in and hugging her. "I'm so sorry. Men can be idiots. Are we setting up in the kitchen?"

Women poured into the house. Each of them had brought chips or brownies or wine. In a matter of minutes, kittens had been picked up and were being cuddled, Jo's blender was whirring and food was being set up in bowls and on plates.

"I don't understand," Noelle said. "Not that I don't appreciate the company."

"I told them," Felicia admitted. "About what happened with Gabriel. Not any details, of course. Mostly because I don't have them. He didn't say anything before he left."

Noelle swallowed against the sudden lump in her throat. "He l-left?" she asked, her voice cracking. "He left Fool's Gold?"

The room went still as everyone turned to look at her. She tried to hold it together, but knowing he was gone changed everything. When he hadn't shown up for his shift, she'd assumed he was assessing. But he wasn't. She wasn't going to run into him. He wouldn't be at the live nativity or the wedding. There would be no more conversations, no more touches or kisses, no chance of him changing his mind. Until that second, she'd been holding out hope so secret, she'd kept it from herself.

"He's gone," she whispered, hanging on to the counter to keep from going down on her knees. "He's really gone."

Then the tears came. They poured down her cheeks as she held in her sobs. Arms held her tight as her friends offered comfort and understanding. She let them take over, let them guide her to the sofa, let them tell her that eventually she would be all right.

She told herself to listen. To remember that she was strong. She had conquered much more than this already. She'd survived against brutal odds. She would get over her broken heart.

Eventually.

ON CHRISTMAS EVE day, Noelle closed the store early. Not only was she fighting the hangover from hell, but she also had a lot to do.

The previous night her friends had been there for her. Unfortunately, they'd invited along Jo's very strong margaritas. After her emotional storm had passed, there had been drinking and eating and calling Gabriel names. Felicia had talked about her trials with Gideon because the man had been pigheaded. Dakota Andersson had told how she'd had to fly to Alaska to convince Finn they belonged together. Each woman had a story of love found, which Noelle appreciated, but she was less sure of her own happy ending. Gabriel had said from the beginning that he didn't believe there was a point to love. She'd been foolish not to listen.

Three pots of tea, some crackers and two aspirin later, the worst of her hangover seemed to have improved enough for her to be functional. She walked from the store to her house, aware of the time. She had an appointment and didn't want to be late.

She let herself inside and greeted her cat family. Then she made sure the evidence of the previous night was all put away.

Right on time, someone knocked on her door. She let in Patience and her very excited daughter. Lillie practically danced in place as she entered the house.

"We've already been to the pet store," Lillie told Noelle. "We have a litter box and the food you're using and some toys and a bed. We got a book on taking care of a kitten and I've read it twice. Mom warned me that she's going to be sad for a few days, because she'll miss her family, but then she'll be okay and I need to be patient."

Lillie's expression turned hopeful. "I'll be eleven soon and I'm very responsible."

Noelle still felt like her heart had been ripped out, but listening to Lillie reminded her there were so many wonderful moments in her life. Friends who cared and things to look forward to. Like giving Lillie her very first kitten.

"Do you know which one you want?" she asked.

Lillie nodded, then pointed to the little black-and-white kitten crawling up the side of the sofa. "Her."

Noelle looked at Patience, who nodded.

"Merry Christmas," Noelle said.

Lillie grinned broadly, then hurried to pick up the kitten. The little cat relaxed into her arms and playfully batted at a lock of hair.

"Thank you," Patience said. "She's so excited."

Noelle laughed. "One down, six to go. Spread the word."

GABRIEL HAD DECIDED to go to Mexico. He headed south on I-5, only to change his mind when he hit San Diego. He spent the night in a cheap motel by a truck stop, then figured he would go east. Maybe Florida would be nice. Halfway across Arizona, he turned around again. By two o'clock on Christmas Eve day, he was at the Oregon border, pulling into a rest stop and wondering when he was going to admit the truth.

He couldn't leave. He'd been driving for two days and he was still within a couple hundred miles of where he'd started.

He told himself to let go. That he had to move on. That there was nothing for him in Fool's Gold. Not friends, not family and certainly not Noelle. The thing was, he'd never been very good at lying to himself. Everything important to him waited there and for the life of him, he couldn't figure out why he was so scared to simply accept that.

At the rest stop, he got out of his car, then stood there with no clue as to what to do next. He wanted to raise his fist, but to whom? And for what? There was no one to be pissed at except maybe himself. He'd left her. That was the raw truth. He'd left Noelle, no doubt hurting her. She'd said she loved him and he'd run like some scared little kid.

He walked to the sidewalk, then back to his door, telling himself he hadn't had a choice. What was he supposed to do? Tell her he loved her, too? Propose again, this time for real? That wasn't going to happen. Six weeks he could give her. He would have been there for her every second. He would have—

Gabriel swore loudly, startling an older woman walking a small dog. She came to a stop, stared at him, then quickly turned and went the other way.

"I'm sorry," he called after her. "I'm not crazy or dangerous."

The woman walked faster.

He got in his car, where at least he could rant without disturbing people and retraced his logic. He would help Noelle die but he wouldn't share in her life. Was that it? Six weeks were okay, but what about eight? Or twelve? Would he agree to one year but not two?

Life was tenuous, he reminded himself. It could be taken away at any second. He'd seen it countless times.

But he'd also seen his father feeling up his mother after nearly forty years of marriage. He'd seen happy couples of all ages, enjoying what they had. Everyone knew that life ended, but they didn't live in fear. They lived with joy. They loved and laughed and when it was over, however long that was, they could say there were no regrets.

He started the car and drove out of the rest stop and back onto I-5. This time he was going south, following the signs to Sacramento. From there he would go east into Fool's Gold. He'd already missed the live nativity, but there was still the Dance of the Winter King and then a wedding. More important…*most* important…was Noelle. Sweet, beautiful, brave Noelle, who loved cats and was overly competitive about window decorations and who sold gourd nativities. Noelle, who was the strongest person he knew and for reasons he couldn't ever understand, loved him. She loved him.

The realization of what he'd nearly missed, nearly lost, swept through him. He clutched the steering wheel, knowing the folly of driving too quickly, but unable to grasp what an idiot he'd been.

He glanced at the clock. He would be there in time. He had to be.

NOELLE ZIPPED UP the wedding gown that had once belonged to her grandmother. She turned back and forth, pleased the dress nearly fit perfectly. She still had a few pounds to put on, but that would come with time. The strength she'd drawn on to survive her illness was still with her. As were her friends and her store and this town. She belonged.

Loving Gabriel wasn't a bad thing, she told herself. Giving her heart had been the last part of her healing process. She'd been willing to risk it all and she would again, one day. She would find the right man and they would be happy together. Until then, she would save her grandmother's dress.

She undid the zipper and slipped on her robe. She folded the dress carefully, using lots of tissue. She had a little time until she needed to get ready for the Dance of the Winter King and the weddings to follow.

She thought of how surprised everyone would be and was pleased she got to be a part of it all. Talk about memories.

Someone pounded on her front door. The noise was determined and insistent.

She hurried to the front of the house and pulled open the door. "What's…"

The rest of her sentence got caught in her throat as she stared at Gabriel. He looked exhausted—nearly as gray as he had been the first time she'd seen him. There were dark circles under his eyes and she wondered if he'd slept at all over the past couple of days. She would guess he hadn't been eating. Signs of his suffering should have pleased her, but they didn't. She wanted him to be well.

He didn't speak. Instead, he walked into her house, slammed the door shut behind him and then pulled her close. He held on to her so tightly, she could barely breathe. A shudder raced through him.

"I could have lost you," he said. "I could have lost us." Then he let her go and dropped to his knees.

He took both her hands in his and stared into her eyes. "Noelle, I'm sorry. I was wrong about everything. Not in wanting to take care of you, but in believing that would be enough. I want to give you everything I have, everything I am. Whatever it takes to convince you, I'll do it. I swear. I love you. I want to be with you, always. I want to be by your side for however long we have. Six weeks or sixty years. I'm sorry I left. I have no excuse except that every soldier has to face fear and some do it with more grace than others. I won't run again. I'll stand and fight. For you. For us. If you'll have me."

There were too many words, she thought, unable to take them all in. Except right in the middle, she would have sworn he said he loved her.

He must have read the question in her eyes because he held on tighter and repeated, "I love you. I've loved you from the first, but I didn't want to admit it. I want to marry you, if you'll have me."

Somehow she managed to pull him to his feet. Then they were holding on to each other and he was kissing her and she was kissing him.

He drew back. "Am I too late?"

She smiled. "It's been two days. Did you think I'd forget so fast?"

His expression turned hopeful. "You'll marry me?"

She smiled. "You know about the cats, right?"

He laughed and pulled her into his arms. Then he swung her around until she was dizzy and slowly lowered her to the ground.

"I stopped at Jenel's store in town. The longest few minutes of my life, for many reasons." He pulled a diamond ring from his pocket and slid it onto her left hand.

"I love you, Noelle," he said, staring into her eyes.

"I love you, too."

"So about the wedding tonight."

She gasped, then looked at the clock by the TV. "I have to start getting ready. I'm the bridesmaid."

"Are you sure? Because I talked to Dellina on my way here and if you want to make it a quadruple wedding, she says she can handle it."

Noelle couldn't believe what was happening. Gabriel was back and he loved her. That was enough. But to get married tonight?

"You've been busy! Are you sure?" she asked.

He smiled. "You think now that I've finally figured out what I have with you that I'm going to be stupid enough to let you get away?" He chuckled. "Don't answer that. Yes, I'm sure. I want to start our life together. I'm going to leave the army and live here in Fool's Gold. I hear there's a new hospital that needs a trauma specialist."

She flung her arms around him, knowing she would never let go. "The wedding is supposed to be a surprise," she murmured.

"Then let's make it a big one."

THE LAST STRAINS of music faded. Evie Jefferson walked out onstage. "Thank you so much for joining us tonight," she said as her dancers waited behind her. "Before you go, we have a little something special prepared."

She moved off the stage and her students began to dance to a special arrangement of the wedding march. Four girls twirled into view, each dressed as a bride. Then two teenaged boys walked down the center aisle, carefully unrolling a white carpet.

In the audience, whispers were heard as the townspeople realized this wasn't a simple encore. As if to confirm the murmurs, Mayor Marsha walked out, a microphone in her hands.

"Good evening. Tonight as we celebrate a season of miracles, I am pleased and honored to tell you there will be four weddings performed here. Four beautiful brides join with four handsome grooms and begin their lifetime journey of love and commitment."

Gladys nudged her friend Eddie. "Another wedding. It's a Christmas miracle."

"I hope one of them is wearing Vera Wang. I just love Vera Wang."

The music changed and Lillie and Carter walked down the aisle together. They separated and stood on opposite sides of a podium someone had put in front of the stage. Four men started down the aisle, each in a black tux.

Seventysomething Eddie sighed. "Now that they're getting married, we'll never see them naked. Wives have a way of objecting to that."

"What about those football players moving to town? We can suggest another calendar as a fundraiser. Butts of Fool's Gold."

"Good plan."

The music swelled to the wedding march. Everyone

rose and turned to watch as four brides started down the aisle. Patience, Felicia, Isabel and Noelle.

The bouquets were done in shades of pink, ranging from very pale to nearly fuchsia. The dresses were all strapless, but otherwise as different as the women themselves.

Dellina watched the ceremony begin from the far side of the convention center. Once the couples started speaking their vows, she turned back to the flurry of activity taking place to get the reception ready. Huge trays of food were being set out for the buffet. The tables and chairs were set up and the kids area prepared. She was exhausted, but pleased. Everything had turned out perfectly.

Noelle stood next to Gabriel and listened to him recite his vows. He slid the diamond band on her finger, sealing their love in a tradition that stretched back for generations. She felt the warm, loving presence of her mother and grandmother, as if they were there, holding her close. And for one brief second, she saw her future with Gabriel. Decades of happiness, children and grandchildren, and the miracle that was the true meaning of Christmas.

* * * * *

*If you love Fool's Gold at Christmastime,
turn the page for a bonus novella.
The holiday magic continues in
YOURS FOR CHRISTMAS.*

This is for Linda Elliott,
who said yes to the man of her dreams
Waymon (Ray), in 1961 on Christmas Eve.
Since his illness and death in 2008,
Linda has returned to comfort reading,
her first love, with a vengeance.

CHAPTER ONE

"Mom, even though I know there's no Santa, is it still okay to have a stocking?"

Bailey Voss smiled at her daughter. Being a single mom was often a challenge, but every now and then she thought maybe, just maybe, she was getting it right.

"Of course," she told her seven-year-old. "Christmas is about being with the people we love and sharing our traditions. A stocking is a tradition."

Chloe beamed. "When can we put out our stockings? And decorate the house?" Her bright, adorable girl paused. "When we move, right? Can we put up our Christmas tree the very first night?"

"We can," Bailey promised, confident she was going to be exhausted after a long day of moving, but determined to make this the best Christmas ever for her little girl.

Chloe had already been through so much, most especially the loss of her dad over a year ago. But she was happy and thriving now. Bailey and her daughter had made a place for themselves in Fool's Gold and they were less than a month from moving into what Bailey hoped was their forever home. Bailey had a great job she loved, Chloe had friends and was doing well in school. A wonderful holiday season was exactly how she planned to finish up her year.

Chloe walked to the calendar attached to the refrigerator and counted out the days.

"Seventeen days until Thanksgiving," she said excitedly. "Then twelve more days until we move and get our tree and stockings." She hurried over to her mother and hugged her. "It's almost Christmas!"

Bailey held her tightly, then stroked her hair. "I'm proud of you, honey," she said, trying to keep from sounding too emotional. "You're working hard in school and you're a big help to me."

Her daughter looked up her. "I love you, Mom."

"I love you, too, sweet girl." She glanced at the clock on the stove and held in a shriek. "We are so late!"

Chloe laughed and pulled back, then ran out of the kitchen. "I'm ready. I just need my coat."

Five minutes later the Voss women were walking briskly toward Chloe's school. After dropping off her daughter, Bailey continued on toward city hall, where she worked as Mayor Marsha Tilson's assistant.

Mayor Marsha was the longest-serving mayor in California. She ran her town with an impressive combination of carrot and stick. Bailey was pretty sure Mayor Marsha could twist the devil himself to her bidding. Today was no exception.

Only it wasn't going to be the devil walking through the mayor's office doors. Instead they would be visited by a tall, broad-shouldered man who got Bailey's heart to fluttering in a way that really couldn't be healthy.

"It's just a crush," Bailey told herself as she waited in line at Brew-haha for her morning latte, then realized that talking aloud in a crowd was a sure way to get her neighbors and friends to worrying about her. She pressed her lips together, then felt them curve into a smile as she thought about how being around Kenny Scott made her feel sixteen again.

She knew that having a crush was no big deal. It was a part of life. As long as she didn't act on it, she would be fine. Because throwing herself at the muscular, former NFL player, and Super Bowl-winning receiver, would be foolish and possibly pathetic.

There was no way she was Kenny's type. Not that she'd ever seen him with a woman, but still. He was gorgeous. Dark blond hair, big blue eyes. He was built like a superhero and strong. A gentle giant of a man. And speaking of big, his hands...

She held in another sigh, placed her order, waved at her friend Patience, who was manning the espresso machine, then moved to wait for her drink.

The truth was that famous former NFL stars didn't date small-town single moms. Especially not those who were battling an extra twenty pounds. Bailey figured she was attractive enough. She'd been blessed with thick red hair and nice skin, but she wasn't like those women in the gossip magazines. She was pretty much the same as everyone else in the normal world. She had a job, she worried about her daughter and much of the time her paycheck barely stretched to cover her bills. She wasn't exactly a hunky-guy magnet.

But that was the beauty of a crush. She could look and dream all she wanted, for free. And if the man in question happened to be coming in for a meeting that very morning, then she was simply going to have more to sigh about later. Which made today a very good day.

As Kenny Scott's friend Jack had once admitted, going to see Mayor Marsha was a bit like visiting the great and powerful Wizard of Oz. But without the flying monkeys or the man manipulating things behind the curtain. Unfortunately for Kenny, Mayor Marsha came by her power the old-fashioned way, and not through smoke and mirrors. If it were the latter, she would be so much easier to refuse.

It wasn't that he was afraid of the woman, he told himself as he walked toward city hall. It was that he didn't like situations where he couldn't say no. And with Mayor Marsha, *no* wasn't a word people generally uttered.

He knew he could tell himself to be strong. That she was merely an old woman. But the truth was far more complex than that. Mayor Marsha knew things she shouldn't, and no one could figure out how. Kenny assumed she had a network of accomplices who fed her tidbits of information. She put them all into some retired NSA computer program that predicted behavior or something. He shook his head as he climbed the steps to the main entrance. Maybe he should simply accept the prevailing wisdom that the mayor wasn't of this earth. Or had precognition. Regardless, she had summoned him and here he was.

He took a flight of stairs to the second floor and walked down the wide hallway. A sign directed him to the mayor's office.

He walked through the open doorway only to get hit by a three-hundred-pound cornerback. Okay, not really, but that was what it felt like. He came to a stop, unnoticed by the single occupant of the office foyer, and told himself that he was imagining the body blow. And the attraction.

He knew the curvy redhead sitting guard outside the

mayor's inner sanctum. He'd seen her dozens of times in town, had talked to her. He even knew her kid. But while seven-year-old Chloe was adorable and only a little dangerous, the same couldn't be said for her mom. Bailey Voss was a walking, breathing temptation. She should come with a permanent warning sign and a quarantine zone. Because when he was within ten feet of her, his brain shut down and he became an idiot.

He couldn't figure out what it was about her that got to him. She was tall and he liked tall, but it wasn't like that was so unusual in and of itself. The long, wavy red hair was sexy, but survivable. He wanted to say it was her big green eyes. There was an innocence there, a trust, and that appealed to him.

Okay, fine. He would admit it. He was just as mentally simple as every other man on the planet. Sex was important and when he saw Bailey Voss all he could think about was getting her naked and having his way with her. He was pretty sure that three or four hundred times would do the trick.

Under any other circumstances, he would ask her out, wow her with his charm, get her into bed and get over her. Or fall crazy in love with her. He was open to either. Only that wasn't going to happen. Not ever. She was a single mom and he didn't date single moms. Not now, not in the future. Because single moms came with kids and while a guy could get over falling for a woman, kids ripped out your heart and took it with them when they left. There was no recovering from that.

He braced himself for the inevitable feeling of being all feet and no brain, then cleared his throat. Bailey looked up and smiled.

That was all it took. One sweet smile and he was a goner. He'd played in the NFL—shouldn't he be better than this?

"Hi, Kenny," she said. "You're right on time."

"I figured if I wasn't, she'd unleash the dragons."

Bailey's smile turned into a little laugh. One of those soft, sweet sounds that made a man think about how he should have matching towels and maybe get something monogrammed. He'd read once that men might have conquered the West, but women had civilized it. Truer words, he thought glumly.

"The mayor said to bring you right in," Bailey told him.

She rose and stepped out from behind the desk.

She was wearing a dress. Some gray tweedy fabric that probably had a name or was the latest style. He didn't care about the color or the style. What he liked was how the dress followed the generous lines of her body. The style emphasized her breasts and her hips. She wore boots with sensible flat heels and still came up past his shoulder.

She moved closer and suddenly he could smell some girlie shampoo or soap. It made him think of Bailey in the shower, which was dangerous and fun at the same time.

She moved toward the closed double doors and he followed. She came to an unexpected stop and he nearly plowed into her. Before he could move back, she turned to face him.

Her green eyes were big and her lashes were long. Her full lips had some kind of gloss on them and he briefly wondered if it had a flavor. Because every now and then when he kissed a woman he got a twofer. A sweet, sexy mouth and a hint of piña colada. It was nice. Women were nice and Bailey was the nicest of them—

He grabbed his self-control with both hands and deliberately took a step toward safety. Early in his career a coach had told him that he had one job on the field. To catch the football and run it to the end zone. Nothing else mattered. The advice had served him well.

When it came to Bailey, he only had to remember one thing. She wasn't for him. If he kept that in mind, he would be fine.

"I should have asked," she said. "Did you want some coffee? We have a pot going."

"I'm good."

Something flashed in her eyes and her smile broadened. He wanted to ask what she was thinking, but before he could, she'd opened the door to the mayor's office and led the way inside.

The space was large with a huge desk and big windows. There were three flags behind the mayor's desk. The U.S. Flag, the California state flag and one that he guessed was the seal of Fool's Gold.

Mayor Marsha was in her sixties with white hair. She wore suits or dresses and pearls. On the surface she wasn't the least bit intimidating, but he'd seen grown men bow to her bidding and be unable to explain why.

Today she had on a red dress. She smiled welcomingly when he followed Bailey to her desk, then rose and shook his hand.

"Mr. Scott, thank you so much for seeing me."

Uh-huh, like he believed he'd had a choice. "Kenny, please."

She motioned for him to sit. Bailey took the chair next to his and Mayor Marsha settled back in her seat.

The older woman studied him for a moment before nodding. As if she'd just made a decision. Kenny briefly wondered how big a pain in his butt that decision was going to be.

"As you know," she began, "we have various service projects for our FWM groves."

"Sure."

Fool's Gold had its own version of scouting. Future Warriors of the Máa-zib. The Máa-zib tribe was the former indigenous tribe of the area. They had been a matriarchal society, so the FWM was for girls from age six to maybe ten. They progressed from Acorns in year one to Sprouts and so on until their final year when they were Mighty Oaks. The girls were in "groves" and there was a Grove Keeper.

Taryn, one of his business partners, was a co-leader of a grove with her husband, Angel. Chloe, Bailey's daughter, was in their grove. Kenny had helped her and one of her friends learn knots this past spring.

"You know the Sprouts?" the mayor asked.

"Taryn's grove? Sure." He looked at Bailey, but she seemed as puzzled as he was.

"Is there a problem with the Sprouts?" she asked her boss. "Chloe hasn't said anything."

"All is well," the mayor assured her. "However, there is a slight logistical problem. Each grove has a service project for the year. The Sprouts want to have a toy drive for the holidays. An admirable and ambitious project to be sure. But with Taryn and Angel traveling for the next month, they have no leader."

"Taryn's not traveling," Kenny said. She would have

said something to him and his partners. He'd just seen her yesterday at their staff meeting.

"She and Angel are going to Fiji for a month," Mayor Marsha told him. "So the Sprouts will need someone to temporarily take over the grove. I immediately thought of you two."

Kenny felt the walls closing in. No way. Not him. He couldn't be responsible for a bunch of little girls. Even if he had the time, which he probably did, he didn't want to get involved that way. It was too close. Too personal. Plus the mayor had said him and Bailey. He couldn't work with her. Not up close. She was too sexy and desirable.

"I'd love to," Bailey said quickly. She smiled at Kenny, then turned back to the mayor. "It's a great idea. This is only Chloe's second Christmas without her father. Last year was so hard on her. I was worried how she would handle the holidays. I think focusing on collecting toys for needy children will help her see the joy in the season."

Kenny swore silently. Totally tempting and nice to boot. Wasn't that his luck? How was he supposed to say no now? He would look like a jerk. Plus, he liked Chloe. He didn't want her sad over Christmas. He believed in self-preservation but not in being a jerk.

"Excellent." The mayor handed them each a folder. "Here are the approved collection sites. The girls will each need to decorate a bin and then the bins will need to be emptied regularly. The toy drive will start the Saturday after Thanksgiving. That gives you time to organize the decorating and placing of the bins. The toys will be delivered to Sacramento on the nineteenth of December. They'll be distributed that weekend."

She gave a few more instructions, then thanked them both for agreeing to help. It was only when Kenny found himself outside the office that he realized he'd never agreed at all. Not that he was going to mention that now.

He sat in the visitor's chair at Bailey's desk and opened his folder. The neatly printed sheets detailed everything that had to be done.

"I know where we can get a cargo trailer," Bailey was saying. "Mayor Marsha had me make sure it was available but I didn't know why until now."

He was having trouble taking it all in, and sitting this close to Bailey didn't help. Once again he could inhale the scent of something a little floral, a little girlie, and it didn't make thinking any easier.

"A cargo trailer will take a lot of toys," he said.

"The town will come through," Bailey said confidently. "Okay, so I see where we pick up the empty bins. We'll need to arrange to decorate them. If the drive starts the Saturday *after* Thanksgiving, we should decorate the Saturday before. Does that work for you?"

She looked up at him and he found himself getting lost in her big green eyes.

"I never said yes," he told her, knowing he sounded like an idiot.

Her mouth twitched. "Don't let that worry you. Mayor Marsha does that to people. Unless you want to go tell her no."

"Not really."

"I didn't think so." She lightly put her hand on his forearm. "It'll be fun."

Her fingers were long and slender and he could feel the heat through his shirt. There were a lot of words for spending the next month or so working with Bailey on the toy drive, but he wasn't sure *fun* was going to be one of them. Torture was more likely.

"I, ah, have a big SUV," he said after clearing his throat. "I can use it to empty the bins."

"Great." She pulled her arm back. "We'll get a schedule together. Discuss it with the girls at the FWM meeting. They can sign up their parents to help with that, too."

"There's a meeting?" he asked.

She nodded. "We're both going to have to be there. I know most of the girls because of Chloe, but they'll have to meet you and we'll discuss supplies for decorating." Her glossy lips curved into another smile. "I can't wait."

"Me, either," he lied, thinking it would have been so much easier to take on the flying monkeys.

KENNY WALKED INTO Taryn's office and stalked over to her desk. "You have a lot to answer for," he announced, doing his best to look intimidating.

Unfortunately for him, Taryn had spent the past few years dealing with three former NFL players and not much got to her. Instead of looking nervous or even guilty, she simply raised her eyebrows and waited.

"You and Angel are bailing," he told her, his tone accusing. "On your Sprouts. There's a toy drive and I got hauled in to the whole thing."

"What are you talking about? How did you know about our trip? We just decided a couple of days ago to spend a month in Fiji. We haven't told anyone yet."

"Someone told Mayor Marsha. I just got back from

a meeting with her. I'm going to be working with Bailey Voss on the toy drive. It's not like I could say no."

Taryn's mouth twitched, but it wasn't nearly as sexy as it had been on Bailey. Because he knew Taryn was laughing *at* him rather than with him.

"It's not funny," he grumbled.

"It kind of is." She rose and walked around her desk toward him.

As usual she wore some fancy designer-suit thing and was barefoot. Because she wore stupid shoes that were too high to walk in all day. She put her hands on his chest and stared into his eyes.

"Thank you for helping my Sprouts with the toy drive."

"You owe me."

"I do. I don't know how Mayor Marsha found out, but she did and you're a really good guy for stepping in."

He made a growling sound in his throat. No way she could mollify him with a few compliments. He was tougher than that.

She smiled. "Seriously. It means a lot to me. Those are my girls and I want them to have a good holiday."

He shook off her touch and glowered. "I said I'd do it, okay? You don't have to convince me."

"No, but I would like it if you'd at least pretend it might be fun. Unless…" The humor fled her violet eyes and worry replaced it. "Oh, Kenny, I didn't think. Is this going to be too hard for you? I can ask Jack or Sam."

Kenny was sure their other two partners would agree. And while that would free up his time, he wasn't one to walk away from something he'd already said he would do.

"I'm fine," he told her. "Bailey has the details figured out. It's the holidays, right? I can help kids who need toys."

Taryn wasn't fooled. She continued to study him. "I worry about you. You need somebody in your life." She held up a hand to stop him from talking. "Not just friends, but someone special. Someone to fall in love with."

"I'm fine." The truth, he thought. He was completely fine. As for falling in love—well, he wanted that, too. But so far it hadn't happened. He liked women but he hadn't found the one. When he did…he would be all in. As long as she didn't have kids. That was his only caveat. No single moms. No exceptions.

"I want you to be more than fine," Taryn told him. "I want you to be happy."

"I will be."

One day, he thought longingly. Because there was someone for everyone. Even a guy like him.

CHAPTER TWO

THE FWM MEETINGS were a lot louder than Kenny would have guessed. He knew that there were only eight seven-year-old girls in the room, but it seemed like there were more. Of course all the girls had brought at least one parent. Adding the Grove Keepers along with him, that was a fair number of people in a small-ish space.

He kept to the back of the room, careful not to make eye contact with the mothers. The dads he could handle. They would either want to talk about a game they remembered or try to prove that his having played pro ball didn't mean anything. He could handle that, no problem.

The mothers made him more nervous. He didn't mind the ones who said their sons wanted to play. It was the women who looked at him the way a hungry cat watches a goldfish that made him glance longingly toward the exit. He'd been propositioned plenty of times. For some people, a wedding ring was an accessory, not a commitment. *He* didn't feel that way.

While he was good at shutting down the lady in question, there was always the risk of hurt feelings. Or a husband feeling he had something to prove. Kenny wasn't in the mood for either. Better to avoid the problem completely.

He kept his attention on Angel and Taryn, who ran the meeting like the experts they were. When he felt the need to look at something more appealing, he let his gaze drift over to Bailey. Now a proposition from her would be most welcome. Then he remembered Chloe and knew he was totally screwed.

Angel, a tall dark-haired man with gray eyes and an air of danger about him, explained about the toy drive. The Sprouts didn't seem to care that their Grove Keeper was a former special ops guy with a scar on his neck like someone had tried to slit his throat. Kenny would guess that day hadn't ended well for the other guy.

Taryn stood by her husband and smiled. "You all know Bailey—Chloe's mom. She's going to be helping with the toy drive service project. But it's a big job, so we have someone else joining the grove for the next few weeks. My friend Kenny Scott."

Kenny waved from his place by the wall. A few of the girls waved back. He saw Chloe looking at him and he winked at her. She giggled.

Maybe he was looking at this all wrong, he told himself. Sure, he had his rules for his dating life, but this wasn't that. He could help the girls with their service project, enjoy the holiday season and walk away without worrying that he'd gotten too involved. That made it a win-win for everyone.

He acknowledged that at some point he was going to have to deal with the fact that holding himself apart from nearly everyone wasn't the best idea. But not a psychological hurdle he had to deal with today.

Taryn explained how the bins would have to be decorated and when that would happen. She also pointed to the sign-up sheets on the wall.

"Parents, this is where you come in. We're going to need all the bins emptied every day. Then either Kenny or Bailey will meet you at the trailer so the presents can be secured. Any questions?"

Taryn and Angel fielded the questions. A couple of the parents walked over to the sign-up sheets and wrote their names. Kenny wondered if it was too early for him to duck out. Before he could decide, Bailey walked toward him.

Today she had on a fluffy sweater and tight jeans. Both made his mouth go dry. Her hair was pulled back in a ponytail and she wasn't wearing any makeup. She looked great.

She bit her lower lip as she glanced at him. "Um, I'd like to ask you something," she murmured. "If you have a second."

Did she want to come to his place for the night? Because his answer to that was a big, fat yes. But somehow he doubted that was what she was thinking.

She drew in a breath. "Okay, so I'm buying a house. It's so strange to think I can afford it and some nights I worry that I can't." She paused and shook her head. "Sorry. The rambling wasn't supposed to be part of the question."

"No problem. Congratulations on the house."

"Thanks. It's my first. The inspection is tomorrow."

She tucked her hands into her jeans' back pockets, which made her chest stick out more. He held in a groan. Seriously, she was killing him.

"I, ah, don't know what happens at a house inspection. Or what I'm supposed to ask. I was going to go by myself, but now I'm worried I'll miss something important. Would you mind coming with me?"

It took him a second to stop looking at her body long enough to realize there was a question in all the words.

"Sure," he told her. "I'm happy to be there."

She relaxed. Unfortunately that meant she pulled her hands out of her pockets, but nothing lasted forever.

"Really? That would be so great."

"Tell me when and where and I'll be there."

She rattled off a time and address. He entered both into his phone's calendar.

"It won't be difficult," he told her. "The inspector's on your side. He or she wants you to know what you're buying."

"That's what my agent told me, but it's still a little scary. I'll feel better having you along."

One of the mothers claimed Bailey's attention. Kenny stood in the back of the room feeling as if he could take on a whole defensive line by himself. Yup, he was the man.

BAILEY SPENT HER morning alternating between worrying about why on earth she'd asked Kenny Scott to join her for her house inspection and being incredibly grateful that he was going to be along. There was just something about being around him that made her feel…safe. As if he knew what he was doing. A ridiculous assumption, she reminded herself. The man was a former professional football player. Why would he know anything about houses?

But ask him she had and she was grateful he'd agreed to join her. Despite the fact that her late husband had been deployed during their marriage and gone for nearly two years, there were still some things she found hard to do alone.

The house was in an older part of Fool's Gold. The neighborhood was well-established, with a nice mix of residents. Young families were buying homes and refurbishing, while older couples still lived in the places where their kids had grown up.

Bailey's house-to-be was two stories with a large front porch. There was a small yard in front and a big one in back, a detached garage and an unfinished basement.

While the one and a half bathrooms hadn't been remodeled in a while, the roof was new and the kitchen's appliances were younger than her daughter. All pluses. Bailey figured she and Chloe could live with the oversized tub and two-tone pink tile in the bathrooms a lot easier than they could handle a leaky roof.

Bailey had loved the house from the moment she'd stepped foot inside of it. It wasn't huge. There were only two bedrooms upstairs and a bonus area that Chloe could use as a playroom. Downstairs there was a tiny office for Bailey, a decent-size living room and the eat-in kitchen. There were lots of windows, big trees in the backyard and beautiful hardwood floors throughout.

What had most appealed, aside from the reasonable price, was the sense of rightness she felt when she'd first seen it. Despite the fact that the house was empty, she'd been able to see herself and Chloe living here for a long time. There had been other contenders—larger homes that were a little newer. But with all that space and shininess came a heftier mortgage.

Today was her day of reckoning, when she found out if her home, barely in escrow, would pass its inspection.

She heard the rumble of a powerful engine and turned to see Kenny pulling up in front of the house. He drove a large Mercedes SUV. She was sure it cost about half of what her house did, but then he could afford it.

It must be nice not to have to clip coupons and save for things like winter tires and unexpected repair bills. In her next life, she thought with a smile. She would remember to be rich.

Kenny got out of his SUV and started toward her. The sun had been playing peek-a-boo with some clouds, but obviously shared her fascination with the man. It slipped into view and cast warm, golden light on the object of its affection. Kenny's hair gleamed, his smile was easy and Bailey felt her heart give a little jump of appreciation.

Even if he didn't know anything about construction or houses or the difference between a screwdriver and a wrench, he would be a nice distraction if she started to freak out, she reminded herself.

"Nice house," Kenny said as he approached.

"Thanks." She waited until he stopped in front of her. "So, do you know anything about houses?"

He grinned. "Regretting your impulsive request I be here?"

"Not at all. Just wondering if my assumptions are correct."

"That because I'm a guy, I know something about electricity and plumbing?"

"Um, yeah. That would be it."

He put his arm around her and turned her toward

the house. "I am more than a pretty face. Growing up I helped my dad with all kinds of projects. I can lay tile, replace a light fixture and repair most plumbing leaks."

"Good to know."

The words sounded so normal, she thought. But on the inside, there was quivering and shrieking. Mostly because of how close she was to Kenny and how warm his arm was around her body. He made her feel small and delicate. Like an ordinary woman, as opposed to the widow and single mom she'd been for the past couple of years.

Before she could do much more than breathe in the scent of him and indulge in a little PG-13 make-out fantasy, a small pickup drove into her driveway. Bailey recognized the name of the inspector her real estate agent had suggested. All thoughts of Kenny fled as the enormity of what she was doing crashed in on her.

"I want it to be perfect," she admitted in a whisper.

"Be willing to settle for sound," Kenny advised. "Everything else is a bonus."

Good advice, she thought as she walked over to meet her inspector.

Paul Jennings was a man in his fifties. He was pleasant, but seemed more interested in the house than making small talk. He had a large rolling toolbox with him and began the inspection by walking around the outside of the house.

"We start from the ground up," Mr. Jennings told her. "Foundation to roof. I'll tell you what I find as I go, then get you a written report via email by this time tomorrow. But before I leave, you'll already know everything I've found."

"I appreciate that," she told him.

"Then let's get started."

Three hours later Bailey knew more about the house she wanted to buy than she'd ever known about any other building in her life. Even better, she was comfortable with her decision. There were a couple of small problems. The chimney needed to be cleaned before she and Chloe could use it, there were three electrical outlets that didn't work and the faucet that connected the water to the washer had lost its turny thing.

A small list of easy repairs, she thought as the older man drove away. There hadn't been any roof leaks, the basement was dry and the furnace put out plenty of heat. Even better was the series of stickers on the side of it, showing that it had been serviced regularly.

"Feeling better?" Kenny asked as they stepped back inside.

She nodded. "Thank you so much. You were great."

He had been. He'd let her take the lead, but had stayed close by and asked plenty of sensible questions. He'd insisted she go into the attic herself to see into the deep corners so she understood about the insulation and venting. Because of him she now knew where the water and gas shutoffs were.

"As soon as I get the inspection report, I'll contact my real estate agent," she said. "We'll get a list to the seller."

"Don't forget about the chimney cleaning," he told her.

"I won't." She glanced at the big fireplace. "I'm going to have to read an article on how to build a fire. There's a special way, right? With twigs and regular wood?"

Kenny sighed. "It's kindling and I'll show you."

"You know how to build a fire?"

"I'm a man of many talents."

His voice was teasing and maybe a little sexy. While Bailey appreciated the thrill of her crush, right now practical Kenny was even more appealing.

"I'd like you to teach me," she told him. "I wonder if the local hardware store has classes on basic home repairs. I don't want to be one of those women who has a house and doesn't know how to do anything. I should be able to learn, right?"

"It's not hard. There are a couple of really good books on the subject. I'll get one for you." He winked. "Along with a set of pink tools."

She laughed. "I'd love pink tools. One of my favorite mystery books has a heroine with pink tools." They wandered into the kitchen. Mr. Jennings had checked all the appliances along with the drains. "My expertise is more cosmetic. I can patch and paint with the best of them, but anything behind the walls makes me nervous."

"What do you want to do before you move in?" he asked.

"The usual. Clean, paint." She set her large tote bag on the counter and pulled out a folder. "Chloe and I have been picking out paint colors." She fanned the squares onto the counter. "Usually I'm a big believer in painting a sample on the wall, but the seller probably wouldn't like that. I've talked to a few friends and they're open to a couple of days of helping me out. The plan is to close on Thursday, then start the intensive patching and sanding on Friday. We'll be painting by Saturday. The move will be Tuesday."

"A well-oiled machine."

"I hope. You know what can happen when you make plans." She pointed to the pale lavender sample. "That's the one Chloe wants for her room. I think it will be really pretty."

"She's getting the room with the dormer windows?" he asked.

"Right, with the little built-in desk between them. I thinking a good sanding will work wonders."

"You're right. The wood is pine. Then a nice clear finish, maybe cover it with a thick piece of glass."

She smiled up at him. "That's what I was thinking," she admitted. "I want to get her a new bedroom set. She's always had hand-me-downs. I've been saving and I've picked out a couple that would be great for her. I'm torn between letting her in on what I have planned and keeping it a secret."

"Let her be surprised. She'll like whatever you get."

"You think?" she asked eagerly. "I want her to love the house. We've always lived in apartments. Will and I never had the money for a down payment. I wouldn't have it now except there's a special program that grants money to people who wouldn't otherwise qualify. Mayor Marsha helped me apply and wrote a recommendation."

She told herself Kenny couldn't possibly be interested in her personal finances, but she couldn't seem to stop talking. "I know it's a great opportunity. I've always wanted to own a house. Nothing fancy, just our own home." A place to be safe, she thought wistfully.

"Makes sense," he told her. "I'm glad you're getting this place. Let me know if you want a guy's opinion on the furniture."

"You'd go with me?"

"Sure. Sounds like fun."

He was being *nice*. Nice was much more dangerous than handsome, she thought. Nice was real. Nice could make her want more than a crush.

Not possible, she told herself firmly. For all she knew, she was Kenny's good deed for the season. She had to remember that she was a not the kind of woman a famous former jock, who was also wealthy and successful in his business life, would be interested in. He probably dated supermodels or actresses. Or both.

"Should I warn you that seven-year-old girls generally adore all things princess?" she asked teasingly as they walked toward the front door.

"I would expect no less."

CHAPTER THREE

WITH TARYN OUT of town for a month, the responsibility of running the offices of Score fell to Kenny. He didn't mind picking up the slack. While the day-to-day minutia wasn't his favorite, he could handle it on a short-term basis. Sam's department took care of the cash flow and payroll and the vacations were already scheduled so Kenny figured he was in for an easy time.

He looked over the master calendar for their clients. There weren't any big presentations due in December and all the advertising had already been scheduled. The company would be closed from the Wednesday before Thanksgiving until the Sunday after, then for couple of weekdays before Christmas and New Year's. Easy duty, he thought, clicking on the partners' private calendar.

He saw Taryn was out for her honeymoon with Angel. She would miss Thanksgiving but be back before Christmas. Jack and Larissa were heading to Los Angeles for Thanksgiving, to be with Larissa's family. He frowned as he realized Sam would also be out of town in late November. He and Dellina were going to Lake Tahoe with Dellina's two sisters and their husbands. Which left Kenny on his own for the holiday.

He leaned back in his chair. His own family was mostly back east. His mom worked for the State Department and was in D.C. His sisters were in New York. He could easily go to either place and be welcome, but wasn't enthused about the idea. For Christmas they were all flying to Bali. Exotic locations were a family tradition. But for once, he was saying no. He wanted to stick around Fool's Gold. See the snow and the festivals. Plus he had his responsibilities with the toy drive.

His cell phone rang and he glanced at the screen. Speaking of responsibilities, he thought as Bailey's name came up.

"Hey."

"Hi. It's Bailey. The collection bins have been delivered. I've confirmed all the supplies we're going to need and wondered if you wouldn't mind picking them up."

"Not at all. Where are the bins?"

"The convention center. They have some space that isn't being used, so I parked them there. It will be easy access for our decorating and plenty of parking. We're at the north entrance. There are signs." She also told him where to pick up the supplies for sprucing the bins.

"I'm writing it down," he told her as he typed the information into his calendar. "We're delivering the decorated containers the Friday after Thanksgiving?"

"That's the plan. Oh, are you around? I didn't think to ask if you'd be traveling."

"I'm not."

There was a pause, as if she were thinking. "Okay. Great. Because I thought you might be with family. Or, you know, a girlfriend."

He leaned back in his chair and grinned. A not very

subtle attempt to extract information. "There's no girl-friend. And I'm staying in town for the holiday."

"Good," she said. The single word was followed by a quick intake of air. As if she was concerned he would think the "good" referred to his single state.

"I, ah, meant I appreciate your help. With the bins and all. I don't think I could have fit them in my car or carried them into the different stores. And with Sam and Jack both out of town, I'm not sure who I would have asked...." She paused again. "Kenny, all your friends are going to be gone. Where are you having Thanksgiving dinner?"

The previous topic had been a whole lot more interesting to him. Was it possible he made Bailey nervous? Better and better, he thought, before turning to her question.

"I don't have any plans."

"You can't be alone," she told him. "You're welcome to join Chloe and me. We're planning to go to the parade and then have a pretty traditional dinner. Nothing fancy."

He wasn't interested in fancy. It was highly overrated. He thought about the beautiful redhead and her adorable daughter and realized the invitation was something he could put on his list to be thankful for.

"I'd like that a lot," he told her.

"Really? I mean good. The parade is at noon. We'll be walking over about eleven-thirty, if you want to join us. Or after."

He smiled. "I'll be there at eleven-thirty. I'll bring pie."

"You don't have to."

"I want to. I'm looking forward to the day."

"Me, too."

THE FOOL'S GOLD convention center was an older building that lacked much in the way of architectural detail. But it served its purpose and right now that was way more important to Bailey than anything in the way of visual interest.

She had eight Sprouts, eight collection bins, plenty in the way of paint, markers, glitter and glue, and milling adults to corral.

The bins themselves were round, about four feet tall and wide enough to take a tricycle. The outsides were a stiff cardboard. Clean but not very holiday-like. That was going to change.

"Big crowd," Kenny said as he walked up to her. "I thought we'd get a few parents, but that was it. There have to be at least thirty people here."

"I put the word out," she said, trying to appear both pleasant and casual without giving away how her body had gone into hyperalert. He was so tall, she thought dreamily. So handsome. So *nice*.

The latter was the most dangerous. Because while his physical appeal was exciting, that kind of a crush wouldn't last. If he'd been a jerk or arrogant or the least bit annoying, she could have dismissed his blue eyes or easy smile. But the niceness was the real problem. The more she got to know Kenny, the more she liked him. He'd been incredibly helpful during the inspection and now he was here to help the Sprouts with their bins. If the man rescued a kitten from a tree, she was going to be a goner.

"People just showed up?" he asked.

"You sound surprised. You're here."

He gave her that slow smile of his. "I had no choice. Mayor Marsha terrifies me."

"I doubt that." She glanced at her watch. "Time to get serious. You want to take charge or should I?"

The smile widened. "I like a woman in charge. Go for it."

Bailey told herself not to read too much into his teasing comment as she walked to the front of the large conference room she'd chosen for the decorating.

"Good morning," she said loudly.

The conversation stilled as everyone turned toward her.

"Thanks so much for coming. Our goal this morning is to decorate our collection bins for the toy drive. There's one bin for each Sprout. We'd like the bins to reflect the individual Sprout's personality and family traditions for the holidays."

She went on to explain about the supplies and then broke everyone into groups. There was a mad rush for paint, glue and glitter. Gideon, a local late night DJ, strolled in with a portable music system.

"Mind if I set up?" he asked.

"I'd love it," she told him.

Kenny walked up to her. "So what am I supposed to do?" he asked. "I don't know anything about decorating a collection bin."

"It's okay. We're just here to supervise. Make sure no one goes wild with the glue sticks. Or you can help Chloe."

She pointed to the small group around her daughter. Madeline, who worked at the town's bridal boutique, had offered to be Chloe's substitute mom for the day. Bailey had been concerned that if she was supposed to be running the event, she wouldn't be able to help

Chloe very much. She'd gratefully accepted the offer of help.

Kenny looked around the large open space, then nodded toward Chloe. "I'll be over there."

"Hiding out?" she asked, her voice teasing.

"You know it."

She watched him go. He was a good guy, she thought wistfully. Before she could allow her thoughts to drift to more places they shouldn't, music filled the room. Gideon had brought a collection of upbeat holiday carols that soon had everyone singing while they worked.

Bailey walked to each of the Sprouts. Allison and her family and friends had come prepared with beautiful printouts of Russian nesting dolls.

"We're going to decorate the background, then glue on the pictures of the dolls," Allison told her. "We'll put clear varnish over the top."

"I like it," Bailey said.

She noticed Allison's mom had on a pretty beaded bracelet. For a second she thought it was an adult version of the bracelets the Sprouts wore—one with beads they earned for various projects.

Allison's mom saw her studying the piece and held out her wrist. "Isn't it wonderful? The beads represent all the colors of cancer awareness." She smiled at her husband. "It was a gift for my birthday."

The man in question smiled back. "You'd been hinting you wanted it for weeks. Don't give me too much credit."

They laughed together.

Bailey nodded and moved to the next group. But before she got there, she glanced back at the couple who had paused for a quick hug.

Their intimacy, their obvious love for each other, gave her a funny feeling in her stomach. Longing, she decided. She wanted what they had. She wanted to fall in love and stay in love for the rest of her life.

If any of her friends knew that was what she secretly longed for, they would be surprised. After all, she'd been married. Happily—or so it had appeared on the outside. But not in her heart, she thought. Will had been a terrific guy...just not for her.

Theirs hadn't been a bad marriage. Just not special. Maybe they'd married too young. Maybe they'd grown apart because of his frequent deployments. There could be a thousand reasons. Her only hope was that he'd never figured out that she wasn't happy.

THANKSGIVING MORNING DAWNED clear and cold. Bailey was up early—in part to prepare the turkey and stuffing, but mostly because she couldn't sleep.

She was going to spend the entire day with Kenny. The realization made her feel like she was sixteen again and had a mad crush on... She stopped applying her mascara so she could laugh without poking herself in the eye. Because the cliché that had come to mind was a mad crush on the football captain. And she would bet that Kenny had been just that. He was the kind of guy who would take charge of the team and lead them to the championship.

Not that she would have been there to see it, she reminded herself as she leaned into the mirror and continued applying her makeup. She would have been working as many hours as she could manage. There hadn't been time for things like football games.

It wasn't going to be like that for Chloe, she told

herself. Chloe was growing up in a community where she connected with people. Bailey wanted her daughter to feel safe and strong. Like she could do anything.

Bailey's grandmother had been willing to take in her only granddaughter when her own daughter had skipped town. The older woman had been loving but firm. The message was clear. Bailey was expected to take care of herself starting the day she turned eighteen. To that end, Bailey had put aside her dreams of a college education and had instead focused on afterschool jobs and learned to be an adult as early as possible. It wasn't until years later that she'd saved enough to go to community college.

She supposed the lessons had served her well. While she'd had to adjust when Will died, she'd known that even if she didn't always feel capable, she had the skill set to survive.

She put away her makeup and tidied the small bathroom. It was the only one in the apartment and they were going to have company. She paused to take in the pink-and-gold plastic shower curtain, the princess-printed towels Chloe loved and the turkey-shaped liquid soap dispenser on the small vanity. Probably not anything a man like Kenny was used to.

She walked into her bedroom and dressed. While the thought of getting all fancy and sexy for their visitor was fun, it simply wasn't going to happen. For one thing, she wasn't the sexy type. For another, she didn't actually own anything that fit that category. She was a single mom who worked for the mayor. Her clothes were either casual or for business. There wasn't room for much else in her life. She didn't date, so there was no LBD in the back of her closet.

She did have on a nice pair of dark wash jeans and a deep brown sweater with flecks of gold and green in the weave. The cotton blend was just thick enough to be warm but not so heavy as to add bulk. She thought maybe the colors were good for her complexion and brought out the green in her eyes. Of course while she was cooking she would be wearing an apron with a turkey on it. Not exactly a pattern designed to bring a man to his knees.

Bailey stepped in front of her dresser and started to take out the hot rollers. She was determined to have pretty waves in her hair. It was the best she could do. Not that Kenny would notice anything more than the fact that they were friends and he liked her kid. She was clear on that. Any crushes went strictly one way. But that was fine because her giddiness was enough for two.

The rest of the morning passed in a blur. Chloe got up and ate her breakfast while Bailey got the stuffing together. The scent of sautéing onions and celery filled the small kitchen. The turkey was already out of the refrigerator and in the roasting pan.

She'd made the sweet potato casserole the night before. It only had to be reheated, which would happen after the turkey had come out of the oven and was resting. The potatoes were peeled and sitting in water. She'd prepared the broccoli for the steamer. All that was left was for her to make her famous cheese biscuits and she would do that after the parade. They only took twenty minutes, which meant they would share space with the sweet potato casserole.

She would make gravy while Kenny carved and, with luck, they would sit down to a perfect dinner. Or just a good one, she thought happily. Because perfect was seriously overrated.

She'd already set the table, as well. The centerpiece was a sterling silver bowl with a candle in it. While they weren't going to decorate for Christmas until after the move, she'd put her favorite gingerbreadmen cookie jar on the old sideboard she'd picked up at a garage sale when they'd first moved to town.

"I don't remember the parade from last year," Chloe told her as she carried her cereal bowl to the sink.

"We went."

Although they hadn't stayed long. Chloe had said she wasn't feeling well and Bailey had brought her home. She'd known that what was bothering her daughter had little to do with a virus and everything to do with the loss of her father.

Chloe had come a long way, Bailey thought gratefully. She would always miss her dad, but she'd remembered how to be happy again. She had friends, she loved school and she was thriving. No mother could ask for more.

"I'm really excited to see it again," Chloe told her. "We're going to meet up with my friends, right? I told you where that was?"

Bailey smiled. "Yes, you did. About fourteen times. I know the exact corner where we're all watching the parade."

Because the Sprouts were going to view the festivities together. Bailey had a feeling there were going to be several speculative glances when the other mothers caught sight of Kenny.

Their guest arrived right on time. Bailey did her best to quell the butterflies practicing a two-step in her tummy. She drew in a breath for strength and maybe courage while Chloe raced across the carpet, yelling, "I'll get it! I'll get it!"

Her seven-year-old flung open the front door and beamed at Kenny. "You came! We're going to the parade and the turkey's in the oven and it's going to be delicious. You get to carve, which means you're going to make the slices for us."

Kenny stepped into the living room. He was tall and broad and the living room seemed smaller than usual with him in it. Bailey had the sense of being all thumbs and feet as she tried to smile and greet him.

"Right on time," she said with a smile.

"I heard there's a parade."

"At noon," Chloe said.

He wore a leather jacket and a scarf around his neck. In one hand he had a bottle of white wine and in the other, the promised pie. Only she didn't recognize the color of the box. She'd assumed he would go to Ambrosia Bakery, but their boxes were white with silver stripes.

He held up the wine. "This should go in the refrigerator."

"Sure." She motioned to the kitchen.

He walked in that direction and she followed. Once there she took the wine from him and fit it into her small refrigerator. He set the pie on the counter.

"Where did you get that?" she asked. "Is there somewhere new in town?"

He raised both eyebrows. "I'm wounded. You're assuming I bought it."

He shrugged out of his coat as he spoke. Underneath he wore a blue sweater the same color as his eyes. A white shirt peeked out from underneath. He had on jeans and boots. He was big and masculine and being this close to him made her thighs a little trembly.

She forced her attention back to his words. "You baked a pie?"

"Uh-huh."

"Not possible."

"It is. I'll have you know I'm an expert pie-maker."

Kenny? Ruggedly handsome, football star Kenny? "When did you learn?"

"When I was a kid. We were in Sweden and had a housekeeper who made the best pies. Her crust was a family recipe." He shrugged. "I was her favorite and for my ninth birthday she taught me how to make it. Once you have that down, the rest of the pie is easy."

Chloe scooted close to him and grinned. "I can earn a cooking bead when I'm a Sapling. Can you teach me?"

"Sure thing, munchkin."

He ruffled Chloe's hair.

The combination of the pet name and the affectionate gesture was nearly as bone-melty as the man's big hands, Bailey thought, aware that being around Kenny was like playing with fire. Exciting and ultimately dangerous. But it was just one day, right? And a holiday. Didn't everyone deserve a little something special on Thanksgiving?

CHAPTER FOUR

"WE HAVE A specific corner," Bailey told Kenny as they walked along with everyone else heading toward the center of town and the parade. Chloe had already spotted Layla and her mom and run ahead. "On Sixth between Frank and Katie Lanes."

"Okay," he said easily. "Why?"

"We're meeting the other Sprouts there. Chloe wants to watch the parade with her friends."

He nodded. "She's a bright, outgoing girl. I would guess she's popular."

Bailey stared at him.

"What?" he asked. "What did I say?"

"Nothing," she said, turning away, fighting unexpected tears.

"Bailey."

Kenny pulled her onto a driveway and stared at her. "Are you crying?"

She shook her head and sniffed. "No," she said firmly as she looked at him. "You're right. She's popular. She has sleepovers nearly every weekend and friends coming by and parties…" She stared at him, hoping her crush would distract her from her emotions, but for once Kenny was simply a friend.

"When Will died, she was devastated. She'd been counting the days until he got home. She'd been so excited to learn to read and write because she wanted to keep a diary for her dad. It was a list of things to tell him. What had happened to her in her day. Every night I helped her write a sentence or two so she could share it with him. Only he never came back."

She remembered the shock for both of them. The pain. And for her, the guilt.

"She started not doing as well in school. She was quiet and had nightmares. I was so scared for her. I took her to a child psychologist, who said she would come out of it, but I wasn't sure." She felt her eyes fill with tears again, and she tried to blink them away.

"Then I heard about the FWM. I signed up Chloe and she became an Acorn." She brushed the moisture from her cheek. "She blossomed and now my best girl is back. I'm so grateful."

Kenny cleared his throat. "I'm glad," he said, and then pulled her close.

The embrace was unexpected and warm and comforting and just a little exciting. Bailey let herself lean against him for a second. He was a lot taller than her and he held her easily. He smelled good, too, she thought. Now if only he would confess his undying lust for her, the moment would be complete.

But he didn't and soon they were walking toward the parade route again.

Chloe found her friends and Bailey greeted the other parents. She introduced Kenny and did her best to avoid the questioning looks. At the bin-decorating party, Kenny had explained he was filling in for Taryn. No one had thought they were together. And they weren't, Bailey reminded herself. He was just a friend coming over for Thanksgiving.

Fortunately the parade started before anyone could pull her aside and ask about things she couldn't answer. The first entry was a banner carried by two high school kids from the marching band. The annual Fool's Gold Thanksgiving parade had begun.

Mayor Marsha rode by in an old convertible, followed by several smaller versions of the famous balloons from the Macy's parade.

"Chloe's going to watch the repeat of that later," Bailey told Kenny. "Just so you're prepared."

"I look forward to it."

All the right words, she thought with a sigh. No doubt he had plenty of practice.

The marching band came next, loudly playing their version of "Jingle Bells." Farther up the street came murmurs. Bailey grinned at Kenny.

"It's Priscilla," she said happily, remembering the only part of the parade that had made Chloe smile last year. "She's an elephant. She'll be dressed as Santa."

He looked over her head, then frowned. "How do they do that?"

"I heard the costume was in sections and held together with Velcro."

He looked over the crowd and shook his head. "Well, I'll be da—" He glanced at the Sprouts crowding around and pointing. "I'll be, ah…"

"Let it go," she told him. "There's no good substitute."

He smiled at her. "You got that right." He turned back to Priscilla. "Not something you see every day."

"No. I heard that she has several custom blankets to keep her warm. The local knitters made them for her."

"Gotta love the town. Did you know about the camel?"

"There's a camel?" Chloe asked eagerly and tried to see.

Kenny picked her up as if she weighed nothing. Her daughter pointed and laughed.

"Mom, look! There's Reno the pony and a camel. They're dressed as elves."

Bailey waited until that part of the parade came into view. Sure enough Priscilla had her elf friends with her, along with wagons from Castle Ranch.

"I've never seen a camel dressed as an elf," she said, shaking her head.

A couple of fire trucks—all decked out for the holidays—were next. There were small trees and lots of stars, including several Jewish stars.

An hour later, the parade had ended and the three of them made their way back to the apartment. The smell of turkey greeted them as they entered the living room. Chloe carefully hung up her coat before heading to the TV to find the replay of the Macy's parade. Kenny helped Bailey out of hers.

Was it her imagination or did his hands linger on her shoulders? She knew the answer, of course, but a girl could dream. And when the man in question was as good as this one, she supposed dreaming was inevitable.

THE FINAL PREPARATIONS for dinner went as smoothly as Bailey could have hoped. Kenny wasn't just a guy who knew how to make a pie, he was also an expert turkey carver. His skill made her wonder about the other women in his life—both who they were and the actual number of them.

The cheese biscuits and sweet potato casserole went into the oven at the same time. She stirred the gravy while Kenny poured wine for the two of them and sparkling apple cider for Chloe.

The table was big enough to seat six. Bailey put Kenny at the end. She sat on his right while Chloe was across from her on his left. Their place settings were surrounded by bowls and platters and steaming stacks of delicious food.

When they'd taken their places, Kenny surprised her by reaching for her hand and Chloe's, then saying grace.

When they'd filled their plates, she turned to him. "You really learned how to bake pies in Sweden?"

"I did." He passed Chloe the stuffing. "My mom worked for the State Department. We lived all around the world until I was twelve."

"Did you miss your friends?" Chloe asked.

"I made new friends."

Her eyes widened. "Was it hard?"

"Sometimes. Especially if I had to learn a new language. But I was used to it." He looked at Bailey. "We moved back to the States when I was twelve. My parents wanted to settle in one place so my sisters and I could have continuity."

"How many sisters?" she asked.

"Three. I'm in the middle."

That must have been nice, she thought. She would have liked siblings. And for Chloe to have had at least one brother or sister. Although the odds of that were getting more unlikely by the year.

"I'd like a sister," Chloe said. "I guess a brother would be okay, too. Daddy always told me…" Her voice trailed off as she stared at her plate.

"What, honey?" Bailey asked gently.

Chloe raised her gaze. "He said that no matter how many other kids you had, that I would always be his best girl. Because I was first." She worried her lower lip. "I feel sad because I don't remember him so much."

Bailey reached across the table and touched her daughter's hand. Before she could figure out what to say, Kenny spoke.

"It sounds like he really loved you."

Chloe nodded.

"And you loved him."

Another nod.

"Isn't that the most important part? Knowing you loved each other?" He reached for the sweet potatoes.

Chloe looked to her for confirmation. Bailey nodded.

"He lives on in your heart. All the people we love do."

"For always?" Chloe asked.

"For always," Bailey promised.

AFTER THEY FINISHED dinner, Bailey kept waiting for Kenny to leave. But he stuck with them through the second half of the football game and Chloe's movie pick of the evening, *The Muppet Christmas Carol*. About eight-thirty, her daughter finally wound down from the excitement and zonked out on the sofa. Bailey tried not to let her heart get all twisty when Kenny carried Chloe to bed.

But there was something magical about a big, strong

guy carrying a little girl. So it wasn't completely her fault that she was both breathless and hopeful when they returned to the living room.

He was going to leave, she told herself. It was time for him to go. They were only friends, so she would be very, very foolish to expect anything other than a handshake. And while she didn't expect more, she was willing to admit she *wanted* more.

But instead of leaving, Kenny returned to the sofa. Bailey settled on the opposite end and faced him.

"Your pie was delicious," she said into the silence.

"Thanks. The whole meal was great. Thanks for inviting me."

"We had fun. You're good with Chloe."

Instead of smiling, he stared past her, as if seeing something she couldn't. "I like kids."

"Do you have any?" she asked, realizing how little she knew about his past. She really had to spend some quality time on the internet, using Google to do some research on him.

"No," he said firmly. "I did."

She stared at him. "Oh, no. What happened? I'm sorry."

He looked at her. "No one died. It wasn't like that."

She didn't understand. If no one had died... She waited, not sure what to ask, or if she should. His expression was tight—both pained and angry, she thought.

"High school was easy," he said with a shrug, his gaze once again looking past her. "I liked girls and they liked me. I was in and out of what I called love every couple of weeks."

"Sounds like fun."

He glanced at her and smiled. "Yeah. *Fun* is a good word for it." The smile faded. "In college, I got a little more serious. The girlfriends lasted months instead of weeks. But no one stuck. Natalie was one of them. We dated for a few weeks. It was great and then it ended. When I ran into her the following spring, it was obvious that she was pregnant."

Bailey stiffened. She hadn't seen that coming.

"She'd never tried to get in touch with me, which pissed me off," he continued. "I could count as well as the next guy. She was about five months along. The kid was mine. I proposed and she refused. She said she didn't want to get married that way. So we moved in together."

He shifted a little, then looked at Bailey. "I'd been drafted at that point. I was excited about graduating and starting my NFL career. I didn't take as much time with Natalie as I should have. I wasn't home much. I didn't run around with other women, but there were a lot of things to do."

She nodded, not sure what he wanted to hear. Or where the story was going.

"The baby—a boy—was born while I was playing. Natalie didn't call to tell me she was in labor. I rushed home as soon as I found out, but Natalie wasn't all that eager to keep me at home, so I went back to work. Time passed. We still weren't married, but we had James and that was enough for me."

He drew in a breath. "I spent all my free time with him. He was a great kid. Smart and loving. I was so damned proud. Things with Natalie were up and down, but I figured that's what happened when you were in a serious relationship. When James was three, every-thing changed."

She looked at him, wanting desperately to hear and almost afraid of what he was going to tell her.

"How?" she asked softly.

"I got hurt. My first serious injury. I missed five games. While I was recovering, Natalie came to me. She said that the reason she'd never wanted to marry me was that she was in love with another man. A married man. He kept promising to leave his wife for her and he finally did. Natalie was leaving me to go be with him."

His expression turned fierce. "It wasn't good news, but I was okay with that. We definitely weren't in love then. I told her I wanted custody of James. That's when she said he wasn't mine. The other guy was the father."

Bailey sucked in a breath. "Was she telling the truth?"

"Yeah. That's the hell of it. I got an attorney and we arranged for a DNA test. But when it came back...I had no legal claim on him. She took him and walked out and I never saw him again."

Bailey wanted to go to him, to hold him and offer comfort. Only there wasn't anything she could say.

She tried to imagine what it would be like if she lost Chloe. But even thinking it was possible was too painful to consider.

"I'm sorry," she whispered.

"Me, too. The thing is, you're great and I like you a lot."

An unexpected statement that should have thrilled her. Except for the single word at the end.

But.

He didn't have to say it. She heard it loud and clear. She was the woman with a kid who wasn't his. Kenny had been burned that way once before. He wasn't going to risk it again.

"I understand," she told him, feeling disappointed and more than a little hurt. "It makes perfect sense."

"I wanted you to know why," he said.

She stood. "And now I do. Thank you. Chloe and I had a great time today."

"I did, too."

He rose and there was an awkward moment as they both stared at each other. He gave her a half smile and reached for his coat.

Bailey held open the front door, briskly wished him good-night, then shut it behind him. When she was alone, she leaned against the door and told herself it was for the better.

Only she didn't feel better. She felt a little sick to her stomach. Because she thought maybe what he'd been saying was that under other circumstances, he might have been interested in her. That he might have thought she was his type. And knowing that made not having any chance at him just a little more difficult to take.

CHAPTER FIVE

ONE OF THE advantages of living in Fool's Gold was that no matter what horrible thing might be happening in your personal life, there was also something in town to serve as a distraction.

Despite having not slept much the night before, Bailey greeted the morning with as much optimism as she could muster. For one thing, she had a great life. She had her daughter, friends and a job she loved, and in less than two weeks, she would be moving into her first ever, very own home. It was enough, she told herself firmly. She didn't need a man—not even one as tempting as Kenny.

She and Chloe had breakfast, then she dropped her daughter off at a friend's house, where she would spend the day. For her part, Bailey was going to head into town. All the stores would be decorating for the holidays and that was fun to watch. There was also a new store opening, and she was meeting Isabel there. Tomorrow, she and Chloe would go look at all the store windows and stay for the town's tree lighting.

Back at her place, she made quick work of cleaning the kitchen, then dove into her closet. She wanted to clear out as many things as possible before the move. She and Chloe had already done her daughter's room. Chloe had given up a couple of boxes of toys to be donated. Clothes that were too small would also go to charity.

When Bailey's cell phone rang, she was trying to decide if she was ever going to lose the twenty pounds necessary for her to get back into several pairs of jeans she owned or if she should simply donate them.

"Hello?" she said without glancing at the display.

"Hey."

All it took was a single word spoken by a specific man. Her slightly fake good mood shattered and the jeans dropped to the carpet. She sank onto the bed.

"Kenny."

A thousand emotions struggled to find room inside. She thought of the child he'd lost and how she would never have guessed he suffered such a tragedy. She thought of the way his smile made her toes curl and how knowing he was a great guy made her crush just a little harder to get over.

"I've got all the bins in place," he said.

It took her a second to mentally switch gears. Right, the toy drive. That was still their responsibility.

"Thank you. There's a schedule for collection. You have that, right?"

"Yeah. I know my days."

"The parents helping do, too. I appreciate your help with all this."

"We're in it together."

The truth, but when said in his low, sexy voice… Well, she wanted it to mean a lot more than it did.

"We're still on for Sunday?" he asked.

He'd offered to take her to Sacramento to look at bedroom furniture for Chloe. She needed to get her order placed and thought the Black Friday craziness would be over by then. Only after last night, she'd assumed she would be on her own.

"You don't mind?"

"I'd like to go with you," he told her. "We're friends, Bailey. I don't want that to change."

Friends was better than nothing, she told herself. Friends was the mature response to their situation. Friends was enough. Although that last one might be stretching the truth a tiny bit.

"Thank you," she said. "I'd love the input. Chloe's going out to Castle Ranch for riding lessons with several of her friends, so the timing is perfect."

"I'll pick you up at noon."

"I'll be ready."

"See you then. 'Bye."

He hung up and she did the same.

This was good, she told herself. She and Chloe would go to church and be back in time for an early lunch before her daughter headed out on her own adventure. Bailey and Kenny would go to Sacramento and buy furniture. It would be nice. Pleasant. Friends hanging out together. Nothing more. No matter how much she wanted a little "more" in her life.

DIAMONDS AND PURLS, a yarn and bead shop close to Brew-haha, had been open all of two hours and was already packed. Bailey sipped her cup of complimentary hot cocoa as she studied the bins filled with what seemed like hundreds of types of yarn. There were different weights and textures, dozens of colors. Yarn that was impossibly soft and yarn that glittered.

On the other side of the store were the beads. Millions of beads, she thought with a grin. Inventory in this place would be complicated.

"I love it," Isabel said, coming up next to her and linking arms. "Doesn't this place make you want to be creative?"

Bailey smiled at her friend. "Are you saying you're going to take a class?"

The tall blonde shook her head. "No. I'm going to *think* about taking a class. There's a difference."

"A big one," Bailey told her. "Chloe and I already talked about taking a beginner's knitting class together."

Isabel tried not to look horrified. "I'm sure it will be fun."

Noelle Boylan, owner of The Christmas Attic, joined them. She, too, was a pretty blonde. Her usually slim physique had a little more curve to it these days, along with a definite baby bump.

"Great store," she said, then sipped her hot chocolate. "I miss coffee. And wine."

"How are you feeling?" Bailey asked.

"Better. Almost four months to the day, like you said."

Noelle had spent the first three months of her pregnancy feeling nauseous. Bailey had gone through the same thing. By the fourth month, everything calmed down.

Noelle grinned. "Gabriel is going crazy, though. I think it's harder for him because he's a doctor. He has just enough training to make him totally freak out every single day."

"But it's nice, right?" Isabel said, eyeing Noelle's stomach. "Having him hover."

"Most of the time. Except when I want to smother him with a pillow."

They laughed. Bailey joined in, even though her feelings were bittersweet. She'd spent much of her pregnancy alone. Will had been deployed. He'd arrived back in time for the birth, but hadn't been with her through her pregnancy. He hadn't seen her as she'd gotten bigger or felt the baby move for the first time.

Thinking about the past made her wonder if things would have been different if he'd been home more. Or would they still have grown apart?

It was a question she could never answer, she reminded herself. Will was gone and she and Chloe were making a life without him.

"The decorating is starting," Noelle said. "For the town's window display contest."

"You've had your plan figured out for weeks," Isabel teased. "What's the big deal about winning this year?"

Noelle's gaze intensified. "Seriously? You have to ask? If I'm entering, I'm entering to win."

"There's the spirit of Christmas," Isabel teased.

Noelle ignored her and turned to Bailey. "One of the windows is going to be a fantasy winter wonderland, but with a twist. All the decorations are funny and quirky. Like a pickle dressed up as Santa."

"Chloe and I can't wait to see it."

"Good." She glanced around the store. "I want to go introduce myself to the owner. Her name is Lora, right?"

Bailey nodded. "Yes. I've met her a couple of times and she's really nice. I'm so glad she and her family moved to Fool's Gold."

Isabel sighed. "You're an annoyingly pleasant person, Bailey Voss."

Bailey grinned. "Why, thank you."

KENNY DROPPED OFF the toys and carefully secured the lock on the trailer. Each of the collection bins he'd visited had been overflowing. He had a feeling the trailer would be full long before their deadline. From what he could see, the people in Fool's Gold had a way of coming through for a cause.

He drove to Bailey's apartment and walked upstairs to her unit. Anticipation burned hot inside, but he ignored the sensation. He'd deliberately made his position clear with her. As much out of self-defense as because it was the right thing to do. Even though he found Bailey funny, sweet and sexy, he couldn't take the chance. Not now, not ever.

She opened her door, her coat in her hand.

"You're right on time," she said with a smile. "It must be all that sports training. Having to be at practice or games when they said."

He nodded because the punch to his gut made it impossible to speak.

There should have been nothing amazing about her. She wore jeans and a green sweater that matched her eyes. She had on some makeup and her hair tumbled past her shoulders in loose curls. Nice but not mind-shattering.

Except she was. The curves alone would drive a stronger man to his knees and Kenny was willing to admit that when it came to Bailey he was as weak as a kitten. Then there was the smile that tugged at the corners of her mouth. A mouth he wanted to cover with his own, explore, tease, nibble and lick. He wanted to taste her, hold her, strip her naked and—

He sucked in a breath and steered his wayward mind back to reality. Naked wasn't going to happen. Bailey was his friend. He should think of her as someone like a grandmother. A lovely woman and nothing more.

"The bins were full," he said as they went down the stairs. "At this rate, it's not going to take long to fill up the trailer."

"I'm glad. I was hoping I wouldn't have to activate the phone tree and make an appeal."

He held open the passenger side door for her. "There's a phone tree?"

She grinned. "Really? You have to ask?"

She was standing close enough that he could breathe in a sweet scent. A little floral with a hint of vanilla. He would bet her skin was soft and warm and for a second he allowed himself to wonder if she was quiet when she made love or if she moaned. Because he liked it best when a woman moaned.

"By the way, Chloe doesn't know," she told him.

He blinked, trying to find his way back to the conversation.

"About the furniture?" he asked, the pieces falling into place.

She nodded and slid onto the seat. "I told her we were shopping for furniture, but she thinks we're getting a new coffee table. I want it to be a surprise."

He closed her door and walked around to his side. "I won't say anything," he promised as he settled next to her.

They headed out of town and got onto the freeway toward Sacramento. There was a sign on the side of the road announcing the opening of the Lucky Lady Casino seasonal ice-skating rink.

"We should do that," Bailey said. "I mean Chloe and me. Go ice skating. I haven't in years. Not since I was a teenager. Do you think I'll remember how?"

"Sure. I skate. I'll take the two of you, if you'd like. I can catch you if you fall."

Bailey glanced at him, then away. "I wouldn't want you to hurt yourself," she murmured.

"Not possible. I'm athletic."

She laughed. "I've heard that somewhere. You used to play sports of some kind?"

"Very funny."

She grinned. "I can be." The smile faded. "Okay, I'll admit it. I'm nervous about buying furniture. I know this is going to sound crazy, but I've never bought this kind of stuff before. Not new, I mean. I've always had hand-me-downs or something from the thrift store. When Will and I were first married, we didn't have any money. And later, we moved around a lot. When Chloe came along, plenty of friends had cribs and changing tables."

"How did you and Will meet?" he asked.

She glanced at him. "In high school. He was a little nerdy and funny and crazy about me. We were friends more than boyfriend-girlfriend. I was focused on saving enough money to go to college."

"Was that your dream?"

She nodded. "I grew up in small town in Ohio. My mom took off when I was a baby and my grandmother raised me. She was a good woman, but she'd been through some tough times. I knew from an early age that I was expected to be on my own when I turned eighteen."

He couldn't imagine that. He knew that if he told his parents he wanted to move back now, they would welcome him with open arms. Not that it was ever going to happen.

"I had a couple of jobs all through high school. I figured I'd work for two years, save enough to get through community college. Will always told me I could do it. He had a different path. He wanted to join the army."

"A different way out."

"Exactly." She shifted in her seat. "The night we graduated, Will proposed. I was stunned. I said no and he left for boot camp. A couple of weeks later, I realized I had stronger feelings for him than I thought. I drove down to where he was and we talked for a long time. By the end of the weekend, we were engaged. After we got married, I went to community college and worked and he was deployed."

"Then Chloe came along."

She smiled. "Yeah. She was a surprise, but a good one."

"Did you get your degree?"

"Not completely. I have my AA, but not my bachelor's. My plan is to start taking night classes next fall. Chloe will be a little older and we'll be settled in our house."

"You'll get there," he said. "You have a plan."

She laughed. "Yes, it's all about having the right plan. I've learned that over the years. Partly I want to do for myself, but also for Chloe. I want her to see me working hard and succeeding. I think it's a good lesson for her."

Everything about Bailey was a good lesson for her daughter, he thought. She was impressive, how she'd kept it all together. He supposed that was one of the reasons he liked her so much.

They drove into Sacramento and found the furniture store. As they walked inside, Bailey pulled a small notebook out of her bag.

"I did some online looking," she told him. "I thought it would make this go faster. I didn't want to be overwhelmed by choices."

"It's kids' furniture. How many choices could there be?"

Her expression turned pitying. "And here I thought you were a man of the world."

He held open the door. "I am."

"We'll see."

Fifteen minutes later, he had to admit he was in over his head. There was a whole floor of kids' furniture. Fortunately they could avoid the section for babies, but still. There was plenty from which to choose.

One entire corner was devoted to princess beds. Some had canopies and others had scrollwork on the head and footboards. There was white furniture and gilded furniture and padded chairs in the shape of high-heeled shoes.

Bailey stared at all the fantasy setups, with gauzy bedding and fluffy pillows. "I so want to get her this," she murmured. "But it's silly. I need to find something she can use until she goes to college. In a few years, she'll hate her princess bed."

Kenny wanted to tell her to go for it, but he knew that wasn't practical. Bailey worked for the city. It wasn't as if she was going to suddenly double her salary in the next few years, and furniture cost money.

"Bedding isn't that expensive," he said. "What about getting a more sensible setup, then buying a fun princess comforter. That wouldn't cost much to replace in a couple of years."

She nodded slowly. "I could do that. Add some pillows." She smiled at him. "How do you know about bedding making a difference in a room?"

"I have sisters and a mom."

"They'll be so pleased to know some of what they said got through."

Her gentle teasing made him want to pull her close. It made him want to kiss her and maybe buy whatever she thought Chloe would like...his treat. Instead he stuffed his hands into his pockets and jerked his head toward the rest of the floor.

"Let's go be practical."

A little while later, they stood in front of what looked to be the perfect compromise.

"Are you sure?" Bailey asked, then nibbled on her bottom lip.

"Positive." Kenny pushed a few more buttons on his phone, then turned the screen toward her. "Look. There are all kinds of hardware available." He pointed to a bright daisy knob. "These are eight dollars apiece but you only need seven or eight of them. You could change them out if you needed to."

She nodded slowly, as if working through the problem. "I like the natural a lot. It's a pretty color and a nice, neutral backdrop for her room. She wants it painted lavender."

The bedroom set was both whimsical and practical, he thought, studying the design. A unique bunk-bed set. The bottom was a full-sized bed with a small night table tucked next to it. On the left side were stairs leading to a twin upper bunk that went across the top of the full, so the beds formed a *T*. The best part was the storage. Each stair was a drawer and there was a big drawer under the full-sized mattress.

"It's more than I had planned to spend," she murmured. "But with the free financing for a year, I could make it work. I just think this one is perfect."

He moved next to her and put his hand on her arm. For a second he allowed himself to get lost in the feel of her warm skin. Then he shook off the guy moment and focused on the problem at hand.

"Don't shoot the messenger," he began. "Taryn wants to get you a housewarming present and she put me in charge."

Bailey stared at him. "I don't know if I should laugh or be afraid."

"That was my reaction, too. I know she would really like to get Chloe a great princess bedding set. Like that one we saw by the stairs."

They'd seen it on the way in. It was all ruffles and lace, done in various shades of pink, blue or purple. There were matching pillows and a great lamp.

Bailey surprised him by turning away. "Did Taryn really say that?" she asked, before holding up her hand. "Never mind. I know the answer. She is so nice to me."

She turned back and he saw tears in her eyes.

She drew in a breath. "If it was for me, I would have told her no, but for Chloe, I accept. I'm going to get this one. She'll love it and it will last her through college and she can have friends over."

He couldn't help himself. He put his arm around her and drew her close. "You're a good mom, Bailey."

"I think I'm like most moms out there. We love our kids and want the best for them."

For a second, she leaned into him. He felt the weight of her body and wanted to pull her even closer. He wanted... Well, he was clear on that and how he couldn't risk it. Not just for himself, but for Bailey, too. She was the kind of woman a man got serious about, and he knew the danger of that.

"Let's go talk to the sales guy," he said, steering her in that direction. "While you're filling out the paperwork, I'm going to check online for some princess-worthy drawer pulls."

CHAPTER SIX

KENNY WAVED JACK into the office. His business partner sat down and waited until Kenny hung up the phone.

"You make your calls?" he asked.

Jack nodded. "They mostly don't care. For some reason they think you can do as good a job. Idiots."

"You'd be happier if they were threatening to leave the company?" Kenny asked with a grin.

"You know it."

Jack was leaving Score at the end of the year. Although he'd been a founding partner with Taryn, he'd been offered a coaching job at Cal U Fool's Gold. And not just any coaching job. He was going to start the football program, from the ground up. A challenging project, but one Jack would see to the end. Kenny was confident the Cal UFG Warriors would have a winning season within three years of their first game.

In the meantime, Jack was contacting all their clients and letting them know he was moving on. Kenny followed up to assure them that he was committed to staying with Score. So far no one had minded about the change.

"It's going to be strange not to be here anymore," Jack told him. "But I'm excited about what's ahead of me."

"Let me know if you need any help."

"You want to coach?"

"No," Kenny said with a laugh. "But I'm happy to listen and offer advice."

"Sam said the same thing," Jack admitted. "You're good men."

Kenny held up a hand. "You're not going to turn into a woman, are you? And start talking about your feelings?"

"No. Sam and Dellina and Larissa and I are thinking of going up to Henri's for a fancy dinner." Jack rolled his eyes. "Larissa says they decorate the whole resort and she wants to see it. Dellina agrees. Sam and I are going along because we love our women. You two want to join us?"

Kenny frowned at his friend. You two? As in…

"You and Bailey," Jack clarified. "Before she left, Taryn mentioned the two of you were working on the toy drive together. She's fun, right?" He shook his head. "Or is it a problem because of Chloe?"

Because Jack knew about Kenny's past and how he avoided single mothers.

"We're friends," Kenny said. "I could ask her if she'd like to go."

"It's up to you. You could fly in one of your models. Of course the dinner would be wasted. Doesn't it bother you how they only fake eat? No actual food passes their lips."

"Just because you're engaged to a regular woman now, don't pretend you didn't date models in your day."

Jack's smile turned smug. "I dated everyone in my day. I've matured and I know better now. I have the best woman on the planet and I'm going to do everything in my power to make her happy for the rest of her life. That and win a national football championship."

"As long as you have your priorities," Kenny said. "I'll talk to Bailey and let you know what she says."

"Good."

Jack rose and left.

Kenny tried to return his attention to his computer, but what he saw instead of the screen was Bailey. He would like to take her to the dinner. As long as they were both clear on the rules.

BAILEY WATCHED KENNY carefully tighten her daughter's skates. There was something so sweet and sexy about a big guy helping a little girl, she thought. Those large hands and those little skates. Not that this was anything but friends getting together, she reminded herself. Kenny was a good guy. Good enough to warn her that he wasn't interested in her romantically.

For a brief moment, she allowed herself to fantasize about telling him she didn't need the romance. That an hour or two in his bed was all the holiday cheer she needed. But as fun as that sounded, she knew it was completely unrealistic. She'd only been with one man in her life. And that was her husband...after the wedding. She was old-fashioned.

As much as she might miss the things a man could do to her body, she couldn't do those things lightly. She might not have to be married the second time around, but she knew she would have to be in love. And falling for Kenny would be an emotional disaster.

So she would simply enjoy the sight of him kneeling on the ice while Chloe tried to stand on the slippery surface, all the while balanced on a blade.

Her daughter hung on to his hands as she got her balance. Bailey finished with her own skates and stood. She wobbled a bit, then found her center of gravity and moved toward Chloe.

Her daughter stared at her. "Mommy, you can skate!"

"Sort of. It's been a while, but it's coming back."

She moved to Chloe's side and held out her hand. "Let's try moving. It's easier than standing still."

Kenny stood. He, of course, had no problem skating. He moved with a grace and sureness that she admired. At the same time she wondered what it must have been like to be so physically gifted. Not that she would ever know.

He was on Chloe's other side. Her daughter took his hand and together the three of them started across the ice.

The rink had been set up at the far end of the resort's parking lot. There was a canvas structure with sides that could be rolled up when the weather was cold enough—like tonight. The temperature had to be in the twenties. They could see their breath and the stars overhead. So far it had been cold, but they hadn't gotten snow.

"Try bending your knees a little," Kenny was saying. "It'll help you balance. If you start to fall, don't wave your arms. Get closer to the ground. Lowering your center of gravity will help keep you balanced."

When they both stared at him, he shrugged. "I used to have Rollerblades. I can't help it. I'm good at stuff like this."

Chloe pulled free of their hands. "I want to try it on my own."

She moved her legs and skated a little away from them. She was surprisingly steady. Either Kenny's athletic prowess was rubbing off, or Chloe had inherited her skill from Will.

The three of them made a few turns around the rink. There were other families out, along with teenagers on dates and younger kids in groups. Chloe caught sight of a couple of her friends and asked if she could skate with them.

"Sure," Bailey told her. "Just don't leave the rink."

"I won't," Chloe called over her shoulder as she hurried away.

Kenny sighed heavily. "They grow up so fast."

Bailey laughed. "They do."

He tucked her arm into the crook of his arm, which meant they were skating close together. She told herself to go with the moment and not read too much into his actions. He was, after all, basically a nice man.

"I have confirmation on the bedroom set delivery," she said. "It's the Monday before the move."

"That's good. So she'll have it for her first night in the new house."

Bailey nodded. She still couldn't believe her good fortune—being able to buy her very own house. Whatever else happened to her in her life, she would always have that accomplishment.

"There's going to be a dinner," Kenny said abruptly. "With Jack and Larissa and Sam and Dellina." He looked at her. "I'd like to take you. It's at Henri's."

Bailey stopped and looked at him. Henri's was a fancy restaurant, at a very nice hotel up on the mountain. Something hot and hopeful bubbled to life inside of her.

"If we could go as friends," he added carefully.

The bubbles all popped. She forced herself not to let her disappointment show.

She should be grateful, she told herself sternly. Kenny had told her he had issues with her being a single mom and they made sense. He wasn't playing games or trying to trick her or being anything but friendly, open and honest.

"Dinner sounds like fun," she said. "I don't have a thing to wear, but I'll figure it out."

"I have a spare jersey." He winked. "It'll be really big on you but with a belt and some accessories..."

She swatted at his arm. "Thanks, but no. And for the record, a belt *is* an accessory."

"Really? I thought it was just a belt."

They stared at each other for a second. Tension crackled between them—at least on her side. She doubted he noticed. Although if he did, maybe he would kiss her. Because while she wasn't up to casual sex, a kiss could be nice. It had been a long time between kisses.

Worried he could read her mind, she quickly turned away. Too quickly, it turned out, as her foot slid out from under her.

She instinctively raised her arms as she tried to find her balance. Kenny reached for her but she was too far away. She staggered a couple of steps, started to fall, then felt a pain in the side of her ankle as she went down.

Her first thought was that the ice was both cold and hard. Her second was that she looked like an idiot. Ankle concerns came in a distant third.

Kenny knelt next to her. "Are you okay? What hurts? Your wrist? Your hip?"

She tried to figure out how to stand without falling again. "I'm okay. I lost my balance." Probably not in an elegant way, either. She shifted to put her weight on her skates, only to gasp as searing heat ripped through her left ankle. Okay, that wasn't good at all.

Kenny reached for her foot. "You hurt yourself."

"Just a little."

"You winced."

"I'm wimpy."

He had her skate off in five seconds and then removed her sock. The skin around her ankle bone seemed a little puffy, but it was a small price to pay for the feel of those strong, large hands touching her.

Kenny had her move her toes, then her whole foot. The sharp pain had faded to something fairly dull.

"I'm pretty sure I can stand," she said, reaching for her sock.

"Let's get you to a bench and take it from there."

He put the sock back on her foot, then stood and reached for her. She shrank away.

"What are you doing?"

"Helping you to your feet."

She was tall and carrying an extra twenty-five pounds. "I'm okay. I'll just crawl over." The bench wasn't that far away. "I don't want you to hurt yourself."

He scowled at her. "I can bench-press over three hundred pounds. I can get you to your feet."

His tone said he'd been insulted. This probably wasn't the time to explain she didn't doubt his strength—that she was more concerned about her own personal bulk. Either way, the ice was really cold and she could see Chloe skating toward them.

"Okay," she said quietly. "I appreciate the help."

He bent down and actually picked her up. Like she was as light as a rag doll. Then the man carried her to the bench.

It all happened so fast, she didn't know what to think. Once second she was on ice, the next she was perched on the bench.

Chloe hurried over. "Mom, what happened?"

"I fell. I'm fine."

"She sprained her ankle," Kenny said. "I want you checked out. We're going to the hospital. They'll take an X-ray, just to be sure." He pulled Chloe close. "Don't worry, kid. I'll be with both you every step of the way."

ONE X-RAY, A car ride and second trip in Kenny's arms as he carried her up to her apartment later, Bailey found herself relaxing on her bed. The E.R. doctor had confirmed a mild sprain. Bailey was to take it easy for a couple of days. She had crutches, a compression bandage and instructions to use ice and an anti-inflammatory. The doctor had assured her she wouldn't need the crutches more than a day or two. He'd also been impressed by Kenny's skill in wrapping the compression bandage. No doubt the former NFL player had a lot of practice.

Kenny and Chloe disappeared into the kitchen only to return a few minutes later with a tray of hot chocolate and several cookies on a plate.

"We need a snack," Kenny told her.

Chloe climbed up next to her mother while Kenny sat in the chair by Bailey's small corner desk. He dwarfed the furniture, which should have looked silly but for some reason she found comforting.

Bailey accepted the mug of hot chocolate and wondered at the improbability of the situation. She'd thought about getting Kenny into her bedroom and it had happened. But somehow this was not the scenario she'd fantasized about.

"Are you feeling okay?" Chloe asked anxiously.

"Honey, I'm fine." Bailey stroked her daughter's hair. "I fell and I feel foolish. My ankle will be a lot better by tomorrow."

"You have to use crutches."

"Not for long. People get hurt and then they get better."

Chloe nodded, but didn't look convinced. Bailey was sure it was harder for her than for most kids. She'd already lost her father—she wouldn't want to see her mother as vulnerable.

"I'm staying," Kenny announced.

Bailey blinked at him. "Excuse me?"

"I'm going to sleep on the couch."

A thrilling thought, but no. "That's not necessary. I'm mobile."

"What if you need to get down the stairs in the middle of the night? Your apartment is on the second floor and there's no elevator. I'm staying." He shrugged. "You can't say no. You're not in a position to throw me out. You can barely walk." He winked at Chloe. "I can't see your mom putting me on her shoulder and hauling me down the stairs, can you?"

Chloe giggled.

"So it's agreed."

Bailey opened her mouth, then closed it. Unexpected

tears burned in her eyes and she knew if she spoke, she would lose control. The last thing she wanted was her daughter to see her cry.

It was Kenny, she thought, smiling and hoping neither of them noticed the sheen of moisture. Actually it was his actions. He was taking care of her and it had been so very long since she'd had a shoulder—however temporary—to lean on.

WHILE THE SOFA looked comfortable enough, Kenny knew it was going to be a long night. Although he had a nice pillow and plenty of blankets, there was no way he came close to fitting. Even if he didn't have his feet hanging off the end, he was still not going to get any rest. Mostly because where he wanted to be was in Bailey's bed, not her living room.

No way, he reminded himself. There were dozens of reasons—the most important of which was in the smaller, second bedroom. Chloe. A bright, sweet kid whom he adored. But at the end of the day, he wasn't going to start to care about her only to lose her. Only a fool would expect a different outcome.

He punched the pillow a couple of times and closed his eyes. He'd nearly fallen asleep when he heard footsteps in the hallway. They were light and hesitant.

He saw up and turned on the light. Chloe stepped into view.

She had on a long flannel nightgown with pink flowers on it. Her bright red hair was pulled back in a braid and her eyes were huge. As he watched, a single tear slipped down her cheek.

He'd gone home to pick up sweats and a T-shirt to sleep in. He pushed aside the blankets and patted the sofa next to him. She crossed to him, but instead of settling beside him she threw herself at him and began to cry.

Bailey had been emotional earlier, he thought as he instinctively wrapped his arms round Chloe's skinny body and held her close. A reaction to the accident, but still. Females and tears were a tough combination.

Not knowing what else to do, he let her cry for a few minutes. He rubbed her back and murmured reassuringly. Finally she raised her head and looked at him.

"I had a bad dream about my dad."

"What was the dream?"

"He was lost and I couldn't find him."

He brushed he tears from her cheeks. "Yeah, that's a bad one. It woke you up, huh?"

She nodded and sniffed.

"Can you keep real quiet for a minute?" he asked.

She nodded.

He picked her up and carried her into her mother's bedroom. Bailey lay asleep on her bed. Kenny returned to the living room and sat on the sofa with her on his lap.

"You see she's okay, right?"

Chloe nodded.

He smiled at her. "You've had a lot to deal with, munchkin. Moving to a strange town, then losing your dad. You're about to move into a new house. And while the new house is going to be wonderful, it's still a change. And sometimes change is upsetting. Even a good one. We like our routines."

She watched him, her big green eyes focused on his face.

"When your mom fell, you were scared."

Chloe nodded.

"You know she's okay, right? That it's just a sprain and she's not in danger." What he wanted to say was Bailey wasn't going to die, but he didn't know if that was too much. "Normally you'd be okay with it, but right now it's harder."

Another nod, this one a little slower. Some of the worry faded from her eyes. "It's like when I'm tired and I get cranky when I wouldn't usually?"

"Yeah. Just like that. There's a lot going on and then you saw your mom hurt. It scared you. It would scare anyone. I think that's probably why you had the dream about your dad."

He touched her nose. "You know your dad loves you. He's always going to love you. Just because he's not here, doesn't mean the love goes away. It's like the blue sky. Just because you're not looking doesn't mean it's suddenly purple or green."

She smiled. "Because he's my forever dad?"

Soft, sweet words that hit him in the gut. Longing so fierce and intense that it stole his breath caught him in a vise grip and didn't let go.

Because that was what he'd wanted with James and what he still wanted. He was one of those traditional guys who had always assumed he would get married and have kids. Not special dreams, but his all the same.

The problem was after Natalie, he'd been reluctant to trust again. There had been girlfriends, but none of them had truly touched his heart. In fact the first woman to get his attention in that way happened to be the mother of the little girl sitting on his knee.

Chloe slid to the floor and yawned. "Thanks, Kenny. I feel better. I'm going back to bed."

"I'll walk you."

He got her settled, kissed her on the forehead, then retreated to the sofa. But he didn't bother lying down. He knew he wouldn't sleep. Not when everything he wanted was so damned close, and yet completely out of reach.

CHAPTER SEVEN

BAILEY WIGGLED INTO her Spanx camisole and smoothed it into place. Tonight was the triple-date dinner at Henri's with Kenny. Not that they were dating. They were friends joining two other couples, one of whom was married, while the other was engaged. No big deal.

Except thinking about that over and over didn't seem to be getting the message to the butterflies currently practicing their *Nutcracker* ballet in her stomach.

She'd been lucky with her sprain. The following morning she hadn't needed her crutches at all. The swelling had gone down quickly and by the second day, there wasn't much pain. She'd been careful to wear flats for the week so she could save her ankle for tonight.

She pulled her holiday sweater over her head. It was black with stylized bows knit into the pattern. All of the bows were white, except for one red one. She had her faux diamond-stud earrings she'd purchased on sale and a pair of too-high sexy black heels she'd gotten at a clothing exchange.

Bailey studied her reflection in the mirror. She'd done her best with her makeup. Her hair was good—long and thick with a curly wave. She thought she looked nice. But what would Kenny think?

She'd given up on the just-friends thing. She had

a crush on him and all the sensible talk in the world wasn't going to change that. The truth was they would be seeing a lot of each other over the holidays. She would enjoy every minute of that. But come the first of the year, she was going on a Kenny diet. She had a feeling that giving him up was going to be a lot harder than giving up carbs, which happened to be the second of her resolutions for January.

She didn't have a choice. Not only had he made his feelings extremely clear, but she'd also actually taken the time to do an online search of him the previous night. The results had not been easy to see. While there weren't many pictures of Kenny with the woman he'd thought of as the mother of his child, there were more than enough of him with beautiful, talented, sexy, *thin* women. Models and actresses. A couple of athletes and a woman who had founded a successful nonprofit while still in her teens.

If one ignored the beautiful and successful part, he didn't seem to have a physical type. There were blondes, brunettes and a smattering of redheads. Some were short, some were tall. But not one of them had been curvy. Or plump. Or fighting an extra twenty pounds. There also hadn't been any executive assistants or schoolteachers or hairstylists. In a word, Kenny didn't seem to favor normal when it came to the women in his life.

Which made the need to get over him even stronger.

She got her coat and her least sensible handbag, which was still a pretty utilitarian black shoulder bag, and walked into the living room. Chloe was staying with her friend Allison for the night, saving Bailey the cost of a babysitter.

Right on time she heard steps on the stairs, then a knock at her door. She opened it to find Kenny standing there, looking way too good to be legal.

He had on a long camel-colored coat and a dark suit. He looked as if he'd showered and shaved. He smiled at her and stepped into her apartment.

"You look great," he said by way of greeting.

"You, too." She frowned as she noticed there were melting white flakes on his shoulders. "Is it snowing?"

He grinned. "Just started. Don't worry. I have all-wheel drive."

Because they were heading up the mountain. What if they got snowed in?

She allowed herself exactly four seconds to imagine herself and Kenny in a hotel room, with a fireplace and a very big bed. Then she gathered her "I'm a mother and I have to be sensible" thoughts and ignored the tempting, naughty ones.

The light snowfall became steadier as they headed for the restaurant. Near the resort, they passed a plow already doing its thing. So much for being snowed in, she thought with only a little regret.

The Gold Rush Ski Lodge and Resort had been decorated for the holidays. The bright lights were visible from the road. Kenny turned onto the property, then followed the signs to the valet.

The Christmas cheer continued inside the main building. There were several trees set up in the lobby, with garland around all the doorways. Carols played from hidden speakers and several of the staff sported festive Santa hats.

"It's this way," Kenny said, pointing to a long hallway.

She started in that direction. He put his hand on the small of her back. Even through her coat she felt the warmth and strength of his hand.

He was just being a gentleman, she told herself. She shouldn't read anything into his actions.

Only a few more weeks, she reminded herself. She would see Kenny regularly through the toy drive and then he would be gone from her life. She would allow herself to be hopeful and even wistful through the holidays, right up until the New Year. Then she would return to her happy, busy, sensible self.

Henri's was a five-star restaurant. Bailey wasn't sure what, exactly, that meant, beyond the food being good. And probably expensive. She's never eaten there before. In fact, she hadn't spent any time up at the resort, except when she'd helped Dellina with a Score party there over the summer.

She had to admit the quiet elegance was very nice. A hostess took their coats, then showed them back to their table. Jack and Larissa and Sam and Dellina were standing next to it, talking.

The four of them turned and greeted her and Kenny. Jack and Sam surprised her by kissing her on the cheek. Her friends hugged her. They were all seated and a server appeared with a bottle of champagne and six glasses.

"There's a lot to celebrate," Jack said, his gaze locked firmly on Larissa, his fiancée.

"I'll second that," Sam added.

They toasted the holiday season. Bailey sipped her bubbly drink and tried not to stare at the bottle of Dom Pérignon—a champagne she'd only ever read about in books or seen in movies.

Kenny leaned close. "You eat red meat, don't you?"

"Of course."

"How do you like your steak?"

"Medium rare."

He grinned. "You get more amazing every time I'm with you. Want to split the chateaubriand for two?"

She'd seen it on the menu. It was a holiday special and cost more than her electric and cable bills combined.

"I've never had it before. I'm sure it will be great. Thank you."

"You're going to love it," he promised.

They sipped champagne and talked about what was happening around town. Dellina was busy with several holiday parties.

"January second, we're out of here," Sam said, taking his wife's hand in his and kissing her knuckles.

Bailey knew they were heading off to Australia and New Zealand for a three-week belated honeymoon.

"I'll be back in time to finalize everything for your wedding," Dellina told Larissa.

Larissa, a pretty blonde with an easy smile, shook her head. "Don't worry about it. I have the dress and we're all set for the venue."

Kenny nodded approvingly. "You're smart," he told Jack. "No way you'll forget your anniversary."

Because Jack and Larissa were getting married on Valentine's Day. It fell on a Saturday next February.

"Chloe's excited," Bailey said. "She's never been a flower girl before. She loves her dress."

The event was going to be an evening affair, here at the resort. Jack had already arranged for rooms for the entire wedding party, including Bailey and Chloe.

Bailey was determined that she would be over Kenny by then. Maybe she would even be dating someone.

Although right now, that seemed impossible to imagine. Who could be nicer or sweeter or more fun to be with? Oh, those first few Kenny-diet days were going to be ugly, she thought. But not something she had to worry about now.

The server reappeared and they placed their orders. Jack talked about his new job at Cal U Fool's Gold and Kenny mentioned a few clients. Talk turned to holiday happenings in town.

"We're doing incredibly well on the toy drive," Bailey said. "We're going to fill up our trailer for sure."

"Let me know if you need anything extra," Sam said.

"Me, too," Jack told her. "Take advantage of us."

"He means financially," Kenny said, glaring at his friend.

"I knew that," Bailey told him. "I will be in touch if we fall short on anything."

Their salads and soups appeared. Bailey had chosen the crab bisque. It came in a beautiful gold-rimmed bowl. There was a little tower of crab in the middle of an empty bowl. The server set it in front of her, then poured steaming bisque into the plate, followed by a drizzle of truffle oil. The combination of smells made her stomach rumble.

Conversation continued. Dellina asked about Bailey's house and she admitted to being nervous about all the work she had to do between closing and moving. Sam entertained them with stories about his bawdy parents and how they were pressuring him to get Dellina pregnant.

Partway through the meal, Kenny draped his arm across the back of Bailey's chair. She felt enveloped by his warmth and wanted to lean in. But when his fingertips lightly rested on her shoulder, she allowed herself to pretend, if just for that minute, that they were a couple.

"WHY DO WOMEN go to the bathroom in packs?" Kenny asked as they drove back to town. It was after eleven and the temperature was in the low twenties. But the snow had stopped and the road was plowed.

Bailey laughed. "I don't know. It's just a thing we do. I guess we want to talk without you guys around."

"I figured. While the three of you were off doing your thing, Jack, Sam and I had our own conversation. What are you doing about the move?"

"I have the name of a company I was going to use. Why?"

"We'll take care of it. You don't have a lot of stuff. I'll rent a truck for the morning of the ninth. You'll only need to pack up the breakables. We'll take care of the rest of it."

She stared at him. "I can't let you do that."

"Technically I don't think you could stop me. I'm bigger than you." He reached across the console and squeezed her hand. "You have plenty going on, Bailey. Think of it as a holiday surprise."

The unexpected gesture floored her. If she didn't have to pay for movers, that would mean an extra four or five hundred dollars in her pocket.

"Thank you," she murmured. "I really appreciate the help."

"It's what friends do." He withdrew his hand.

They drove through town and parked in front of her building.

"You don't have to walk me up," she told him.

"No way. I was raised to walk a lady to her door."

He came around the side of his SUV and helped her out, then followed her up to the front door. Bailey braced herself for what was going to be an awkward moment. Because they weren't on a date. There wouldn't be any kissing. So what was she supposed to do? Shake his hand?

They reached the door and she got out her key. For a second she thought about offering coffee. Only it was late and he might think she was hoping for more than coffee, which she was, but it was probably for the best if that information wasn't confirmed.

"Thank you for tonight," she said when she'd opened the door. "For the dinner and the offer to move our stuff."

"You're welcome."

She stared into his face. He was a good-looking guy, but that was the least of it, she thought with a little sigh. His actions were turning out to be even more impressive.

"Good night," he said and started to turn away.

"'Night."

But before she could step into her apartment, he spun back, put his hands on her shoulders, bent down and kissed her.

The soft, warm contact of his mouth on hers caught her by surprise. She didn't know what to do, so she stayed where she was. A second passed, then another. His lips moved against her—lightly, sweetly. She leaned in a little.

Deep inside she felt wanting and hunger. Fire burned hot and bright. But there was more than that. There was a sense of rightness, of belonging. As if she'd been waiting for this moment, for this man, all her life.

He drew back. "Good night, Bailey."

She nodded and watched him go down the stairs. Then she went into her apartment and closed the door.

KENNY WENT OVER the account information. He had a couple of client meetings in January. And a list of new clients he wanted to start wooing. That was the part he liked best. Meeting with a client for the first time and blowing them away.

He could usually get a meeting. That came from having a recognizable name. But people who didn't know him often assumed he was just a dumb jock. They didn't expect much, which gave him an advantage. One he wasn't above using.

His phone buzzed.

"Yes?"

"You have a visitor, Kenny," the receptionist said. "Her name is Chloe."

He smiled. "Send her back."

He got up and walked into the hallway. His smile widened when he saw her. She had on a coat and scarf, with a backpack over her shoulders. Long red hair hung down below her hood.

"Kenny!" She flew toward him and hugged him. "It's snowing again. Isn't that the best? We're going to have snow for Christmas."

"I know. Pretty cool." He showed her into his office.

It took a couple of seconds for her to drop her backpack on the floor, then shrug out of her coat. He saw the reindeer barrettes in her hair and felt a distinct tugging in the center of his chest. Chloe was a sweet kid and she got to him.

"How about a cup of coffee?" he asked, keeping his voice serious.

Chloe giggled. "I'm seven. I don't drink coffee."

"Right. Good point. Let's go get a hot chocolate."

Her green eyes widened. "You have hot chocolate at your office?"

"Sure. We have one of those coffeemakers with the pods. It'll do anything."

They walked into the break room. He showed Chloe how to use the Keurig brewer. She watched as her drink poured into a mug. There was a plate of cookies on the table. While his coffee brewed, they each picked a cookie, then took them and their drinks back to his office.

She sat on one side of his desk, while he took the other.

She blew on her drink before tasting it, then she smiled. "This is really good."

"I'm glad. So what's up?"

"I want to make a jewelry box for my mom," she told him. "For Christmas." She dug some sheets out of her backpack. It showed how to decoupage a box and then seal it. "I've saved money for the box and I have lots of pictures to put on it. But my friend Allison's mom said I'll need help to get it finished. Can you help me?"

Self-preservation meant saying no. Chloe's big green eyes told him that wasn't going to happen. He was in dangerous territory, but that couldn't be helped.

"Sure thing. We can go get the supplies now, if you want. Then work on it over the next few days."

She smiled. "Thank you. I also need to get my mom some presents for her stocking." She shrugged. "I know there's no Santa, but stockings are important. She doesn't have one. Just me. Don't you think my mom should have a stocking?"

"I do. Have you thought about what to put in it?"

"It's supposed to be fun stuff. Candy and little toys. Maybe a lip gloss." She pulled several crumbled dollar bills out of her pocket. "Is this going to be enough?"

She might as well have reached into his chest and pulled out his still-beating heart, he thought as he stared at what looked like three dollars and change. Kids were tough—and the best part of life.

"Yeah," he told her, trying to keep any emotion out of his voice. "That's plenty."

Because he would pay for whatever Chloe wanted to get. Not just for the girl herself, but for her mom, who'd done a great job with her daughter.

"THANK YOU," BAILEY said, telling herself it would be bad to start sobbing. Her real estate agent had been incredibly supportive. Breaking down in tears, however happy, would only frighten the woman.

Her agent smiled at her. "Merry Christmas, Bailey. You're a homeowner."

Bailey nodded and walked out of the office. She clutched her house key tightly in her hand. It had really, really happened. She officially, legally and every other *l-y* word she couldn't think of right now, owned the house. It was hers. Escrow had closed.

Outside the sky was clear and the sun shining. There were holiday decorations everywhere. She wanted to stop everyone she passed and tell them the good news. She owned her own home!

But rather than frighten her fellow citizens, she walked toward through town and up toward her new neighborhood. She wanted to see the house for just a few minutes before she went to pick up Chloe from school.

Five minutes later she stood on the sidewalk and told herself to keep breathing. That this was really happening.

She stared at the house she'd bought and felt a rush of gratitude. Moving to Fool's Gold had changed everything, she thought happily. She had a great job, friends and a future. The mayor had given her the rest of the day off, along with Monday and Tuesday so she and Chloe could get moved and settled before the holidays. A few friends were coming by over the weekend to help her paint. Chloe's bedroom furniture would be delivered on Monday. What more could she ask for?

Right then, a familiar dark SUV pulled into her driveway. Her already thundering heart kicked it up a couple of speeds as Kenny climbed out.

"Congratulations," he said. "You did it."

"How did you know I'd closed?"

"Your real estate agent called me. I asked her to."

Bailey tried to summon some indignation, but just couldn't. "So much for her working for me."

He flashed her a grin. "She thought I was charming."

"I'll bet."

He moved to the rear of his vehicle and popped the hatch. Inside were gallons of paint, tarps and brushes, along with bags filled with cleaning supplies, Spackle and sandpaper.

She sighed. "You picked up my hardware store order for me? Thank you."

"You're welcome. Come on. You can help me carry it inside."

She took a few shopping bags while he grabbed three paint cans in each hand. She followed him to the front door and tried not to let her gaze linger on his butt. Although she had to admit it was a pretty impressive butt. Kenny looked great in a suit, but in jeans and a leather jacket, the man was devastating.

He bumped his shoulder against the front door.

"Oh, let me unlock that," Bailey told him.

"Not necessary."

The door swung open. Before she could figure out how that was possible, she saw over a dozen women waiting in her new living room. Larissa and Isabel stood together, with Dellina right behind them. Noelle and Patience, Heidi, Annabelle and Charlie, the Hendrix triplets, Consuelo, and even Mayor Marsha was there. They were all dressed in jeans and sweatshirts.

"Surprise!" they yelled.

Bailey blinked. "I don't understand."

Isabel hugged her. "We're here to help. We're going to clean and sand and paint and put down shelf paper. By Sunday night, your house is going to be ready for you to move in."

Larissa laughed. "Don't look so surprised. We love you. We were planning on helping when Kenny talked to me about it. The two of us arranged everything."

"I'm on lunch duty," Noelle said, patting her stomach. "I can't do paint, what with being pregnant. But I'm happy to run errands."

Bailey looked at all her friends and felt their affection wash over her. Turning to Kenny was a different story. She was afraid of what he might see in her eyes if she looked at him just now.

"I don't know how to thank all of you," she said honestly.

"Child, we're your family now," Mayor Marsha told her. "All right, everyone, let's get to work."

By the time Bailey had collected Chloe from school, her house was controlled chaos. Charlie Stryker, a firefighter in town, had taken control of the work parties. The bathrooms and kitchens were being scrubbed from top to bottom. Kenny had been joined by Jack and Sam. They were hard at work, prepping the walls.

"I want to complain about the traditional division of labor," Charlie said when Bailey walked in with her daughter, "but the guys are doing good work. So I won't."

Bailey listened to the happy conversations from every corner of the house and knew that she would treasure this memory always. As for the man who had made it happen…well, that was a problem for later.

CHAPTER EIGHT

THE DAY BEFORE the move, Bailey packed up her kitchen. At least the breakable items. Pots, pans and flatware she simply placed loose in boxes. She wasn't going to move across the country—just a few blocks away.

The weekend had been a lot of work, but so much had been accomplished. The house was clean and painted. Chloe's bedroom was a beautiful lavender color, with the doors, windows and trim all done in white. Bailey had picked a soft blue-gray for her bedroom, and a muted sage-green for the rest of the house.

She straightened, putting her hand at the small of her back. There were aches and pains from all she'd been doing, but it was worth it. Right after lunch she was meeting the delivery guys at the new house. They would deliver and put together Chloe's bedroom furniture. Tomorrow was the move and then she and her daughter would be in their new home.

She pulled the step stool over to the cabinet above the refrigerator, then climbed up. There were only a few serving pieces up there—ones she used for special occasions, like Christmas dinner.

As she lowered the items to the counter, she smiled. There was a crystal bowl she used every year. It had be a wedding gift from her grandmother. The bowl had been in the family for nearly a hundred years. While she loved that bowl, for some reason, Will had loved it even more. Her smile faded as she remembered how hard last Christmas had been and how she hadn't bothered to get down the fancy serving pieces. She just hadn't been able to face them.

Now she touched the bowl and remembered all the good times they'd had as a family. She might not have been madly in love with Will before he died, but she would always remember how he'd been a good husband and father.

She picked up the crystal bowl to wrap it and saw there was an envelope tucked inside. Her name was on the front, in Will's handwriting.

She started to shake. After picking up the envelope, she walked over to the kitchen table and sat down. She opened the envelope and found a Christmas card inside. She opened it.

Bailey, I'm putting this where I know you'll find it on Christmas Eve. I'm heading out tomorrow and I won't be back for six months. I'm sorry to be away from you and Chloe, especially at the holiday. Know that I'll always love you both, so much.

Her eyes filled with tears. She hadn't found it on Christmas Eve, she thought sadly. Hadn't known he left it. Now, looking back, she wondered if having his card would have made last Christmas easier or more difficult.

She turned the card over in her hand, then got up and took it into her bedroom. She had a box of Will's things she was saving for her daughter. When Chloe was a little older, they would go through them together.

She placed the card inside and closed the box. Then she got back to her packing.

KENNY WAITED BY the elementary school. He was a couple of minutes early, with his SUV in line with all the parents picking up their children. In Fool's Gold most kids walked home from school, so he was surprised at the number of drivers. Then he noticed all the sports equipment and stickers for things like dance and drama and figured the kids being picked up were heading to an activity.

He was there for Chloe. Bailey was finishing up the last of her packing before the move tomorrow, so he'd scheduled his stocking shopping trip with Chloe for that afternoon. Bailey had been grateful to have more time to get work done and had tried to give him money to pay for the stocking contents, but he'd refused. He wanted to be a part of their Christmas morning, however remotely.

The doors to the school opened and the first children appeared. He got out of his SUV and stood by the passenger's side so Chloe could spot him easily. He watched as groups of girls and boys walked together, talking and laughing. A few headed for the cars, but the rest kept going toward home.

He'd wanted this, he admitted to himself. Hell, he thought he'd had it with James. He'd imagined what it would be like to take his son to his first day of school. He'd had big dreams for that kid.

Of course he'd wanted him to be a football star and get the girl, but mostly he'd wanted to watch him grow up and have a good life and be happy. While he still wanted that to happen, he would never be a part of James's life.

As the sea of children continued to move around him, he let himself feel the emptiness that was always there. The pain of what he'd lost—what couldn't be recovered. In a way it was worse than if James had died, because he knew the boy was out there. Growing up without him. Connecting with the man who was his biological father.

Kenny knew that James had been young enough to forget him. By now he was only a distant memory. Eventually he would be lost completely. Natalie wasn't going to ever tell her son what she'd done. No one shared stories that made them look bad.

Which left him alone. He knew he should move on. Find someone else. Start a family. And he would. It was just there hadn't been anyone who sparked his interest. Not until Bailey—which left him totally screwed.

"Kenny!"

He looked up and saw Chloe waving frantically. She hugged her friend goodbye, then ran toward him. She was small and skinny and completely adorable. As she got close, she dropped her backpack and launched herself at him. He caught her and held her close.

"You're here!" she said, hugging him tight. "I knew you would be. I was so excited that I had trouble paying attention and my teacher had to give me a yellow card."

She leaned back enough to look into his eyes. "That's only one card away from red and if you get three red cards, your parents are called in. My mom would *die* if I got red cards."

"Have you ever?"

"No. I like school and I like following the rules. But today was hard."

He lowered her to the ground. She picked up her backpack and grinned again. "We're going to go shopping!"

"I know."

He opened the back door for her and she climbed in. When her seat belt was secure, he walked around to the driver's side and got in. While he wasn't going to announce it with as much enthusiasm, he had to admit, he was a little stoked about their afternoon, too.

"I have a list," Chloe told him. "I want to get a special Christmas ornament from The Christmas Attic and gloves. We saw them in Aunt Isabel's store last week and Mom really liked them. But she said because of the house, she wasn't going to get them." In the rearview mirror, he watched as Chloe's expressive face turned serious. "Buying a house is a big responsibility. We're going to be careful with our money so we can afford it. I'm helping. I'm practicing turning off the lights when I leave the room, so we're not wasting electricity."

"That's very thoughtful of you."

"Mom and me are a team. Being in a family means taking care of each other." She bit her lower lip. "I think it was easier when my dad was with us. Because they could take care of each other." She glanced at her lap, then back at him. "Do you think my mom is pretty?"

A question with an implication he should have seen coming, he thought, pulling out onto the road.

"I do."

"She says you're not her boyfriend. That you're just friends."

"That's true."

"What's the difference? Is it kissing? Because you don't kiss my mom and Uncle Ford kisses Aunt Isabel all the time."

"Some of it is the kissing," he said, ignoring the memory of the incredible kiss he and Bailey had shared. She'd about brought him to his knees with a chaste kiss. He didn't want to think about what would happen if things got hotter. Not that they would, because he wasn't going there.

He tried a not-so-subtle distraction by asking which of the stores she wanted to go to first. Lucky for him, it worked.

They went to The Christmas Attic. He'd never been inside before and despite the name, he wasn't expecting quite so much...Christmas. There were trees and ornaments, stuffed animals, decorations and Christmas music playing.

"I know what I want," Chloe said as she took his hand.

"Good because this place scares me."

She giggled. "It's okay. You're safe with me."

The trees were all done with different colors and styles. He paused by one done in primary colors with Máa-zib tribal ornaments. Chloe made a beeline for one that was decorated in silver and red, and plucked a quirky ornament from one branch, an elephant on rockers.

"This one," she told him.

He took it from her and they went to pay. The tall blonde at the cash register wrapped it in tissue.

"I wondered if you'd be back," she said to Chloe. "You've been eyeing this one for a while."

Chloe nodded. "You won't tell her, will you?"

"Of course not." The woman looked at him. "Hi. We met at the painting party. I'm Noelle."

"I remember. Hi."

Her brows rose. "Helping Chloe with her shopping?"

The question wasn't a problem. It was the speculative tone that had him shifting his weight. "Uh, yeah." He passed over a twenty.

"Nice."

He held in a groan. There were parts of this shopping expedition he hadn't thought through.

She handed him his change, gave the bag containing the ornament to Chloe and wished them a merry Christmas.

Their next stop was Isabel's store. Fortunately she was too busy to speculate. She rang up the leather-glove purchase with only a harried smile. Kenny took that bag, then guided Chloe outside.

"What's next?" he asked.

"Candy." Chloe smiled. "You have to have candy in your stocking. There's a store by Morgan's Books that sells fudge. My friend Allison said they have Christmas candy in little bags. That would be nice."

"Sounds good." Kenny glanced at the other stores in the square. One in particular caught his eye. "Chloe, can I put something in your mom's stocking?"

"Sure. What?"

He pointed to the sign that read Jenel's Gems, and said, "Let's find out."

Like every other business in town, Jenel's Gems was decorated for the holidays. There were twinkle lights and a Christmas tree in the corner. The inside of the glass display cases had shiny ornaments scattered around.

Jenel, a pretty blonde with an easy smile, approached. "Hello. How can I help you?"

"We're buying something for my mom," Chloe told her.

"How nice," Jenel said. She turned to Kenny. "What kind of jewelry does your wife like?"

Kenny froze. "She's, ah, not my wife. We're friends. I was thinking of maybe a..." His gaze fell on one of the cases. "A necklace."

"Of course." Jenel moved behind the counter. "We have a large selection. Why don't you look them over and tell me what appeals to you."

Chloe joined him. Together they studied the circles and hearts. There was a silver snowflake, but Kenny didn't think Bailey would wear that.

"I like that one," Chloe said, pointing to a stylized heart that was hanging a little on its side.

Jenel pulled it out and put it on a velvet tray. "This is sterling silver. An eighteen-inch chain. It comes in different sizes, and different materials."

He studied it. "I like it better than the hearts that are straight," he said.

"Me, too," Chloe told him. "It's happier that way."

"What else have you got like this?" he asked Jenel.

"Let me show you."

She brought out similar hearts in yellow gold. One had a few little diamonds on one side. The last one she showed them was the same heart covered in pavé diamonds, on a platinum chain.

"Look!" Chloe said, pointing to the heart. "It's sparkling in the light. That's so pretty."

"I agree." He looked at Jenel. "We'll take that one."

"Of course. Would you like me to gift-wrap it?"

"Please."

Chloe clapped her hands together. "My mom is going to love that. I can't wait to see her open it."

"You won't say anything, though, right?"

She pressed her lips together and made an *X* on her chest. "I promise."

"Good. Are there any presents under the tree?" he asked.

"I don't know," she said. "I'll go look."

As soon as Chloe was out of earshot, he turned to Jenel. "I'd like that small silver heart, too," he said quietly.

Jenel nodded. "For the little girl?"

He nodded.

"I have the perfect chain. When she outgrows it, we can exchange it for a longer one."

"Good. I'll pay for these now and pick them up later." He didn't want Chloe to see the second box.

After he'd signed the credit card slip, he walked over to Chloe. On the way, he saw the display of diamond engagement rings. For a second, he wanted to stop and look. He wanted to dream about possibilities. Because Chloe wasn't the only Voss female tugging at his heartstrings.

Only he wouldn't give in. Wouldn't think about what could be. He was successful in life because he learned from his mistakes. And lesson one was not to repeat them.

BAILEY STOOD ON the walkway in front of her apartment, prepared to give thanks to whomever had arranged for perfect weather on her moving day. The sun was out, the temperatures had climbed to nearly fifty and there wasn't any wind. She couldn't have asked for more.

At some point she was going to have to pause and be grateful. Which she would…just as soon as she managed to recover from the shock of her moving crew.

As promised, Kenny had come through with a rental truck and a few friends to help. But somewhere along the way, the few friends had turned into something so much more.

Sam and Jack were there, along with all the guys from the bodyguard school. In addition, there were Dellina's brothers-in-law, two of the three Stryker brothers, Tucker Janack, Josh Golden and Raoul Moreno. She thought it was very possible there were more men milling around her place than she had boxes.

Kenny climbed halfway up the staircase, then turned back to the crowd. "All right, here's how we're going to do it. We'll empty from front to back here and load from back to front at the new place. If you pick up a lamp or a table, remember where it came from. You'll be responsible for getting it in the right place. Chloe's furniture is being dropped off at the donation center. She has a new set waiting in her new house. Everything else is going with us." He paused. "Oh, and if you break it, you're buying a new one."

Jack glanced at Bailey and winked. "Want me to drop the TV?"

"Only if you want to buy me a new flat-screen," she teased.

"The Super Bowl is coming. You'll need a big TV for that."

She laughed. There was no point in mentioning that football wasn't a sport that especially interested her. Except when it came to Kenny, she thought. Of course, when it came to Kenny, many things interested her. Which was all fine and good, but she had a move to focus on.

Kenny led the way up into her apartment. Faster than she would have thought possible, it was empty and the truck was loaded. He drove it to her new place while everyone else walked over. As the truck pulled into the driveway, Bailey saw it was barely ten-thirty in the morning. At this rate, she was going to be moved in today with no problem.

Getting everything into her house went just as quickly. She stood in the hallway by the stairs and directed the guys. Kenny was upstairs and occasionally yelled down questions.

Around eleven-thirty Dellina and her two sisters showed up with lunch. There were sandwiches and soda, along with brownies and cookies. Bailey had arranged the lunch a few days ago and had called that morning to up the order when she'd seen how much help she was going to have. Given how much the guys were doing for her, it was the least she could offer. By twelve-thirty, the men were gone and Bailey faced the daunting task of unpacking.

"We're not leaving," Dellina told her, as she put sandwich wrappings into a large trash bag.

"That's right," Fayrene, her sister, added. "We're going to help you unpack."

Bailey shook her head. "I don't want to keep you. I really appreciate the offer, but I can do it."

She would be up all night, but she would get it done.

"Don't be silly," Dellina said. "We'll go room by room. We'll pull stuff out of boxes and you tell us where to put it. We'll be finished before Chloe's out of school."

Dellina turned out to be right. With four of them unloading boxes and Bailey directing them on where to put things, they got dishes into the cupboards and food into the pantry. When the kitchen was done, the rest of the house was easy. She'd spent the previous afternoon driving over carloads of their hanging clothes, so that was already in place. Their few DVDs were lined up in the entertainment unit. Chloe's stuffed animals were in place up on the shelf Kenny had installed over the weekend and the cleaning supplies were placed neatly on the shelves in the laundry room.

At two-forty-five Bailey hugged her friends good-bye and walked toward Chloe's school. She was tired and happy and still in shock over how the day had gone. Yes, her feet hurt and her back hurt and there were a thousand things to do, but she and Chloe had their forever home and nothing was ever going to be better than that.

Chloe raced out of school and ran up to her. "Did it happen? Are we in our new house?"

"We are. I'm very excited."

"Me, too!"

They walked back to the house. Chloe told her about school and how all her friends wanted to come over.

"We'll have a party," Bailey promised, thinking how

great it was going to be. With Chloe's new bedroom set, sleepovers would be easy.

They rounded the corner and she saw Kenny's SUV parked in her driveway. Her chest got tight, her heart raced and the rest of her sighed in anticipation. She didn't know why he'd stopped by, but that was okay. Seeing him was its own reward.

But as she got closer to the house, she saw he wasn't alone. He sat on their front porch, with a large, fresh-cut Christmas tree leaning against the railing. Chloe shrieked and ran up to stare.

"Our tree," she said reverently. "You remembered!"

Bailey followed at a more normal pace, but she was shouting on the inside. "You got us a tree."

"You promised Chloe one as soon as you got the house. I figured you might be too busy today, so I picked up this one. I hope you like it."

Like it? She loved it. And…well, maybe him as well.

She wasn't sure. Her feelings were still all over the place and she didn't want to assign a name to something so wonderful and happy. There was also the complication of Kenny not wanting to get involved with her. But all that was for later.

He stood and held out both his hands. "Come on. Let's take the tour. Then we'll get the tree set up. If you're nice to me, I'll help with the lights." He glanced at Bailey. "I thought we could order in pizza. You won't want to cook tonight."

"Thank you," she said. Simple words that didn't come close to expressing her gratitude for all he'd done for her.

She put her hand in his and he squeezed her fingers. Chloe danced on his other side.

"I want to see," she squealed. "I want to see *everything.*"

CHAPTER NINE

BAILEY HELD HER hands palm-up. "I honestly don't know how this happened," she told Isabel. "It's not like he asked me. It was just sort of expected."

Isabel laughed. "As long as you're going."

"I don't have anything to wear." Dinner with Kenny's business partners was one thing, but the Score Christmas party was something else. For starters, several clients had been invited. She didn't know what to say to a man who owned a company that rented out private jets to rich people. Or a couple that owned a worldwide rum brand.

But Kenny had mentioned the party a couple of times and she'd finally realized that she was his date. Not that they were dating. Or kissing. There hadn't been a single kiss since that one. This despite the fact that she saw Kenny nearly every day. She tried to tell herself the man had extraordinary control, only she was afraid the truth was much less flattering. He really *was* just friends with her.

Either way, she was going to the Score Christmas party, which was going to be an elegant affair up at the resort. Dellina had dropped hints about the decorations for the ballroom and what the guests would be eating. The invitation had stated black tie very clearly. And as Bailey didn't own a tux, she was forced to find a dress.

Which was where her visit to Isabel's store had come in.

"I have you covered," Isabel promised.

Bailey nodded, trying to telling herself everything would work out. Only she didn't see how she could afford a nice dress, along with the accessories. It wasn't like she was buying something for work, where she could justify the cost knowing she would wear it weekly for the next two years.

Isabel went into the back room of her store, then returned with a long dress. Bailey felt her breath catch as she stared at the stunning gown.

It was simple—a black lining with gold beading. The neck was round and not too low, the cap sleeves added interest at the shoulder.

Isabel handed her the dress and pushed her toward the changing rooms. "Try it on."

Bailey did as she requested. She noticed there was no price tag, which made her nervous. But she stepped into the dress and pulled it up. The long zipper closed more easily than she expected. As she was on the bridal side of the store, there were no mirrors in the dressing room, so she had to go out to see how she looked.

Isabel smiled when she saw her. "I knew it. Try on these."

"These" were a pair of simple black pumps with killer four-inch heels. Bailey managed to step into them and stand without hurting herself. She stepped up to the bridal mirror and glanced at her reflection.

"Wow."

"I know, right?" Isabel stepped up behind her. "The fit is incredible. You look like a movie star."

Bailey thought maybe her friend was exaggerating,

but she would accept the compliment. The gold beading added a warmth to her skin that made it glow. The color was perfect with her red hair. The dress itself hugged her curves, but in the best way possible. She looked like a redheaded Kim Kardashian.

"I love it," she admitted. "But how much is it?"

Isabel wrinkled her nose. "Don't get mad, but it's not one of mine. It's a rental. I found the site online and had them overnight the dress to me." She handed Bailey the invoice. "Considering the retail value of the dress, it's a bargain."

Bailey had to agree. She could rent the dress for the week for less than a hundred dollars. "Thank you."

"You're welcome. The shoes are Taryn's. She also sent over a bag and some jewelry." Isabel grinned. "Because she loves you."

"I love her back." Bailey glanced at the high heels. "I should have recognized them as being from her collection."

She stepped down and they opened the box that had arrived from Taryn that morning. Inside was a Judith Lieber black-and-gold clutch and a pair of diamond-stud earrings.

"I don't want to know what those cost," Isabel murmured.

"Me, either." Bailey told herself she wasn't going to cry. "When did she get back from her trip?"

"Yesterday."

And Taryn had done this for her today. "I'm going to have to give her a kidney or something to say thank you."

Isabel hugged her. "It will make her happy to see you looking like a princess."

"I think I'd rather be a sex goddess."

"That, too."

BAILEY DIDN'T KNOW where to look first. The ballroom had been decorated in white. White trees, white twinkle lights, white flowers on white tablecloths. There were perfect red accents—a red ribbon running down the center of each table. A single red rose at every other place setting. Formally dressed serving staff circulated with glasses of champagne. She was out of her element, but prepared to have the time of her life.

Having an incredibly handsome man at her side certainly helped, she thought. Kenny had shown up on time, looking movie-star gorgeous in a tailored tux. But what really got her heart beating fast was the look on his face when he saw her. The moment of appreciation and raw desire had gone a long way in upping her confidence quotient.

Now, as they circulated through the party, he kept his hand on the small of her back. When they stopped to talk to clients, he kept his hand possessively on her hip. She told herself not to read too much into his actions, but she couldn't help the little ripples of excitement that zipped through her.

The guy who owned the jet company turned out to be pretty nice. His wife, a stay-at-home mom, used her phone to show off pictures of their kids.

"I see Taryn," Bailey told Kenny a few minutes later. "I need to talk to her for a second."

"Don't go far."

"I won't." Later there was supposed to be dancing. Bailey hoped Kenny planned to dance the night away with her. Who wouldn't want that in her future?

She excused herself and crossed the room toward her friend. Taryn had on a black, strapless, fitted evening gown that sparkled and dazzled nearly as much as the woman herself. Her hair was long and straight, her makeup dramatic. Large diamonds gleamed from her ears and around her wrists. She looked exotic, wanton and powerful.

Bailey gave herself a second to admire the view, then approached her friend. Taryn saw her and hurried over.

"You look fantastic," Taryn said. "My God, every guy in the place is going to want to haul you off and have his way with you."

"Oh, please," Bailey said. "As if. You look amazing."

Taryn dismissed the compliment with a flick of her wrist. "This old thing? We just got back two days ago. I didn't have time to shop. Not that anyone here has seen the dress, but still."

Bailey laughed. Obviously her month away hadn't changed Taryn at all. It was good to know that some things were consistent. "Thank you for my accessories." She held up the bag and pointed to the earrings. "You're very sweet to me."

"Don't say that out loud," Taryn told her, glancing around as she spoke. "You think I *want* people to know I'm nice?"

Bailey grinned. "Sorry. I won't say anything. How are you? How was your trip?"

"Wonderful. Romantic. Angel is a god—not that I want him to know." She took Bailey by the arm and led her to an alcove in the corner. "I need to talk to you."

Gone was the teasing and sassy attitude. Taryn's

eyes were wide and filled with an emotion Bailey didn't recognize. On anyone else she would have said it was fear.

"What's wrong?"

Taryn drew in a breath. "I think, I mean I'm pretty sure…" She swallowed. "I'm pregnant."

Bailey laughed. "That's wonderful. You scared me. Aren't you happy?"

"Happy? No. Terrified. I'm not like you. I'm not sweet or giving or huggy. I want to be a good mom, but what if I screw up? What if my kid doesn't like me?" Tears filled her eyes. "You don't understand. I had horrible parents. I don't know how to do this."

Bailey wrapped her arms around her friend. "You'll be fine. Trust me. You have everything you need inside of you. You're warm and caring. I'm wearing the shoes that prove it. You know how to love. That's all children want. To be loved. You'll provide a stable home and lots of attention. It's going to be fine."

Taryn stepped back. "I'm not convinced. Can you teach me how to be more like you?"

Bailey held in more laughter. "Sure. We can start right away so you're ready."

"Okay. Thank you. I'm not going to tell anyone else until I'm in my fourth month. Just to be sure everything is okay. But I wanted to tell you." She sniffed. "Do you think they make couture maternity clothes?"

Bailey laughed. "I'm sure of it."

PART OF GROWING up with a parent in the State Department and living overseas meant learning to adjust to different cultures and traditions. Kenny had gotten good at adapting when necessary. It was a skill that had served him well on the football field and in life. But no matter how he smiled and talked with his business partners, his friends and clients, he couldn't shake the sensation of something not being right.

Maybe it was the tux. He would rather be in jeans. Maybe it was the party itself—too many people having too much fun. Only he liked parties and he enjoyed the holidays and hell, wearing a tux now and then wasn't a big deal. So why did he keep feeling as if his collar was too tight and that he should be scanning the room for exits?

The most obvious reason was standing about two feet away, laughing at something Jack had said. In a word—Bailey. She looked stunning in her black-and-gold evening gown. Sexy and beautiful and more temptation than any man should have to resist.

The problem wasn't that he wanted her. He could accept the longing, the heated blood, the need to pull her into a dark corner and kiss her until neither of them could breathe. That was fine. Desire was easy. Familiar. Comfortable. No, what had him unable to relax was more complicated and a lot more terrifying.

It was that he *liked* her. He liked hanging out with her. He liked listening to her talk and the sound of her laughter. He liked how she painted a room and baked cookies and took care of her daughter. He liked how he felt when he was around her. He liked that she made him feel protective. He wanted to take care of her, to be with her. He wanted to be a part of her and her daughter's lives, and that was where it all went sideways for him.

The battle of what he wanted and what he knew was safe wasn't easy. Telling himself that she wasn't his ex didn't help the situation. Because in the end, he could still lose her. That was bad enough, but to also lose Chloe—he didn't think he could survive the loss of both of them.

Still, when she walked up to him, he couldn't help leading her onto the dance floor.

She fit into his arms perfectly. With her heels, she was taller than usual, so her body nestled against his. Her smile called to him, as did her beautiful eyes. How was he supposed to resist her? How was he supposed to save himself?

After the holidays, he told himself. Then he would back off. Because while there was some danger, it wasn't as if he was in love with her. Not yet, at least.

"WHAT DO YOU think?" Bailey asked as she walked around the dining room table. It was old—probably from the 1920s. A beautiful dark wood with just enough carving to make it interesting. There were six matching chairs, also in good condition. The cushions needed recovering but she knew how to do that. The best part of the set was the buffet. There was a big scratch on one side, which was probably the reason the set hadn't sold yet. But in Bailey's dining room, the buffet would slide into an alcove. With only six inches of clearance on either side, no one would see the scratch.

Chloe studied the pieces. "It's really nice, Mom. I like the way it shines. Could I help pick out the fabric for the chairs?"

"Of course. We'll get new cushions and then cover them ourselves."

"You're going to teach me how?"

She pulled her daughter close. "I will. It's going to be a great weekend project."

Her old table still worked, but it was lost in their new dining room. Plus, she'd always wanted a buffet. She already had a pretty vase she could set on it.

She knew the four-hundred-dollar price tag was a bargain. This set was made of solid wood. It would last another couple hundred years. There had been a sign out front offering delivery in town for only twenty-five dollars. She had the money from what she'd saved on the move.

Chloe squeezed her hand. "It's okay, Mom. We have a nice house now."

Bailey smiled at her daughter. "You're right. The new house deserves a beautiful dining room. Let's get it."

They went and found the lady managing the sale. She put a Sold tag on the furniture and arranged for delivery. Bailey and Chloe wandered around a little more.

The old farmhouse was filled with plenty of furniture, along with dishes, paintings and other household goods. Bailey lingered over a box of old records. Kenny liked oldies, she thought. And she'd yet to find a Christmas present for him. What did you get the man who not only had everything, but also had the ability to buy it again and again?

She flipped through the albums, not sure what he liked. She saw an album by the Doors. There was something scribbled on the front of it. She pulled out the album and carried it to the window.

"Really?" Bailey asked in a whisper as she studied what turned out to be a signature. She was pretty sure it was Jim Morrison. Was he the lead singer of the Doors? Hadn't he died young or something?

Her working knowledge of music from the 1960s was sketchy at best, but as the album was priced at five dollars, she was willing to take a chance. She could call Gideon, the owner of Fool's Gold's radio stations and an oldies fan himself, and ask him if this was something Kenny would like.

"Mom, look!"

Chloe held up an old-fashioned Christmas ornament. It was of a football player. He was holding the ball in his arms.

"It reminds me of Kenny," her daughter said. "Let's get it for the tree."

"Sure," Bailey said automatically, doing her best to remain calm on the outside. But on the inside, alarms went off. Because until this very second, she'd only been worried about her own heart, when it came to Kenny. She hadn't thought that Chloe could be falling for him, as well.

Panic set in, and with it a fierce need to protect her daughter. Because Kenny had made it clear he wasn't interested in forever and anything less would devastate Chloe. She'd already lost her father—she didn't need the pain of losing someone else nearly as wonderful.

"Mom?"

Bailey forced a smile. "It's adorable and yes, we need it on our tree."

How to fix this, she wondered. A problem she would wrestle with when she got home, she promised herself. Because she had to keep Chloe safe.

They paid for the dining set, the album and the ornament, then they started toward her car. She'd just reached it when her cell phone rang. She glanced at the screen and saw Kenny's name. For a second, she thought about not answering, but that was neither helpful nor mature.

"Hi," she said, telling herself to ignore the now-familiar quivering that accompanied either seeing him in person her hearing his voice.

"Bailey, I don't know what to say. They're gone."

His voice was thick with tension and disbelief. The quivering disappeared and worry took its place.

"What's gone? What's going on?"

"The toys. I emptied the barrels this morning and drove out to load them in the trailer. The lock is broken and the trailer's empty. All the toys are gone."

CHAPTER TEN

IT DIDN'T TAKE long for word to spread and people to start showing up at the empty trailer. A couple of women Kenny didn't know stood talking on their cell phones. A few of Bailey's friends he recognized but couldn't name were standing together looking stunned.

Kenny stayed by his SUV. He could see inside the large empty space. There was nothing left. Not even part of a carton or some torn packaging. Whoever had taken the toys had done a thorough job.

He knew this kind of thing happened all the time. People stole from food banks and took deliveries off neighbors' porches. But he hadn't realized it could happen here. In Fool's Gold. Things were supposed to be better here. There wasn't a lot of crime. From what he'd heard, people barely locked their doors at night. It was that kind of place.

Only not anymore. And if someone could steal toys meant for disadvantaged children, then other bad things could happen. People could get sick and die. Pets could be lost. And green-eyed redheads could decide they didn't want to have anything to do with him. Bailey could walk away and take Chloe with her, and he would be left with nothing. His heart stolen, just like the toys.

Mayor Marsha arrived in a small red car. She got out and walked over to him.

"It has to be someone from out of town," she said by way of greeting. "I refuse to believe that a person I know would do this to the Sprouts. Those girls are going to be heartbroken."

Something he hadn't thought of, he realized. What would Chloe and her friends think when they found out what had happened? They'd worked hard on their project. They'd decorated the bins and had spent time asking for donations.

"Then there's the matter of the children in Sacramento," the mayor continued. "We have to make sure they have a good Christmas."

Bailey arrived. Chloe was with her, the seven-year-old's eyes filled with tears.

"Are they really all gone?" she asked as she rushed up to him.

"Afraid so."

Chloe turned to her mother. "Mommy, I don't understand."

"Me, either." Bailey put an arm around her. Together they stared into the empty trailer.

"It was nearly full," Bailey murmured. "People were so generous."

She looked devastated. He wanted to go to her and hold her tight. He wanted to make things right. Which meant he was in deeper than he'd realized and he'd better retreat while he still could.

"I'll write a check," he said.

Bailey and the mayor stared at him.

He motioned to the empty trailer. "I'll write a check

to cover everything taken. We can go buy more presents."

"I don't think that's necessary," Mayor Marsha said. "I think the town can fix this problem."

"I agree." Bailey smiled at him. "But thank you for being generous."

He wasn't. Didn't she see that? He was trying to buy his way out of a difficult situation. Because he could. Because he couldn't risk giving anything else.

"Let me know if you change your mind," he mumbled and returned to his SUV.

"Kenny, wait." Bailey hurried after him. "We have a lot to do to make this right."

He shook his head. "Angel and Taryn are back in town. It's their project. Let them fix it."

He didn't turn around. He didn't want to see the shock on her face or the hurt in her eyes. He didn't want the proof that he'd hurt her. Even though he knew he had.

As BAILEY HAD expected, the town rallied. The trailer was moved into an empty warehouse with locked doors and an impressive security system. The police department offered to patrol the area regularly. Once word went out, presents started pouring in. The bins filled up so quickly, Bailey arranged times for people to go directly to the warehouse with their donations. During those collection times, one of the guys from the bodyguard school was on hand as extra security. Not that there had been a problem.

Bailey took the last of the packages that Denise Hendrix had dropped off and walked to the large trailer. Angel, on duty with her today, carried it inside.

Chloe studied all the toys in place and smiled. "We're going to do it, Mom. We're going to fill the trailer again."

"I know we are."

Her daughter leaned against her. "I'm glad people are helping."

Angel jumped down from the trailer, then squatted in front of Chloe. "What do you think about the people who stole the presents?" he asked.

"I don't know," Chloe admitted. "I guess they're bad. They stole at Christmas. They stole toys."

"I agree." He stared into her eyes. "There are always going to be bad people. But the thing to remember is that most of us aren't like that." He pointed to the toys. "How many families have donated toys?"

"A lot."

"Right. And maybe two or three people stole them. There's more of us than them. Good people can make it right, if you give them a chance. Remember that. Everyone who loves you and your friends came through when you needed help. But more important, people in this town who have never met you wanted to help."

"Because they're nice?"

"Yeah." He stood.

Bailey listened to him explain what had happened with a clarity that made her grateful. She and Chloe had had several conversations on the topic, but she had a feeling this one had been the one to get through.

Her daughter took her hand. "I'm glad we're helping those kids in Sacramento and I'm really glad we have such a nice town."

"Me, too."

Angel walked to the trailer and swung the doors

shut. "All right. You two can head out. I'll lock the doors and arm the alarm."

"Thanks."

She led Chloe to their car. There were only a couple more days until the toy delivery, but she wasn't worried. They would make it. Then it would be Christmas and the start of a New Year.

Usually she enjoyed the holidays. Since having Chloe, they'd become nearly magical. She'd had high hopes for this season, at least until three days ago. Because ever since the toys had been stolen, Kenny had disappeared.

He hadn't called her or stopped by. They hadn't spoken. She hadn't even caught sight of him in town. Taryn hadn't said anything, so Bailey knew that he hadn't been in an accident or gotten sick, but he had disappeared.

She wanted to tell herself that there were a thousand explanations. The problem was, she couldn't think of a single one that explained why he hadn't been in touch with her. If only to say he was busy. Or driving to Bora Bora.

It wasn't that he'd left her to deal with the toy drive on her own. It was that she'd missed him. In the past few weeks, she'd grown used to seeing Kenny every day. She liked talking to him and simply being in his company. Her feelings for him had grown to the point where he was part of her world. Letting that go was going to be difficult.

Ignoring her own bruised heart, there was also Chloe to worry about. So far her daughter hadn't mentioned Kenny, but it was only a matter of time until the questions started. And Bailey had no idea how she was going to answer them.

TARYN TOOK A sip from her Score mug and shuddered. Kenny looked back at the Keurig in the break room. The used pod was still in place. He raised his eyebrows.

"Hot chocolate? You?"

She sighed. "I know. But it's the season, right?"

"You drink coffee. Or water."

"Now I drink hot chocolate." She grimaced. "Or not."

He studied his business partner. Something was different, he thought, but he wasn't sure what. Taryn was wearing one of her stylish suits with stitching and darts and whatever made it contour to the shape of her body. She was barefoot, as per usual. Her ridiculous high heels looked good, but she only wore them walking into or out of the office. During the day she was barefoot.

She looked happy, he thought. But there was something in her eyes. Maybe a secret? Not that he was going to ask. Right now he was a big believer in everyone keeping their thoughts to themselves.

She set down her mug and walked to the bowl of fruit on the counter. She picked up an apple, washed it, then took a bite.

"So what's new with you?" she asked when she'd chewed and swallowed. "How's it coming with the toys? I heard the town has responded as you'd expect from this ridiculously nice place. Toys are pouring in by the bucketful."

The one thing he didn't want to talk about. No—the toys were symptomatic. Bailey was the real subject he wanted to avoid. Yet he wanted to hear how she was. It was less than a week until Christmas. Was she settled in her house? Was Chloe excited about her presents? What were their traditions? And how was he going to make it through without being with the two of them?

"Kenny?"

He saw Taryn frowning at him. "What?"

"Are you okay?"

"I'm fine."

"That's a complete guy response. Talk to me like a human being. What's going on? Are you feeling all right?"

"Sure. Never better."

She didn't look convinced. "You didn't answer me about the toy drive."

"You seem to have all the answers."

She dumped her mug into the sink and quickly rinsed it, then picked up her half-eaten apple, grabbed him by the hand and dragged him into her office. When they got there, she bumped the door closed with her hip and positioned herself in front of him.

"What?" she demanded. "You're not getting out of here until you tell me what's going on. And don't think I won't beat it out of you."

"Nothing's going on. I don't know what's happening with the toy drive because I'm not doing it anymore."

"Why not? I thought you were helping Bailey?"

"You and Angel are back. Why don't you take it over?"

"Bailey said she wanted to finish it with the Sprouts. I thought you felt that way, too."

He paced to her window, then turned back to her.

"It's stupid. The whole thing. I said I'd write a check. We could have just bought the toys."

"Now you sound like Jack did six months ago. Money doesn't always solve the problem. Besides, people like to give. They like to be a part of the solution. What's wrong with you? Is it your family? If you want to go with them to Bali, you know we'll be fine here."

"It's not that."

"Then what?"

She asked the question gently. While Taryn was all about the threats, in her heart, she was a marshmallow. She took care of all of them—she had from the very beginning. Taryn was the glue that held Score together.

She walked up behind him and put her hand on his arm. "Kenny," she said softly. "Tell me."

He continued to stare out window. "I can't do it. I can't. When I lost James…" He swallowed. "I loved him and it was like he died. Only worse, because I knew he was around and I couldn't be with him anymore."

She stepped closer and wrapped her arms around him. He pulled her against him and hung on.

"I could have sued for visitation," he continued, remembering long talks with his lawyer. "I had a good case. But what was the point? He was three. He would forget me. What would happen when he was six or eight? I would just be some guy he had to spend time with. It's not like I was his real dad."

"I'm sorry," she whispered.

"Me, too. I can't go through that again, Taryn. I can't love some kid only to lose her. When those toys were stolen, it changed everything. I'd started thinking that bad stuff couldn't happen here. Stupid, huh?"

"No. There's something about this damn town. It makes you crazy. Worse, it makes you hope."

"You've got Angel. You can relax."

"I know, but I want you to be happy, too." She looked up at him. "Bailey isn't anything like Natalie. She would never deceive you. She'd never hurt you."

He stared into her violet-blue eyes. "I agree she's a better person, but she's also still a mother. Chloe comes first and if things went south, I'd lose both of them."

"So that means you're not even going to try?"

"I won't take the chance."

She shifted so she was standing in front of him—both her hands on his chest. "Kenny, you would run into a three-hundred-pound defensive end without blinking."

He shrugged. "That's just physical pain. The body heals. The heart's not such a sure thing."

"I agree there's a risk, but the reward could be everything you've ever wanted. Don't you want to be the one person Bailey can depend on? Don't you want to be with her always? Don't you want to watch Chloe grow up into a beautiful young woman and walk her down the aisle, then hold her babies one day?"

It was like she'd stabbed him with a knife. He could see that as clearly as if it was happening right in front of him. Bailey and Chloe and the third generation of redheaded Voss women.

He allowed himself to dream for just a second, then he shook his head and physically stepped back. "I can't."

"You won't. There's a difference."

"Not a big enough one to matter."

CHAPTER ELEVEN

BAILEY, TARYN AND the Sprouts stood on the sidewalk by the shelter in Sacramento. All eight girls were solemn as the director thanked them for their help.

"So many of the families we work with don't have enough money to buy Christmas presents," she was saying. "They're struggling to keep food on the tables and lights on in the house. This Christmas, when you are with your families and opening your presents, I hope you'll stop to think about what a good thing you've done. Thank you, girls."

Chloe reached for Bailey's hand. Several of the girls were wiping away tears.

Behind them, volunteers unloaded the toys that had been collected. Taryn sniffed.

"All this emotion," she grumbled. "It's just so..." She looked at her Sprouts and smiled. "I'm proud of all of you. You didn't let one person ruin something special."

Allison sighed. "It's like a Christmas miracle. We delivered toys to needy children. My mom wants us to have this for our project next year."

"We'll talk it with the Grove council," Taryn promised. "Okay, let's head back to Fool's Gold. Rumor has it, there's going to be a celebration at Brew-haha."

Several of the girls cheered. Chloe released Bailey's

hand and walked with her friends. Taryn fell into step with Bailey as they walked toward their cars.

"I hate all this stupid happiness," Taryn muttered.

Bailey grinned. "You need to get over that. Happiness is part of the tradition. It's good for you."

"No, it's not. Worse, I'm fighting hormones. I cried over a commercial last night. It was horrifying."

"There's so much more to come."

Bailey knew that Taryn was holding off on telling people about her pregnancy and couldn't wait for the news to come out.

"The toy thing was good," Taryn admitted. "Needy kids and all that." She paused. "You want to talk about it?"

There was no need to ask what the "it" was. Or who.

"There's not much to say," Bailey told her.

"Are you okay?"

"No. But I'm faking it as best I can." She lowered her voice. "I miss him."

"He misses you. It's just...he has some baggage."

"I know about Natalie. He told me. So in my head, I understand why he's cautious. But it still hurts to have him gone."

Taryn got to her car and unlocked it. Bailey did the same. The girls climbed in and began fastening their seat belts. When all the doors were closed, Taryn looked at her.

"Have you told him how you feel? I can't promise it will make a difference, but it might." She shrugged. "I'm assuming you're serious about him. If all you want is something short-term and hot, then tell him that, too. I'm sure he would be interested. Kenny's a good guy. We all want him to be happy. It would be great if he could be happy with you."

Bailey nodded and got in her car. On the drive back to Fool's Gold, she thought about what Taryn had suggested. While Bailey knew that Kenny was afraid of getting involved with her, she'd never considered that he might not know how she felt. She'd never hinted that her liking had turned into something else.

Would that change things? Would he be willing to take a chance if he knew she loved him? There was only one way to find out. Unfortunately it meant laying her heart on the line.

For the next hour Bailey tried to figure out what to do. In between Christmas carols sung loudly with the Sprouts, she considered her options.

When they reached Brew-haha, several of the parents were waiting. The girls ran inside and shared what had happened at the shelter. Patience, the owner, had hot chocolate and cookies waiting for them. Bailey took Taryn aside.

"I want to go talk to Kenny," she whispered. "This is going to go on for at least an hour. Do you mind if I duck out for a bit?"

"Go," Taryn urged her. "I'll stay with Chloe. If you're not back by the time this wraps up, I'll take her to Noelle's store. It's always fun to watch the shoppers the Saturday before Christmas."

Bailey hugged her friend. "You're the best."

"I know. It's a burden, but one I've learned to live with." Taryn gave her a little push. "Go!"

Bailey did as instructed. She told Chloe she was going to run an errand, then ducked out of the store and hurried toward Kenny's house. It had snowed a couple of days ago, then warmed up enough for the streets and sidewalks to clear. The few snowmen in the yards were melting. But the weather was supposed to cool down again at the beginning of the week and it looked like they might have a white Christmas after all.

Bailey still wasn't sure exactly what she was going to say when she got to Kenny's place, but she rang the bell anyway. She tried not to be intimidated by the large house.

It took him nearly a minute to answer. When he did, she saw the shadows under his eyes.

He didn't speak and neither did she. She took in the old L.A. Stallions sweatshirt and worn jeans. He looked like he hadn't shaved or slept, for that matter. Was it possible he was missing her as much as she was missing him?

"I need to speak to you," she said at last.

He stepped aside to let her in.

She walked into the foyer of the big, two-story house. She could see a living room and part of a dining room, but that was all. Not that the house mattered. It was just that now she was here, she was nervous. And scared. But she was also determined.

He shoved his hands into his front pockets and waited.

She'd been hoping for a little encouragement, but apparently that wasn't happening. He still hadn't spoken. Was he too polite to simply tell her to get out?

She drew in a breath. "I want to say something. It may not make a difference, but maybe it will. When I'm done, I'm going to leave. I don't want you to say anything. That should be easy, seeing as you're not talking now."

She paused to see if that comment would spur him to action. It did not.

"Okay, then," she murmured. "Here goes. Like I said, I don't want you to respond. I would ask that you think about what I am about to say. I want you to consider it and live with it and then come to a conclusion."

She suddenly realized she hadn't thought this through at all. How was he supposed to tell her no, in a way that wouldn't crush her soul? Or be heard in front of the whole town or something?

"If I don't hear back from you by, um, New Year's, I'll know that you're not interested. Or that you don't agree. Or whatever."

"I have no idea what you're talking about."

The words, quietly spoken, caused the nerves in her stomach to start doing laps.

"I know. I'm getting to that. You need to not talk again, okay?"

He nodded.

She laced her fingers together and twisted them around. Was she a fool for thinking he could care about her? Were they too different? Was he too much the athletic superstar? She was just a single mom with a kid. And there was the weight thing. Did he think she was fat?

She told herself to get out of her head and into the moment. She loved this man. If she wanted to have a chance with him, she had to tell him that.

"I don't know exactly what happened," she began. "Why you disappeared. I know it has something to do with Chloe and me. Maybe you're thinking you've gotten too close. That if you care, you could be hurt.

If you do care, then that's true. But it's also true that you could hurt us, too."

She paused to gather her thoughts. She wasn't sure how to convince him, but not trying was no longer an option.

"I want to say that I loved Will desperately until he died, but that's not true. We were drifting apart when he was killed. I don't know if it was because he was gone so much or if we simply grew up and apart. But whatever my feelings, Will was a good man and I want his daughter to know that about him."

She found herself staring at the center of Kenny's chest and forced her chin up until she was looking into his eyes. She couldn't read anything there, but that was okay. She was going to get through this.

"You're right—I am a package deal. You'll never be Chloe's biological father and the possibility exists that if something happened between you and I, then you would be at risk of losing another child you'd come to care about. I know that has to be really scary. I want to tell you I know how you feel, but we both know I don't. I can't. But here's what I do know. I know that you're a wonderful person. You're caring and gentle and funny and kind. You are the kind of person others admire. You make my heart beat faster whenever you're around and you make me feel safe."

Heat burned on her cheeks, but she kept talking anyway. So what if she was embarrassed? She had to tell him the truth—they both deserved that.

"I'm not like the models and actresses you've dated. I get that. I'm just a regular kind of person who lives in a small town. Nothing flashy. Nothing special. But

I know what it's like to be alone and I know what it's like to want to belong."

Now for the hard part, she thought, wishing she was just a little more confident in his response.

"Kenny, I've fallen in love with you. I'm pretty sure Chloe has as well. I want us to be together. I want to be the love of your life. I want…" She shrugged. "I want a lot of things. More kids. A dog. But mostly I want you. And I'm hoping you want me back."

She reached out to touch him, then dropped her hand to her side. The man hadn't said a word. Sure, she'd told him not to, but did he have to pick this moment to listen? She couldn't tell what he was thinking, but worried it couldn't possibly be good.

"That was all I had to say," she whispered, returning her gaze to the center of his chest. "Please think about it. If you're not interested, then you don't have to do anything. If I don't hear from you by New Year's, I'll get the message."

She looked into his blue eyes again. "I hope whatever happens, we can stay friends. And if it's not me, then I really hope you find someone you can give your heart to. I want you to be happy, no matter what."

She turned to the door, then spun back. "Merry Christmas," she said, and then she left.

KENNY SAT ALONE in the dark. Tomorrow was Christmas Eve. For everyone in town it was a magical time. The presents were bought, the dinners planned, and there was the promise of snow tomorrow night. What could be better?

He hadn't been out of his house in days, hadn't seen anyone. The weekend had made that easy and the Score offices were closed today through Christmas. It gave him time. The question was, what was he going to do with it?

Bailey had laid it all on the line when she'd come over on Saturday. She'd bared herself, heart and soul. All she'd asked was that he think about what she said. And he had. Endlessly.

She said she loved him. Those words—how he wanted them to be true. He wanted all she had to offer. Her and Chloe and more babies and a dog. Yeah, it was a perfect picture. But was it real?

Could he trust her? That was what it came down to. Was he willing to try again, to love, knowing he could lose it all? Chloe would never be his. If the worst happened, he would lose her, too.

But the alternative was not to have her at all. It was to not try. To give up before he'd begun and that wasn't who he had ever been.

What was safe battled with what he needed as much as he needed air. The pain of not having wrestled with the potential of losing. The hours passed from night to dawn and he was no closer to an answer. But maybe that was because he'd always known how this was going to end.

"THAT WAS THE best!" Chloe crowed as they walked home, hand-in-hand, in the lightly falling snow. "The show and the day."

"I agree. It was magical."

Bailey walked next to her daughter as they made their way home from the annual performance of the Dance of the Winter King, followed by evening services at church. It was snowing, but not too cold. Or maybe they were warmed by the season itself.

Her daughter smiled up at her. "This was the greatest Christmas Eve ever!"

"Wow. Thank you. What was your favorite part?"

"I don't know. All of it. I loved the live nativity."

"Me, too."

Bailey smiled as she remembered the eccentric animals filling the manger next to the Baby Jesus. There had been goats, an elephant, a pony and a camel, all compliments of the Castle Ranch. This year there had also been the unusual addition of a small service dog, Cece. Her holiday sweater had kept her poodle-self warm, and she'd been up for snuggles and kisses. The rest of the manger animals had preferred to simply have their pictures taken.

Afterward, she and Chloe had wandered through downtown, taking in all the decorations. Carolers had gone from store to store. Most of the businesses had stayed open to offer cookies and hot chocolate to singers and residents alike.

After dinner, Bailey and Chloe had gone to see the Dance of the Winter King, a seasonal production with great music and dancing. Chloe had loved it all. Bailey had enjoyed it, too, but she'd also been aware that Kenny wasn't with them.

She hadn't heard from him since she'd announced she was in love with him, and then had left his house. While she'd known that she might not get him to change his mind, she'd been hopeful. Okay, more than hopeful, she thought wistfully. She'd imagined him striding into her office at city hall and sweeping her into his arms, à la that old movie *An Officer and a*

Gentleman. Or simply walking up to her somewhere in town and saying that while he couldn't love her today, he thought he might be able to eventually.

In her more sensible moments, she reminded herself that the obvious answer was he wasn't interested. She imagined a politely worded note of "thanks, but no thanks." Despite the fact that she'd said he didn't have to respond, she'd never seriously considered there would be nothing.

She reminded herself there was still a week to go. A week in which she could dream and hope. But come January first, she was going to go on those two diets she'd promised herself. One for the extra weight and the other for Kenny. She would figure out how to deal with both. And she was determined to be successful.

Chloe leaned into her and yawned. "Is Kenny coming over tomorrow?"

"I don't know."

Because Bailey hadn't said anything to Chloe yet. When her daughter asked, she said he was busy with the holidays. If there was even the slightest chance of it working out, then better for her daughter not to suffer needlessly.

"He has to. We have presents for him under the tree. And you have something from him in your stocking."

"Do I?"

She'd forgotten about that. What had he gotten her? And if he walked out of their lives forever, should she return it?

They turned the corner and started up their street. Snow continued to fall. Neighbors walking home from the church service waved to each other. Calls of "Merry Christmas" filled the night.

"I love our new house," Chloe said sleepily. "And my bedroom, and my bed."

"I'm glad. I love it all, too."

Chloe looked up at her and smiled. "I love you, Mommy."

"I love you back, sweetie."

They walked to their house and started up the driveway. On the porch, something moved. Bailey stared, not sure what—

Kenny rose and took a couple of steps toward them. It was dark and the porch light was behind him so she couldn't see his face.

A thousand questions crowded into her brain. Why was he here? Was it good news or bad news? Surely he wouldn't break her heart on Christmas Eve, would he?

He looked good, she thought, greedily taking in everything about him. If felt as if she hadn't seen him in years, instead of days. He had on a long, heavy coat. Snow clung to his head and his shoulders. He held a Santa hat in one hand.

"Kenny!"

Chloe broke free and raced toward him. He caught her and lifted her up into his arms. Chloe hung on so tightly, Bailey wondered if she would ever let go.

"We went to the live nativity and there was a poodle in the manger! Then we saw the Dance of the Winter King, which was so great. And then we went to church and now you're here. We've missed you. You're coming over for Christmas, aren't you? Mom wasn't sure, but you have presents."

Kenny kissed her cheek, then lowered her to the ground. He stepped toward Bailey.

She stayed where she was. Snow fell all around

them. She was probably freezing, but she couldn't feel a thing except for the hope rising inside of her. The world was still, except for the beating of her frantic, hungry heart.

"You were right," he said quietly, staring into her eyes. "About all of it. I am afraid of what I could lose. How could I go on without you or Chloe around?"

She wasn't sure if she was supposed to answer, so she simply waited. Chloe came and stood next to her, but was also silent.

He turned the Santa hat around in his hands. "I don't bring much to the table. I'm kind of beat up from playing football. My knees are bad and my track record with relationships isn't much better."

She wasn't sure how those two thoughts related, but she was happy to keep listening. Because to her, it didn't sound like he was saying goodbye.

"The thing is," he continued, staring directly into her eyes, "I'm in love with you." He dropped his gaze to Chloe. "With both of you. And I need to ask you something."

Ask what? To date her? To have dinner with her? To—

He returned his attention to her. "Bailey Voss, will you marry me?"

Bailey felt all the air rush out of her lungs. Chloe shrieked and began jumping up and down.

Kenny raised one shoulder. "There's a lot we have to work through, I know. Details about where we'll live and family stuff and—"

"Yes," Bailey said as she stepped into his embrace and kissed him. "Yes."

She held out one hand and Chloe joined them.

Kenny wrapped his arm around the little girl, as well. They stood in the snow and hung on to each other.

Later, they went inside. It was all a blur to Bailey. The actual movement and the removing of coats. Somehow they were piled together on the sofa, Bailey on one side of Kenny, Chloe on the other. The tree lights were on and there was a fire in the fireplace.

"This is nice," he said.

She laughed. "Yes, it is."

He glanced at Chloe. "Someone needs to get to bed so that Santa can deliver presents."

Chloe smiled. "There is no Santa, but I'll go to bed anyway. I'm tired." She wrinkled her nose. "You two want to have some grown-up time."

Bailey thought about the magic that was Kenny's kisses and knew that grown-up time would very much be welcome.

She walked her daughter upstairs and helped her get ready. When Chloe was tucked in bed, Kenny joined them. He sat on the edge of the mattress and stroked Chloe's cheek.

"Will is always going to be your forever dad," he said quietly. "I'm going to stand in for him, but I'm not taking his place."

Chloe sat up and hugged him. "You're going to be my forever dad, too. Okay?"

Kenny held her and nodded. He kissed her forehead. She lay back down and was asleep before they had left the room.

Back downstairs, Kenny drew Bailey into his embrace and kissed her.

"I love you," he told her.

"I love you, too." She tilted her head. "What brought you to your senses?"

One corner of his mouth turned up. "I tried to live without you. I couldn't last two days. Whatever happens, it's worth it."

She touched his cheek. "Kenny, I want to spend my life with you. I'm yours. I'm hoping that you'll consider adopting Chloe, so she's yours, too. Not just in your heart, but in the eyes of the law, too."

He stared at her. "You'd do that?"

"Of course. I love you. Not just for Christmas, but for always."

He kissed her, then drew a small box out of his jeans pocket and handed it to her. She opened it and saw a sparkling diamond solitaire winking back at her. The beauty of the ring took her breath away, but the wonder of knowing this amazing man loved her was a feeling she wanted to hang on to forever.

"I love you, Bailey," he whispered. "Merry Christmas."

He slipped the ring on her finger and lowered his mouth to hers. Somewhere in the distance, bells began to chime. Christmas Day had arrived.

* * * * *

New York Times bestselling author

RAEANNE THAYNE

**welcomes you to Haven Point, a small town full of
big surprises that are both merry and bright.**

Nothing short of a miracle
can restore Eliza Hayward's
Christmas cheer. The job she
pinned her dreams on has gone
up in smoke—literally—and
now she's stuck in an unfamiliar,
if breathtaking, small town.
Precariously close to being
destitute, Eliza needs a hero,
but she's not expecting one who
almost runs her down with his car!

Rescuing Eliza is pure instinct
for tech genius Aidan Caine.
At first, putting the renovation of
his lakeside guest lodge in Eliza's
hands assuages his guilt—until he
sees how quickly he could fall for
her. Having focused solely on his
business for years, he never knew what his life was missing before
Eliza, but now he's willing to risk his heart on a yuletide romance
that could lead to forever.

Available now wherever books are sold.

Be sure to connect with us at:

Harlequin.com/Newsletters
Facebook.com/HarlequinBooks
Twitter.com/HarlequinBooks

New York Times bestselling author

NORA ROBERTS

brings you two classic stories about finding love
in the most unlikely of places...

Available now wherever books are sold!

Be sure to connect with us at:

Harlequin.com/Newsletters

Facebook.com/HarlequinBooks

Twitter.com/HarlequinBooks

REQUEST YOUR FREE BOOKS!

2 FREE NOVELS
FROM THE ROMANCE COLLECTION
PLUS 2 FREE GIFTS!

YES! Please send me 2 FREE novels from the Romance Collection and my 2 FREE gifts (gifts are worth about $10). After receiving them, if I don't wish to receive any more books, I can return the shipping statement marked "cancel." If I don't cancel, I will receive 4 brand-new novels every month and be billed just $6.24 per book in the U.S. or $6.74 per book in Canada. That's a savings of at least 22% off the cover price. It's quite a bargain! Shipping and handling is just 50¢ per book in the U.S. and 75¢ per book in Canada.* I understand that accepting the 2 free books and gifts places me under no obligation to buy anything. I can always return a shipment and cancel at any time. Even if I never buy another book, the two free books and gifts are mine to keep forever.

194/394 MDN F4XY

Name	(PLEASE PRINT)	
Address		Apt. #
City	State/Prov.	Zip/Postal Code

Signature (if under 18, a parent or guardian must sign)

Mail to the **Harlequin® Reader Service:**
IN U.S.A.: P.O. Box 1867, Buffalo, NY 14240-1867
IN CANADA: P.O. Box 609, Fort Erie, Ontario L2A 5X3

Want to try two free books from another line?
Call 1-800-873-8635 or visit www.ReaderService.com.

* Terms and prices subject to change without notice. Prices do not include applicable taxes. Sales tax applicable in N.Y. Canadian residents will be charged applicable taxes. Offer not valid in Quebec. This offer is limited to one order per household. Not valid for current subscribers to the Romance Collection or the Romance/Suspense Collection. All orders subject to credit approval. Credit or debit balances in a customer's account(s) may be offset by any other outstanding balance owed by or to the customer. Please allow 4 to 6 weeks for delivery. Offer available while quantities last.

Your Privacy—The Harlequin® Reader Service is committed to protecting your privacy. Our Privacy Policy is available online at www.ReaderService.com or upon request from the Harlequin Reader Service.

We make a portion of our mailing list available to reputable third parties that offer products we believe may interest you. If you prefer that we not exchange your name with third parties, or if you wish to clarify or modify your communication preferences, please visit us at www.ReaderService.com/consumerschoice or write to us at Harlequin Reader Service Preference Service, P.O. Box 9062, Buffalo, NY 14269. Include your complete name and address.

ROM13R

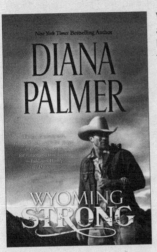

SUSAN MALLERY